beneath a starlet sky

Also by Amanda Goldberg and Ruthanna Khalighi Hopper

Celebutantes

beneath a starlet sky

Amanda Goldberg

and Ruthanna Khalighi Hopper

St. Martin's Press

New York

BENEATH A STARLET SKY. Copyright © 2011 by Twinheads LLC. All rights reserved. Printed in the United States of America. For information, address St. Martin's Press, 175 Fifth Avenue, New York, N.Y. 10010.

www.stmartins.com

Library of Congress Cataloging-in-Publication Data

Goldberg, Amanda.
  Beneath a starlet sky / Amanda Goldberg and Ruthanna Khalighi
Hopper. — 1st ed.
      p. cm.
  ISBN 978-0-312-54442-3
  1. Women fashion designers—Fiction.   2. Theatrical agents—Fiction.
3. Female friendship—Fiction.   4. Cannes Film Festival—Fiction.   5. Cannes
(France)—Fiction.   I. Hopper, Ruthanna Khalighi.   II. Title.
  PS3607.O4375B46 2011
  813'.6—dc22

                                                                    2010054465

First Edition: May 2011

10   9   8   7   6   5   4   3   2   1

To our family, with love and gratitude

In the future, everyone will be anonymous for fifteen minutes.

—Banksy

beneath a starlet sky

1

cannes-dy land

the smattering of movie posters that read, FORGETTING PETUNIA HOLT, EVEN THE DOG THOUGHT YOU WERE A BITCH, PETUNIA HOLT, and SATAN COULD BE YOUR SISTER are lit up in an explosion of lights from the cacophony of cameras going off like fireworks on the vertigo-inducing Palais steps, the most famous red carpet in the world. Tonight's premiere is one of the hottest tickets in town. The town being Cannes. Because this is the Cannes Film Festival, the *grand-père* of all movie festivals. It's surreal that my brother Christopher's first feature film is at the center of this white-hot vortex. I'm about to chuckle at the tag lines— brilliant viral marketing; there are twenty-seven *Forgetting Petunia Holt* fan clubs on Facebook at last count—until I think of my best friend, Kate Woods, and how she's going to feel when she sees them here. Bad enough that the promo campaign was already spinning into overdrive back in L.A. I try and push her out of my thoughts and revel in all the attention my brother's getting.

The wide expanse of the Palais steps is crammed with journalists, photogs, movie execs, and well-wishers, all angling for time with my big brother. As the flashbulbs erupt in Christopher's face, he seems to be transformed in the bright white glow, his usual mess of hair smoothed back, his traditionally slumped shoulders rolled upright in his tux jacket. Christopher may look like he's following in the steps of our father, Paulie Santisi, the two-time Academy Award–winning director, but in fact he's finally stepping out of the very large, dark shadow Papa casts and standing tall on his own two, trademark red Converse high-tops.

Please let Christopher get a positive reception. Please. I suddenly remember how they booed Sofia Coppola's *Marie Antoinette* at Cannes—how could they *do* that to all those delicious Manolo Blahniks *and* Kirsten Dunst? I have a panicked vision of the crowd booing and the French critics having a field day at my brother's expense and I feel an instantaneous knot in my stomach. The only thing the public loves more than a *Hollywood Kid Of* success story is one with a *Hollywood Kid Of* miserably bombing. These French audiences at Cannes are notoriously harsh—Lars von Trier and Vincent Gallo, sure, but all that Gallic disdain for Wim Wenders . . . and *Pamela Anderson*? My stomach drops when a journalist sidles up to Chris with a question.

"So, who is Petunia Holt?" the journalist asks, shoving a mic in my brother's face. Christopher swore on his Leica that once belonged to François Truffaut that he would never reveal the truth. I hold my breath and wait for his reply.

"You're about to find out," Chris says coyly, pointing to the theater where the lights will shortly go down for the screening.

I breathe a huge sigh of relief until I hear, "Darling!" My mother calls from across the Palais steps, her *Wristwatch Wives* camera crew, all decked out in tuxes, in tow. Yup, that would be my mother joining the ranks of Bethenny and the Countess in her new *reality show*. How'd she get clearance for her cameras to be *here*?

I yank on the arm of my Best Gay Forever (BGF). "Quick, Julian, let's get out of here. I can't deal with her freaking cameras right now."

"Too late," he says as my mother comes bounding toward me, a painterly floral print, ruffled Chanel shrugging off of one of her slender shoulders. Her blond hair is in a tousled Bardot beehive.

"Hi, Blanca," Julian says, giving my mother double air kisses. "You look absolutely ravishing."

"Thank you. Isn't Karl an absolute genius," my mother says, fanning out the billowy skirt of her gown for Julian. "I promise that I'll be wearing one of your designs, Julian darling, the night of Fête-ing Santisi."

"Fête-ing Santisi?!" I repeat.

"I was going to call the party the Santisi Cannes-Cannes or the Santisis Conquer Cannes but Fête-ing Santisi just feels more all-encompassing with my TV show, your debut bridal collection, Julian, and Paulie and Christopher competing to win the Palme d'Or," Mom says.

"I think Fête-ing Santisi is perfect, Blanca," Julian says. What a suck-up. Or maybe he's just angling for more publicity for the bridal couture line our company's about to debut, with Mom's camera crew ten feet away.

Wristwatch Wives is Mom's latest reinvention. She was on a meditation retreat hanging off the side of a cliff at Esalen on her 108th chant of So-hum when it came to her. She realized that she'd been supporting others (read my father) in their creative pursuits for long enough. She was tired of Hollywood women being treated as nothing more than expensive accessories. And *Wristwatch Wives* was born—the show that showcases the famous Wives Of, the Powers Behind the Throne.

"Did you get the script, Lola?" my mother whispers out of her cameramen's earshot.

"*Script?*" I ask. "What script, Mom?"

"For the party, darling," my mother says in a low voice.

"You have *got* to be kidding. You don't actually expect us to follow a script, do you?" I say. "Mom, what part of 'reality TV' do you not get?"

Mom draws me into a tighter huddle. "Lola, I've been working my bum off on this party, not to mention all the money I'm spending, which your father doesn't even *know* about, so it has to *perfect*. And the only way for it to be perfect is to script it. I got one of the writers from *Keeping Up with the Kardashians*."

"Ooooooh, I love *Keeping Up with the Kardashians*," Julian says. "Did they tell you what's going to happen next season?" I shoot Julian one of my infamous death daggers.

"Lola, please, this is important to me. I've even been editing old family movies together for the party. They're just so wonderful. They're such a beautiful expression of our closeness," Mom says.

"Closeness to what, Mom? The Hollywood sign?" I say.

"Oh, please, Lola, this party is going to be not only a celebration of our family, but a celebration for *all* families. In these difficult economic times, family is all that we have," she says. She delivers this last line while beaming at Alex, her lead cameraman. I can't tell if she's speaking to me, or to the camera.

"Did you come up with that on your own or did your new scribe write that for you?" I ask, when I find myself being dragged out of earshot again, stage left.

"Okay, look, Lola, this episode is going to air during sweeps and I just found out that one of the other wives is letting the cameras film the delivery of her surrogate's twins who, it turns out, has been having an affair with her husband," my mother pleads. "And I'm sure the footage of

Christine and her husband and their team of lawyers signing the paper-work for a trial separation is sure to be a big ratings bonanza. And Francesca has footage of her sixteen-year-old daughter getting more than just the standard post-op nose job visit with her *married* plastic surgeon. That's why I really need this party to be *perfect*."

"Oh, great, Mom, so we're just pawns in your scheme to steal the WWW limelight," I say.

"Darling, please just smile and do this for me, *please*," she says, linking my arm in hers. "Now let's go find Christopher. I'm so nervous for him," my mother says a little too loudly before barreling through the throng of journalists and photogs and landing us smack-dab in front of my brother, her camera crew struggling to keep up with us. "Darling," my mom says, dropping my arm, spreading her suntanned arms wide, and hugging Chris. "I'm so proud of you," she says, stretching her hands around his neck. It's not much of a reach; she's nearly as tall as his six feet two inches in her towering four-inch silver stilettos.

"Thanks, Mom," Chris says, smiling, at which point my mother doesn't just begin to cry, she begins to weep like they're putting down Old Yeller.

"You okay, Mom?" Christopher asks, a bit startled.

"Shit, the battery just went out, we need to switch them out," I hear Alex say to his Assistant Camera, at which point my mother instantaneously turns off her Oscar-worthy waterworks and turns to face them.

"So you didn't get that?" Mom asks squarely.

"I don't think so," the cameraman says.

"Well let's do it again then," my mother says. "Byron, I think I need a touch-up," she says, summoning her hair-and-makeup guru while they reload the battery. Damn if she doesn't execute a perfect second take. Why she didn't take her famous seventies' supermodel looks into acting is beyond me. Too tall for Robert Redford? Or maybe she's been flexing those acting chops after all, putting up with my dad's antics all these years.

"Okay, I gotta go," my brother says, giving my mother a little peck on the forehead before heading into the theater.

"Wait, I wanted to get a shot with your father as well," my mother calls after Christopher, who doesn't turn back.

"Where *is* Papa? Why aren't you with him?" I ask, searching the crowded steps for my father.

"He's allergic to the cameras," Mom says.

"He's allergic to *your* cameras," I point out. "He doesn't seem to be allergic to those. Those cameras he seems to love," I say, spotting my father in the middle of a firestorm of flashbulbs.

I overhear one of the many French journalists surrounding my father ask, "What do you think of your son's movie?" and my breath catches in my throat.

"Haven't seen it," is the curt response.

"And how do you feel about being in competition here at Cannes against your only son?"

My father takes off the straw fedora he's paired with his tux and strokes his graying beard. "There's no competition, he's my son," he says, and just when I think my father's actually going to act like a father for once, he adds, "He's got no experience, this is his first movie, and I've been making movies for four decades." Geezus. Can't he just let this freaking moment be about Christopher? This is a man who probably fought for his name above the title on Chris's birth announcement.

"Dad is such an asshole," slips out before I can stop myself. "Did you hear what he just said about Christopher?" I ask my mother.

"No, darling, I didn't," Mom says. "Alex, were you rolling?" my mother asks her cameraman.

"Oh geezus, did you just get me saying that about my father?" I ask him.

"Oh don't worry about it," my mother says, linking her arm with mine again and pulling us in the direction of the theater, "We'll cut it out in the editing room." But I can't help but imagine my verbal gaffe in promo all over Sweeps Week.

Inside the Palais, I lean back in my plush red velvet seat. I'm nervous for my brother as his premiere is about to begin.

"Stop fidgeting," Julian says softly. "You're going to destroy the sequins."

"Sorry," I whisper trying to smooth out the couple of them I inadvertently gnarled on my cobalt blue, one-shoulder minidress Julian made especially for tonight.

"OMG, Lo, is that Rob Pattinson?" Julian asks, gesturing with his eyes toward the row in front of us. "He's even more gorgeous in person," Julian says breathlessly. "Is he or is he not a god among men? Maybe we should pray to him to let everything work out with our fashion show. C'mon, Lo, pray with me." He closes his eyes and folds his hands in prayer, "Please, dear Rob, let us—"

"Stop it, Julian, breathe!" I say, trying to prevent Julian from having a full-on twelve-year-old-girl freak-out.

"Sorry." Julian takes my hand in his. "The movie's going to be great," he says in a hushed voice.

"Thanks," I say, squeezing his hand, wishing it were Lev's. But Luke Levin, MD, my live-in love of the last nine months, is back in L.A. Lev, whose first love is the ER and whose knowledge of pop culture ended the day he started his residency at Cedars-Sinai three years ago. (He thinks the HD in HD-TV stands for "high dose," and the last movie he saw was *Crash* because he thought it would have an interesting take on trauma center stabilization techniques. I mean, how adorable is that?)

Exactly one year, two months, and twelve days ago (but who's count-ing?) I fell headfirst off a gurney (and out of my Louboutin stilettos) and in love with the good doctor who saved me from more than a broken ankle on Oscar Night. He not only fixed my busted foot, but cured me of an undiagnosed case of Actorholism, my near-fatal addiction to dating the world's most narcissistic men. He got me straight on an IV drip of anti-actor (IV in my case stands for *inter-vention*), and straight onto him. Not that kind of straight onto him. Well yes, that kind, too, but that came later.

That's right. I, Lola Santisi—the CEO of a struggling fashion line, former Hollywood ambassador, and daughter of Hollywood Royalty without a kingdom—or even a condo—to call my own—scored a real, live Doctor in Shining Armor with a kingdom to call *our* own. Okay, maybe not a kingdom, but a really nice house in—*Sherman Oaks*—which makes it absolutely perfect because it's on the *other* side of the hill from Hollywood.

I clutch Julian's hand, thankful to have any hand to hold right now.

Finally the theater goes dark and *Forgetting Petunia Holt* appears in simple Courier font against a black screen.

An hour and forty-five minutes later, as the movie ends and the lights go up, I spot Kate, standing in the back of the theater alone. She must have snuck in when the lights went down. When we lock eyes she's already bolting for the door.

"Oh my god, she came," Julian says, following my eye line.

"I've got to go," I say, scurrying through my row. "Kate," I yell once we're outside. "Kate!" I catch up with her and lay a hand on her shoulder.

"What?" she says, finally turning to face me, her red lips pursed. If looking good really is the best revenge, then my best friend is getting hers. She's wearing one of the prettiest, sexiest black silk slip-dresses I've ever seen. It's spliced with tulle to create these supersexy peekaboo panels flaring out from her taut midriff and down her perfect legs. Her chocolate hair is in a soft wave and her dewy skin is positively radiant.

"I'm not sure what to say." I look down at the red carpet underneath us, not sure whether I just said that out loud or I'm just thinking it.

"Relax. I'm here to sign the actress who plays Petunia Holt—Gigi Summer. She's going to be huge. Bryan told me to bring back a signed contract or not bother coming back." Kate is a rising star at Bryan Lourd's Creative Artists Agency. But we both know that's not why Kate's *really* here tonight. Her voice is detached, unemotional, all business, her feelings swept right under that red carpet she's standing on. She shifts on her needle-heeled stilettos. I grab her arm to steady her, startled by this rare moment of imbalance from my best friend, who's trying so hard to mask the heartache she must be feeling.

I know that nothing I say will make it better for Kate so I don't say anything at all. Instead I wrap her in a hug. She doesn't even try and push me away. She actually hugs me back. Hard.

"I love you," I whisper in her ear.

"Thank you," she says, not letting go of our embrace.

Suddenly the theater starts to unload and I spot Christopher through the throng. I look over at my brother and then over to Kate. Chris. Kate. Chris. Kate. God I hate this. Why did I ever think a romance between my best friend and brother would ever work? I want to go and congratulate my brother, but it feels like such a betrayal to my best friend.

"Go. Tell him what an amazing movie it is," Kate says, as if she's somehow read my mind. But just as I'm about to head toward him, he's suddenly standing right in front of us.

"Chris," I shout, throwing my arms around him. "It was incredible. I'm so proud of you." I look back at Kate and mumble an added, "Sorry."

"It's going to be a huge success," Kate says.

"Kate, it's really . . . can we talk for a min—" but just as Christopher's trying to finish his sentence, Gigi Summer, his leading lady, sidles up next to him in a glittery strapless short dress with a nipped-in waist and a balloon skirt showing off her long legs. She gives him a kiss on the cheek. Was that a kiss-kiss? Or just a friend kiss? "Gigi, hi!" Chris says after a beat. "Have you met my sister, Lola?"

I'm about to return the greeting when Kate immediately thrusts her hand out to Gigi. "Congratulations. You were really great."

"Thank you, I owe it all to my director," she says, giggling in Christopher's direction. "I'm Gigi." She reaches out to shake Kate's hand.

"Kate," she says. "Woods."

"Oh . . . wow . . . *you're* Kate," Gigi says. Maybe she's not that good an actress after all because she's unable to stop the surprise from showing on her face. After a few silent, tense beats, she says, "Wow, this is kind of awkward."

"Not for me," Kate says, seeming to relish in Gigi's discomfort. "I hear you're at Gersh. I suspect you'll be looking for new representation soon. Here's my card. CAA sees you in some huge projects. I'd love the chance to talk with you more about it." She fishes one of her business cards out of her black cut-crystal clutch and hands it to Gigi.

"Thanks," Gigi says, overwhelmed. "It was nice to meet you. I'll . . . I'll definitely give you a call. And nice to meet you too, Lola." To her credit, Gigi looks as puzzled as she is excited. "Well . . . I'm going to go and mingle. Are you coming, Chris?" she asks.

"In a minute," he says. He reaches out and gives Gigi's hand a lingering squeeze as she melts into the crowd.

"Kate, I really hope we can talk at some point, I want to explain," Christopher says.

"Go enjoy your moment in the sun, Chris. You should be talking to all the journalists, not me. You need to capitalize on this," Kate says, safely back in agent mode, which is far less painful than ex-girlfriend mode.

"I hope you're coming to the after-party," he says.

"I'll try," Kate says, but we both know she won't.

As Christopher disappears into the crowd, I turn to Kate.

"Are you okay?" I ask as her cell phone starts ringing.

"Saved by the bell," she says. She reads the caller ID. "Okay, Lola, here's the other disaster I'm dealing with. Hello," she says, clicking on the speaker.

"The eagle has landed in Cannes. Let all prepare to rejoice and let Kate be down waiting for me in the lobby of the Hôtel Du Cap in ten minutes," Nic Knight's voice booms. The only thing worse than thinking it was a good idea for my brother to date my best friend is thinking it was a good idea for Kate to put one of her most loose-cannon clients, Nic Knight, in my father's own bid for the Palme d'Or, *San Quentin Cartel*. Nic makes Sean Penn, Mickey Rourke, and Robert Downey Jr. 1.0 look like paragons of sobriety and self-control.

"I'll be there soon, Nic," she says, before hanging up. "Do you believe this shit?"

"What's with the fake accent? He sounds like Ricardo Montalban," I say.

"More bullshit. He says he's gonna stay in character until after the premiere. I've never met a more pretentious, full-of-himself actor in my life, and I've met a lot of 'em. But I'm just glad he actually made it here. He let his passport expire, and you have no idea the strings I had to pull to get him a new one in twenty-four hours. Not to mention Nic violated parole *again* by causing a public disturbance when he went commando into the hot mugwort tea pool of the all-*women's* spa in Koreatown and missed another mandatory drug test. I had to bribe his parole officer with premiere tickets and a free trip to Cannes just so he can personally make sure Nic stays out of trouble."

"I was going to offer you a trade but now I'm not so sure," I say. I've been having major headaches with a certain supermodel who seems hell-bent on finalizing her fittings for a jail cell instead of for Julian's runway show, which is only four days away.

"I gotta go, I'll call you later," Kate says.

"Good luck with Nic," I say before Kate walks away down the Palais steps.

I head off to find Julian when my own cell starts chirping.

"Hello?" I ask.

"I just left Grace Frost's office," Coz, the Senior Bitchitor at *Vain* magazine says over the phone line. "I simply cannot imagine why you've been calling her. I'm returning the call on her behalf."

I feel my stomach plummet to the floor along with our chances of being in *Vain,* the hottest fashion magazine around. I wouldn't have even dreamed of calling the editor in chief herself, except that Coz left me no choice. I *had* to call Grace Frost. Julian's new bridal collection *deserves* to be on the cover of *Vain.* And without it, I'm not even sure if there will be a JT Inc. any longer.

"I, um, well, I can explain," I stumble and imagine Coz on the other end of the phone, basking in this moment from behind her big black sunglasses.

"As much as I'd derive immense pleasure from listening to you grovel for the next few hours, I'm actually really busy so I'm going to cut to the chase," Coz says. "I called my friends at *Vogue, Elle, Bazaar,* and *Marie Claire* and I know that there are no other offers for a Julian Tennant cover. Did you imagine for one second that I wouldn't check?"

"I—" I shouldn't have lied to Grace Frost's assistant. But can you blame me? I'm desperate and I'm not Criss Angel or God or Stacy London, so what else could I do? It's taken me my entire twenty-seven years to find a career that I love and I'm actually good at, so I'm going to do whatever it takes to get the world's most talented designer that I can't seem to make famous no matter how hard I try on the cover of *Vain.*

"I'm *still* speaking. I'll let you know when it's your turn," Coz says. God I hate her. "We're going to give you the cover and a twelve-page layout inside to coincide with the release of *Four Weddings and a Bris* in August."

"You're *what?!*" I ask, flabbergasted. Julian beat out John Galliano, Vivienne Westwood, Marchesa, and Jason Wu to be one of the four designers to create wedding dresses for Baz Luhrmann's latest musical extravaganza, also set to premiere at Cannes. It stars Hollywood's hottest supernova, Saffron Sykes, the Best Actress Oscar winner who has Spielberg, the Coen brothers, *and* Clint Eastwood all fighting to work with her—and pay her twenty mil—all at the ripe old age of *twenty-five*. Could it possibly be that Coz is our miracle worker after all? "Is this a joke?"

"Does it sound like I'm joking?" Coz says icily. Other than *sounding* as if she's got a pair of her Dior studded platform skyscrapers shoved up her flat bum, I can't tell if she's serious or not. Could she be serious? "*Are* you listening?" she demands.

"I'm here," I say, still in shock.

"Just so we're clear, I'm not doing this for you or Julian," she says, as if she's *ever* done anything for me—or Julian. Except waterboard our careers. "I'm doing it for Chili."

"Chili?" I repeat. That's Charles "Chili" Lu, fashion's rising wunderkind, who Coz thinks is the second coming. And did I mention the kid is only *sixteen*? Yes, sixteen. He's accomplished more in his sixteen years than I have in all of my twenty-seven. Chili was the first winner of *Cutthroat Couture,* the reality TV show brainchild of *Vain*'s very own *Coz,* its most tart-tongued judge. He also created wedding gowns for Baz's film. Except Baz and Saffron weren't clamoring for gowns with iPod portals and solar panels after all. So Baz replaced Chili with Julian and Coz forced us to hire the Christian Siriano wannabe as Julian's assistant after convincing Baz that it would be bad PR for his movie to draw attention to firing a designer on a film where the costuming is *everything*. Chili's transition over to our team would make all appear to be smooth sailing.

"Grace agreed that it was a complete travesty that Chili's divine wedding gowns ended up on Baz's cutting room floor, so she thought it was a wonderful idea to let his gowns see the light of day in *Vain*."

I know that Coz is speaking but I can't compute what's she's actually saying.

"What about Julian?" I'm finally able to get out.

"Saffron and Cricket will do the cover together. Saffron will wear Chili and Cricket can wear Julian," Coz says. My Best Actress Forever (BAF), Cricket Curtis, landed the part of Saffron's wisecracking sidekick in *Four Weddings and a Bris*. "I've already booked Patrick Demarchelier, Gucci Westman, and Orlando Pita and called the Du Cap and arranged to shoot in their gardens. Chili and I are flying out tomorrow. *Jusqu'à demain. Bisous. Bisous*," she says, and then just as abruptly hangs up.

I try and recover from the Coz tsunami that just hit me. So what if Julian has to share the cover with little Chili Lu? At least Julian is going to *be* on the cover of *Vain*. This could catapult Julian into becoming the *next* Vera Wang. He could rule the Hollywood brides. Everything I've killed myself for as CEO of Julian Tennant Inc.

Oh god. Oh no. I still haven't actually *asked* Cricket or Saffron if they'd be willing to pose for the cover. What if they say no?

My head is spinning. I feel faint. I speed-dial Cricket. It goes straight to voice mail. I leave her a very long rambling, bumbling, begging message.

I contemplate hurling myself down the Palais steps, the most prestigious red carpet in the world, but decide against it. I'm fairly certain that the throng of international paparazzi and fans camped out at the bottom of the steps would only break my fall. Not to mention the last thing I want is another video of me all over TMZ.

I drop to my knees on the red carpet and clasp my hands together.

Please Rob Pattinson, please Rob Pattinson, let Cricket and Saffron agree to pose together for the cover of *Vain*. *Please.*

"What are you doing?" Julian asks. "This is the red carpet, not a mosque."

I look up at Julian. "I can explain."

2

being bi-lolar

Six months earlier

pull the sheets off the Ligne Roset Nomade couch in Julian's living room and stow them in a closet already crammed with fabric samples. "Nomad" is exactly how I feel. Julian and I *still* don't have new office space, and I haven't been able to find an affordable apartment, even in this dismal market. Which means I'll have to keep living *and* working (at least Monday through Friday) with Julian under his twenty-foot ceilings until we find a new studio, I find my own apartment—or I strangle Julian with one of his Hermès ascots. I rub my sore neck and do a couple quick Down Dogs to get the kinks out. After more than a hundred days on that sofa, I feel like I need a body brace. Everything in Julian's monochromatic, minimalist SoHo loft is *Elle Decor*-worthy but none of it is actually comfortable, most especially not the sofa, which is like sleeping on a slab of dessicated tofu, which only makes sense because Julian's a die-hard vegan. So far he's rejected every space we've looked at, citing bad feng shui, an unlucky address in numerology, or wonky chi. Naturally, he won't even look in the Meatpacking District because he "doesn't want to hear the ghostly screams of those poor murdered creatures."

I've done my best to transform Julian's living room into a picture-perfect showroom for our meeting this afternoon with Coz, the Senior Bitchitor from *Vain*. She's doing a "From Fashionista to Recessionista" story, and I'm desperate to get her to include some of Julian's fall samples. I've changed the outfits on the mannequins ten times, straightened the hangers at least fifty times, repositioned the vase of peonies a dozen times, and removed any trace that the living room-slash-showroom is also my bedroom-slash-office. The cool, polished-concrete floors feel good on my bare feet as I head to the pristine stainless-and-white-marble kitchen in my cotton nightie.

I flip on an electric teakettle and ready two white mugs with PG Tips, organic raw honey, and soy milk. Of course, there's nothing in the fridge except a massive collection of take-out containers from every vegan restaurant in Manhattan. I don't care what anyone says: soy chicken, turkey, beef, shrimp, pork, riblets, whatever—it all tastes like spongy Play-Doh. There, I said it. I hate tofu. I don't get this cultish enchantment with meat pretenders. Maybe I've just been spoiled by Lev, who actually has *real* food in his fridge and makes me the most delicious meals when I'm in L.A. I've been so busy with the company, I haven't had time to shop for anything, let alone go apartment hunting. I *need* to find my own place where there isn't a ban on meat. And then I need to convince Lev to move to Manhattan and into said apartment with me. Suppressing a shudder, I swallow god only knows what made out of soy from The V-Spot.

My cell chirps.

"Hello," I say.

"Hey, Lo," Cricket says. Her voice is trembling.

"Cricket?! It's five-thirty a.m. in L.A. Is everything okay? What are you doing up so early?"

"I can't sleep. I'm freaking out. Do you realize it's been six months already?"

"Cricket, you're lucky you're alive," I remind her. "You were going a hundred-fifty miles an hour when you spun out." And got fired off of *Days of Thunder 2* when she skidded off the practice track with Jeff Gordon in Fontana and totaled a hundred-fifty-thousand-dollar custom racing car—and her career.

"Well, I don't *feel* lucky. This was my big break and I blew it, Lo. I was supposed to be the Next Nicole Kidman and now I'd be grateful if someone could get me a job babysitting her kid." Cricket pauses, takes a deep breath, and then, as if she's delivering the worst news imaginable, says, "I took that job with Margery Simkin last week."

"Why do you sound so horrified?" I ask, unaccustomed to hearing Cricket sound anything less than sunny. Kate and I have been enjoying the personal portable solar radiation machine we call Cricket for a decade. In fact, Kate and I call 2000 B.C., as in, Before Cricket, The Dark Years. As in, before we became one name: Lokaticket. "Margery was the casting director for *Avatar*. Maybe she can get you a part in *Avatar 2*."

"That's what I was hoping, but I'm nothing but a lowly assistant. I'm stuck picking up Margery's Labradoodle from daycare and doing *off-camera* readings opposite the actors who are auditioning for the parts I should be auditioning for. Lo, I studied with the Royal Shakespeare Company. I have a degree from Juilliard. Do you know what my last audition was for? *Cialis*. A commercial for freaking erectile dysfunction."

"That sucks. I hope you were up for the lead," I say. It's not just that Cricket's a highly trained actress, it's that she's really, really good. When

Kate signed her to CAA as one of her first clients and Cricket nabbed that lead, it looked as though she'd finally gotten the break she deserved.

"I had five callbacks. And I still didn't get the part because I was too tall next to the guy they ended up casting," Cricket says, then quietly adds. "Lo, I'm barely making the rent."

"Do you need some money, Cricket?" I ask her, though I'm barely scraping by myself. Being CEO of Julian Tennant means living paycheck to paycheck at this point. Keeping my business and my relationship afloat has meant emptying out my bank account on travel—bicoastal love affairs are killer—along with fifty million other expenses.

"Oh, Lo, thanks for the offer, but I'll be okay. I'm just stressed. CAA's going to drop me, I know it. I feel awful for me—and for Kate. Thank God I was able to get out of escrow on that house I bought. I'm going to be in this teensy little guesthouse *forever*." Cricket's been living in Viggo Mortensen's 125-square-foot studio guesthouse on his property in Venice for the last five years. Aside from our friendship, it's been the only constant in her life. Unless you'd call her string of romances a constant. Cricket falls "deeply in love" every other month. If it's not the yoga instructor from her vinyasa flow class at Yoga Works, then it's the struggling screenwriter she met typing hopefully away in the corner of the Palihouse, or her scene partner in Larry Moss's acting class.

"Okay, yes, that sucks, but there are worse things than getting to see Viggo's ass every time he goes for a midnight skinny dip," I remind her.

"Don't you get it?" Cricket wails. "I'm never going to have a bathtub, washer and dryer, or a parking spot. I really believed I was *finally* going to make it and now here I am—still."

"Cricket, it's going to be okay," I say, hoping I'm right, worried that I'm not. It took tremendous luck and balls for my BFF Kate to talk Jerry Bruckheimer into taking on Cricket, a complete unknown, for the lead in his next blockbuster. And not even a bat of an eyelash for him to fire Cricket after the car crash, which totally wasn't her fault. "There'll be something else. You've just got to be patient. Kate's not going to give up on you. I won't let her. She'll find you something even better."

After the accident, when Cricket told me and Kate that she was going to take her busted ribs and pour herself into a new part, we applauded the optimism and light that we'd grown accustomed to her bringing to even the darkest moments. Then, when she told us she'd be playing *Hamlet* in an all-women's Shakespeare troupe, we thought maybe she'd lost her mind in the accident along with her chance at the Big Screen.

We thought wrong. On opening night, when Kate and I found the theater on Santa Monica Boulevard nestled between an S&M paraphernalia shop and an erotic bookstore, we opted for the back row for fear that Cricket might catch us asleep during the three-hour show—and because that's where the seats looked cleanest. To say that she blew our hair back would be an understatement. More like, every hair on our bodies was standing on end by the end of the three hours. We were on our feet clapping hysterically with rivers of mascara running down our faces. Kate tried to get as many agents and casting directors to see it as possible, but getting people to the theater in L.A. might be as hard as persuading Heidi Montag to stop staging plastic boob near-nip-slips. Let alone, the Dragonfly Theater on Santa Monica Boulevard in West Hollywood—a.k.a. "Boy Town"—where the main attraction is *Point Break Live!*—the stage adaptation of the Keanu Reeves movie. Kate at least got the *L.A. Weekly* there to review it. And they called Cricket reminiscent of a young Meryl Streep— okay, so the ads for *Girls, Girls, Girls* and *Add Three Inches* on the same page was a little distracting. Still, it was a damn good review. Even if Lokaticket were the only ones to ever read it.

"Enough about me," Cricket says, sniffling. "I'm so deeply sick of myself. Tell me about you? How are you?"

"I'm doing okay. But I should really get going. We have the *Vain Bitchitor* coming this afternoon to see the collection, and I have a ton to get through before I get on my plane back to L.A. tonight."

"Okay, well, knock 'em dead. Call me later and tell me how it goes. I'm going to go light another career candle and do an acting invocation. Thanks for talking me off the sill—again. Talk to you later."

Click.

Poor Cricket. I've never heard her this upset before. I have to call Kate. It's not that she doesn't care about Cricket. It's that she's been killing herself to prove to Bryan Lourd that he made the right call taking her in as a junior agent last year. She's got her two hottest clients, Saffron Sykes and Nic Knight, on the front burner. I've got to convince her to take Cricket off the back burner.

I open Julian's bedroom door, set the PG Tips teas on the nightstand, toss the drapes open, and throw back the sheets to find Julian sound asleep in nothing more than a pair of tighty whities and a black satin sleeping mask with the words DO NOT DISTURB stitched in hot pink.

"Rise and shine, sunshine," I say, jostling him awake. "We've got a huge day ahead of us."

"Tom Ford and I didn't get to bed until after three. We were working on the new 'Dogshmere' collection all night and we're *exhausted.* Just give us a few more minutes of REM. *Please,*" Julian begs, flipping over onto his stomach. He buries his head in his pillow and reaches over to the adjacent pillow to pull a sleeping Tom Ford closer to him. Julian's newly rescued Mini-Pinscher is dead asleep in the crook of Julian's neck.

"Julian, I think it's great that you're teaming up with PETA to do a knitwear collection for dogs, but you need to finish hand-dyeing the gowns for Nic Knight. They've got to go on the plane with me today. We have to go over the agenda for our conference call with LVMH at noon. The stock market is still down and so are sales for all the designers. Coz is coming this afternoon. Saks wants you to do a personal appearance next week. And my plane leaves at eight p.m., which means I have to be there by six to give them time to do the full cavity search."

A loud sigh gutters from Julian's lips as he flips onto his back. He lifts off his sleeping mask, his raven hair the embodiment of bed head, then throws his hand out expectantly for his morning tea. "Lo, Tom Ford's dog groomer also does Barbara Walters's Havanese, Cha Cha, and she's going to hand-deliver Barbara the custom outfits I've designed for her dog. If Barbara likes them, I bet she'd put me on *The View* and do you know what that could mean for our company and PETA?"

"Julian, it'd be amazing but it's a real long shot. In the meantime, what about the PA at Saks?"

"Last time you made me do a personal appearance at Bergdorf's I ended up wasting the entire day trying to help that woman find a dress for her twenty-year high school reunion—and she ended up buying a Chanel. Jesus, Lola, when are you getting your *own* apartment so that I'm not forced to have my CEO breathing down my neck the minute I wake up every single day? I can't take it anymore. You've turned into—*Kate.*"

"If you mean that I'm actually a competent, capable *businesswoman,* then yes, Julian, I've become Kate. While you're out at the Boom Boom Room till four a.m. drooling over Chace Crawford, one of us has to actually *run* this company. I'm the one doing the spreadsheets and P&Ls while you're schmoozing Rachel Zoe at Bungalow 8. I signed on to be the CEO of Julian Tennant Inc. And suddenly I'm also the director of PR, head of marketing, production manager, design assistant, your personal assistant, *and* the receptionist."

"I liked you so much better when you were just my best friend," Julian says, struggling to sit up on his elbows.

I throw Julian a death dagger. He's probably gotten at least a million thrown at him by now over the seventeen years we've been friends. He's been my BGF since we were ten and collided while reaching for the last Rifat Ozbek studded belt at Neiman's.

"I'm sorry," Julian says. "I don't really mean that. That was the me pre-caffeine talking. I'd never have gotten my first gown onto the Oscars red carpet without you. There'd be no JT Inc. if you hadn't gotten LVMH to back us. I'd have nothing without you, Lo. I'm just so afraid that we're going to lose it all again."

I sit down on the bed next to him. "I'm not going to let that happen, Julian. Because of you I finally have a career that I love and I may actually be good at, but this is really, really, really serious. Three more boutiques that were carrying the collection just *closed*. Women aren't spending like they used to and stores and brands are folding every day. LVMH isn't going to carry us forever if we can't get the numbers up. We need to figure out something to subsidize the lack of sales until this economy bounces back—if it ever bounces back."

"Lo, I think this Dogshmere collection could be as big as Juicy. Maybe they won't shell out for a fifteen-hundred-dollar dress, but people will still buy for their pets no matter how dead the economy is. I'd eat Tom Ford's Flint River Ranch myself before I'd cut corners on his food—or his outerwear," he says, nuzzling his dog closer. "And what about all those Russian billionaires? That Sweet Sixteen gown I made was killer. It actually made that little matrushka doll look like she had a *waist*." I was sure that getting Julian to make a coming-out gown for that Russian financier's daughter would help us break into that Billionaire Boychik club.

"Sure, we've gotten referrals, but they're not generating nearly enough sales or press coverage. And even the rich Russians aren't as rich as they used to be," I say, and can't believe what I'm about to say next. "I heard that American Airlines is looking for someone to redesign their uniforms. How about I try and get us a meeting?"

Julian waves the thought away. "Because nothing says couture like spill-proof double knits."

"Julian, every designer is making concessions. Ralph Lauren is designing couture work gloves for Home Depot, and Alexander Wang is doing a capsule collection for Fruit of the Loom. Proenza Schouler is making their PS1 bags in canvas for Walmart."

Julian sniffs. "Lola, I don't want to do gimmicks to promote myself. I'm an artist. I just want to design," he says. "Don't you think we'll be able to get major press off the gown I'm designing for Nic?" Nic's the lead in Papa's first film since he won his second Oscar. *San Quentin Cartel* is about a transvestite drug lord operating the largest cocaine cartel in Colombia from a four-by-six San Quentin jail cell. It had taken a lot of begging to get Papa to agree to let Julian do the designs.

"I hope so, and I hope you don't think it's gimmicky, but I'm going to pitch *Vain* to put Nic Knight on their cover in full drag in your gown. I don't think they've ever done that before. It could be revolutionary and create a huge buzz for us and them."

"I actually think that's a genius idea, Lola, do it!"

"I will, this afternoon, but let me pitch your fall collection first, because that's where the money comes from. You know how hard it's been to get Coz to come look at your stuff; she's been putting us off for months. I want her to bite on the collection first. Then we'll try to sell her on Nic in drag."

"Okay, any news on the Luhrman gig?"

"Nothing yet. Julian, I'm doing the best I can and so is Kate," I say. Julian was thisclose to being one of the four designers hired to create wedding dresses for Baz's musical extravaganza, *Four Weddings and a Bris,* shooting down in Australia now with Kate's other huge star, Saffron Sykes. It killed him when the final slot went to Chili Lu, the exuberant prince of "cyber couture," whose slashed silk sweatshirts with live Facebook status updates have scored him legions of devotees from the Olsen Twins to Miley Cyrus. Even Michelle Obama was spotted pulling up deep purple dragon carrots from the White House garden while wearing one of his Glitter Twitter "garden" dresses, which simultaneously broadcast the news of the harvest to her followers. Who cares that he's supposed to be the fresh, brash new voice of fashion? He's only in the *tenth* grade, for crying out loud.

But I've got the audacity of hope. It seems as though little Chili Lu can't drape, gather, cinch, ruche, and sew like the second coming of Coco Chanel after all. Rumors are leaking out that Chili's gowns for *Four Weddings and a Bris* are a disaster, and that Baz has been quietly shopping around to replace Chili. I've been killing myself to get Julian the gig this time.

Julian fumbles around on the nightstand for his sketchbook. "Lo, just look at these and tell me they wouldn't be perfect for the movie." He's right. Julian's strapless ivory chiffon siren gown with petal-like ruffles fanning to a beaded flyaway train and his fairylike, frothy, tulle-and-lace bustled dress *deserve* to be on the big screen. I really want us to get this movie. I want it as much as I want to move out of Musée de Julian and find my own apartment where I'm allowed to drink liquids that aren't all *clear* because Julian's worried about staining his all-beige furniture.

"Julian, you know I agree. Listen, I'm about to call Kate about Cricket. I'll see what I can find out about when Baz is going to make his final decision."

"Lo, just make it happen, *please*," Julian begs. "I just really, really, really, don't want to have to redesign the American Airlines uniforms. If I could design costumes for one of your dad's films *and* a Baz Luhrman film in the same year, it would be the coup of the century."

"I'm going to try to make it happen, but for god's sake, don't breathe a word around Coz," I remind Julian. "If she finds out that you could be replacing her precious Chili in Baz's film, we'll be lucky if your name is ever in *Vain* again."

"That woman is dreadful." Julian shivers. "I have no idea what Grace Frost even sees in her." He tucks Tom Ford in closer; the tiny dog gives a faint sigh. "Now can I just have ten more minutes of REM. *Please.*"

"Julian—"

"I'll do the appearance at Saks," Julian interrupts.

"Fine. I have to call Kate anyway," I say. "But I'm coming back in *ten* minutes."

I walk back out into the living room and grab my phone. As I glance out of the floor-to-ceiling windows at the falling January snow, a chill runs down my spine. What if Baz chooses another designer over Julian—*again*?

I pick up the phone to dial Kate, who's been lobbying Baz on our behalf since she's got Saffron as her "in." Saffron is Kate's biggest client to date and it was a huge coup when she signed her away from the William Morris Endeavor Agency two weeks after Bryan invited her to join CAA. Aside from the fact that I know Julian will design a dream wedding dress, Kate owes me.

I did something for my BFF that I've rarely done in my twenty-seven years: I asked my father for a favor. It's not that our father doesn't love his kids. It's that he made it in Hollywood totally on his own and he's tough as tacks because of it. He was a Jewish kid from Georgia who stuck out like a sore thumb among the peach farmers. The only place he felt at home was in the Coronet Theatre on Main Street, watching Humphrey Bogart and Lauren Bacall, Jimmy Stewart and Kim Novak, James Dean and Liz Taylor, light up the screen. Every penny he made working after school and weekends at Saul's Shoes, the shoe repair shop owned by his first-generation Russian émigré father (who, according to Mom, made Mussolini look like Mr. Rogers), was spent escaping into that darkened theater. Papa still can't stomach the smell of shoe polish. It takes him back to those tough days before he got on that bus to Hollywood and changed his name from Sitowitz to Santisi to be more like his idol Marcello Mastroianni—who he also happened to resemble when he was young—and thin.

Kate begged me to beg Papa to hire her client Nic Knight for the lead in *San Quentin Cartel*. Which I did. Nic, whose drug-addled antics had squandered any box office cachet he'd once had and made him uninsurable to boot, especially after his umpteenth failed stint in rehab, when he famously ran starkers down the aisles of a 747 during a flight to the Grenadines. Nic, who traded his Golden Globe for a hit of Ecstasy, who's punched out the paparazzi more times than Sean Penn, and who once asked Chris McMillan to trim his pubic hair. After weeks of badgering, my father finally agreed to hire Nic only *after* he spent ninety-three days at Utah's Cirque Lodge rehab, traded in his old friends Johnnie Walker, Jack Daniel's, and Mr. Belvedere for a gang of eastern ayurvedic practitioners/sober coaches, paid for his own insurance, *and* agreed to have his AA sponsor on set daily. The gamble seems to have paid off. Rumors on the set are that Nic's scenes are incredible, maybe even Oscar-nomination-worthy. I'd like to think that Julian's gowns help keep him in character—which was the very angle I used when I asked my father for a second favor: hiring Julian. Now it's time for Kate to return the favor for me. I press "2" on speed dial.

"Christopher and I haven't had sex in a week," Kate barks into the phone after one ring.

"Jesus, Kate, what ever happened to hello?" I say. "And you're talking about my *brother*."

"I'm talking about my—" Kate struggles to get the word "boyfriend" out—even after eleven months and being in love with him since she was sixteen. To say Kate has intimacy issues would be an understatement. In Kate's case, the apple didn't fall very far from a pretty barren parental tree. Her mother and father were divorced for three years before they told their teenaged kids. They maintained separate bedrooms because their father "had a bad back and needed his orthopedic mattress," while Kate's mother had "insomnia" and had to have her waterbed—it was the only thing that soothed her. The kids were the last to find out about the split. The announcement came on the heels of her mother's decision to marry the tennis instructor she'd secretly been dating for five months. This was after Kate found out that she'd been secretly dating the personal trainer for fourteen months before that. Kate's mother now lives in South Beach with Hubby No. Five. I was with Kate for every one of her mother's weddings—until this last one, when Kate had finally had enough of playing Maid of Honor in her mother's Beaming Bride Redux. Meanwhile, her father's living in Southampton with Countless Girlfriend Under the Age of Twenty-five. They split holidays with the kids.

"And you were the one who convinced me it was a good idea for us to live together," Kate continues.

"Because that's what adults do when they're in love and in committed relationships, Kate. And besides, if you didn't *live* together, you'd *never* see each other."

"I barely see him as it is. We're on totally different schedules. He's been doing night shoots for the last three weeks. I don't understand why musicians can't film videos during the day." Kate expels a long sigh. I picture her twisting her glossy chocolate tresses around a finger. "He's so talented, he should be shooting a feature film instead of wasting his time with music videos and commercial shoots for Jennifer Aniston's new line of "Smar*ter*" Water and Ashley Tisdale's new protein bars for tweens, but he doesn't want to hear it from me or let me help him. His *Burning Man* doc was so good and it's been so nicely received, but he hasn't seemed to want to capitalize on the momentum. And the sex—"

"Kate, please. I don't want to hear about you and my brother having sex," I interrupt. The only "L" word Kate is interested in is that of her "Libido"—it's so much easier than that other one: "Love." Kate doesn't go for easy in any other area of her life. She's a fighter. I mean, the way she took on Katzenberg for Cricket, for instance, or the way she's taken on Baz Luhrman for me. She's no coward. She's one of the bravest people I know. But when it comes to her personal life, it's as though the Great Wall of China took up residence around her heart.

"Lola, it's six a.m. I've already done an hour of cardio, rolled all my NYC and European calls and I'm *still* stressed," Kate says. "Is it so bad that I just want to sleep with Christopher before I have to spend the day with Nic and your father on set? I thought the whole point of living with someone was so that you could have sex at any time. But since Christopher isn't here I have to settle for my vibrator."

"Okay, I'm going to pretend like you didn't just say that. New topic: How are the reshoots going?" I ask. A sore point. The studio is forcing Papa to reshoot some of Nic's scenes because he tested low with the fourteen- to-nineteen-year-old demographic during some prescreenings.

"The studio is obsessed with those moronic test-screening feedback cards. Now your father is blaming *me* for convincing him to cast Nic instead of Emile Hirsch, and the studio's hired some kind of 'cool hunter.' Who gives a shit about what some pimply teens think? We're talking Nic could win another Oscar and there's already been buzz about Cannes. Plus he looks hotter than Penelope Cruz. And Hollywood loves a comeback story. Can't you just tell your dad to leave Nic's scenes alone?"

"You're kidding, right? Do you know how hard it was for me to ask him about Nic the first time? Kate, just be glad you got Nic back to above the title, especially after he was caught in the wardrobe trailer with that coke. Did he really think he was fooling anyone by saying it was baby powder and patting it under his armpits? Lucky for him that the judge let him pull a Paris Hilton and trade community service for prison."

"Yeah, I know." Kate sighs. "He's hard enough to control; I just don't want anything to happen to freak him out. So how's his gown for the prison break scene? Am I going to see you on the set next week?"

"The gown is unbelievable. It's an orgy of hand-embroidered flowers, paillettes, and tiny crystalline beads. I'm flying it back to L.A. tonight, with a few backups." I take a deep breath and go for it. "Kate, I hate to ask again, but do you know if Baz has made a decision yet about Julian?"

"No, not yet. I told you, I'll let you know the second I hear anything."

"Okay, okay. We really *need* this movie," I say, my desperation seeping from every pore. "Also, I'm really worried about Cricket. Do you think there's any chance Baz will consider her?" Not only did Chili Lu's gowns not work; the actress *wearing* those two gowns didn't work either—apparently she made Megan Fox's performance in *Transformers* 2 seem Oscar-worthy. Baz has been very quietly on the hunt for a fresh new face he can use to plug this hole in his movie—and to quiet the bad buzz that's snowballing before Perez Hilton and TMZ tank it before the first screening. I don't want Cricket to know, but Kate and I have been campaigning for him to test her for the role.

"I'm *trying*, Lo," Kate says, exasperated. "I already sent Baz Cricket's head shot and reel, but there's only so much I can do. Now, I have to go take care of *myself* since your brother isn't home."

Click.

I walk back into Julian's bedroom to rouse Sleeping Beauty.

"Julian, it's been ten minutes. Get up," I say, stirring him.

"Just ten more minutes. Please," Julian begs.

"No, Julian. You have to get up. *Now!*" I demand.

Suddenly there's a loud knock at the front door.

"That's probably the rose point lace you ordered," I tell Julian. "Listen, I'm running to the door, but I want you in the shower by the time I get back. Quick, quick," I say, rustling the sheets. "I need to get ready. I don't need to be worrying about getting you out of bed." I close the bedroom door behind me.

I shield myself with the huge stainless door so that I can sign quickly for the delivery.

"Coz," I yelp as I fling open the door. She doesn't bother to wait for me to invite her in, and I'm absolutely humiliated to be found in my skivvies at nine o'clock in the morning.

"I heard the lingerie look was in, but I didn't realize you were taking it so literally," Coz says from behind the mammoth black shades shielding her ice blue eyes. "Is that one of Julian's?" she asks. Her bone-straight platinum hair, right out of Michelle Pfeiffer in *Scarface,* grazes shoulders any Olympic javelin thrower would kill for.

I feel about one centimeter tall. I crane my neck to try and meet her gaze, but my head only comes up to her waist. Coz has to be at least seven feet tall with those snake skyscrapers on her feet. I'd give all of my mother's vintage Alaia for legs as long as hers.

"Hi Coz," I say, trying to pull down my nightgown over my tush. "We weren't expecting you till this afternoon."

A loud sigh escapes her red-painted lips. "Ash, you said you moved the appointment to nine a.m.," Coz says icily to her assistant, a lanky, plaid bow-tied, Kanye West look-alike cowering behind his BlackBerry.

"I did," he says, frantically scrolling through his e-mails. "Oh, I'm just seeing now that my e-mail didn't go through," he says sheepishly. "Sorry."

"Ash, one more screwup and you're dead to me," Coz says flatly. "*Gone, gonzo, good-bye* if you mess up again," she says, turning away from her shrinking assistant and training her attention back on me with a faraway look in her eyes. "Well, we're here now, so do you mind if we just have a quick look, Lola," she says. It's not a question. She breezes past me in a floor-length white mink coat that's the same shade as her milky skin. I'd better hide all the red paint or Julian, my die-hard PETA-ite, will go Jackson Pollock on that thing.

"Just give me a second to get changed and get Julian. The collection is over here if you'd like to start looking at it. Julian's calling it 'Bondage Ballet,'" I say, gesturing toward the fall samples, the spiraling lace and violet, caramel, mint, and chartreuse tulle dance dresses cinched in with hip-jutting, fetishistic patent belts to create the perfect hourglass silhouette.

Julian walks out of his bedroom nearly naked, except for those tighty whities, with Tom Ford in one hand and his sketchbook in the other. "Can I see the lace samples?" he asks, not noticing Coz and Ash hidden behind the racks of gauzy sheer skirts.

"Hi Julian," Coz says, stepping into view.

Julian's sketchbook and Tom Ford thud to the floor.

"Wow. This is like one of my recurring nightmares, except it's *real*," Julian says, patting at his messy raven locks. "Coz, honey, you've caught me pre-caffeine and clothes. You weren't supposed to be here for hours."

"Ash completely screwed up my schedule. I'm so sorry, Julian," Coz says, her voice wiped clean of any trace of actual regret. "But believe me, I've seen far worse."

"Excuse us," I say, grabbing Julian by the arm and dragging him out of sight and into the bedroom.

I change faster than Adriana Lima backstage at the Victoria's Secret show and reappear in a pair of midnight blue, high-waisted flared cords and a cream J. Crew cashmere cardigan.

"Julian's playing with the ultrafeminine romanticism and fluidity of ballet in stark opposition to the stiff, structured, binding lace-up corsets," I say, holding up a breathtaking, floor-grazing, asymmetric, sheer-gauze gown with a trailing train and an intricate interior bustier that Julian's planning on showing with thigh-high dominatrix boots.

"Ash, be sure to put the new accessories editor at the top of the call sheet," Coz says, turning to her assistant. "What's her name? Whatever," she says, brushing away the inquiry. "I need to talk to her about the July issue." Clearly the gown I'm holding in front of her face isn't having the slightest impact. But I continue anyway.

"Julian has a flair for making chiffon flow and flutter in a way that defies gravity," I say, pointing to another gown.

"And Derek Lam," Coz interrupts me and turns back to her assistant, "to set a meeting to go by their studio for the July feature piece." Clearly this nightmare woman would like to be anywhere but here. Unabashedly, I press on, despite my face, which I can feel has turned a deep crimson.

"I think some of the dresses could be perfect for your 'Fashionista to Recessionista' story since the bondage is really a metaphor for how we're all bound by the failing economy while the dreaminess of ballet suggests hope for the future," I offer. Okay. I know I'm really reaching. But I'm desperate here.

"Mm-hmm," Coz says absently from behind her giant sunglasses that she has yet to lower while checking her iPhone. "Yeah, you know, I don't think they're going to work, but maybe there'll be something next month," she says, her focus still trained on the screen as she scrolls and taps. Funny. That's what she said last month when I'd been given a two-minute phone audition to discuss the JPEGs of some other Julian inspirations. And the month before. And the month before that. I thought her visit would change everything.

"Oh," I say, deflated. "Listen, I also wanted to talk about *Cut-Throat Couture*. I think Julian would be a perfect guest judge for the show."

"*Everyone* wants to get on the show," Coz says. "We've got Zac Posen, Stella McCartney, Erin Wasson. The slate's already full."

Sure it is. I'm sure if Marc Jacobs wanted to be a guest judge, she wouldn't tell him that the slate was already full. What is *with* this woman? What does she have against Julian and me?

"Did you know that Naomi Campbell modeled in Julian's student fashion show at Central Saint Martins?" I say of *Cut-Throat Couture*'s infamous host. Her dust-ups with fellow judge Donatella Versace have been getting all of the big buzz on the show. In their latest run-in, with one million YouTube hits and counting, Campbell removed a six-inch stiletto from her arched foot and threw it at Donatella's head, nearly taking out her bleached blond extensions as it grazed her temple.

"Naomi's never mentioned it to me," Coz says flatly.

"They became friends when Julian interned for Oscar de la Renta. It was a big deal when she walked in his show," I say.

"I guess they're no longer close since she hasn't walked for him in years," Coz says. Just as I'm fantasizing about grabbing the red paint from Julian's closet *myself*, Julian resurfaces in a pair of dark denim jeans with a charcoal gray, square-shouldered blazer, a white button-down, and a pair of chunky oxblood saddle shoes. Tom Ford has on a miniature hand-tied bowtie.

"Julian, darling, the collection is gorge," Coz tells him, still swiping at her iPhone. Too bad there isn't a "Bitchitor" App on there that would make her mink coat instantaneously go up in flames—or at least alert PETA of her whereabouts. "I wish I could stay longer but I'm off to meet Mrs. Herrera and I can't keep her waiting."

As Coz heads for the front door, she pauses to pick up Julian's sketchbook, which he'd left in a heap on the floor. "I didn't realize you were designing wedding gowns now," Coz says, flipping page after page of Julian's sublime sketches for *Four Weddings and a Bris*. Uh-oh.

"Coz, that's a personal sketchbook," I say, trying to stop her. But it's too late.

"These are nothing," Julian says, rushing over to take the sketches from Coz.

"*Really?*" Coz says. If she removed those sunglasses, I'm certain I would see one of her albino brows raised. Oh god. This is bad. She totally knows that Julian is in the running to replace little Chili Lu. "Frankly, Julian, those sketches are sophomoric. You're better than that," she says, her already translucent skin turning an odd shade of purple-white. Did those monster shoulders just deflate a bit or am I imagining things?

"You don't want to keep Mrs. Herrera waiting," I say. "You should really go," I say, practically pushing her out the front door, with Ash trailing behind her.

We wait until the sound of footsteps retreats. "That was a complete disaster," Julian says, flopping onto the sofa. "You didn't even get the chance to pitch Nic in drag for the cover."

"I'll call her tomorrow, once the smell of brimstone dissipates. That woman is awful," I say, plunking down beside him. "I feel like we need to sage the entire loft."

"You get the sage. Tom Ford and I are going back to bed."

"No, Julian. You can't. We have our conference call with LVMH and you need to finish Nic Knight's gown so I can take it on the plane with me tonight."

"Lola, I *adore* Lev, but how long can you keep flying back and forth to L.A.? At some point you're going to have to choose."

"Julian, don't start with this. Please. Not now."

Seven exhausting hours later, as I plop myself into the standard-issue smelly taxi en route to JFK, I stop to ponder Julian's question. Do I really have to choose? Just when I finally found a *real* man in Tinseltown, I had to move to Manhattan to become the CEO of Julian Tennant Inc. Why are the gods of career and love conspiring against me? Why don't they want me to have it at all—or at least all on the same coast? Screw that. I'm not about to let three thousand miles stand in my way.

I've had to fly back to L.A. from NYC every other weekend for the past thirty-something weeks just to see Lev. I've got more frequent flyer miles than Phil Keoghan. Or Hillary Clinton. But I've never been happier. Or more dead tired.

I reach into my black nylon overnight bag for a pair of Lev's old scrubs and his ratty Harvard sweatshirt to change into. Julian would go into anaphylactic fashion shock if he saw me in Lev's clothes, which is why I have to change in the back of a dirty taxi every other Friday. I'm fairly certain every taxi driver in Manhattan has seen me in my underwear at this point. But the thing is, I'm really *happy* in his ratty sweatshirt and scrubs. If Anna Wintour saw me in *this* she'd seriously regret ever putting me on her Best Dressed list a couple of years ago. But all the designer duds and Louboutins in the world couldn't rival *this* kind of happiness.

Next I slip off my knee-high, lace-up, tobacco, high-heeled boots and put on a pair of navy—*Crocs*. Yes, *Crocs*. I almost had a shoe seizure when Lev gave them to me. When Julian saw them, he almost fainted onto his copy of *Women's Wear Daily*. But the thing is, they're actually really *comfortable*. Something I never knew footwear could be. And they're not *that* ugly. Okay, they are *that* ugly, but it's not like I'm parading down any red carpets in them. The only carpets I tend to walk on when I'm in Los Angeles these days are the ones in Lev's house that he brought back from Africa when he was volunteering with Doctors Without Borders. He has mementos from every country he volunteered in with DWB scattered around the house—a laid-back, mismatched, eco-friendly place in L.A. where all of my belongings are stored in his garage. (I gave up my rented Spanish jewel box across from the Chateau Marmont.) Lev's reupholstered hemp sofas from the salvage yard, reclaimed wood coffee table, navy canvas beanbags, and bedside tables made from recycled tires may be totally unchic by Julian's standards, but his place feels like a home instead of a museum.

I shove my boots deep into the bottom of my carry-on where Lev won't find them. He still has *no* idea that I've jumped back on the stiletto wagon, something I'm not so sure he would be thrilled about given my newly healed broken ankle. And Julian believes that I ceremoniously torched the Crocs months ago. So here I am again, a double agent in the worlds of fashion and love.

I dial Lev's cell.

"Hey babe," Lev says.

"You can't believe the day I've had," I say as I launch into a full-throttle diatribe about my dressing down by the money-crunchers at LVMH, the awkward pas-de-deux with the Personal Shopper department at Saks after Julian asked if they could remove all the leather and fur from the floor during his personal appearance, a battle royale with my Excel spreadsheet, an argument over piecework with my favorite subcontractor, and more. "Lev, I'm just not sure we can pull this off. I'm getting squeezed on the prices like you wouldn't believe."

"You're going to find a way to sort everything out, just like you always do. I know how hard you've been working and I'm really proud of you, Lola," Lev says when I'm done with my rant.

I've never been with a man who's believed in me the way Lev does or been *proud* of me. Heck, I just learned to be proud of *myself*—after ten-plus years on Dr. Gilmore's chintz couch. I let his words pulse through me. "Thank you," I finally say.

"Is there anything I can do to help?"

"Do you think you could slip me just a teensy overdose of Ativan for Coz? Sorry, I know that was mean. I'll figure out something," I say, hoping I really will. "I haven't even asked about your day. How's it going?"

Lev lets out a groan. "There was a drive-by shooting on the 405 and we had four GSWs. I stabilized three of them, but I had to do an open thoracotomy on one of them."

"*What?* Oh my god. I feel like such an asshole. Here I am going on and on about *fashion* and you're talking about gunshot wounds and slicing someone's chest open."

"Didn't you tell me that people *kill* for fashion? I've gone to enough events with you to see firsthand how bloody things can get," Lev says.

"Is everyone going to live?" I ask nervously.

"Yes, looks like it."

"And here I thought mine was the only life you'd saved." As I say the words I can hear Dr. Gilmore's voice in my head, "*You* saved *yourself. You* conquered your Career Deficit Disorder *and* your Actorholism. *You* stood on your own two Louboutins." I *know* that she's right and that there are no Doctors in Shining Armor in *real* life, but when I went flying off those four-inch stilettos, it sure was nice to have Dr. Levin help me up. "I can't wait to see you," I say.

"Me too," he says. "Shoot, I've got to run, I'm being paged."

"I love you," I say.

"I love you too," Lev says. "I'll be the guy waiting for you at the airport." *Click.*

Screw you, geography. I'm determined to have it *all*: the Doctor Boyfriend and the career. It's official. I'm not only bicoastal, I'm *Bi-Lolar: The condition by which I swing like a pendulum between the diametrically opposing poles of the fashion world with my Best Gay Forever and the real world with my Doctor Boyfriend. The strong gravitational pull between these two converse worlds on opposite coasts resulting in a major identity crisis to the point that I don't know which shoe fits me anymore: the Louboutin stiletto or the Croc.*

3

You know, it's not like my mom gave us any warning. I just picked up her message when the plane landed. It's so last minute. I can totally get us out of it," I say, begging. I'm changing in the bedroom while Lev is sprawled out on the couch in the living room. We just got the news that Mom wants us to go to their house for dinner.

"Lo, I'm going to have to meet them sooner or later," he says. "I say we go."

Lev and I have been together for almost a year now and my parents have never even asked to meet him. But it's not like Lev's crazy residency schedule gives him much spare time, either. Not to mention, I can't remember the last time the Santisis ate together as a family. Actually, I think it was probably when I was five for Swifty Lazar's Oscar Night

Party at Spago? Or maybe it was when I was seven at the old Morton's after my father's premiere of *The Assassination*. No, no, it was Christopher's bar mitzvah.

"I just don't understand why the urgency tonight," I call out as I slip into my dress and reach for a box I've stashed deep inside the closet. "I mean, after all this time, why the sudden command performance of *Meet the Parents*? Maybe we should call and say we can't make it. I mean, you're exhausted, I'm exhausted. It's not easy being bi-Lolar."

"I know it's a lot for you having to travel out here every other weekend," he says, "but this is where my life's work is. This residency is getting me for all it's worth. But let's just do this. I'll finally get to see where you come from. C'mon, it'll be fun."

"Let's see if you still feel that way after you meet my folks," I say, stepping out into the living room. I twirl in front of Lev in my new white crepe shift. "What do you think? It's one of Julian's."

Lev whistles in appreciation. "You look just as beautiful all dressed up as you do in my old scrubs," he says.

"Thanks, sweetheart," I say. "And here's the thing," I add, opening up the box I've hidden behind my back. "A dress like this really doesn't go with Crocs. It needs something like these." I show him the sky-high stilettos. His face clouds. "I know you don't like high heels, Lev, but just think! We never would have met without them. And the truth is . . . as much as I love my Crocs, I love my Louboutins too." *Don't make me choose,* I think. *Don't make me choose.*

Lev rolls his eyes and grins. "Lola, I just want what makes you happy. If wearing ridiculously high heels makes you happy, then I'm fine with it. Just promise me that if you do another face plant in them, I'm the only one you get to play doctor with."

"It's a deal," I say, slipping on my shoes. Maybe being bi-Lolar won't always be so awful.

"Careful, you could get a nose bleed from the change of altitude," Lev teases me as we drive in his ten-year-old Volvo over the hill from the Valley to Hollywood. I've deliberately avoided going anywhere near Hollyweird when I'm in L.A. these days. A recovered Actorholic doesn't need to visit the bar. "I don't know that I've actually ever driven through these gates," he says as we make our way into Bel Air for dinner at *Chez Santisi*.

"Just make me a promise," I plead with the fear of my crazy Hollyweird parents as I look into his green eyes, "Don't hold it against me?"

"I promise." Lev laughs and reaches over to seal it with a kiss.

My single hope for tonight is that my parents will actually notice that I'm really happy—and in a functional relationship for the first time in my life—which is anything but Hollywood now. Now let's just hope they behave.

"Make a right here," I say, pointing to Chez Santisi, a sprawling Spanish-style house that was built for the silent movie star Colleen Moore in the 1920s. My mother is constantly redecorating and remodeling the place with items from her world travels: the enormous ornamentally wood-carved front door that originally belonged to a Hindu temple, the tumbled marble mosaic tile in the Olympic-sized swimming pool from Morocco, the Venetian blown-glass chandelier in the entryway. "Home Sweet Home," I joke as we pull up the long gravel driveway lined with jacaranda trees.

Stepping out of the car, I smooth the fabric of my dress.

"You're gorgeous, Lola Santisi, in Crocs or Labootininis," Lev says. And I love him even more for *still* having no idea how to properly pronounce Louboutins. We step up to the huge front door and ring the doorbell. "What's that music?" I say as we wait for the door to open. It sounds like— *Fiddler on the Roof.*

"Shabbat Santisi shalom," my mother says excitedly as she flings her arms open to embrace Lev. Her usually frizzy blond hair has been tamed into a smooth up-do. And she really overdid the makeup tonight. Her blue eyes are loaded down with smoky shadow and reams of mascara. "You must be Lev."

"*Shabbat Santisi shalom?!*" I say. "What's going on, Mom?"

"We're all so busy these days, it's easy to forget the importance of family," Mom says. The family she leaves behind for Deeksha retreats in India, colon cleanses at We Care in Desert Hot Springs, and when she's home— the Byron & Tracey Salon for daily hair and makeup? *That* family?

"It's lovely to meet you, Mrs. Santisi. If I'd known this was a Shabbat dinner I would have brought matzoh ball soup," Lev says.

"That's so sweet of you, Lev. And please, call me Blanca. But I actually made the matzoh ball soup myself," my mother says proudly.

"You what?!" I exclaim. "Who are you and what'd you do with my mother?"

"Oh, Lola, you're such a silly!" she says, smiling off into the distance. Who is she looking for? "Do you like my outfit? It's a Bedouin gown I picked up in Israel when I was on that pilgrimage to the Red Sea," she says, the gazillion gold bangles up and down her arms clanging together as she runs her hands over the beaded caftan. Pilgrimage? What pilgrimage? The only pilgrimage my mother takes is to Rodeo Drive for the trunk shows. "Alex, Alex darling, where *are* you? You're missing the moment," my mother suddenly yells.

"Alex? Who's Alex, Mom?"

But before my mother has time to answer, a scruffy-haired, thirty-something man in gray cords and a black hoodie wielding a video camera comes running into the room, accompanied by an equally scruffy guy carrying a boom and another carrying a light.

"Oh, darling, didn't I tell you? Alex is my wonderful, wonderful cameraman. Now, don't you mind him one bit. Just pretend he isn't even here." Mom turns to Alex. "Are you rolling?" Alex buries his eye behind the lens and gives her a thumbs-up.

Suddenly my mother throws herself around Lev. "We are so glad to finally *meet* you," she says. "Welcome to our humble home! Shabbat Santisi shalom!"

"Mom, can I have a word with you outside?" I ask.

"Darling, there's nothing that you can't say to me here, in front of Alex's camera. This is a *reality* show. The *realer* the better."

Stupid, stupid me. I actually believed that this evening was about Lev and me. Of course it's not. It's about her—and *Wristwatch Wives*.

Mom is coproducer and costar. There's also Christine Buchenwald—the forty-five-year-old—okay, maybe fifty-five, but after that last face-lift, you wouldn't guess a day over forty—wife of Peter Buchenwald, the movie producer who's famous for his womanizing and thirty-year habit as a functioning cocaine addict as well as his blockbuster movies. Christine went from being the Daughter Of a Famous Movie Tycoon, to a terrible marriage and Wife Of a Famous Movie Tycoon. Then there's Lucinda Mayes, otherwise known as The Newby. She's the twenty-eight-year-old Wife Of Stan Mayes, the founder of the hottest agency in town, and the agent behind the careers of some of the most powerful actors in Hollywood. And finally, Francesca Della Rosa, the ex-wife of the owner of Della Rosa restaurant. Despite their divorce and Gabriel's prompt second marriage to a super-model, he and Francesca remain in constant communication. As in: "Clooney needs a table for six at eight." Click. They share custody of their two teenaged daughters, who often grace the pages of *Vogue* and *Bazaar*, photographed in the Hollywood Hills Lautner House Gabriel left to Francesca in the divorce. Since the divorce,

Francesca's gotten involved in her own venture: a restaurant in Hollywood to be opened in conjunction with—surprise—the premiere of *Wristwatch Wives.*

"Mom, outside. Now," I demand, dragging her by her Bedouin gown until we're outside the front door and away from Alex's prying lens. "The cameras? Tonight? So *this* is why you finally wanted to meet Lev? To get footage for your damn show? And here I thought that for once you actually cared about whether I was happy. Lev is really important to me, Mom."

"And this show is really important to *me*, Lola," my mother says. "*Wristwatch Wives* is my shot at something. Honey, you're getting a shot at your dream as CEO of Julian Tennant. And I want that for you so much," my mother says, grabbing both my hands in hers, looking me deeply in the eyes, then kissing me on the forehead. "I really do," she adds softly, looking beyond me. She drags me away from the front door then breaks her motherly revelry. "It's always been about your father. I want out of that shadow," my mother says, dropping my hands. And if anyone can understand wanting that—it's me. "Besides, what could I do? I just found out that Francesca got footage of the family's intervention for the daughter's Oxy addiction. She is *such* a show-off. And Lucinda's filming the opening for her new line of vegan detox jewelry. And Christine's got couples counseling *and* her colonoscopy, like that hasn't been done before. All I've got is a lot of Papa swearing about that ridiculous Nic character and Christopher moping. I've worked too hard to end up on the cutting room floor," she says. "The network says if we don't grab viewers in the first two weeks, we're dead for pickup for the next season." Mom grabs up my hand again and drags me back to the front door, her face softening in a smile. "Just think: if you end up marrying Lev, we'll have all this footage of the first time he met your family to show your children."

"Why do you keep looking above my head?" I ask. And as I follow her eye line I notice something new by the front door, and it's not a mezuzah: it's a camera. "Jesus, Mom!?"

"Oh, just pretend they're part of the woodwork. Now can we please just go inside and try and have a nice time? I've been working all day on this dinner," my mother says. "Please, honey, for me?"

"Okay, Mom, I guess," I say, thinking about how my mother has indeed always been the silent force behind my father, who's always grabbed 100 percent of the spotlight. It would be nice for my mother to have her shot at creating something. "But let me just check with Lev to see if he's okay with it."

"Thanks, sweetheart," Mom says, fishing around in her caftan pocket. "And would you mind having him sign this little release, please?"

"I'm so sorry," I whisper to Lev as I walk back inside. He's leafing through the *New Yorker* he found on the coffee table next to the new *People*. I quickly scan *People*'s headlines: "Rock Royalty's Super Couple Om and Nano: Saving the Planet—One Tree at a Time" catches my eye above "Cut-Throat Couture's Coz Dishes on the New Season." Just seeing her name sends a chill down my spine. I flip the mag over. One anxiety moment at a time. I try to shake off my work anxiety and focus on the anxiety at hand. "I didn't think she'd be filming tonight," I whisper to Lev. "Are you okay?"

"Yes. Stop worrying about me. I'm fine. Are you okay?"

"As long as you don't let go of my hand," I say as we follow my mother into the dining room, where the gang's already seated at the dining table. Christopher is slumped back in his chair, one hand placed on Kate's thigh, the other brushing back his disheveled sandy hair. Kate's sneaking a peek at the BlackBerry she has resting in her lap, her intense blue eyes accentuated by her slicked-back chestnut ponytail. The strumming of my father's impatient fingers on the table is the only sound in the room. He hasn't taken his white Panama hat off, and I see that he has bare feet beneath the orange sarong he's wearing. He looks like when he woke up this morning he mistook Bel Air for Havana.

"Hey guys," I say as Kate and Christopher get up to give us a hug. I can't help but notice the tension between them.

"Dad, this is Lev," I say nervously. It was so much easier when I brought Actor Boyfriends home. It was just expected that they'd sit there in rapt adoration of my father, and that he'd write them off as idiots—which they were. With Lev it feels different.

My father puffs away on his cigar with one hand and extends the other, "Welcome to the zoo," my father says, shaking Lev's hand. That's it: it feels like Lev is a zoologist visiting the animals.

"I'm very glad to finally be meeting you, Mr. Santisi," he says.

"Paulie, call me Paulie," my father says.

"I'd like to do a Shabbat prayer. Please, everyone, hold hands," my mother instructs as she lights the ridiculously expensive Diptych candles she uses for her weekly Goddess meetings instead of Shabbat ones. I look sideways at her with those eerie camera lenses peering on and I'm beginning to wonder who the director is at this table. It's certainly not my father, who takes that moment to clamp down on that cigar between his teeth.

"Why is this night unlike any other night?" my mother says, her head bowed solemnly into her chest.

"Mom, I'm pretty sure that's Passover," I interrupt.

"Oh geezus, Blanca," my father bellows. "Is this all really necessary? You already took these fucking cameras to Al's birthday party last night at DeNiro's house. Enough is enough. Can't we just eat?"

"Mom, when did you decide to take up Judaism?" Christopher chimes in.

"I've always been very identified with my Judaism," my mother says, shooting Christopher a slightly warning glance.

"Yeah, you love Goldie Hawn," I say.

"And the lox from Nate 'n Al's," Christopher adds.

"I never take off my Star of David," Mom says, stroking the Jen Meyer gold design around her neck—which I've never seen her wear before. Ever. "And I go to mass as often as possible," she adds vehemently.

"Mom, you mean 'services,'" I say. "It's not called mass. Mass is for Catholics. We're Jewish. They're called 'services.'"

"Now please, all of you, shut up and let me get back to praying," my mother demands with a sideways glance to the cameras as she bows her chin back to her chest.

"Get that fucking thing out of my face," my father yells at Alex, who's gotten a little too close. "Come on, Blanca," he continues. "This is absolutely ridiculous. Can we please just eat and get this done with."

"All right, all right," she says, waving her arms in the air and rushing into the kitchen, quickly reappearing with a tureen of matzoh ball soup. "Honey, could you give me a hand with the platters on the counter?" she asks.

"Where's Lorena?" I ask, looking around for Nanny No. 9—the last nanny in the string that raised Chris and me and stayed on after we left to be my parents' housekeeper.

"Never mind," my mother says, quickly swatting away my inquiry because she obviously wants to appear to be a Hollywood-Housewife-Who-Has-No-Help. Is this a joke?

"Let me help you, Mom," I say, getting up from the table and returning with the two silver platters.

"Mmmmm, lobster ravioli," Kate says. "This looks fabulous, Blanca!"

"And pork cheeks," my mother adds as she leans over Lev to serve him.

"Even the shiksa knows this isn't what you'd call a kosher meal," Kate whispers to Christopher.

And then Lev leans into me and whispers, "Isn't it a bit odd to be eating pork at Shabbat dinner?"

"If that's all you think is odd, we're in good shape," I whisper back, putting my hand on his knee beneath the table and mouthing "I'm sorry." But before I can get a sense of whether he's holding up okay, my father starts in.

"So, Lev, I guess you're some kind of doctor?"

"Actually, Paulie, I'm in my final year of residency at Cedars-Sinai. I'm planning to be a trauma specialist," Lev says. "I'm basically living in the ER these days."

"So, I guess you get a lot of the crackheads and drunk frat kids, right?" Papa chuckles. "You probably get paid shit, right? You know Frank Luks? He's my cardiologist. Best fucking cardiologist in the country. He makes like, five hundred, six hundred grand a year. You ever thought of cardiology?"

"Papa, Lev's job is incredibly important," I say. "Do you realize how many lives he's saved? What does it matter how much he—"

"Lola, it's fine," Lev says, clasping my hand, then turning back to Papa. "Paulie, cardiology's a fine specialty, but my heart's in emergency medicine. The field has made the most incredible advances in just the last five years. Last week we saved a guy with a dissected aorta who wouldn't have had a chance at a less cutting-edge ER. You should've seen how the team worked—it was like . . . almost like we'd choreographed it. It's literally the stuff of life and death."

"I bet it was incredible to watch," Mom says, her eyes glittering. "Lev, what you do sounds very impressive."

"Thanks, Blanca," Lev says. "I really feel like I make a differ—"

"Yeah, fine, whatever," Papa huffs. Class dismissed. He turns immediately to my brother.

"So, Chris, when are you going to stop with these ridiculous commercials and get down to some real work," he demands.

"Oh no," I mutter beneath my breath.

"Those 'ridiculous commercials' pay the bills," Christopher says, tearing into his pork cheek a little too vigorously with his knife.

"Paulie, do you know how many of my clients would give their left arm to be directing some of the spots Chris is doing?" Kate is a lioness protecting the den.

"It's commercial tripe," my father persists. "It's beneath him."

"Please, Dad, not now," Chris says, gesturing to the cameras circling about. Which seems to put a muzzle on my father—for the moment.

"Who wants rugelach?" Mom trills, jetting to the kitchen and returning with a tray of them and a stack of photo albums tucked under her arm. "I baked it myself! Lev, may I serve you some?" They taste suspiciously familiar. They're in fact the rugelach from Nate 'n Al's I've been eating since I was a kid. Ironically, they're the one testament to our Judaism that my mother could actually stand by, as they were always in the house. She plunks the array of photo albums onto the table.

"Uh-oh." I sigh as Christopher lets out a moan from across the table.

"Really, Mom? Do we have to do this?" he asks.

But Lev's already grabbing one of them as Kate does the same. He immediately starts laughing as he opens to a shot of me at six years old dressed in one of my mother's magenta flowered DVF wrap dresses that's plunging down to my bellybutton and that's so long it's dragging on the floor, a gold five-inch Versace heel peeking out from beneath it. My eyes are bright and hopeful as I smile widely for the camera beneath a huge hat emblazoned with a silver G.

"So that's how you walk in those heels of yours. Practice started early on," Lev teases, rubbing my back.

"What I want to know is where is that hat?" I say, leaning in to take a closer look at the signature charcoal gray seventies Givenchy that's nearly covering my entire face.

"That's a total mini-version of Lo, isn't it," Kate says, running a red painted nail over the photo and turning to Chris, who nods in agreement.

"She's always had a light around her," my mom says to Lev as I feel my face turn crimson. I'm suddenly the vulnerable six-year-old girl in the picture. "A sense of humor, and, of course, impeccable taste. Raiding my closet to play dress-up was a regular occurrence in the Santisi house," she adds maternally. "I felt it nurtured Lola's creative spirit."

"Look at this one." Kate flips to a shot of Christopher and laughs. "The aspiring director." It's a nine-year-old Chris sitting in our father's director's chair with a camera in his hand in a miniature version of the outfit that he'd wear today: little Levi's, a plaid button-down, and red Converse.

"That was on the set of *The Assassination*," my father chimes in. "It was summer, and the days we shot in L.A. Chris came with me to the set every day. He could see the monitor from where he sat. So he got to see everything we shot," my father says, a hint of pride in his voice.

"I helped the script supervisor. Well, I'd sit next to her and she let me pretend that I was helping," Chris says, looking at me with an unusual shyness about him. I have the sudden urge to leap over the table and wrap my arms around my brother. Underneath Chris's coolness, he's still that insecure nine-year-old boy trying to win over his father—or at least get him to look sideways in his direction.

"There isn't one photograph of you in here where you're not holding a camera," Lev says to Chris.

"I gave him his first Leica," my father says, leaning back in his chair and lighting his cigar.

"He said, 'Take pictures of what you see'—I was six years old," Chris says, rubbing his refined hands over the knees of his worn-in Levi's.

"And there isn't one photo of you without that sketchbook," Lev adds, turning his inquisitive green eyes to me.

"I told them both to document their feelings," Mom says. "It wasn't easy for them growing up in Hollywood with busy parents."

"'Busy' is a nice way of putting it," I say under my breath. Totally consumed with their lives would be more accurate. It was pretty much Chris and me against the world. Still is.

"Lola told me she wanted to be a fashion designer when she was seven," my father says, popping an entire rugelach in his mouth.

"He showed up the next day with a Moleskine journal and said, 'Draw what inspires you,'" I say to Lev. "It's the same kind of journal I carry with me everywhere to this day."

"Oh, Lev, you've never seen this one." Kate offers up the photo album. "This is the famous mother-daughter Santisi shot."

"It kinda says it all," I mutter.

"This is where Lola's love of fashion began," my mother says, laying a protective manicured hand on the photo Papa took the night I was born. "She was born on Oscar Night, you know." Mom's still in her Thierry Mugler one-shoulder black-and-silver sequined minidress in the delivery room at Cedars. I'm sucking on my mother's boob and she's sucking on a Camel Light. "She's given me fashion advice for the Oscars ever since," she says, flipping to a family photo from the night my father won his first Oscar for *The Assassination*. The Santisis: a more slender version of my father in the forefront, the warrior chief puffing proudly on a Cohiba, wave of dark hair, olive skin, and salt-and-pepper beard. My mother, standing slightly behind my father in the cream Chanel I picked out for her, blond hair smoothed into a gentle wave as she tugs absent-mindedly on a diamond-studded ear with one hand and waves a Camel Light at the camera lens with the other. Us kids at their feet: eleven-year-old Chris aiming his camera at whoever's taking the picture so that his face is covered by his mop of golden brown hair. He's paired his tux with Converse. And me, eight years old in the white taffeta Lacroix pouf I paired with a black camisole with white polka dots and black patent Mary Janes—and of course—my sketchbook tucked beneath an arm to document my favorite Oscar gowns.

"Oh my god, look at this one," Kate laughs as she flips to a shot of the two of us as teenagers.

Kate has her Polo-clad arm draped over my plaid grunge-shirted shoulder and we're on the Texas set of my father's movie, *Bradley Berry*. We had as much in common as Lindsay Lohan and Rachel McAdams in *Mean Girls*. She was a chocolate-haired, blue-eyed, lacrosse-playing, straight-A preppie who took notes furiously on a steno pad as a PA on the set. And I was a fishnet-stocking-wearing, Converse-All-Star, black-eyeliner-wearing, PE-failing, straight B-minus preppie-hater who was perpetually serving detention at Crossroads, my alternative high school, for tardiness. And the only notes I was taking were in the margins of *Teen Vogue*. But we bonded after she saved me from my first broken heart over Actor Boyfriend No. 1. And I was there—I cringe to think—the night Kate lost her virginity to Christopher on that Texas set. Those days all he was into was the Super 8 camera he toted with him everywhere.

"You were smoking hot at sixteen." My brother leans in to look at the shot. "Even if you were a total prep," he adds, kissing Kate on the ear as he does.

"Not my best look," she adds.

"Who's this?" Lev asks, flipping to a weathered black-and-white photograph taken on a gritty sidewalk in front of a sign that says HUGO'S CIGARS.

"That was my father's shop in the Bronx," my mother says, leaning back in her chair as if readying herself for a plane's takeoff, resting her palms in her lap face-up on her Bedouin number. "My parents moved from a small village in Southern Spain when I was three years old. I must be about five years old in this picture." My grandfather stands proudly, dark hair slicked with pomade, a cigar resting between his lips, my grandmother beside him in a simple flowered housedress, her dark hair in a matching bob to my mother's, an only child standing in front of them. I barely recognize this little girl as my mother, startling blue eyes looking shyly at the camera in a simple white dress and with the natural dark hair of her childhood before she became a blonde. "We had nothing," she says matter-of-factly.

"You had your beauty," my father adds, smoothing out his orange sarong, "and your brains."

"It's what got me out," she says. "My mother always told me to educate myself. She took me to get my first library card the second we got into the country. Every second that my mother could get away from the Johnson's house, where she was a housekeeper, she'd take me to the Bronx library. We'd sit in the stacks and read. When I went off to model in New York at seventeen, my schooling was at the Museum of Modern Art, the Whitney, the Met. I would spend days on end in the museums just soaking it up.

"And then of course I met Paulie when I was just twenty-three years old, and he opened up the world to me. He gave me Becket and Pinter and took me to art house movie theaters to see De Sica and Fellini and Hitchcock. If my New York modeling days were undergraduate studies, then Paulie's been my graduate school."

My father leans into the photo for a closer look. "Blanca's father was a tough bastard."

"He was very handsome and a famous philanderer," my mother adds. I look to my father and can only wonder: Do we all end up with our fathers in the end? Then I look to Lev and in my mind let out a very emphatic: NO. "My mother forgave it because it was cultural, really, and maybe generational, and of course she was crazy about the bastard."

"And because he loved her and she knew that," my father says quietly, tipping off his Panama hat and looking at it in his large hand, then just as quickly popping it back on. "Blanca's mother made the best empanadas. She won me over with those." He chuckles.

"Are they still alive?" Lev asks as he unrolls the sleeves of his button-down shirt and crosses his arms in front of his chest. Did it get cold in here or is he uncomfortable, I wonder, as I scoot my chair away from my father and closer to Lev, wrapping an arm around him.

"Very much so," Chris chimes in, "with the rest of the retired Jews from the Bronx and Brooklyn living Happily Ever After—in Boca Raton."

"When I was able, the first thing I did was get them out of the Bronx," my Mom says. "My father had a dream of living by the ocean. When I took him to find a house in Florida, we walked out to the beach, he dropped to his knees and kissed the sand. My mother had to help him up and as she did she said, 'Blanca, it's so pink here.' Then she looked out to the sea and said, 'I'm going to get a lot of reading done.' My father has a chess club. My mother has a book club. They take salsa classes together. They have a mojito on their balcony and watch the sunset every night."

"It's good of you, Blanca," Lev says simply.

Suddenly looking at my mother's heavy eyelids, weighed down by all of that makeup, I have one of those rare moments where I see her as a human being and not just as my mother. It hits me in the gut just how hard it was for her growing up, and that in the end—despite everything—she took care of her parents. And I can't help but look to my father and think how eerily similar this through-line seems to be. But then I've gotten so lost in this rewind of The Santisi Chronicles that I've momentarily forgotten the cameras circling around like vultures looking for crumbs. And I see my mother again, for all of her complexity: one moment totally caring and the next totally self-involved. Looking at the family shots, her image sticks to me like a second skin, that habit of absent-mindedly tugging on her ear with a faraway look in her eye. That look: Discontent?

Longing? Ambition? This Sephardic Jewish girl from the Bronx who made it to Hollywood by route of a modeling career, by route of Paulie Santisi, dreaming of more for herself than being married to Famous Director. But as the cameras for *Wristwatch Wives* buzz about, I wonder, is this really what she wants?

"I think everyone's had enough of a walk down Santisi Lane," I say, pushing back my chair and taking an armful of dishes. At least I have. "Kate, help me with the dishes."

Kate and I are clearing the table when she shuts the kitchen door and faces me.

"Lo," she says, gripping my arm so hard I can feel my veins clamp shut. "Your father's right. Chris has to do something. He's doing absolute crap. It's driving me nuts."

"But I thought you liked his commercials! You said—"

"Lo, who cares if *Adweek* called him the new Michel Gondry? He's still shilling for Lexus and Grey Goose when he should be making movies. It's like he's afraid of success. Why doesn't he give a crap about doing anything worthwhile anymore?" I can't tell whether those are tears of anger or frustration filling her eyes. "Can't you talk to him? He won't talk to me anymore! We don't talk!"

"Kate, please, not now. I'm barely saving my own career at the moment. We have so much riding on Nic Knight wearing the Julian Tennant gown in *San Quentin Cartel*—thank god for that—and we need this Baz Luhrmann gig *desperately*. Of course the damn recession had to hit right when Julian Tennant finally got the official stamp of backing by LVMH. It was our big break but it seems like all that's breaking is the bank." I stop myself from having a full meltdown right there on my parents' kitchen floor because I can see my best friend is feeling awfully desperate herself. "Look, Kate, okay, don't worry, I'll talk to Chris—" and then there it goes. Lev's beeper going off. Now, this is a sound that

I've learned to dread, especially when we're eating Chinese out of the containers while curled up on the couch in our PJs. But tonight it's as though the bells of St. Peter's are reverberating through the house. As in, saved by the bell. Get us out of here!

"Jesus, that fucking beeper again. Lo, how do you stand it?"

I squeeze my best friend's arm. "Kate, I'll talk to Christopher, I promise," I tell her. "C'mon, we've got to get Lev out of here before Papa tells him how much his world-famous dermatologist makes, and before my mother breaks out my bat mitzvah video." I lead Kate back to the dining room, where Lev is scraping back his chair.

"I'm sorry to have to say this, but I'm wanted back at the ER," he says. "We've got two gunshot wounds and one is bleeding out."

"Oh, how *fabulous*," my mother squeals, followed by a confused silence from all of us—except for the camera crew, who are quickly packing up their equipment. "Lev, this is the perfect opportunity to share the important work you do with the entire country," she says as if she's Lesley Stahl and this is *60 Minutes*.

"Oh, no, that's not going to work," Lev says matter-of-factly, which makes me love him even more than I thought was humanly possible, because this is a man who will stand up to my parents. "No one in the ER except essential medical personnel. Sorry, Blanca."

"Well, maybe we could just stand outside the operating room? Alex is very discreet. He worked on *Keeping Up with the Kardashians*."

I can't help smiling. Another reason I love Lev: He has no idea who the Kardashians are. "Blanca, I'm sorry, but it's a definite no." I'm witnessing a miracle. Lev doesn't care who my parents are, whether they can get him into the *VF* Oscar party or into Cut for dinner on short notice.

Mom tries to take her defeat graciously. "I understand, dear. But will you come back and tell us all about it?" And by "us," I'm pretty sure she means Alex's crew.

"Absolutely," Lev assures her. "Blanca, Paulie, so glad to have gotten the chance to meet you," he says, giving my mother a hug and trying to do the same with my father, which turns into an awkward handshake-meets-side-of-the-body arm-slap. "Lola, I'll drop you on the way."

"Lev, please go ahead. You're needed for far more important things. I'll get a ride home with Christopher."

"You sure?" he asks, looking to Christopher for the signoff and then back to me.

"Absolutely positive," I say, disappointed that I won't be able to make up for our time at Chez Insane Asylum with some time alone but relieved just to get him out of here. "I'll walk you to the car."

When we're safely outside with the palm trees and wisteria, he wraps his arms around me.

"Thank you so much for enduring that," I say into his chest.

"Oh please, it was fun for me," he says, "and now I understand what you're talking about. I just hope they filmed my good side."

"You're the best," I say to him. I sigh out loud at the healthy distance Lev has from this Hollyweird thing and feel so, so grateful for my Doctor Boyfriend. This man who comes from the other end of the world from here, from a "normal" family, the kind as a kid I'd always dreamed of being a part of: parents who cheered from the sidelines of soccer games, whose family actually ate dinner together and talked about the state of the world over Cheerios at the breakfast table, all from behind their white picket fence in Cambridge, Mass, where his mom and dad were doctors and took turns as president of the PTA. This was the world I wanted to live in. The *Brady Bunch* was my freaking favorite show. Of course it turned out that Mr. Brady was gay and Greg had a massive crush on Mrs. Brady, but they all looked so *happy* on TV. Even if there's no such thing as "normal," I can't help but think for the first time in my life I've made a healthy choice in a guy. That maybe I've got a shot with him at getting off of Planet Hollywood.

"And I still love you," he teases. "Do you still love me, even though I'm not raking it in like Frank Luks, world-famous cardiologist?"

"I love you," I say softly as he kisses me good-bye and then runs to his car, calling out as he goes, "See you at home." *See you at home.* And those words sound like a song. I watch his car until it's out of sight.

"You are sworn to absolute secrecy," my brother says to me on our way back to Lev's house after we drop Kate off at their place. She's got a 7:30 A.M. breakfast meeting at The Polo Lounge and needs to finish the Todd Phillips script, *Flake,* that she's pitching Nic Knight for. "It's about a schlumpfy guy who's an assistant manager at Applebee's who falls for a gorgeous blond pastry chef at a five-star restaurant and fakes a Le Cordon Bleu diploma to impress her. Nic's perfect for the lead and I want to get him into comedy."

"You have to promise me," Christopher says, emphasizing it by pulling to the side of the road as we make our way over Coldwater Canyon into the Valley. He pulls up behind the thirty or more cars collected at Britney's driveway on Mulholland Drive. The paps' telephoto lenses are resting on their window sills like rifles aiming for a shot at her.

"Chris, you're freaking me out now," I say. "Yes, I'm sworn to secrecy. Now what the heck's going on?"

"Have you sensed Kate pulling away from me recently?" Chris asks without looking at me.

"No," I lie. This is where your brother and your best friend in a relationship is not exactly ideal. "So what's the big secret? Is this about Kate?"

"Well, no, I mean yes, well no, not really, yeah, kinda, you could say—"

"Would you just *tell* me already!"

"It's about Kate. The movie I've been making. I haven't told anybody; it's a closed set. It's a comedy. Inspired by Kate. It's called *Into the Woods*. I just finished the final edit. It's a romantic comedy about two opposites—the guy's a pot-smoking slacker who isn't living up to his potential and the girl's an overly ambitious businesswoman—of course they fall madly in love and hilarity ensues."

"Wait, a movie!? You've been making a *movie*? How come you didn't tell me—or Kate?"

"I think it might be really good," he says, looking out at the night sky. Well, this explains the certain gleam that he's been walking around with for a while. I thought up until this moment that was the look of my brother in love—of his being quote unquote "Into the Woods." But this look isn't exactly about being in love with Kate Woods. More like, it's the look Einstein had before he came up with the theory of relativity—or Calvin before he came up with jeans.

"Chris, this is such fantastic news," I say. Maybe my brother's living up to his potential after all. "But I still don't get why you want it to be a secret."

"No one knows, Lo, okay," he says, looking at me for emphasis.

"I got that part. I got it. No one knows, okay. I will not utter a word."

"Except for my production crew and actors who've all signed confidentiality agreements to keep it under the radar—and now you. If Papa knew, he'd either slam me or bury me in advice. You know Kate. She'd be absolutely *obsessed* with helping me with contacts and everything. I've got to do this completely on my own. I really need to prove myself—not just to Kate and Papa. But really to myself."

"I understand," I say, as in *totally* understand. As in, I wouldn't be at all surprised if I'm walking around with that phrase stamped on my forehead.

"The only problem is that I've plunged myself into huge debt doing this independently. My credit cards are a joke," Chris says, shaking his head.

"Um, when do you plan on telling Kate?" I have no idea how she'll take the news, especially with it being based on her life. Kate's the most private person I know. And if I know my best friend, she's not exactly going to be thrilled about the whole *debt* thing, either. The only kind of debt she'd be interested in is the kind where Colin Firth stands up and says, "This Oscar is for my agent, Kate Woods, to whom I owe a great *debt*."

"I want to wait until I hear back from Cannes to see if it's been accepted before I tell Kate. Just to get a sense of what kind of league I'm in."

"*Cannes*," I say, dumbfounded. "You sent it to Cannes?" I mean, I want to be supportive, but the Cannes Film Festival? Now my brother's dreaming.

"Okay, so it's a real long shot. But maybe the South by Southwest Festival? I dunno. We'll see. I'm just hoping it has a life. And Kate really doesn't need to know about it until I see what kind of a future there is for it and I've pulled myself out of this mess I've gotten myself into," Chris says, resting the weight of his forehead on the steering wheel. "She really doesn't need to know I fucked up here."

"Chris," I say, as afraid to know the answer as much as he's afraid to tell me, "Just how much debt are we talking about here?"

The answer floats up from the steering wheel. "A lot, Lo. Like three hundred, four hundred thousand."

The darkened canyon on the hillside is dotted with those L.A.-centric houses teetering on stilts like a dare. Like my brother. Teetering on the edge of something and taunting Hollywood: "Oh, you just try to knock me down." Yes, it seems insane in the Land of Earthquakes. And yes, I might be crazy, too. But no one in our family got anywhere by playing it safe—or being sane. So here goes.

"I think I can help," I say, reaching for my bag and pulling out my phone. Glancing at my watch I quickly calculate the time difference, then dial anyway. When the thick Russian accent picks up groggily on the other end of the phone, I don't mince words. "It's Lola Santisi. Remember you always said you wanted to break into Hollywood? Well, now's your chance."

4

the colossal billboard on Ventura Boulevard nearly makes me crash my Prius into the car in front of me. I slam on the brakes and crane my neck to get a closer look. My mother is posing like she's back on the cover of *Vogue*—shoulders thrust back, the plane of her cheekbone catching the light, red nails curled around a canted hip. The caption above her head reads, BLANCA SANTISI: THE HOLLYWOOD DIRECTOR'S WIFE. Below her silver Manolos runs her tagline: WHO WILL SHE CUT OUT OF THE PICTURE THIS TIME? WRISTWATCH WIVES DEBUTS THIS FALL! It's entirely creepy to see my mother's face that large—and that airbrushed— but at least she's wearing Julian Tennant, which was the whole reason I signed my release in the first place. And it's amazing to see Julian's nude sequin-smothered sheath splashed across a 10×20-inch canvas. I can't imagine what Papa thinks when he drives by that surreal image of my mother looming over Los Angeles every day on his way to work.

I snap a quick photo with my iPhone and e-mail it to Julian. Hopefully it'll cheer him up. He's convinced himself he's lost the Luhrmann gig *again* since we still haven't heard anything—even though I've been using *The Secret* and *The Secrets of Abraham,* and Mom's phone psychic Lynda *did* see a wedding dress when we spoke. I can't think about that now; I need to focus on the fitting I'm about to have with Nic Knight— and my father. Everyone's going to want the stills of Nic in drag wearing these stunning JT gowns. I still can't believe my father came through for me—and Julian—in such a big way. Maybe people really *can* change.

It's not that my father hasn't tried to be supportive in his own limited way. As I wind my way down Ventura Boulevard, I'm flooded by a memory of being eight years old. My father stalked up to me where I was leaning up against the gate of our house in my purple-sequined leotard dress with full tutu and matching slippers. Chris had just taught me how to ride sans training wheels the red, sparkly, banana-seat Schwinn that was the envy of the neighborhood kids. And I was taking a break from my proud moment. My father had been holed up in his office for weeks writing his next movie; he'd surface in silence only for a cup of coffee. He'd drink it while standing over the sink with a glazed look in his dark eyes as he gazed out the window. He wasn't looking at the jacaranda trees. He was looking into the world he was creating. Christopher and I knew not to disturb him during these phases, tiptoeing by his door on our way to watch reruns of *Three's Company* and *The Cosby Show,* the smell of cigars and the sound of his voice acting out scenes wafting out from under the door. And now here he was, still in his striped pajamas at four o'clock in the afternoon, appearing as if back from the dead, hair disheveled, dark circles under his eyes, and glasses askew. I knew this return to the living meant he'd finished his script, but wondered what he wanted with me.

"I hear you're playing Snow White," he called out from a distance.

"Yeah," I nodded nonchalantly. I mean, it was cool to get the lead in the school play, but it was mostly about the blue-and-red silk dress with white puffed sleeves and black wig with red headband that I got to wear. I wasn't that thrilled about all of the memorization. But the costume—now, that was inspiring. I'd already talked through my design concept with Mr. Fisher, my sewing class teacher. He was my first GDF—Gay Design Friend—and we were totally thrilled about our concept. "The red piping's going to be a challenge, Lola, but we'll figure it out. You're a real talent," he whispered in my ear as I took my lunchbox to head out for recess. I was supposed to meet Julie Roth for lunch in our usual spot on the grass under the palm trees but I'd have to cancel. I needed some time alone with my sketchbook to sort out my ideas.

"Let's work on it," my father said, handing me the pages he'd obviously gotten from Nanny No. 5. I threw my bike up against the gate, and we got to work rehearsing my lines. It was dark outside three hours later when my father finally declared it a wrap for the day.

"Good work," Papa said to my four-foot-tall self as he took my hand and we headed back toward the house. "Want some pizza?"

"Yeah, thanks, Papa," I said, looking up at him. "And I'd really like to show you my ideas for what I want to wear."

"Great," he said. "Costuming is very important."

I got a standing ovation that year as Snow White. And it wasn't just the costume, which was perfection. Papa will be the first to tell you, it was the best acting work I've done.

"Lola Santisi," I say to the Warner Brothers security guard as I hand him my driver's license. "I'm going to the set of the Paulie Santisi movie, *San Quentin Cartel*." When the guard points me in the right direction, it occurs to me that I should have called Kate first to make sure Nic Knight is actually on the set and not in the slammer. Kate told me on the drive home from our trayf Shabbat that she had to spring him from jail, yet again, the day before. Nic was cited for indecent exposure. *Again.* He was buying a wallet at Louis Vuitton in Beverly Hills when he felt the urgent call of nature and *peed* on a row of one-of-a-kind Murakami bags instead of using the plush marble bathroom on the second floor like every other human being on the planet. Thank g-d it was on his day off and somehow Kate kept it away from the media—and my father. I don't even want to know who or how much Kate paid to keep it quiet. If Nic wasn't so supremely talented, he'd be behind the gates of the L.A. County Psych Ward instead of Bel Air.

Wrestling with the garment bags all the way to Nic's trailer, I balance them on my knee and knock on his door. Unlike most quadruple-wide luxury star trailers, Nic's trailer is tiny, all the furniture stripped out save for a small cot at his request. He's so Method that he decided to replicate the jail cell where most of the movie takes place.

When no one answers, I go ahead and let myself in, expecting to find Kate pacing with BlackBerry in hand and Nic working on his lines. Instead I find Coz and her protégé little Chili Lu looking awfully cozy on the cot. *What are they doing here?*

"Hey Lola," Coz says coolly, despite the mink vest she's wearing over her caramel-colored, paper-thin leather pinafore, crossing one chocolate knee-high lace-up stiletto boot over the other. Judging from her outfit you'd never know it was seventy-five degrees outside. I swear she has ice running through her veins. I've never seen that woman break a sweat— ever. Unlike me, who is suddenly drenched in sweat thanks to the molten lava coursing throughout my entire body.

"Hey," I say, confused, trying to maintain my composure. "Well, this is a surprise. What brings you here? And where's Nic?"

"On set shooting still," Coz says.

"Yo, I'm Chili," says a skinny teen from beneath his Flock of Seagulls-esque shiny black hair.

"Lola," I stammer.

"Nice to meet you." He looks up at me with big, brown, puppy-dog eyes from behind his Buddy Holly black glasses. I would kill for his pore-less, perfect skin. In his skinny black jeans, oversized gray T-shirt hanging on his diminutive frame, and red vintage Air Jordans, he actually looks even younger than *sixteen*. "You look *hoot*."

"Thanks," I say, trying not to wince at the catchphrase that Chili trademarked (because plain old "hot" is so Paris Hilton over) the catchphrase that strides abreast a million Bedazzled T-shirts that practically flew off the shelves of Fred Segal at seventy-five dollars per. And did I mention the kid is freaking *sixteen*?

"Nic should be back soon if you wanna hang," Chili says, scooching over on the cot to try and make room for me between him and Coz. I look to Chili and then to Coz and think there's nothing I'd like to do less. Suddenly Nic's trailer feels exactly like a prison, and I'm desperate to break out.

"I think three's a crowd on that tiny bed. So, what brings you here?" I try again.

"Oh," Coz says, lowering her signature black shades and casually smoothing her platinum hair. "Your father didn't tell you?"

"Tell me what?" I ask.

"I called him because I had this mind-blowingly *brilliant* idea that we should put Nic on the cover of *Vain* in full drag," Coz says.

"Isn't it *strawberries*!?" Chili chimes in. Oh God. The *other* patented Chili catchphrase. According to him, "*Strawberries* are so much *hooter* than bananas." "It's going to be the *hootest* cover ever."

"Wait, *what*? That was *my* idea, Coz. Remember, when I called you right after you came to the loft? I pitched that idea to you about putting Nic on the cover of *Vain* in *Julian Tennant*. I told you that Julian was designing the gown for the prison break scene, the most pivotal scene in the movie, and that everyone would be talking about it. You turned me down. You told me Grace would never put a man on the cover."

"I have no idea what you're talking about, Lola," Coz says.

Am I being gaslit here? Am I actually losing my mind? Or is Coz out of hers? And then it dawns on me. Nic Knight is going to be on the cover of *Vain* in Julian's gown. Who cares whose idea it is? Let Coz have all the credit. All that matters is that it's happening. Maybe Coz isn't the devil's spawn after all. Breathe, Lola, breathe.

"Well, it *is* an awesome idea, Coz," I say neutrally. "Nic is going to look fantastic on the cover in Julian's gown. It'll be amazing publicity for both of us. Here, we actually made several gowns for the scene; let me show them to you," I say, starting to unzip the garment bag in my arms.

"You seem confused. Nic's going to wear one of Chili's gowns on the cover. That's why we're here," Coz says flatly.

"Sorry? Why would he wear one of Chili's gowns when Julian designed the gown for the movie?" I ask.

"Because Julian didn't. Chili did," Coz says. She seems to be deriving immense pleasure from every viperous word.

"Do you want to see them, Lola? They're so *hoot*. You're going to go *strawberries*," Chili says, oblivious to the drama swirling above his five-foot-three head.

This has to be a bad dream. I'm going to wake up any second. Please let me wake up.

"There must be some misunderstanding," I insist, looking around the trailer as if I might find the very tiny answer there hiding in a very tiny corner. Or at the very least a Lilliputian Candid Camera?

"Your dad is smart and wants to be where the buzz is. And the buzz is with Chili, not Julian. It's all about reality TV," Coz says. "And Chili *rules* reality TV. Did you know that Bravo's thinking of doing a spinoff? *Hoot Chili.* Aldo says that Chili's numbers are through the roof."

"Who's Aldo?" I ask. "What numbers?"

"Oh, you don't know Aldo? Aldo Threepersons the cool hunter?" Coz says. "I'm surprised. Isn't it part of your job to know the latest trends?" Coz sounds almost bored as she slides the knife in and twists it. "Aldo has *brilliant* ideas for the fourteen- to nineteen-year-olds."

"Yeah, your dad's *hoot,* Lola," Chili chimes in, "but Aldo says I'm totally kicking his ass in the prime demographic. Plus Aldo's totally down with my designs. I've already licensed them to Second Life so Nic will totally be the first drag avatar. Isn't it *strawberries!*"

"Are you kidding me?" I ask. It's true Papa wouldn't know a Twitter from a woofer or a tweeter, but why is he ceding creative control to a kid who couldn't recognize "couture" if he saw it on the PSATs?

"Aldo's work is *genius.* He came up with the new counter show to *NYC Prep.* It's called *NYC Un-Prep.* It's the downtown high schoolers' response to those dull Upper East Siders," Coz says, as if this guy were Einstein. "And to think he's only fifteen."

"Well, I'm sure he'll be even more *genius* when he hits puberty," I say. "Now, if you'll excuse me, I've got to dash."

I barely notice the welter of extras and PAs and ADs and grips as I make my way through the set to find my father. All I'm seeing is red. This was *our* job. And we didn't waste our time on these gowns for nothing. When I finally find my father talking to the script supervisor, I don't hesitate. I will risk his wrath because I'm fuming.

"Can I talk to you for a second," I tell him. It's not a question. The script supervisor bows her head and backs away, like she's departing a royal. Which I suppose, in her universe, Papa is.

Papa raises an eyebrow at my impertinence. "What's up?" he asks curtly, clearly preoccupied with the entirety of this movie on his shoulders.

"Did you forget you gave Julian the job of designing Nic's gown for the reshoots?" I ask, trying to keep my voice from cracking. "I just found out that you gave the job to Chili Lu instead. Why would you do that? You *promised* me! You *knew* what that publicity meant to my company! You *knew* how hard it was for me to ask you for help!"

"Oh geezus, Lola, it's just a fucking dress," he says, strumming his fingers on the notebook he's gripping.

"It's just a fucking dress to you, but we spent a lot of time and energy redesigning several gown options for you."

Papa pinches the bridge of his nose at the tiresome business before him. "Look, I'm sorry, but I've been told that everyone's talking about this Chili kid and I really need the younger demo. Our test-screening numbers were in the shitter for the kids who buy the most tickets. I'm sorry," he says matter-of-factly, turning back to his work. "Business is business." Discussion over.

As I make my way through the set back to my car, I can't help but feel like I've taken a giant leap backward. I thought I'd grown out of feeling crushed by my father. But he's just as self-centered as ever. I can feel the smoke coming out of my ears as if my head might explode. I'm so furious that it doesn't even occur to me that I left the gowns in Nic Knight's trailer until I've left the lot and am speeding back down Ventura Boulevard. I don't even consider going back for them. They're of no use to us now.

My phone trills and I click on my Bluetooth. Oh thank god, it's Kate. "I was just about to call you! Did you know that Nic is going to be in Chili instead of Julian for the reshoots? And the *cover* of *Vain*! That Coz is such a conniving bitch. How could you not tell me, Kate—"

"Look, I just found out twenty minutes ago myself, and I've been on calls every second since. I'm sorry. But there's great news! Cricket got the part! She's going to be in Baz's movie!"

"Kate, that's amazing! Is Cricket thrilled to pieces? You must have lobbied so hard for her," I say, my emotions whipsawing as I struggle to feel happy for my friend while still crushed by Papa's self-absorption.

"Actually, we got lucky. Vanessa Hudgens was his next pick, but she dropped out when she got the chance to replace Amanda Seyfried, who dropped out of *Mamma Mia 4* so she could replace Anne Hathaway in *Footloose 3*, who dropped out to replace Beyoncé in *Chicago 2*. And I have to confess that it was actually as much Saffron's doing as mine. Apparently she saw Cricket's headshot and tape and totally went to bat for her. She said she loved the way Cricket glows on screen, thinks she's a knockout."

"Well, this is great for Cricket. She really needs this. How did she react?"

"I called you first, because guess what else! Guess who's making those two wedding gowns? Julian!"

I can't help it. I'm squealing like a contestant on *Rock of Love*. "Omigod! Omigod! Kate! How did you pull that off?" Finally! Finally we get a break! This is just what we needed!

"Saffron and I really put the screws to Baz. He'll be calling Julian any second with the news, so just pretend you don't already know it."

"Oh my gosh, Kate, this is fantastic. You don't know how badly we needed this news after having Chili steal the *San Quentin Cartel* design gig away from us."

"I wouldn't blame Chili, that kid's clueless," says Kate. "But your dad and Coz? Two pieces of work. Anyhow, I've got to go make more calls. Remember, when Julian calls you, act surprised."

It's almost impossible to keep my excitement under wraps ten minutes later when he calls. "Julian," I say, "what's new?"

"Hey," he says glumly. Guess he hasn't gotten the news yet; I debate whether I should just go ahead and tell him when he adds, "Katy Perry just signed a two-million-dollar deal with Target for a line of doggie sweats. I can't believe it. I did all that work on the Dogshmere collection and Tom Ford's groomer never even got my designs to Barbara Walters. We should have had that deal."

I feel like I have to tell him about Baz's movie now. He sounds so distraught. This will cheer him up. I'm about to tell him when he says, "Oh, and we're designing the wedding gowns for Baz. We got the gig." He sounds like he's just been told they've stopped making Dolce & Gabbana underwear.

"Why don't you sound more excited, Julian?"

"Because guess who I'm stuck with as an assistant? Chili. Coz has somehow convinced Baz that it'll be more great publicity for the film. I think she'll do anything to protect that little freak. She wants to stop all the bad buzz about how Baz fired him because his designs were so ridiculous. Why risk embarrassing gossip, which could only distract from the movie? I have no choice but to go along."

"Don't worry, Julian, I'll handle Chili, you just focus on getting those gowns designed," I say, though I'm feeling queasy at the thought of being in the same room with that kid ever again. So Coz already knew we'd gotten the Luhrmann gig. I contemplate telling Julian about the epic disaster with Coz, Chili, and my father, but decide it can wait. Why is that damn Coz so set on ruining my entire life and Julian's? She may have ruined things with Nic Knight, but I'm not going to let her ruin this Luhrmann movie.

"Honey," I call out as I throw my bag and sunglasses on Lev's couch and make my way toward the kitchen. The smell of garlic and lemon is wafting toward me, and I realize that I didn't have time to eat today.

"Hi, hon," Lev says, putting down the wooden spoon he's using to stir the chicken piccata and wrapping me in his arms.

"I'm so happy to see you," I say, nuzzling into his neck.

"Me too," he says.

"How was your day?" I ask, grabbing a slice of carrot from the cutting board and pulling myself up onto the counter next to Lev.

"Well, actually, it was kind of eventful. I got a job offer."

"What do you mean?" I ask.

"Have you ever heard of Shonda Rimes?" he asks.

"Of course, she created *Grey's Anatomy*." He gives me a blank look. I'm going out with the only Dr. McDreamy in the country who's never heard of Dr. McDreamy. "It's this incredibly popular medical show. Seriously, you're like the only person who doesn't watch it."

"Well, she's got this new show called *Para-Medic*. Here, she gave me this description of it." Lev slips a piece of paper out of his pocket, unfolds it, and hands it to me. I read it out loud.

"'A lovably irascible doctor treats victims of paranormal events—alien abductions and the like—while engaging in a will they/won't they relationship with his comely, scrappy sidekick.' Hm. It sounds like a spin-off of *Grey's Anatomy* meets *House,* with a little *X Files* thrown in." Lev gives me another blank look. "*House* is the one with the sexy diagnostician who gobbles Vicodin. *X Files* was the one with David Duchovny and Gillian Anderson, and the smoking man and . . . oh, never mind. So what does Shonda want you to do, anyway?"

"She wants me to be the medical consultant for the show," he says. "It would only be a few hours a week."

"Honey, that's so cool," I say, but I have a strange feeling in my stomach at the thought and I don't know why. It's probably just my own work anxiety creeping in. I brush it off to try to stay focused on Lev. "How did this happen?"

"I actually ran into her at the ER the night I met your parents. She came in for food poisoning, and I guess she liked me. She called the ER to track me down today and made me this offer. I figure it'll be good extra income to help pay off my medical school loans."

"Honey, it's fantastic," I say, leaning in to give him a kiss as he hands me my chicken and braised carrots and we head for the couch to eat in front of the TV. We've gotten very into watching *Planet Earth,* but then I remember I recorded *Cut-Throat Couture.*

"I know it's not really your thing," I say, "but do you mind if we just watch this one episode? I've been trying to get Julian on as a guest judge designer. Coz turned me down, but I'm not giving up."

"Sure, babe, why not?" Lev says, and I cue up the DVR.

"Welcome to *Cut-Throat Couture,*" intones a plummy voice over pulse-pounding beats as images of the contestants alternate with models high-stepping the runways. "In the competitive blood sport of high couture, designers' reputations get cut, but the price tags never do. Which of these sixteen contestants is willing to pay the cost for achieving their dreams of designer deification—and which will see their ambitions *slashed to ribbons?*" The screen fills with sixteen faces; one by one, six of the images are electronically sheared away by a pair of lethally gleaming scissors as a violin offers screeching accompaniment. "Only ten designers are left to compete for our grand prize—one hundred thousand dollars from *Vain* magazine to launch their new line, a personal tour of Naomi Campbell's closet, and—best of all!—a private fifteen-minute audience with editor-in-chief Grace Frost!" The camera pans back as the contestants gasp and swoon in anticipation of such a papal blessing. "Now it's time to meet our judges! *Vain*'s creative director and one of the most powerful opinion-makers in the world of fashion, Coz Cahill!" Coz's face fills up the television screen; she nods coolly, the studio lights bouncing off her platinum hair, as the ten wannabe designers clap wildly. "And one of

fashion's original supermodels—and still its queen—Naomi Campbell!"
Naomi crosses and recrosses her miles of legs: "Hullo, dahlings!" "And
legendary designer and muse, Donatella Versace!" Donatella gives a flick
of her white-blond Barbie tresses and wiggles long, lacquered nails at the
contestants, who beam with giddy joy. "Ciao, my babies!"

"Hello contestants," Coz says from the stage in a gilded dégradé
crocodile-embossed skintight jersey minidress. "Only ten of you are left.
Your work has been . . . adequate. We are expecting more from you.
Which of you will step up? And which will be the next to get *slashed*?"
I flinch involuntarily as the violins screech again. "Today we have an
exciting new challenge for you." A screen drops down behind her, which
quickly fills with images of a towering, steaming . . . dump. The camera
closes in on shots of festering garbage, screaming gulls wheeling around
split-open bags and rusting appliances. "Everyone, reach under your
seats and open up your gift bags." As the challengers pull out bulky rubber boots, thick plastic yellow gloves, and gas masks, their expressions
change from gleeful anticipation to grim caginess.

"For your challenge today," Coz tells them, "we will be taking you to
the world-famous—or infamous, according to some—Fresh Kills land-
fill. As part of our ongoing 'Green the Runway' theme, you will have
exactly ten minutes to collect as many items as you can and recycle them
into a look that can go day into night. You will be judged on creative
repurposing, originality, and attention to sanitary considerations. And
joining us today as our guest judge is the totally original and way hot
new designer and winner of *Cut-Throat Couture* last season." The camera
pans to the guest judge for dramatic effect as Coz pauses to introduce—
"Our very own Chili Lu." The contestants are all smiling ear-to-ear and
clapping as though Chili is the next coming of Christian Dior, if Dior
ever wore a leather newsboy cap studded with USB ports and satin-and-
hemp manpris with solar panel pockets.

"Hello! Don't you all look positively *hoot!*" Chili shouts, bouncing up and down on the tips of his Air Jordans. "I can't tell you how *hoot* it's been working with Queen Coz. Thanks to her, my career is in the stratosphere! I cannot *wait* to tell you all the things that this Chili's got bubbling!"

That's it. I can't take it anymore. I quickly click over to *Planet Earth,* where a lioness, her pelt burnished almost to platinum under the searing African sun, ambushes a lone springbok. One quick slash and the prey tumbles into the long grass, its legs kicking their last.

"'Hoot'? Is that even a *word?*" Lev asks. "Why'd you switch channels? Don't you want to see how it ends?"

"I think I just did," I say.

5

excuse me, miss, is it possible to get another Milo bar please," I say to the redheaded Qantas stewardess.

"I'm sorry, but there aren't any left," she says. "It seems you've eaten them all."

"All?!" I gasp in horror. "Are you sure?!"

The slim stewardess nods her head. "I'm so sorry. We only had thirteen on board. Did you want any Tim Tams? Or some Jaffas? Or perhaps some Caramello Koalas? I could run to first class and swipe some."

"Oh, no thanks," I say, shame stricken. I did start eating all that candy somewhere over Hawaii, and now we're about to land in Sydney. But thirteen bars?! I really need to start redirecting my nervous, sleep-deprived, overworked energy somewhere other than food. Can you blame me? There's so much riding on these wedding gowns for *Four Weddings and a Bris* that Julian and I carried on the plane by hand. Especially now that Coz sabotaged the costumes for my own father's movie.

You'd think since I spend the majority of my life on planes these days I'd be able to actually sleep. But no. Not when we're about to meet with Baz Lurhmann and I have all these reports due for LVMH and our company is on the brink—*again.* I used to catch up on movies and magazines when I'd fly; now I'm stuck writing sales reports, promotion proposals, e-mailing fabric vendors, trying to cut production costs, and praying to God, Ganesh, my guardian angels, and Oprah and Gayle that nothing (read Coz) screws things up on this Lurhmann movie.

Why didn't I take an Ambien like Julian? He's been passed out next to me since before the wheels even went up. Lucky him. He gave up on hypnotherapy, Vedic meditation, Reiki, acupuncture, and ujjayi breathing to get over his fear of flying, and got his shrink to prescribe him a clutch of pills, not to mention a note to the airline that he must travel with his "emotional support service dog." Tom Ford's been curled up in his lap since takeoff. He spent weeks perfecting his "Winehouse," a near-lethal Ativan-Xanax-Ambien cocktail that he's taken for the last three days in preparation for flying all the way to Australia. And he *still* tried to back out this morning. Or was it yesterday morning? How many freaking hours have we been on this plane?

I turn my attention back to my MacBook where all the numbers on my Excel spreadsheet start to blur together.

"Rise and shine, Princess," Julian says, shoving me awake.

"What?!" I say, wiping the drool from my face.

"Did you have a good sleep?" Julian asks.

"No, I didn't. I think I was only asleep for five minutes."

"I told you you should have taken a Winehouse," he says. He takes out a mirror from his black woven Bottega carry-on, spritzes his face with rose water, and smoothes back his dark hair.

"Julian, I don't think I'd ever wake up if I took all of that. I have no idea how you can even formulate a sentence right now," I say, rubbing the sleep from my throbbing eyeballs.

"Well, no offense, Lola, but you look like shit. Next time I'm forcing you to take something."

"How bad is it?" I ask fearfully.

Julian holds his mirror in front of me. "Oh god," I say, squinting at my reflection in the mirror. "Is that really me?! I look like I belong on *True Blood*. What's scarier is that I actually feel even worse."

"Do you want to borrow my fedora and aviators?" Julian offers.

"It's useless," I say, looking at myself again. "But it doesn't matter how horrendous I look; all that matters is how gorgeous the two wedding gowns look and that Saffron and Baz love them, which they will. Lynda said she saw it. And she hasn't been wrong yet." I mean, Mom's phone psychic totally called my ideas for retro *Flashdance* torn sweatshirts and organic braces made from reclaimed toaster oven heating elements. Not to mention my sensitivity to quinoa.

"Lo, I'm a little concerned about how often you've been calling Lynda."

"This coming from the man who paid someone to meditate for him," I say.

"I did feel way more centered and Zen," Julian says. "Until I got the bill."

"Lynda's so amazing, she keeps giving me free sessions."

"I bet your mom is paying her and just not telling you," Julian says.

"You think?"

"Yes," Julian says. "But who cares as long as she keeps seeing good things for us. Thank you again for getting Chili to stay in NYC. Did Lynda see that?"

"That was all me. There's no way I was letting little Chili Lu near Baz and Saffron again. Anyway, he brought it on himself. What did he expect when he put solar panels on the veils? Of course they were gonna catch fire. I told him his penance was staying home and making new ones."

"Brilliant, Lo," says Julian.

"Thanks," I say. "I think. He asked if he could build miniature video cameras into the veils with a live feed to Facebook."

"He really is a technical genius. I have no idea what he's talking about half the time, and some of his ideas are brilliant but some of them are completely unworkable," Julian says. "What bride wants a train that Twitters? Or a Goretex gown? He told me, that way, if the bride cries, the dress won't get stained. I tell you, Lo, if someone made me wear Goretex on my wedding day, I'd cry for sure. Ridiculous! Plus I'm just so fed up with this kid. He's constantly messing up—taking in Saffron's dress too much, spilling on the gowns. I can't wait until he's out of our lives."

"Try not to worry about Chili, Julian. I need you on your A game for this meeting."

"Do you think it was safe to leave him in the studio all alone?"

"I didn't. I told him we had termites and the fumigators were coming and he'd have to complete the veils at home."

"What would I do without you, Lo? Thank you," he says, planting a huge kiss on my cheek. "Now let's go nail this meeting."

And as the tires hit the tarmac, I can't believe that we have to turn around and get back on this plane in twenty-four hours because Julian and I need to be back in L.A. for a *Lucky* magazine shoot ("Sexy and

Streetwise: Hot New Designers You Can Afford Right Now!"). It's certainly not *Vain* but I feel *lucky* to have any publicity at this point.

Saffron Sykes looks like she's riding that crane to the moon. Julian and I are standing off to the side of the cavernous soundstage of Baz Luhrmann's musical extravaganza, *Four Weddings and a Bris,* watching the stunning actress film her big scene. Her raven mane topples down to her waist in perfect, stick-straight lines as she traverses across the sky in a faded Parma violet, billowy chiffon gown that looks like God, or Karl Lagerfeld, draped it himself. When the crane stops at her mark, she begins singing a love song softly, her flawless golden skin glowing dreamily against the backdrop of a perfect azure sky. The magical realism is quintessential Luhrmann at his best. Entering this set is like walking into Alice's Wonderland. It's like being transported to a fantasy world in hi-def color, and if you touch it with your finger it might disappear. It's like being on mushrooms without having to endure that horrific taste or that gummy film on your teeth.

I can't take my eyes off Saffron. She's completely mesmerizing. And to think Saffron owed it all to Ron Howard—and exceptionally good genes. She started off as Ron's *dog walker* to pay off her school loans from Juilliard. When Natalie Portman fell out of his *American Graffiti* remake, he decided to give Saffron a break. Saffron still sees Ron's dogs. She lets their new dog walker bring them over to swim in her pool since the Howard's house is a few doors down on Carbon Beach in Malibu.

As Saffron's sublime song ends, the crane swooshes her down to the ground and places her in front of Cricket, who looks positively radiant.

The hairs on my arms stand on end as I watch my BAF acting across from the biggest star in the world in a Baz Luhrmann movie.

"I just can't stop thinking about you," Cricket says.

"I know," Saffron responds. "I don't know if I can go through with the wedding."

And the thing is, Cricket's totally holding her own. *I* know that Cricket could make reading the phone book interesting and that she could create chemistry with a doorknob—or a chihuahua. But now the world will, too, I think to myself at the sight of Cricket looking at Saffron with dewy eyes. Saffron wipes away Cricket's tears with a delicate finger and then suddenly leans forward and kisses Cricket—on the mouth. Yes, *mouth*. Baz has been keeping the plot of the movie totally under wraps. And now I know why. No wonder we had to sign all those confidentiality agreements before we could even step foot on set. What could be juicier than the queen of the screen in a lesbian wedding? Whoa. I can't believe that Cricket didn't say a peep to me. Or Kate.

"And cut," Baz says from behind the camera. "That was wonderful, ladies. I think we got it."

"Lo," I hear a whisper from behind me. Cricket has a gorgeous billowing aqua gown that seems to be floating on her skin. She seems to be floating, too. No doubt absolutely in heaven being in Australia and on Baz Luhrmann's set. She throws her arms around me and exclaims, "I've never been so happy in my life!"

"Oh sweetie, I'm so happy to hear that. That scene was—incredible," I say.

"I've been dying to tell you about my part but I just couldn't. I'm so sorry, but now you know why the plot of the movie has been so top secret," she says, leaning in and then whispering, "I'm a lesbian in it," she says.

"Yeah, I kinda got that part after I saw you put your tongue down the throat of the biggest movie star in the world."

"How was I?" she asks.

"Amazing. Totally convincing. I'm so proud of you, Cricket," I say, thinking about how much she's been through to get here, all of those commercials for diarrhea and sexual dysfunction, all of those years at Juilliard and with the Royal Shakespeare Company, all of it to barely make the rent every month. "How are your ribs feeling? Being up on those harnesses flying around in the air can't be good for you."

Cricket rubs her sides gingerly. "The doctor told me they'd take a long time to heal, but I had no idea they'd take *this* long. They're absolutely killing me, but it's a true exercise in mind over matter. Which basically means, I'm taking lots of Advil," she says.

"Whatever you're taking is working for you. You look absolutely glowy," I say.

"That gown is what's killing me," Julian says. "My god, it's unbelievable!" He stoops to inspect the delicate pansies trapped beneath nude netting on the bodice of the gown and the breathtaking pansy details in the lace underlayers of the skirt that are echoed in lace ankle-wrappings in Cricket's sandals.

"It's Lagerfeld, right?" I say.

"Yes, isn't it something?" Cricket says. "Don't I get a hello, Julian?" she adds, reaching out her willowy arms.

"Sorry, sweetheart," he says, enveloping her. "I was having a Fashion Paralysis moment."

"I'm so happy to see you guys," Cricket says. "I can't say I'm lonely here. We've become like a big family in just two short weeks. But there's nothing like real family," Cricket says, pulling us in for a group hug. "Let me take you to the costume department; come on, follow me." Cricket leads us through the small corridors of the set, stepping over large cords and between lights and a hive of workers. "You guys are meeting with Saffron today, right?"

"Yes, we need to get her approval on the gown."

"She's . . . well, she's absolutely magnificent," Cricket stammers. "She's just the real thing. She's so unbelievably talented and she's so *present* and just so incredibly beautiful—"

"Sounds like someone has a girl crush," Julian says teasingly.

"Totally!" Cricket chirps.

"Yeah, I get those girl crushes all the time," Julian says. "So much easier to have a crush with no actual sex involved."

Saffron stands before us draped in Julian's exquisite off-the-shoulder gown, an ivory antique Valenciennes rose point lace that makes her skin look so golden it could be the sun itself, the waves of fabric hitting her curves in all the right places.

"I think it's . . . well, it's . . ." Saffron pauses as she walks up to the mirror, turning around slowly to get another look at the back, the raw-edged georgette rosettes and the train wafting gently behind her.

Julian keeps pacing back and forth and back and forth behind Saffron, biting the fingers of his left hand while inspecting the dress nervously from a distance.

"It's flawless, really, isn't it," Saffron says, more as a statement than a question. *Flawless?* I love the sound of that. I couldn't think of a more apt word myself. And she's not speaking in third person or asking her Maltipoo to bark if he likes the gown, like some other clients I don't care to mention.

"It's truly flawless. It's spectacular on you," Baz says as the art director snaps Polaroid shots of the gown.

I can finally breathe again. They like it! They actually like it! Of course they do! I knew they would. Julian and I exchange quiet smiles. I have to stop myself from throwing my arms around Saffron and Baz and asking for a group hug.

"I think it's just absolutely extraordinary," Cricket says. "Saffron, you are absolutely, positively, the most gorgeous woman in the whole world in that dress. You look like a goddess!" I feel slightly embarrassed for her. Note to self: point out to Cricket later that she should probably tone down her obsession with the superstar.

"I'm only sorry that I don't get to be the one to marry you in that gown. You look ravishing, S," Markus Livingston says, stepping into the room and putting a proprietary hand on her dreamy shoulder. With his dark hair sweeping boyishly over chiseled features, his green eyes sparkling, and his skin tanned as though he's just been surfing for a week, Saffron's male costar and boyfriend oozes charm and sex appeal. No wonder *Star* put the two lovebirds on their cover under the headline "X Marks the Spot for Saffron Sykes." *In Touch* screamed, "Markus Spices It Up with Saffron!" TMZ, classy as always, went for the S&M angle when it posted video of the two shopping for leather coats at Maxfield on Robertson.

"Thanks, M," Saffron says with a smile. "It's a perfect combination of modern but still classic. It's feminine without being too soft. It's bold without being pretentious." I can't help but notice that this could be a description of Saffron Sykes herself. She seems almost too good to be true. I'm almost waiting for the other stiletto to drop. Or at least for her to change her mind. Or ask to call in an aura analyst. Or a wedding gown intuitive. Could one of the biggest stars in the world really be this nice? This is a woman who takes things seriously. Not just her acting work, that much is obvious. But everything she does, she does with complete conviction. You won't see *this* PETA poster girl eating a NY strip at Cut. Or the coauthor of *Go Green or Go Home,* a book she wrote with Al Gore, driving a Mercedes G-Wagon. I'm on the verge of forming my own girl crush when Julian approaches Saffron.

"We're so happy that you like it," he says with a wide, relieved smile.

"Julian, it's genius," she beams back. She turns to Baz. "It's this gown. Are we agreed?" As Baz nods, she claps her hands with joy. "And Lola, I understand I have you to thank for getting this beautiful gown to me."

"My pleasure, Saffron; we're so honored you've chosen Julian Tennant," I say.

"Well I've heard a great deal about you from Cricket," she says. "Best girlfriends are one of the most important things in life," she adds kindly, looking at Cricket and then back to me with an outstretched hand.

"You're so right," I agree.

"Let me help you guys with those," Cricket says as we load up the backup gowns to head out after we say our good-byes. She grabs several of the garment bags and we make our way to our rental car. "Well, that seems like it was a big success," Cricket says once we're outside.

"Mission accomplished," I say, a wave of relief washing over me.

"I think I'll actually sleep tonight without a pharmaceutical cocktail," Julian adds as he opens the trunk and we carefully lay out the gowns.

"I wish I could at least have dinner with you guys," Cricket says, "but I don't think I'll see you again before you leave. We shoot all night tonight."

"We're so exhausted from the flight anyway, sweetheart. We just need to crash," I say, wrapping my arms around Cricket and whispering in her ear, "I'm so happy for you. You're in your element here."

"I'm happy for you too," she whispers back. "This is going to be fantastic having Saffron in Julian Tennant," she says with a little squeeze. Cricket opens the car door for me and, once I slide in, closes it gently behind me. She blows a kiss as we take off, looking her usual otherworldly self, her white blond hair blowing gently in the Australian breeze, waving good-bye to us until she becomes a speck in the distance.

My eyes are at half mast when I finally get back to the hotel room. I can barely keep them open as I dial Lev's number to say goodnight.

"Hi honey," I say when he picks up.

"You sound exhausted," he says immediately.

"I am. That flight is brutal, and I can't remember the last time I actually slept. I don't know how you can function on so little sleep on a regular basis."

"You just get used to it, but I don't recommend it. How's it going there?" he asks.

"Everything is great. Saffron loves her gown. So we're in good shape," I say.

"Well, mission accomplished! I'll let you go to sleep then. Sounds like you need it badly," Lev says.

"No wait. First tell me what's going on with you," I say.

"Oh, not much. Actually, something funny happened on the set of *Para-Medic* today. I was there in my scrubs and I guess I looked the part, so Shonda gave me a few lines."

"Oh, that's funny," I say with a little forced laugh, because something about it doesn't strike me as funny at all.

"Yeah, it was fun."

"Oh good," I say halfheartedly.

"Honey, I better let you go; you sound like you're already asleep."

"Okay, love you," I say.

"Love you too," Lev says before hanging up.

The second I close my eyes, I'm out. I'm not sure how much time has passed when the phone rouses me from a deep sleep. I check the number. "Christopher? What is it?"

"She dumped me, La-La," Christopher says on the other end of the phone.

"What?" I ask, pulling myself up in bed and trying to shake myself awake.

"She told me she's just not cut out for monogamy and that we're just too different. She said the only relationships she's any good at are the ones with her clients and that she needs to focus on those," Christopher says, choking over the words.

"Oh, Chris, I'm so sorry," I say as he lets out a disturbing guttural sound. I haven't heard my brother cry since we were kids and I'm at a bit of a loss. I'm usually the broken-hearted one calling my brother after some Actor Boyfriend shredded my heart to bits. But this time it's my older brother who's had his heart shredded to bits by—my best friend. And it's not only going to be hard for my brother to get over Kate, but I wonder how I'm going to get over my best friend breaking my brother's heart. "It's going to be okay. You're going to be okay," I say because it's all I can think of.

"I don't know, Lo, I just don't know if I will be." Chris chokes, then bursts into tears again. I have to wonder myself if he's going to be okay.

"You will be. It's going to be okay. You're going to be okay," I say over and over because I hope that if I say it enough times it will actually be true.

Chris and I have barely hung up when the phone rings again. It can be only one person, and I make a concerted effort to take the edge out of my voice when I answer.

"We broke up," Kate says.

"I know, I just got off the phone with Chris. I'm so sorry," I say.

"No, don't be sorry," Kate says gruffly. "It was my choice. I'm just not cut out for the whole relationship thing." The Great Wall of Kate buttressed and cordoned off. There's not going to be any getting through, so I simply ask, "What happened?"

"We're just too different," she says. "I just thought it would be different. I didn't think it would require so much work—and *talking*. And I didn't think it would bother me as much as it does that he's happy doing music video shoots and commercials when he should be making movies. And the sex . . ."

"Kate, relationships do take work, and you do have to actually communicate, but he really loves you and I thought you really loved him and—"

"How's it going in Australia? How do Cricket and Saffron seem to be getting on?" She's already changing the subject in a typical Kate Wood's technique: avoidance. I can't believe Kate's trying to shift into agent mode. I'm not playing.

"Everything looks really great. But Kate, I'm really not up for talking shop with you at three o'clock in the morning Australia time. If you want to talk about your relationship falling apart, that's one thing. But I'm not going to do this."

"There's nothing to talk about. I don't know how to do relationships. That's it."

I think about telling Kate about Christopher's movie, *Into the Woods*, and wonder whether if she knew about it, it would make a difference, but I don't want to betray my brother's trust. Of all the things I could say to Kate, about relationships, about my brother, about her fear of commitment, I simply say, "Okay, well, I have to go to sleep." Kate's a lost cause.

"Don't be mad at me," she says matter-of-factly.

"Just give me a second to adjust," I say.

"Oh geezus, what? I'm breaking up with your brother, for crying out loud, not you!"

"Yeah, Kate, I'm pretty sure I got that part," I say, losing that battle with the edge in my voice.

"Do you, Lo? Do you get that?" she asks, then adds quietly, "I need to know for sure."

"Yeah Kate," I say softly, knowing that Kate and I—for all our differences—will always be together. "I get it."

"Okay then, good luck there. Go to sleep," she says, hanging up.

Click.

I don't know if it's summer or winter or what time or day it is as I step out of the car from LAX in front of Lev's house in Sherman Oaks. I don't even care. All that matters is that I'm back home. I never knew what it was like to have a home to be happy to return to. This feeling that I'm safe. That I can trust someone. That I have someplace where I can just be. And breathe.

When I open the front door no one seems to be home. But then I realize that there are candles lit everywhere. I'm so tired that I didn't notice before. What are all of these candles for?

"Honey," I call out. "Honey!" I yell again, following a trail of tea lights leading into the bedroom. When I walk through the bedroom door, Lev is standing there by the large picture windows with his back to me and his arms stretched out toward the garden as if greeting it like an old friend.

"Honey, what are you doing? Is everything okay?" I feel like maybe I've walked in on a private moment, but Lev turns toward me, a small black box with gold borders balanced on an upright palm, and drops to one knee. Before he can say anything, I start shouting, "What is happening?! What is happening right now?!"

Lev beams at me. "I've been thinking about our life, about our lives together, about us, and that's what it is, it's about us, that's all it is. It's that simple to me. I love you. I want for us to be together forever. To have our children, our family, for you to be my wife."

"What is happening?" I keep screaming because my body is up there, above me, floating above me, though all I've ever wanted is right there in front of me on the floor, on one knee.

"I've applied to Lenox Hill Hospital so that we can live in New York for your work. I'm asking you to marry me," he says, his eyes shiny with tears. "Will you marry me?"

"What is happening?!" keeps coming out of my mouth and tears spill like uncontrollable geysers out of my eyes.

"Will you answer me?" he says, smiling and crying and laughing.

"Yes!! Yes!! That would be a big fat YES!!" I yell, coming back to the ground and joining him, my love, my Lev, joining him in the smiling and crying and laughing for the rest of my days. For always. For us. For all I've ever wanted. Bye, Bye, Bi-Lolar. Adios Actorholism. Sayonara Santisi. Hello Lola Levin. Hello . . .

6

remind me again why I agreed to let my mother throw us an engagement party *on camera*," I say as Lev and I turn onto my parents' jacaranda-lined street.

"Because it's good exposure for you and Julian. The camera is totally gonna love *that* outfit," he says, giving an appreciative whistle and eyeing my super-pale lemon-beige, short lace dress and ostrich booties that Julian made especially for tonight. Lev has totally gone over to the dark stiletto side. "And besides, your mother wasn't going to take no for an answer even if she had to get us here bound and gagged."

My hands instantly turn clammy as I notice the colossal number of cars parked on both sides of the road. They can't all be here for us? Can they? How many people did my mother actually invite? I made her promise me it would be small, but now I'm realizing I should have gotten an actual number.

"Thank you for still loving me," I say, kissing Lev. "And I just want to apologize in advance *again* for the next couple of hours. Please don't hold any of it against me."

"It's going to be fine," Lev whispers in my ear.

"You keep saying that, no matter what I throw at you," I tell him. "First you're agreeing to Mom sticking her cameras in our faces. Then you have Christopher on your couch on suicide watch. How are you so okay with this?" Lev has been babysitting Chris ever since he moved out of Kate's apartment. He was so flattened by their breakup that I was afraid for him and got Lev to propose the arrangement. I think I was as surprised as Chris when he agreed.

"Okay, I'll admit it was rough at first, but he's actually been a pretty decent roommate," Lev says. "And he stuck to his end of the bargain." Lev has gotten Christopher up and dressed by ten o'clock every morning, off to do reshoots for *Into the Woods,* and then later into the editing bay by eleven. In return, Christopher has been springing for the takeout from Jerry's Deli and Baja Fresh and doing laundry for Lev while he pulls extra shifts at the ER to save up for our honeymoon.

"I'm a little worried about him seeing Kate today," I confess. "He's made so much progress. I just don't want him to roll back."

Lev squeezes my hand. "We had a talk about that last night. He's tougher than you think, Lo. He'll be okay."

I take a deep breath and grab Lev's hand as we drive through the open wrought-iron gates. There are hundreds of flickering luminaria lining the gravel driveway up to the house.

"Hi, would you like to check out the new Chevy Volt before you step inside?" a young man in a tux asks, standing in front of a spinning white car that's holding center stage at the top of the driveway.

"Excuse me?" I say.

"One lucky guest tonight is going to be driving home in a brand-new Extended-Range Electric Vehicle that is redefining the automotive world," he says.

"What's going on?" Lev whispers in my ear.

Oh no. Oh nonono. "I'm not sure, but I think my mother got our engagement party sponsored—by Chevy," I say, taking in the wedding bells painted on the hood of the car as it spins around and around. "We could just turn around and walk away. Act like this never happened."

"Ow," Lev says, releasing his hand from the vise grip I have on it and shaking it to get the blood back. "No, this party is for us, Lo, and we're going to enjoy ourselves." Lev sets his mouth in grim determination and ushers us through the carved wooden front door. Four women in flowing red minidresses and stilettos are playing the theme song from *Gone with the Wind* on stringed instruments that look like they were sprung from a *Transformers* set. Omigod—did Mom really book Escala, Simon Cowell's discovery from *Britain's Got Talent*?

"My darling daughter and gorgeous soon-to-be son-in-law," my mother says, stretching out her freshly lipo'd arms to us in a divine white bias-cut satin dress with a strategic flutter of ruffles down the back. As my mother looks over her shoulder to make sure that Alex, her cameraman, is filming her good side, I realize that the dress she's wearing is one that Julian designed for *Four Weddings and a Bris* that we didn't end up using in the movie. Only my mother would wear a wedding gown to her only daughter's engagement party. I wonder if she'll try and wear one to my wedding as well. Note to self: elope.

"Mom, everything looks beautiful," I say, trying to ignore the cameras pointed in my face. Millions of clear balloons float on the ceiling, and the pearl-filled vases spill over with white roses, hydrangeas, and orchids. There are more flowers in the house than at Huntington Botanical

Gardens. "You've really outdone yourself! I thought this was just supposed to be a small engagement party."

"*Premiere* engagement party, darling," she corrects me, which I'm assuming means she wants to keep the option open to be able to throw *another* party. "And this is nothing compared to what I'm envisioning for the actual wedding," Mom says, scanning the crowded living room. Is that Amy Adams talking to Emily Blunt? And why is Michael Cera in our living room?

"Hi Blanca," Lev says as my mother reaches out her hand to him as though she's the pope and he's supposed to kiss the ring, which in Mom's case is an eighteen-karat borrowed Winston. Instead, Lev wraps her in a hug.

"Oh Lev, you're so wonderful," Mom says in a new over-the-top singsong voice she's acquired for the cameras that sounds eerily similar to the British accent Madonna started using when she first moved to London. "I always imagined Lola would end up with someone in Hollywood, never a nice Jewish doctor." My mother lets out a hearty fake laugh in the camera's direction. "Now come get something to eat. The winner of last season's *Top Chef* is one of the caterers and he made the most delicious foie gras. Don't you just love Escala? And there's an even more special treat for you two later!"

"I'm surprised you couldn't get Heidi and Spencer here," I joke, thinking, *I'm so not a celebrity, get me outta here.*

"Darling, I'm so sorry. They're fulfilling Heidi's lifelong dream of bringing plastic surgery to Africa. Otherwise they'd be here," my mother says, oblivious to my sarcastic tone. "But they said they'd co-officiate your wedding ceremony, so we've been looking at dates."

"What, Mom, no!" I say between clenched lips. "We don't want those two marrying us." And Africa doesn't need them either, for crying out loud.

"Well, maybe that sweet Stephen Baldwin, then," Mom trills. "He's just so . . . *enthusiastic!* I'll look into it first thing tomorrow morning."

"Mom, thanks, but—" My mother is already staring intently behind my shoulder at more arriving guests. "Have fun, darlings, I have to go say hello to *Anjelica.*" The final emphasis is for Alex's benefit as he dutifully marshalls his camera crew so they can film the triple air kiss.

I turn to Lev. "Honey, this is a nightmare! What is she *thinking* of?"

Lev rubs my arm. "Okay, sure, this is ridiculous. But just try and breathe. Your mom clearly went to a lot of trouble for us; let's try and enjoy it."

"Not for us, for her show," I say. "Let's get some champagne."

"Wouldn't you rather have a Levtini or Lolatini?" asks the bartender, plying his shaker amid a blizzard of Ketel One signage. "And don't forget your commemorative coaster," he says, pressing a woolly disk into my hand along with my drink. There are spidery outlines of me and Lev on the front. "Darryl Hannah made them herself from the fleeces of sheep she personally rescued." A chocolate fountain burbles and splashes beneath a plaque for Teuscher with our names spelled out in giant three-foot chocolate letters. "Did you want a lasagna pinwheel?" asks a waiter, proffering a huge tray emblazoned with a Food Network logo. "Rachael Ray says they're absolutely yum-o. Or perhaps some of Paula Deen's Beer in the Rear Chicken?" My face is flush with embarrassment as my mother laughs it up with Goldie and Kurt center stage in the middle of the living room—or should I say—camera right.

I'm gearing up to buttonhole her when my father pokes his head out from around the corner in the dining room. All I can see is the top of his straw fedora and the tip of a burning cigar, which he removes from his mouth and points at the nearest cameraman.

"If you even *think* of pointing that fucking camera in my direction I will ruin you," he says. "Bing," he says, jolting the cigar in the cameraman's direction. "Bang," this time waving it in small circles at the cameraman's chest. "Bong," he says, taking dead aim with the cigar between the cameraman's eyes. I have a disturbing image of a solitary burn mark between the man's eyes when a far more disturbing image catches my eye: Coz and Chili are in attendance. And they're talking to Nic Knight. Coz is wearing the shortest, tightest dress I've ever seen smothered in Swarovski crystal and is towering over Nic and Chili in her sky-high suede boots with a stack of silver buckles running up the side. I can hear Chili's shrieks of "Oh my god, Nic you are so *hoot!*" and "Isn't this party *strawberries!*" and Nic's fake Colombian accent from all the way over here. Nic's so Method that he's now refusing to break character until the movie is out in theaters. Which means he's in drag now, in a sage green sarong with matching organza sash draped bandolier-style across his chest, with an iPhone6, BlackBerry Torch, N8, Flip, and cigarette lighter winking out of sheer mesh pockets. Chili's high-tech haute couture strikes again.

What the hell are they doing here? I have the sudden urge to borrow my father's cigar. Bing. Bang. Bong. And Coz and Chili could be gone. I'm determined to make it through this party without having to speak to either one of them. As in: fully *committed.*

"Okay, that's it," I say. "I really need to go speak to my mom."

"Of course," Lev says as Julian comes running up to us in a three-piece herringbone toothpick-thin suit.

"Oh my god, you look gorgeous," he says, spinning me around. "But what are Coz and Chili doing here? Look at my chest, those people give me hives," he says nervously unbuttoning his shirt to show me his splotchy skin. "Wait. Let me take another look at you. Maybe we should make a long version of this for your wedding. Did you get the new JPEGs I sent you? I sketched five new gowns for you last night. You're going to be the most gorgeous bride in the world. And I'm going to be your maid of honor, right?"

"Julian, please, slow down! We *just* got engaged. Please don't waste your time sketching dresses for me. We don't even have a date set yet. You need to be focusing on your line."

"Are you kidding me, you're my muse and you're getting *married!*" he says. "Hang on, I haven't gotten a close enough look at this thing," Julian says, grabbing my left hand and holding up the engagement ring to his inspecting eyeball. "I must say, I'm impressed by the good doctor." He tosses my hand back at me and winks at Lev. "What is it, like a two-karat princess cut?" he asks. "Honey, after everything you've been through, you deserve it." He gives me a kiss on the forehead. "You really deserve it."

And you know what, I think I actually believe him.

"Thanks, Julian," I say.

We're startled by a loud bray of laughter across the room as Nic minces around, miming putting one caller on hold while texting another. "You're killing me!" Chili practically screams. "She *said* that? That's so *strawberries!*"

Julian shudders. "Why would your mother invite Coz and Chili?"

"I don't know, but I'm about to find out," I say, heading toward my mother, who's laid a soft hand on Larry King's speckled forearm.

"How do you do it, Larry?" she purrs. "You're always so calm and masterful on camera. You're just such a natural. I practically shake every time Alex starts filming. What's your secret?"

"Nonsense, Blanca," Larry tells her. "The camera's always loved you. Remember the Studio 54 shoot? You were more dazzling than Jerry!"

"That was a century ago, Larry," Mom tells him. "It's all about the young ones now, with their Cities and their Hills and their god knows what. My first producing credit and I'm so afraid we're gonna tank. Who's gonna want to look at me now?"

"The whole world," Larry promises her. "We'll make sure Piers has you on the show so the whole world knows about the most stunning Wristwatch Wife."

"Larry, it's so nice to see you," I tell him, slipping my arm through my mother's. "Do you mind if I borrow Mom for a bit?"

"Not at all, Lola," Larry beams. "Congratulations on your mother's new show! You must be thrilled for her!"

"Oh, absolutely!" I say, steering Mom down the hallway. I whirl to face her. "Why would you invite Coz and Chili?" I whisper into her ear. "What were you thinking?"

Mom seems genuinely puzzled by my dismay. "Coz told me that you made friends after you worked with Chili on *Four Weddings*." *Friends?!* The woman stole the Nic Knight design right out from under us! Her sole purpose seems to be to put up every roadblock she can possibly throw our way. Friends we are not. "And aren't you trying to make nice with her, darling, so Julian can be on her show and we can get his dresses into *Vain*?" she asks. "You know, she tried to get me to wear a Chili dress tonight, but I absolutely refused." Oh, what a jerk that woman is trying to get my own mother to wear Chili and not Julian to *my* engagement party. "Besides, Coz really isn't that bad, darling. She's going to do a piece in 'GAGA' for *Wristwatch Wives*. And with all she's doing with Nic to promote your father's movie, putting him on the cover in full drag, we had to invite her. Not to mention, she had this wonderful idea to have Chili design the bag that the party favors go in."

"Party favors? Don't tell me you're giving people swag bags at my engagement party!"

"Darling, don't get all frowny; it doesn't look good on camera," Mom chides me, looking around quickly to make sure Alex isn't getting this on film. "Please. Work with me on this. I really need some decent footage. You know how uncooperative Papa's been. And all the other Wristwatch Wives are total camera hogs. That Francesca is such a bitch. She's just put her daughter into rehab for anorexia—again. How *convenient*. The girl's been doing nothing but Master Cleanse for the last three months and *now* she notices? And Lucinda's maid oh-so-conveniently turns out to be an illegal alien, so now she gets a big deportment court scene. It's not fair."

I'm not sure what to be more scared by at this point. That Papa is bearing down on Lev, threatening each cameraman en route with his cigar. Or that my own mother would sell her soul to Coz for a mention of *Wristwatch Wives* in *Vain's* "Girls Are Gossiping About." But right now I need to prioritize. "Mom, we're not done talking about this, but I need to talk to Lev now." I rush to Lev's side.

"Hi, Paulie," Lev says as my father lurches up to him.

"So, Levin," he says, waving his cigar toward my fiancé. I'm chagrined that Papa hasn't yet retired it as a lethal weapon. "You think you're good enough for my little girl?"

"I don't know, Mr. Santisi," Lev says. "Lola's so wonderful, I'm not sure anyone is good enough for—"

"You still in the ER, right?" Papa cuts in. "That's shit money. If you want, I could make some calls, get you something decent. Did I mention I know the top cardiologist at Cedars-Sinai?"

"You did," Lev says levelly. "But that won't be necessary. I assure you I make more than a decent living. And I'm sure you realize that as a CEO, Lola's more than capable of making her own—"

"Oh yeah, the clothes thing." Papa dismisses my career with a wave of his cigar as he turns toward my mother, who is furiously beckoning him from across the room. "Who knows how long that's gonna last?" he mutters as he saunters away.

"La-La!" Christopher says, crossing the floor in a few long lopes and wrapping me in a bear hug. Oh thank god for my brother. He's always had a sixth sense for when I need him. "Still can't believe my little sis is getting hitched!" He kisses the top of my head and shoots a grin at Lev. "How's it going, man?"

"I'm great, Chris. Some party, huh?"

"You look *really* good," I say to Christopher once he's released me from our embrace. And he almost does. He's lost a little of the hollowed-out look he had in the first few weeks after Kate dumped him. He's still way too skinny, but at least he's shaved and dressed in clean clothes.

"Yeah, taking off to finish the movie was just what the doctor ordered," he says to Lev. "I'm just finishing up the final edit."

"It's good to see you, Chris," Lev says, giving my brother a hug. "When are we gonna get to see this movie?"

"Soon," Chris says with a gleam in his eye. "Lo," he adds quietly to me, "Crimini's been amazing," he says, placing his hand on my arm. "Seems like he might take over the costs of the movie."

"Oh my gosh, Chris, that would be so great," I say. I knew my Russian financier was dying to bankroll more than Julian Tennant–designed Sweet Sixteen ballgowns.

"Everybody into the screening room!" says Mom, clapping her hands for attention. She nods at Alex to make sure he's got cameras rolling. "We have an extra-special surprise for Lola and Lev!"

It takes a few minutes to settle everyone into the plush maroon-velvet seats of the screening room Mom had built for Papa. Then Mom steps to the front of the room and clears her throat gracefully.

"Lola, Lev, a number of people couldn't be here today to wish you both well, so we're doing the next best thing. Lights!" As Papa's twelve-by-twenty-foot screen purrs down from the ceiling, the room goes dark. Then the screen springs to life.

"Congratulations, Lily and Liev!" growls Jack Nicholson, arching one of his famous eyebrows, his wolfish grin on full display. *Lily? Liev?* "I can't believe Paulie and Blanca's little girl's getting married! And hey,

Blanca, if you ever get tired of that old gasbag, maybe you'll give it a whirl with me!" Okay, this is ridiculous. I've met Jack maybe once, twenty years ago, at Mr. Chow.

"Sweethearts!" croons Elizabeth Taylor, her famous violet eyes twinkling mischievously on the screen. "I'm just so thrilled to hear about your engagement! I loved all seven of mine! Lorna and Luke, great happiness to both of you, and may your first marriage be your last!"

"Kids!" shouts Joan Rivers in the next screen tribute, her smile pulled into a strangely frozen rictus. "When Blanca asked me to congratulate you, I could *not* have been more thrilled. Maybe you could convince Melissa to take the plunge next? Now, Lil, if you want to wear any of the Joan Rivers Classics Collection on your special day, you just let me know, okay?"

I can feel my face go hot. I'm sure Mom was trying to impress me—or the cameras—but I'm mortified by this empty display. "That's it," I tell Chris and Lev. "I'm outta here."

"Wait, Lo," Chris tells me. "Look!"

And up there on the screen is Cricket's glowing face—her clear green eyes and soft blond curls cascading around her shoulders. I haven't heard from her in ages. She's been impossible to reach ever since reshoots for *Four Weddings* ended. She's been traveling around the world with Saffron and Markus, who invited her to join their dream getaway gratis. Last I heard she was in Phuket, at least according to Perez Hilton, who's been documenting Saffron and Markus's every move. So far only the back of Cricket's head has actually made it online. Perez did draw question marks and a wheel appearing above it with a caption reading "What's the third wheel doing on Saffron and Markus's love vacation??" I gotta hand it to Mom; she did the impossible tracking my BFF down.

"Congratulations, Lola and Lev!" Cricket says. "I'm so happy for you both. I only wish I was there to give you a big celebratory hug. I always knew you'd find your soul mate." *Soul mate.* I say the words inside my head over and over. *Lev is my soul mate.* "I can't believe I'm not there with you right now celebrating your engagement." Cricket's eyes well up. "But I'll be home soon. And I promise I'll be right by your side when you two walk down the aisle. I love you both so much, Lola and Lev!"

I'm fighting back tears myself when "Gone with the Louboutin," pops onto the screen above two animated stick figures holding hands, one wearing a single four-inch Louboutin and one Croc, the other clad in green scrubs.

Christopher squeezes my shoulder. "This one's from me," he says.

As "All You Need Is Love," by The Beatles plays, Lev and I watch as the story of our relationship unfolds frame by frame through animated stick figures: meeting in our therapist's waiting room without ever even exchanging names. Lev fixing both my busted ankle on Oscar night, and also my broken heart. "We have to stop meeting where things are broken." Chris's voice imitates Lev's voice and then mine, a high-pitched female voice, "I think you just unbroke me." Us reading the Sunday *New York Times* (me reading the Style section and Lev combing the magazine for health features), walking along the beach in Malibu, taking a yoga class, Lev trying to teach me to cook, me trying to teach Lev about fashion, Lev giving me my first pair of Crocs, me traversing back and forth and back and forth and back and forth across the country to be with Lev.

"This is amazing, Chris," I say.

"Keep watching, La-La," Christopher says.

Tears well in my eyes as I watch Lev's stick figure get on one knee and propose as a halogen bulb appears in my figure's chest to illustrate how brightly I'm beaming. "This is not a Hollywood Ending" appears on the screen. As Lev and my stick selves kiss, my leg kicks up to reveal—a four-inch Croc. I'm laughing and crying as I hug Christopher. Lev joins in and the three of us are still hugging when the lights come up amid rapturous applause from the audience. And there in the crowd is Kate, looking spectacular in a form-fitting Missoni dress in gradating shades of blue that offsets her blue eyes and fit physique perfectly. She's surreptitiously wiping away tears.

Lev and I are both holding our breath as we look to Kate and then to Chris and then back to Kate. Chris suddenly looks a bit pale.

"Hey you," I say, walking over and wrapping Kate in a hug.

"Hey Lev," she says holding out her arms to him. "Christopher."

"Kate," Christopher says. "You're looking . . . good." The air seems to hang tensely between the two former lovers.

"Come on." I grab Lev's hand. "I think I spotted someone giving out Swarovski crystal Kleenex cases and I'm having a major mascara malfunction." I lead Lev out of the room to give Kate and Chris some space.

"Excuse me, can I have everyone's attention," my mother says, tapping her champagne glass. "I hope you enjoyed our little video tribute. And now I'd like everyone to come outside for a special performance. It's Sid, the winner of *American Idol!* Who, I'm pleased to say, will be appearing next month on *Wristwatch Wives!*"

Oh god. Only my mother would have done this. The claim to fame of this year's *Idol* winner is that he or she won't confirm whether he or she is a he or she. There's no way I'm staying for this freak show.

"I think I just heard your beeper go off," I say, linking my arm through Lev's and pleading with him with my eyes to get us out of here.

"Yes, it seems I'm wanted back at the hospital immediately," he says, following my lead.

"Come on, you two. I want you front and center outside for the performance," my mother says, coming up beside us.

"Um, actually, Mom, we have to go. I'm sorry, but Lev has to get back to the hospital," I say.

"What? Right now? Darling, it's your engagement party!" Mom says, eyes darting toward where Alex and the rest of the crew are training their cameras on Sid as he or she steps up on the makeshift stage. "You can't leave your own engagement party. You *have* to stay." Mom's tone has gone from commanding to practically pleading. "I've gone to so much trouble. I don't care if I have to call the head of Cedars right now," she says. Lev looks at me and then over to my mother, just as my father approaches. "Paulie, they want to leave their own engagement party already," my mother says beseechingly.

"You know, Blanca, Paulie," Lev says, shaking his head in a signal of having lost his battle with his patience, "I have to be honest because this is killing me on Lola's behalf." His voice is steady, but it's clear that he's quite upset. "This doesn't seem to be an engagement party for your daughter. I don't know much about Hollywood, but I do know something about self-promotion and I must say that this whole thing reeks of it," he says coolly, looking first to my mother square in the eyes and then to my father, all the while with his hand placed protectively at the small of my back. As he stands there waiting for them to respond, I realize that I've never been in this position before. I've never had anyone stand up for me to my parents. And I like the view from here.

My parents seem to be speechless, briefly. Uncomfortable, which is something they rarely are, by being told the truth, which is something they are rarely told. Then my mother wills herself to break the spell. "There's no time for this. We have a performance that needs to go on," she says, sashaying away and toward the stage. Which seems like a fitting place for her to be heading.

"You ready to go, Lo?" Lev asks turning toward me.

"Yeah, one song—for Mom—and then let's go," I whisper and for the first time in my life I've completely forgotten my father's presence there until he abruptly wraps me in a hug.

"I'm happy for you, sweetheart. He's a good man," he says into my ear and then just as quickly lets me go. When Lev reaches out to shake his hand, my father dismisses it. Instead, he gives Lev a hug for the first time, patting him on the back several times as he does. Then just as quickly he bolts through the living room and disappears.

"It's such an honor to be here tonight," Sid says, running black lacquered fingernails through his or her asymmetrical haircut. "Paulie," he or she calls out to the crowd, "I'm a huge fan, though I have to admit, I'm more scared to perform in front of you than Simon Cowell. Thank you for having me here tonight. My album drops next week. I hope you'll all buy it!" He or she scans the audience. "Holy shit. Is that Nic Knight? Wow, man, I love you," he or she says.

"I love you too," Nic yells back.

"Wow, this is so surreal. Okay, this one's for you, Layla. Congratulations on your engagement." *Layla? Did he or she just call me Layla?* As Sid starts in on the Derek & the Dominos classic, Nic Knight suddenly storms the stage, grabbing a guitar from a stand. As Nic's guitar lets out deafening feedback, Mr. or Ms. Idol awkwardly tries to incorporate this unexpected guest into the performance, becoming more and more stilted as Nic starts provocatively dancing with him or her, playfully flashing his sarong. Mom stands off to the side, grinning contentedly as Alex captures the footage.

As the crowd starts cheering, I run inside to grab my purse and am stopped in my tracks by the sight of Kate and Christopher slipping into the downstairs bathroom.

"This is a bad idea," I hear Kate whisper as Chris pulls her in by the wrist. "Ssh . . . just stop . . . talking for once," he replies. I duck out of the hallway before they can spot me, grab a swag bag and Lev, and lead him out of Crazy Town.

Inside the car, I reach into the swag bag and pull out Season One of Coz's *Cut-Throat Couture*. Next is a T-shirt bedazzled with glittery button batteries that spell out "Chili Lu Loves Lola and Lev." Give me a fucking break. As we pull our car past the spinning Chevy in the driveway I toss the swag bag onto the driver's seat, where it rotates crazily as the strains of "Layla" fade into the distance.

My body isn't even sure what time zone I'm in when I rush inside Bar Pitti on 6th Ave and Bleecker with sweaty palms. With the economy in such dire straits, I'm certain I'm not the only one with sweaty palms in lower Manhattan at the moment. When I find Stefano Rabinski from LVMH sitting at a corner table, he's already tearing into his wild boar ragu. He waves me over.

"I ordered you the meatballs." The famous veal ones that launched a hundred lawsuits. "Lola, I'm going to cut to the chase: With the recession as it is, no one's buying high-end retail. And if you can't get sales up, it doesn't make sense for us to continue to invest. It's not personal. I actually like you and Julian. It's a numbers game." His silky smooth Italian accent does nothing to soften the devastating blow.

I think it's safe to say that my insides are shaking to the point of internal seizure. It seems my outsides are as well as I reach for a glass of water with a quivering hand.

"The release of *Four Weddings* is right around the corner, and it's going to be really great exposure for Julian," I insist.

"Maybe," Stefano says, biting into a piece of bread. "But we've actually lost money on the movie so far. Between having to pay for your gown samples and the actual production of the gown for the movie and flying you both to Australia. The company is spending and not earning, Lola. It's really that simple."

"We're doing everything we can, Stefano, but please, just hang in there. We'll make it happen," I say, but can't stop wondering how. *How are we going to make it happen?*

I'm not even sure if I've eaten at all, or what else Stefano and I talked about by the time we say good-bye. All I feel is the buzz of panic in my ears. As I step out of Bar Pitti into a torrential downpour I barely notice that I'm instantly drenched. I speed-dial Kate.

"Kate, what's happening with *Four Weddings*?" I ask the second she picks up.

"No hello? Geezus, now I know what I sound like," Kate says. "Great news, I was going to call you, we just found out that it's premiering at Cannes in May." Yes! Okay, think, Lola, think. There has to be a way to use the mega press coverage from Cannes to save JT Inc. I just don't know what it is yet. "Hang on," I say to her, as I'm pelted in the face by lethal raindrops, trying to open my umbrella while negotiating the angle of my cell phone on my shoulder at the same time that I'm raising my arm up in the air to hail a cab, which seems at the moment to be as likely as Kanye West and Susan Boyle doing a duet.

"Oh *shit*," Kate says with emphasis, and I hear something crashing as though it's landed on her midcentury Lawson Fenning coffee table.

"What's wrong?" I ask, finally getting my umbrella open, though I'm not sure it even matters since I'm already drenched from head to my open-toe black leather booties.

"Christopher's fucking drum, that's what's wrong," she says. "I told him to come get it, but he keeps spacing it out."

"Maybe it's because he doesn't really want to and is hoping you'll get back together," I offer.

"That's not happening," Kate says flatly. "But Cannes is. You and Julian should come."

"You know, I think you're right. I think we should, too," I say, though

I have no idea how we're going to pay our way there. Waiting to cross Houston, I get splashed in the face with dirty rainwater from a taxi rounding a corner. That's just freaking great. Could this day get worse? "I gotta go, I'll call you later."

Click.

And then, ten soggy blocks later, it hits me. I feel like how I imagine Henri Poincare did when he first discovered chaos theory. Or those guys when they invented Google. Or Gaga when she discovered the flank steak.

I squish into Julian's loft and immediately strip off my soaked khaki trench, shrunken white button-down, cropped navy trousers, and black booties.

"Are you trying to seduce me, Miss Santisi?" Julian says, eyeballing my mismatched lace bra and cotton panties.

"I just had to walk all the way home from a completely disastrous lunch with Stefano," I say, heading into the bathroom for a robe.

"How bad was it?" Julian asks timidly, grabbing a slumbering Tom Ford off his spot on the sofa as I curl into the plush terry. "Are we talking one Xanax or two?"

"We're talking I should hide the whole bottle because you might be tempted to take them all."

"Oh god. Don't tell me yet. I'm not ready. I don't think I can handle it," Julian says, petting Tom Ford a little too aggressively. The dog issues a low whimper.

"Julian, Stefano is threatening to pull their financing. This is serious."

"I told you not to tell me yet. Why did you just tell me?" Julian says starting to pace in circles, clutching Tom Ford to his chest. "What are we going to do, Lo?"

"First of all, you need to stop pacing. You're making me dizzy, not to mention poor Tom Ford," I say. "But I think I have our answer. I just found out that *Four Weddings and a Bris* is premiering at Cannes. Saffron's wearing your gown in the movie. And that's where we begin. We maximize that opportunity and turn it into sales." I pick up Julian's sketchbook and quickly flip through the stack of gorgeous wedding dress drawings. "Between all the gowns you designed for the film and what you've been working on for me, you already have an entire line of wedding gowns here. Forget the spring collection you've been working on. We're going to turn your amazing bridal gowns into a new collection and premiere it at the Cannes Film Festival to tie in with the premiere of the movie. Move over, Vera Wang! Maybe we could even get Saffron and Cricket to walk in the runway show!" I say excitedly. "Sure, the economy's in the toilet, but people aren't going to stop falling in love and getting married and they will *always* splurge on their dream dress."

"That's why you're my CEO," Julian says, with a newfound glimmer in his eye. "Because you're freaking brilliant."

"We don't have that much time before Cannes," I say, suddenly struck by just how much work—not to mention money that we don't have—it's actually going to take to launch a brand-new bridal collection.

"After what we pulled off at the Oscars last year, we can do anything," Julian says. "Yes we *Cannes*!"

I let that one go. "I'm going to call Stefano now. Keep sketching!"

I feel like I've been on *Survivor: Fashion Island* these past few weeks. I've barely slept, eaten, or showered. I've had to cancel all flights to Levinland indefinitely. I've been working my ass off to make sure this Cannes opportunity comes to fruition and—fingers and toes crossed—gets sales up for Julian Tennant Inc. and saves my ass. That is, saves our company from going under. Stefano has made it crystal clear that this is our final immunity idol.

I've had to max out yet another credit card to pull together the scratch we'll need to complete the collection and seal the deal with Nadia, the biggest supermodel of the moment. I've been begging and pleading with her agent to make her the lead model in Julian's show, which would not only add great cachet, but garner a ton of media attention. I'm close, but I'm not there yet.

But the big clincher is, I've finally set up a meeting with Om and Nano—a.k.a. Namo—music's hottest, greenest, and most ardently vegan couple. With their ubiquitous fund-raising concerts, they're even bigger than Beyoncé and Jay-Z. Julian had a dream in which Om and Nano did a cover of "Like a Virgin" at Cannes, with Om in a JT wedding dress. He'd been using *The Secret* to attract them to the idea. I went the more practical route. I'd been to kindergarten with Om's stylist, who I tracked down on Facebook, who put me in touch with her record label, who put me in touch with her manager, who put me in touch with her agent, who put me in touch with her lawyer, who finally put me in touch with her publicist, who told me that Om, a die-hard fellow PETA-ite, was, in fact, already a fan of Julian. They've agreed to perform for a wildly reduced fee, so long as JT Inc. covers the carbon offsets for the plane ride and we print our programs on recycled hemp.

Which brings me to where I am right at this minute: in the office of chief Bitchitor Coz herself, choking on my last shreds of dignity and pride to try and save JT Inc. Because the last piece in the puzzle is *Vain*, the coverage we truly need more than anything to make it all come together for Julian. I've practically had to prostrate myself before Ash, who was still feeling guilty about messing up the time for Coz's visit to see Julian's collection, to get this sliver of a five-minute appointment.

As I sit across from Coz, back resolutely turned away from the spectacular view down Broadway in her prime office in the Condé Nast building, I'm realizing this challenge is far more gruesome than any on the real *Survivor*. She's tougher than any tribal council, and trying to convince her to do a piece on the debut in *Vain* exceeds any challenge I've been dealt.

Did I just imagine that, or did Coz just guffaw in my face? No, that was an actual guffaw. I imagine her eyes rolling back in her head beneath those sunglasses that are practically covering her entire face. Does she ever *not* wear sunglasses?

"Do you know how valuable exposure in our magazine is? Come up with a reason why *Vain* would want to do this and get back to me," she says, sauntering by the rack of sublime bridal gowns Julian practically killed himself finishing for this meeting. "I have another meeting. I'm sure you can find your way out," she says, pushing back from her desk, a minimalist disk of highly polished ebony. As she marches to the door, the metallic silver-and-black stripes of her tank dress accentuates her Amazonian stature. Looking at the tear sheets spread on the desk, the framed *Vain* covers gracing the walls, the racks upon racks of couture, it comes to me. I will *not* let Coz desert me in this office and blow us off yet again. Julian's too talented for this. I'm too good for this.

"Wait," I yell after her. "I'll get you a cover with Om. Nano and Om together, if you want them."

Coz freezes midstride. With her toothpick-thin back staring at me, I swear I see the outline of her ribs shudder at the thought that she'd get Namo on a *Vain* cover. She'd be the first, as Nano and Om have refused everyone from *Vogue* to *Vanity Fair* since they don't approve of the carbon footprint magazines leave. I don't know what makes me think they won't refuse me, but at the moment it seems like my only lifeline. We seemed to have switched game shows and I'm now a contestant on *Who Wants to Be a Millionaire*. When Coz turns back around, she has a sly smile on her lips.

"Lola, if you could make that happen, I would be forever indebted to you," she says with a syrupy sweetness. "You would have the Julian Tennant spread. Now I really must run to this meeting."

Once she's gone, I carefully unhook Julian's gowns from the rack and head out, wondering how the heck I'm going to get Nano and Om to do the cover. And what I was thinking, even suggesting that I could?

"Hey hon," Lev's face fills my MacBook screen. These video chats are the only dose of Lev I've gotten in the last month. "You're not going to believe this. They gave me a scene on *Para-Medic!*"

"What?! They gave you a scene?" I attempt to laugh it off as a fluke, though the hairs on my arms stand up on end.

"It's just one scene," Lev says. "It was really fun, but actually, I'm pretty bad. They already sent me the clip by e-mail. I'll forward it to you now so you can have a good laugh."

"Oh yeah, sure, I'd love to see it," I say, not really meaning it at all. "How's Chris?" I ask.

"Well, I actually think he may be turning a corner. He's been spending a lot of time with this girl, Gigi. The one who starred in his movie. She seems really sweet and he actually seems kinda sorta happy."

"Gigi? Oh, well, good," I say, feeling a ping of loyalty toward Kate and then remembering that she's the one who dumped my brother.

"Sweetheart," Lev says as I hear his beeper going off. "I'm being paged."

"You go, honey," I say.

"To be continued later?" he asks.

"Absolutely."

"I love you," he says.

"Love you too."

I quit iChat and check my inbox for Lev's e-mail. There it is. It's just *one* scene. I force myself to press PLAY.

The camera shows a close-up of an OR nurse patting away the sweat from the forehead of a surgeon bent over a surgical field. "Thanks, Carol," he says absent-mindedly. "Okay . . . almost got it . . . and . . . we're out." He flips something into a kidney-shaped plastic tub with a *ping*, steps back from the prone patient, and nods to an associate. "Doctor Sotomayor, will you close, please? I'm outta here." The surgeon strips off his surgical gloves and flings them into the trash, pulling off his sterile mask as he strides toward the exit doors to reveal . . . my own Lev.

Two feds wired with ear buds spring to their feet at his approach. "Doctor MacArthur—how did it go?"

"Very well. I don't get too many chances to work on six-chambered hearts. Where's this guy from, anyway?" Lev/Dr. MacArthur asks.

"Sorry, doc." The first fed shakes his head curtly. "Need-to-know basis only. So, what's the prognosis?"

Lev/Dr. MacArthur grins. "Oh, excellent, I'd say. Considering he was dead for more than three days." He reaches into his pocket and holds out a tiny cylinder that pulses with a gentle green glow. "I removed this from his aorta."

"Let me take a look at that, doc," the second fed demands.

As the second fed reaches for the device, Lev/MacArthur deftly palms it back into his pocket. "Not so fast," he says. "I thought you'd want to know that I've removed one of these before . . . from a certain presidential candidate."

"Who?" the first fed demands.

Lev/MacArthur smiles raffishly. "Sorry. Need-to-know basis only, gentlemen," he chuckles.

Now, Lev is a nice-looking guy. A Paul Rudd type. But he's the sort of guy whose personality makes him exceptional. Kate once said to me when

I was in a depressive Actorholic collapse that the dashing good looks of actors were overrated. "A guy should be: Sexy. Funny," she told me. "That's it. You don't want him to be *too* good-looking. Trust me." And I didn't fully understand until I met Lev. But all of a sudden, looking at the small computer screen, it's as though my brain is malfunctioning to the point of: cannot compute. Lev is sexy. As in Clooney/Duchovny sexy. And then a one-word message is flashing across the screen of my brain: Telegenic. He has that "it" factor they call *telegenic*. And another horrible, horrible truth dawns on me: He's a natural.

7

Welcome to Gasp, Lola," the hostess says. "I'd be happy to escort you to your table as soon as you . . ." She looks down meaningfully at my feet.

"Oh, oops, sorry!" I say, slipping off my black patent leather Mary Jane Jimmy Choos and placing them in the woven willow box the hostess holds out. She shudders slightly as she hands them off to be shuttled outside. No animal products are allowed inside the hot-hot artisanal breatharian restaurant in West Hollywood, the latest brand extension of Namo.

"You can retrieve them later," the hostess tells me a bit frostily, "*if* you still want them. For now, please follow me." I scurry to keep up with her as she threads herself expertly among the tables where couples seem to be tinkering with some kind of laboratory equipment.

"Since this is obviously your first time at Gasp, let me tell you a bit more about our philosophy," the hostess tells me as she seats me at my table. "Gasp is a platinum LEEDS-certified restaurant dedicated to promoting Nano and Om's life mission of leaving minimal impact on the earth. We've teamed with some of Hollywood's most caring celebrities to help us with our outreach. Our seat cushions are made from one hundred percent reclaimed Chip and Pepper and Seven jeans from Alicia Silverstone and Darryl Hannah. Our tableware has been reforged from the models David Lynch used in *Inland Empire*. The tables are hammered steel from Sean Penn's old motorcycles. And our menus are printed using beet juice ink from Suzanne Somer's personal compost pile." She hands me one to peruse. "I'll let you know as soon as Nano and Om arrive. Enjoy your lunch!"

While squinting at the menu—the dim lighting suggests the solar panels outside need adjustment—I nod my head along to the infectious whoosh and drone of "Buzz Buzz Ting" as it pipes in over the loudspeakers. Nano and Om's latest hit—a mash-up of a tinkling Nepalese prayer wheel and buzzing bees "personally rescued from Colony Collapse Disorder by the musicians themselves" according to the press materials—has displaced Lady Gaga and Katy Perry as the favorite of dance clubs everywhere.

"Lola? It's so lovely to finally meet you!" A pale hand is placed across my own. I look up to find a young woman who can only be Om beaming at me. She's sporting the requisite shaved eyebrows, bone-china-white cheeks, and painted geisha mouth that is her signature look, along with a simple organic cotton black sheath wrapped around her phthistic limbs. Battered vegan flip-flops skim her delicately arched feet. She's so skinny I swear I can see the blood pulsing through her veins. By her side is an equally slender six-foot-tall beanpole whose long, pale limbs are barely contained by the unconstructed black organic cotton jacket and coolie pants he wears. Nano reaches out a hand to me.

"Lola! It's so totally cool that you came all the way out from New York to meet with us!" he says. "And thanks for being down with paying for the carbon offsets for the flight. We love the idea of performing at Julian's show! Hold on a sec, I have totally got to Tweet this." Nano brandishes a pointy stick. "It's a bamboo stylus for my BlackBerry. Totally sustainable. Next year Om and I are teaming up with Apple for a whole line of PDAs made from completely recycled parts. Leo says we can start with his old Priuses." He starts tapping on the PDA.

"We've got more than a million people following us on Twitter," breathes Om.

"Check it!" says Nano, brandishing his PDA.

MEETING CEO FOR BRILLIANT DESIGNER JULIAN TENNANT! SO EXCITED!

"Wow! Well, we're so excited that you're excited," I say.

"As soon as I found out that Julian's vegan, I knew he'd be the right one to design the clothes for our next tour," Om tells me. "His clothes are so ethereal, it's like you could almost disappear in them!" Looking at Om—what is she, a size 00 tops?—I can see this is a major goal for her.

DESIGNER JULIAN TENNANT OUR NEW VEGAN HERO!

"You know, Cannes works out perfectly for us," says Nano. "Since we're going into the movie business ourselves next year." He squeezes Om's arm. "We're going to be making a series of documentaries with Sir Paul and Stella to promote more sustainable practices in the music and fashion industries. You know, Lola," Nano says urgently, tapping the motorcycle table for emphasis, "we each have to bear personal responsibility for the size of our footprints on the planet. We've got to make them smaller . . . if we have to make them at all."

I think longingly of my Jimmy Choos. Really, those little stilettos hardly make a dent. "I think it's wonderful, what you're doing," I say, but Om and Nano are already looking down at their PDAs.

LOOK FOR US AT CANNES! PERFORMING FOR JULIAN TENNANT!

SHOULD STELLA AND JULIAN DESIGN TOGETHER? TELL US WHAT YOU THINK!

A waitress materializes next to us. "Are you ready to place your orders, or do you need a few more minutes to decide?" she asks.

Decide? On what? From what I can tell, there's absolutely nothing *on* this menu.

"I think we'll have the tasting menu," Om tells the waitress. "Lola, will you join us?"

Tasting? Tasting *what?* "Um, of course, I'm just not sure I . . . I mean, what exactly is—?"

"Oh, you've never done breatharian?" Om trills. "You're going to *love* it. It's the ultimate in sustainable noneating. The tasting menu is awesome. You breathe into these test tubes, and the condensate from your own lungs is passed through liquid nitrogen, then—" She stops short and furrows her nonexistent brow. "Oh, Nano, you know what I just thought of? Is nitrogen, like, *alive?*"

Nano pats her forearm consolingly. "No way! It's totally a nonliving gas thingey." Om exhales, then bends over her own PDA.

USE MORE NITROGEN! NOT ALIVE, NO CARBON FOOTPRINT!

"So, okay," Nano continues. "So then they use the liquid nitrogen to freeze your breath, and then they mist it over all these, like, ancient herbs: chia, quinoa, and epazote. Then you do, like, these breath mist shots. You'll love it. It's a total rush."

"And it does amazing things for your skin," says Om, stroking a cheek with the ghostly pallor of Morticia Gomez. "I tell all about it on my blog, Squoosh. Um, hold on a sec." Om taps on her PDA again.

GASP! OWN BREATH NATURE'S BEST CLEANSER

"It's better than locavore," pronounces Nano. "It's lungavore."

"It sounds . . . amazing!" I say, hoping my trill will float up to the mist-filled heavens and mix with their trills. "I can't wait to try it!" The waitress rushes off for our test tubes while Nano taps into his PDA.

ORGANIC CORIANDER BREATH SHOT ON THE WAY—SO TOTALLY AWESOME!

Om grabs my hand and starts stroking my forearm. "We really see Julian as the linchpin to our brand extension. Our music put us on the map, but there's so much else Nano and I need to do. After Cannes and the tour, I see Julian redoing the uniforms for our restaurants—we're definitely looking to franchise—and designing the wardrobe for our documentaries and videos. Plus we're going to want him to help us design a line of cruelty-free organic cotton clothes. Time is running out to save the planet. Julian is going to be such an important part of our team!"

This seems like as good a time as any to just go for it. "I know that you don't do magazines because of the carbon footprint they leave, which I totally respect," I say. "But I know that *Vain* would love to put you on the cover—and just think of the people you could reach with your message of a more sustainable future," I say, hoping not to sound too desperate. "The piece could be on Julian's vegan and sustainable designs for your tour. The whole emphasis will be on how you're changing the way people think about fashion and consumption of precious resources."

"You know, it's not a bad concept," Om says turning to Nano. "I think we should consider it."

"We've never done a magazine cover before," Nano says. "But Julian would definitely be the right designer for us to do one with. The message is right, the partnership with Julian seems right." I'm more hopeful than I've felt in a long time. I'm going to get Coz that damn cover because I have to get that feature piece in *Vain* for Julian. My life depends on it.

An hour and seventeen Tweets later, I've reclaimed my Jimmy Choos

(I caught Om peering at me intently as I slipped them back on my feet) and am heading back to Lev's house. I can't tell whether I'm lightheaded because of the incredible coup with Nano and Om, or because I'm completely starving, even after five shots of my own frozen breath, or because I got stuck with a $525 bill for—air? Whatever, Julian is going to *freak*.

I dial Julian's cell and he picks it up, screaming.

"Are you following Nano and Om's Tweets? I'm all over them! They *love* me! Lola, you're a miracle worker! Listen to this: JULIAN TENNANT MAJOR NEW STAR. THANK YOU, LOLA, GENIUS CEO!

"Oh, Julian, isn't it terrific? One more thing nailed down for Cannes. And more business to get LVMH off our backs. This thing with Nano and Om could be *huge*. How's it going on your end?"

"I'm exhausted. I think I bought out every bugle bead M&J Trimming has ever made. But the collection is really coming together. And I sent Chili to the post office to mail those invitations you addressed. I swear, Lola, it's a full-time job babysitting that boy. Isn't there anything else you can do to keep him busy?" I picture Julian raking his fingers through his feathered black locks.

"Julian, you know I'm trying and he is working for us for *free* and we could really use the extra set of hands. I asked him to make five hundred veils by hand as party favors for each guest. This time he wants to incorporate some doohickey that will download the entire bridal collection via Bluetooth to an iPhone or BlackBerry."

"But Lola, we only have space for two hundred fifty people," says Julian.

"Chili doesn't know that," I say. "Listen, I've got to run. I want to call Stefano and tell him the good news about Om and Nano."

"Honey, you've been incredible," breathes Julian. "Ooh—wait! Just got another Tweet from your new BFFs. Listen to this: CAN'T WAIT TO BE NEW VIRGINS FOR JULIAN TENNANT! Isn't that amazing? Add that to your to-do list: Sign up for Nano and Om's Tweets."

"Will do. Bye, Julian, I'll check in with you tomorrow." I hang up and before I can dial Stefano my cell trills.

"What about the Kobe beef? Nadia is waiting for the JPEGs."

I grit my teeth to keep an exasperated sigh from expelling. "Ivan, you can't be serious."

"Honey, I'm very serious," says the booker from IMG Models. "If you want Nadia to walk your show, she needs her beef. And after that dreadful episode with Fendi—can you *believe* they tried to convince her that Tuscan tenderloin was *any* kind of substitute?—Nadia insists on seeing photos of the actual Wagyu cattle so she can make her selection."

The sad thing is that Nadia's latest demand isn't even her craziest one. I've already had to agree to have her hotel room stocked with Flintstones chewable vitamins—Wilma only—a dozen acai berry suppositories, a case of chilled Cristal, ten pounds of carrots, a ginseng root "pulled from the ground by a real native," whatever that means, and an entire watermelon. Each. Fricking. Day. I take a deep breath and remind myself that Nadia is the biggest supermodel du jour. This is the woman who single-handedly caused a run on PF Flyers and Carhartt shortalls after she wore them to the Met Costume Gala. We desperately need her, now more than ever. I will a smile into my voice.

"I spoke to the maitre d' at La Tantra, and it will be his pleasure to make sure Nadia gets her Kobe beef daily," I tell Ivan, "so I don't think it will be necessary to ship it in from Japan. And I spoke with the Hotel Martinez and they assured me that all the produce in Nadia's room will be organic and locavore, so we won't need to ship it all in from Marin. I know Nadia is deeply concerned about her carbon footprint." I cross my fingers and pray the earth doesn't swallow me whole with this last whopper. The only footprint Nadia is deeply concerned with is the one left by the Viviers, Choos, and YSLs she receives gratis by the boatload. I can't believe I'm actually having this conversation right now. This is not what I signed up for when I became the CEO of JT Inc. "So, do we have a deal, Ivan?"

I bite my lip while Ivan summons the cicada trill of clacking computer keys. "Oh-kay," he finally announces. "We're good. But seriously, Lola, Wilma Flintstones only, okay? Nadia can't take the blue dye in the Dinos."

"I'll sort them personally," I assure him, stifling my gag reflex.

It's nearly 9:00 P.M. when Lev finally comes home. I've been so swamped that I didn't even hear his Prius pull up.

"Honey," he yells as he walks through the front door.

"Lev!" I say, throwing myself into his arms. "I'm so happy you're here. I've really missed you."

"Me too," he says. "Are you hungry? I'm completely starving. Pulled another double shift today. So I picked up a bunch of spicy tuna hand rolls from Katsuya for us."

"Thanks. I'm starving, too," I say, biting into a roll straight out of the plastic take-out container before we even make it to Lev's beat-up wood kitchen table. "Mmmm, these rolls are amazing."

"How'd it go with Giga and Dharma?"

"Nano and Om. And it went great. They not only agreed to perform for practically nothing at Julian's show, they basically want him to do all the designs for their tour, their restaurants, their entire empire! And they're considering doing a *Vain* cover in Julian, which means that we'd get that feature spread that we need so desperately."

"Oh, Lola, that's fantastic news," says Lev. "Speaking of which, I have some fantastic news of my own."

"Hang on, we don't even have drinks. Is this something that could require a toast? Did you hear back from Lenox Hill Hospital?" I ask, suddenly flush with excitement.

"No, I haven't heard back yet, but hopefully soon. I know how much you hate the commute," Lev says.

"So . . . the suspense is killing me, what's the news?" I say, reaching into the cupboard for two wine glasses.

"They want to give my character on *Para-Medic* an arc," he says. "They've offered me a part."

"They *what*?! Well, you're not going to take it, right? You said no. Tell me you said no," I say, the words pouring out of my mouth before I can stop them, my heart racing. This was not part of the plan. The plan was to move to New York and to get out of Hollywood and all the superficial crap surrounding it. Not to dive in headfirst. It's as though I'm seeing my world shift before my eyes. I steady myself against the cupboard.

"Well, actually, no, I think I *am* going to take it," he says. "I mean, why wouldn't I?"

"Because you're a *doctor,* not an actor." I wait for him to say it himself as I stare into his green eyes in shock, wondering if this is really happening. Please. Tell me. This is not happening.

"Of course, I'm not an actor. I know that. But this thing on *Para-Medic* isn't full time and the truth is it was kind of fun. Plus, they're offering me a sizeable amount of money that I could really use to pay off my student loans and maybe we can even *buy* an apartment in Manhattan instead of renting. I just don't see how I can say no. The funny thing is, *playing* at saving lives pays more than *actually* saving lives."

"Yeah, that's really funny," I say, thinking: there is *nothing* funny about this.

"I'm doing this for us, Lola. Can't you just be excited for me?"

Nauseous, anxious, dizzy, terrified, unable to breathe, is more like it. I just can't believe this is really happening. "I'd rather rent for the rest of our lives. Lev, I've spent my entire life trying to get away from actors and

Hollywood and I finally did that when I found you and I love you and I want to preserve you and us exactly as we are."

Lev pushes his chair back from the table and shakes his head. "You know what, Lola? I'm actually really bummed by your reaction. This is a once-in-a-lifetime opportunity and it's only for one season. I've already explained to Shonda that it can't get in the way of my practice. I am so sick and tired of working nonstop and still having all these loans to pay off. You obviously have no idea what that feels like. I was actually thinking that you'd be happy for me." Lev sets his plate down and stares at the kitchen table.

I take a deep breath and do a reframe. I mean, he's right, we could use that money to get a great place in New York. He's thinking about *us*. It's not a bad thing to have some financial security going into our marriage. Okay, my heart rate seems to be settling.

"Sorry for overreacting," I say, realizing that I'm dumping all of my old heartbreak onto him—all of those terrible, narcissistic Actor Boyfriends. Lev is none of those things. "I was really out of line. You have every right to be excited about this. I mean, it's exciting. Again, honey, I'm so sorry."

"It's fine," Lev says flatly, pushing away from the table. "Listen, I'm really tired. I'm going to head off to bed."

"Aren't you going to have any more sushi?"

"No, I'm all done," he says. "Just lost my appetite." He leaves the kitchen before I can say another word.

We barely speak the next morning as Lev drives me to the airport so I can catch my flight back to New York. The second Lev's car pulls away from the curb I contemplate calling Dr. Gilmore. I seriously regret giving her up. But Lev and I couldn't *both* continue to see her, right? I know that she wouldn't approve of this stupid Eau du Freak-Out that I'm still wearing. It smells so, so bad. Oh dumb, dumb, desperate, panicked me. As I make my way through security feeling terribly alone, with the realization that I've lost my therapist for good, my worst fear of all is that I'll lose my doctor too.

"It's four in the morning in NYC, what are you doing up?" I'm so grateful to hear Kate's voice that I don't even care that she's yelling at me over the phone line.

"I haven't been able to sleep ever since Lev said he was going to take that job on *Para-Medic*. Did you ever watch that clip I sent you? The worst part is, he's actually *good*. What am I going to do, Kate? I'm freaking out," I say, kicking the covers on Julian's couch off me.

"Do you know who's going to negotiate his deal?"

"Kate, I'm talking about my fiancé becoming an *actor,* the worst possible thing that could ever happen to me, and you're asking who's going to negotiate his *deal*?"

"I'd be willing to do it for five percent instead of my usual ten," Kate says. "Look, Lola, as long as he's doing it, he should get the best deal possible."

"*Kate!*" I scream.

"Oh okay, fine, I'll do it for free, but only because it's you."

"Kate, I don't want you to do it *at all*. I don't want Lev to *act*. Period."

"Lola, Lev isn't SMITH. And he's not Jake Jones. He's not like any of those other narcissistic asshole actors you dated before. Look, Lo, I know how badly you've been hurt. SMITH was the worst—he shattered you. And I'm no Doctor Gilmore, but I think a good therapist would tell you that this isn't just about the ridiculous actors you've been with in the past, it's about your parents, too. But don't spray your abandonment issues all over Lev. He doesn't deserve that. He deserves better and so do you. You deserve Lev. He's a good guy and he loves you. It's going to be okay."

Maybe she's right. Lev isn't the Sexiest Man in the Hemisphere. Or a flaky action hero-cum-asshole. Maybe Lev's right. Maybe I'm just being a total idiot here. Kate's always had a way of cutting right through my BS and holding up a mirror for me. Sometimes I wonder if we're best friends because we're like the mothers we never had.

"Thanks, Kate. You're a good analyst. When do you get to work on yourself?" I joke—kind of.

"Same diagnosis. I blame my parents. Pretty much works for everyone, wouldn't you say?" Kate says before getting back to business as quickly as possible. "Does that mean I can do his deal?"

"Call Lev and ask him. I'm staying out of it," I say.

"Okay," Kate says. "Meanwhile, I have some news that should lift your spirits. I was waiting until you were up to call but you beat me to the punch. Saffron and Markus are doing an appearance on Oprah's special to promote the movie. And guess who's going be appearing with them— our own Cricket Curtis!"

"That's amazing!" I say breathlessly.

"You have no idea how *insane* that negotiation was. Oprah's specials are the new Holy Grail. I've spent the last seventy-two hours getting Oprah's people to agree to get Cricket and Markus on since Oprah really just wanted to spend the whole hour with Saffron, but I dug in. And Saffron really pushed for Cricket, too."

"I have to call Cricket immediately and get her to wear Julian," I say.

"You don't think we've already thought of that? What do you take us for?"

"Oh of course, sorry. Kate! This is so fantastic! I have to get Cricket a slew of outfit options. Where is she? Where do I send them?"

"I'm e-mailing you the shipping address in Chicago right now," Kate says.

"Great, I'll get on that immediately. This is going to be huge for us!

I mean, Lady O. Come on, it doesn't get any better than that. There's no amount of money LVMH could even spend to rival the kind of exposure—and god willing, sales—we're going to get from Cricket wearing Julian on *Oprah*," I say, starting to feel a shift on the horizon. Things are looking up. First Om and Nano. And now *this*. Even more good news to pass along to Stefano and less likelihood that they'll pull our financing. This may even get them off my back about the Cannes budget, which they've been making me slash like I'm freaking Timothy Geithner. "Kate?"

"Oh sorry, what'd you say? I'm just reading *The Hollywood Reporter* online."

"Kate, this is just so fantastic," I say again.

"*Forgetting Petunia Holt,*" Kate says emphatically and then repeats the refrain with more emphasis, "*Forgetting Petunia Holt!*"

"What?!" I ask. "What are you talking about?"

"*Forgetting Petunia Fucking Holt!* Jesus, Lola, why didn't tell me?"

"What are you talking about, Kate?" I say.

"Don't play dumb with me, Lola," she says, her voice arctic. "It's right here in black and white. 'Christopher Santisi is in negotiations with Fox Searchlight to acquire his directorial debut, *Forgetting Petunia Holt,* a dramedy that's *Easy Rider* meets *Into the Wild* meets *The Hangover*. After being dumped by the love of his life, Justin Cooper goes on a road trip to the desert to forget Petunia Holt.' Should I keep reading?"

"No, stop. Please stop. Kate, I had no idea," I say. What has my brother done?

"You had *no* idea?" Kate says.

"No!"

"None?!"

"Well . . . uh . . . umm . . . Christopher did tell me he was making a movie inspired by you. He was calling it *Into the Woods*. He started it when you two were together and he swore me to secrecy because he wanted to surprise you. He must have changed the name of the film after you broke up with him."

"So you're saying this is my *fault*?"

"No, of course not. Look, Kate, I'm sure the movie isn't as bad as the title seems. I mean, *Easy Rider* meets *Into the Wild* meets *The Hangover*— what does that even mean? Maybe it doesn't really have all that much to *do* with you. And nobody knows that Christopher used to call you Petunia." Nobody except Kate, myself, Lev, and Christopher. And Holt is Kate's mother's maiden name.

"So you haven't seen the movie?" she asks.

"No. Not a single frame," I say.

"I just can't believe he'd do this to me. How could he do this?" she says in a soft voice. It's the most vulnerable I've heard her since she and Christopher broke up.

I suddenly realize that this is a nightmare for Kate, who can barely even deal with her private life privately. And now it's going to be up there on the big screen for all the world to see? But this is fantastic for Christopher. I hate this feeling that something that's so good for my brother can be so bad for my best friend. What am I supposed to say? How am I supposed to console Kate? "Maybe you should call Christopher," I say, "talk it through."

"No, I can't do that," she says. God forbid Kate should talk about her *feelings*. Especially to Christopher.

"Are you sure?"

"Yes, Lola, I'm sure. And what's he going to say anyway?"

"I'm having breakfast with him tomorrow. He's in town shooting a music video for *The Killers*. I'll try and get more info on the movie," I say and regret it immediately. I'd rather wear an acrylic bodysuit than be in the middle of this thing between my brother and my best friend.

"Thanks, Lola," Kate says. "I wonder how much Fox Searchlight is offering him for the movie and who's doing the deal," she says and just like that, Kate is back to being Kate.

"I'll call you after breakfast," I say.

"With details. And preferably numbers."

"Goodnight, Kate."

"Goodnight, Lo."

Click.

"Forgetting Petunia Holt?!" I say to Christopher over French toast with caramelized apples at the Mercer Kitchen. "Please tell me it's not as bad as it sounds."

"I didn't make the movie to hurt Kate, La-La," Christopher says. He runs his hands through his thick mop of messy light brown hair. I can still see some lingering fragments of pain in his pale blue eyes. Pain that my best friend caused him and I'm still not certain I've forgiven her for that. "I was originally making it as a fucking love letter to her, you know that, but then she ended it." He pushes the scrambled eggs around on his plate and takes a sip of fresh-squeezed OJ. "It just kind of evolved into what it is now and it's actually been very cathartic. I don't think I would have survived this breakup without this movie, and no one's going to know that it's Kate. It's much more about me than it is about her."

"I just wish you would have told me so I could have warned her it was coming," I say. "You know, you really should have called her yourself."

"I know. I know. But it's so hard to talk to her, you know how she can be," he says, fidgeting with the zipper on his gray hoodie.

"So when do I get to see the movie?" I ask.

"Well . . . I just found out an hour ago that I got into competition at Cannes!" he exclaims. "So I guess you can see it then."

"What?! Christopher, we need to celebrate *immediately*. I can't believe you let me go on and on and didn't say anything. This is the most amazing news! I'm so happy for you." I reach over the Wenge wood table to give him a kiss on the cheek. My phone vibrates on the table. "Chris, it's Mom calling; let's tell her about Cannes," I say as I click on the speakerphone. "Hi Mom, I'm with Christopher and you're on speakerphone."

"Hi darlings," Mom says. "I have some really exciting news. I'm so happy you're both together."

"Christopher just told me the most amazing news as well. Chris, tell Mom," I say.

Chris leans over the cell phone. "I just found out that my film is going to be in the dramatic competition at Cannes."

"Your film," my mother exclaims in shock. "What film?"

"The film Chris has been secretly working on for the last—how long's it been, Chris?" I ask.

"A long time," he says quietly.

"Oh darling, that's incredible, I'm so proud of you," Mom says. "Both my men, together at Cannes!"

"Mom, what are you talking about?" No. No no no. I have a sinking feeling.

"That's my exciting news, darling. We've just learned that your father's movie got into the dramatic competition too! Can you *believe* it! Two Santisis at the same competition! Think of the publicity! I'm going to have to throw the most spectacular party at Cannes! I better call Alex right away and make sure we can add more camera crew. There'll be some amazing footage for *Wristwatch Wives*. Darlings, isn't this the most happy day?"

I look over at Chris. His face is ashen, his mouth set in a tight line. "Yeah, Mom," I say. "We're all just so . . . happy."

8

'd like to welcome the lively, the lovely *Saffron Sykes*," Oprah bellows in her trademark O style, enunciating every letter of Saffron's name to a cheering crowd as she takes to her killer stingray stiletto'd feet and claps. From behind a closed stage door Saffron appears in all of her Amazonian glory, striding across the stage in a sun-bleached silk floral dress that exposes those golden gazelle legs.

Saffron beams at the audience, waving and smiling. With her glossy raven hair pushed back in a loose knot she embodies that elusive, carefree "done but undone," effortless vibe that's become her signature; that she's just like you—*if* you were an Oscar-winning screen goddess blessed with phenomenal genes. Oprah and Saffron embrace like they've been best friends since preschool. As Oprah tries to quiet the applauding studio audience, I try and get Julian from the other room where he's been manically working on Om's gown. I'm totally terrified he's going to get carpal tunnel again from the nonstop sewing.

"Julian, get your ass in here! Oprah's on!" I yell.

"One sec. I just have to finish this pleat," he shouts back.

"Hi Oprah," Saffron says settling into the cream sofa and crossing her mile-long legs. "I'm so excited to be here."

"You look fantastic. Love the dress," Oprah says. *Please love Cricket's outfit just as much*—I beam her telepathically. Lady O and I are deeply connected. She just doesn't know it.

"Thank you so much. It's Alexander Wang. I don't think I'm ever going to take it off. I just love it." Saffron coos like a giddy schoolgirl. Lucky, lucky Alexander Wang. I'm sure that dress is going to sell out everywhere.

Oprah leans forward conspiratorially. "So Saffron, I saw *Four Weddings and a Bris* last night and loved it. You've got some pipes on you. I had no idea."

"Thank you, Oprah. It was such a huge honor to work with Baz. I've been a fan for such a long time and we've been trying to work together forever, but nothing seemed right until now," Saffron says.

"You're premiering the film at the Cannes Film Festival. There's no place more glamorous than Cannes, is there?" Oprah says as Julian walks into the room.

"I didn't miss Cricket yet, did I?" Julian asks.

"No, not yet," I say.

"Saffron looks stunning," Julian says. "Is that Alexander Wang?"

"Lucky bastard," I say as my cell trills.

"You watching?" Kate says on the other end.

"Of course I am. Where are you?"

"I'm here with Cricket in the Green Room backstage at Oprah. She's getting her makeup touched up before she goes out."

"Hi Lo," I hear her call out excitedly from a distance.

"Hi Cricket," I squeal like a five-year-old despite myself.

"She looks stunning. Really Lo, this dress is incredible. One of my favorites of Julian's," Kate says of the black-and-gray Aztec-printed micropleat minidress Cricket decided on.

"I overnighted practically everything we have in the loft and thank god she's sample size and that something actually worked," I say, feeling a wave of excitement. "This is such a huge opportunity for us, Kate. Thank you for looking out, as usual."

"How's everything else coming?" she asks. "Any movement?"

"I haven't told Julian," I whisper while he heads toward the kitchen during a commercial break. "I dangled a carrot to Coz that I could get Om and Nano for a *Vain* cover if she'd give us the spread we need."

"But they won't do magazine covers, Lo," Kate says nervously.

"That's why this is such a big deal. When I met with them they were on board with the idea. They feel like kindred spirits with Julian as fellow vegans. Having them will seal it for us with Coz. It would be their first magazine cover ever. And it would be *Vain*'s."

"That would be huge. I'm sure Coz nearly peed her pants. It sounds like you're doing everything possible—it'll all come together," Kate says. There's a silence before she asks, "So how was seeing Chris?" I'm not sure how she wants me to answer. That it was great? That I'm ecstatic for my brother? That he's finally having a shot at his dream? That his movie . . .

"Got into Cannes," spills out of me. "He's in the dramatic competition—against our father."

It's so quiet I think the phone line's gone dead before Kate speaks.

"Guess it'll be one big, happy party, huh. This is just great," she moans. "I'm really not looking forward to this."

"Kate, would you just call him!"

"No, absolutely not," she says self-righteously. "I don't have time."

"You have time to call me!"

"Well *you*—you're—a necessity."

"What does that make Chris?" I ask.

"A pain in my ass," she announces. What I want to say is, More like a pain in *your* heart. But I don't. Now's not the time. Instead, I'm flooded by a memory. Kate and I were seventeen and visiting my grandparents in Florida during spring break. We spent most of our days on the beach baking in the sun and spraying Sun-In on our hair until it turned a strange shade of orange. One morning I woke up in the twin bed next to Kate, angsting over some cute guy I'd seen on the beach the day before who had the temerity to ignore my pathetic attempts at flirting. We'd just learned about that Sartre guy in my English class at Crossroads. So I decided to throw down some knowledge that I thought Kate might appreciate. "Hell is other people," I said coolly, pulling the covers over me and propping myself up on a pillow.

"Sartre, *No Exit*," Kate said without skipping a beat as she slid into her bikini and threw on her Polo shorts. "Good one," she nodded. Though I knew she really wasn't that impressed. I was going through one of those phases where I was wearing too much dark eyeliner and throwing around literary references as often as possible. When my mother would ask, "Why are you wearing so much black?!" I'd give her a Chekhov and announce, "I'm in mourning for my life." Thing was, Kate knew me too well.

"This quote unquote dark phase you're in doesn't suit you. You're the lover. *I'm* the hater. That's Lola-and-Kate. Period. Grab the Sun-In. Let's go to the beach," she said, pulling me out of bed by the arm.

Kate was right about me: the whole "dark" phase *was* a total front. She was wrong about herself: the whole "hater" thing was her front. For one, I happened to know she was in love with Christopher. I snapped out of my phase by senior year and went right back to my usual: giving people the benefit of the doubt. Kate, well, she was a kid cynic who grew into a Harvard-educated cynic who joined the club of thriving and prospering Hollywood-agent cynics. Kate and Chris, they never really shook each other, even though it took them another decade to find their way back together after that first blush of teen romance. And then it took Kate no time at all to sabotage it. The biggest difference between Kate and me is that I keep expecting the best out of people and she keeps expecting the worst. But here's where we're the same: we'll protect the heck out of the people we care about—until the end. And I think it's about time Kate gave the human race a little credit, starting with Chris. Scratch that, starting with herself.

"You know, Kate, you don't have to be afraid of being honest with Chris about your feelings," I say. "It's okay for you to express your—"

"Gotta run." She stops me as I'm just getting started. Boom. Kate's cement-wall-to-the-face. "Talk later."

Click.

Forget it. I have too much on my plate to play Kate's shrink right now. There's just too much riding on Cannes to let this distract me.

"How's Om's gown coming?" I ask Julian as he saunters back in with two steaming teacups and hands me one.

"It's going to be amazing. She's going to out-Madonna Madonna. Have Natalie Portman's people committed to the vegan satin slide yet?" Julian asks.

I tap a note into my iPhone. "I'll check on that," I say. "They've been stalling me big time. Has Chili told you how many RSVPs we have so far?"

"Nope. And he's still at his trig exam. What *is* trig, anyway?"

I always forget that Chili's some freak prodigy who's still in the tenth grade. "I'll send him a text about the RSVPs now," I say, tapping into my cell.

When I turn back to the television screen Oprah's back from commercial saying, "So Saffron . . ."

"Yes, Oprah."

"The thing that all of America wants to know, and I'm just the middleman here because it's not me that wants to know, but the audience is dying to hear what's happening between you and your hunky costar Markus Livingston. There have even been rumors of a surprise wedding in Cannes."

"I thought I was already married to Bradley Cooper, according to the tabloids," Saffron jokes. "Oprah, the only wedding taking place at Cannes is the one onscreen in the movie, and I don't want to give anything away because Baz is going to kill me, but it's *way* more interesting than my real-life wedding would ever be."

"Do you want to get married someday?" Oprah asks.

"Before I made this movie, I might have said no, but yeah, I'd like to get married. I'm a huge romantic, and who doesn't love being in love?" Saffron asks.

"Are you in love now?" Oprah asks.

"Oprah! I can't believe you just asked me that. Well, um, I'm in love with this movie," Saffron deftly answers with a wry smile. "We had so much fun making it. And it was such a huge treat to play Markus's fiancée in the movie. He's got a wicked sense of humor and the man oozes sex appeal. Am I right, ladies?" Saffron says to the cooing studio audience. "And Cricket Curtis is phenomenal."

"Markus and Cricket are both here and coming out in a few minutes, so maybe we'll be able to pry some more info out of them," Oprah says. "Back in a minute." They cut to commercial.

"What's the real deal with Saffron and Markus? Did Cricket tell you?" Julian asks.

"Not a peep. But I haven't really gotten to talk to her properly since they got back from their trip. They flew straight to Chicago from Greece."

"I still can't believe Saffron and Markus took Cricket with them on their love cruise around the world. That Markus is so hot. I'd like to see him in a Speedo," Julian says.

I decide to check out Twitter to see if anyone's Tweeting about Oprah. I sent out an e-mail blast, Facebook, and Twitter, so I can't wait for the reactions. Suddenly, a flood of Tweets fills my screen.

SAW NANO EATING BIG MAC. MEAT IS MURDER.

MOTHER EARTH IS DYING OF THIRST AND OM TOOK HALF-HOUR SHOWER THIS MORNING.

NANO TEST-DROVE ESCALADE. NO OIL FOR BLOOD.

CAUGHT OM CARRYING JIMMY CHOO SHOPPING BAG. LEATHER LIAR.

NANO ATE GRAPES FROM PERU. BIG STOMPING CARBON FOOTPRINT.

OM THREW OUT CFLS BECAUSE SHE SAID THEY DIDN'T "FLATTER HER SKIN TONES" AND WEARS MAKEUP TESTED ON HELPLESS BUNNIES.

I scroll down the screen. What the hell is going on? Nano and Om are lobbing electronic spitballs at each other at lightning speed. "Omigod, Julian, Nano and Om are having some kind of Twitter war. I don't know what's going on. Look at this," I practically yelp, handing him my iPhone.

Julian just stares at the screen, mouth agape.

"I'm sure it will blow over," I say. "It's probably nothing. I mean everyone fights over Twitter these days, right? Aren't Anderson Cooper and Ashton Kutcher always getting into epic battles?"

"Yeah," Julian says, though it's clear he doesn't really mean it.

"*Oprah*'s back on," I say, relieved for the distraction. Saffron's now seated beside Markus.

"It was a nice change of pace to be in a movie where I didn't kill anyone or have to jump out of a plane at twenty thousand feet," Markus is saying, flashing that heartbreaking smile of his that's surrounded by photo-shoot-worthy stubble.

"I think fans of *The Suicide Squad* are going to be quite surprised that you can sing," Oprah says.

"Well, I'm no Justin Timberlake, but I tried my best," Markus says in his super-sexy gravely voice, running his hands through his legendary brown locks.

"Are you enjoying this? Having the number-one grossing action film of all time with *The Suicide Squad,* a Golden Globe nomination, and now starring opposite Saffron Sykes. Are you enjoying this? Because you look like you are," Oprah says.

"Oprah, I am loving it," he says, flashing a huge grin. "Loving it. I wake up every morning thinking, 'you lucky bastard.'"

Oprah lets out a hearty laugh and then says, "We'll be right back with Cricket Curtis." Yes! Finally.

During the commercial break I check my iPhone again. No more Om and Nano Tweets. Thank heavens whatever the hell *that* was blew over.

"Please welcome newcomer Cricket Curtis," Oprah howls and I look up at the TV screen.

I grab Julian's hand. As the camera pans across the stage to reveal Cricket from behind a stage door suddenly the screen goes black and then—

"We interrupt this program to bring you breaking news," Diane Sawyer says. What?! No, no, no, no, no. Not now. Not when Cricket is on *Oprah* and she's wearing Julian! What's happening? *What is happening?* The camera pulls back to show an angry mob scene behind Diane's shoulder. Punches are being thrown, cars rocked and—good lord, did somebody just set fire to that bench?

"A riot has broken out in Los Angeles. Police are on the scene, and we've received reports of a death. Let's go to Naomi Walker of local affiliate KABC-TV for more on the story."

The local reporter's voice is barely audible over the screaming crowd. "It's a nightmare, Diane. I'm standing in front of Cut, Wolfgang Puck's famous steak restaurant in the Beverly Wilshire hotel, where a paparazzo has just been reported stampeded to death. More than an estimated four hundred people have gathered here based on reports that megastar and diehard vegan and animal activist Nano was spotted eating red meat," she says.

A grainy video shows Nano flailing wildly at the mass of paps flanking him outside Cut while cops circle him wielding batons. "Jesus *bleep* Christ!" he screams. "Get offa me! All I wanted was a *bleep* steak! That bitch's been making me eat twigs and berries for four *bleep* years!"

"As hundreds of paparazzi clamored to get a shot of Nano eating a New York strip, one man may have lost his life," Naomi intones. "Police are attempting to disperse the crowds, which as you can see continue to grow." The reporter flinches at the sound of breaking glass behind her.

"That is horrific. Do they know what set the whole thing off?" Diane asks.

"The crowds apparently arrived on the scene after a text swarm. Om and Nano have over a million Twitter followers, fifty thousand in Los Angeles alone, and this was in response to a very public altercation that started just minutes ago."

"Death by text and Tweet. Just one more sobering example of the brave new world of new media we live in," says Diane. "And now I understand we have L.A. police commissioner William Bratton on the line to comment on today's fatal development. Commissioner Bratton?"

Julian grabs the remote and starts flicking through the channels. Nano's face fills every station. "Am I asleep? Please tell me that I'm asleep and this is just a bad nightmare because this can't be happening. *This cannot be happening,*" Julian says, his voice cracking.

I attempt to speak, but no sound comes out of my mouth. A paparazzo stampeded to death? All because Nano ate a fucking steak? Cricket's appearance on *Oprah* has been preempted because Nano ate a fucking steak? It's too much for my brain to process. Diane Sawyer is still speaking, but the only sound I can hear is a deafening buzzing in my ears.

"We are so screwed. We are so screwed," Julian repeats over and over and over in a soft whisper. "Cannes is right around the corner. We are so screwed."

"Maybe it'll blow over," I say, though I don't believe it will.

"Blow over?! Lola, Nano is one of the biggest stars in the world and a paparazzo is *dead*. This is *not* going to blow over," Julian shrieks as my cell starts buzzing.

"Oh god, it's Stefano," I say. "He's in town and I told him to be sure to watch Cricket on *Oprah*."

"Don't answer it," Julian says.

I look at the phone and then over to Julian. Phone. Julian. Phone. Julian.

"Put down the phone, Lo," Julian says.

I look at my cell in my palm and let it go to voice mail.

"I should have answered that. What are we going to do now?" I say.

"We are so screwed. We are so screwed," Julian repeats like a mantra.

Breathe, Lola, breathe. It's going to be okay. I attempt to do a reframing. Om and Nano have broken up before. They'll get back together again this time too, right? And then they'll perform at Cannes just like they're supposed to. Maybe the people on the West Coast will still get to see Cricket on *Oprah*. It's not like the media can cover Steak-gate *all* day, right?

As the minutes crawl by, we hear from three photographers, two stunned onlookers, a paramedic treating some scrawny vegans for smoke inhalation, the manager of Cut, Wolfgang Puck, a few cops. And a one word text from Kate:

FUCKED.

"We are so screwed. We are so screwed," I mutter and wish I hadn't actually said it out loud because it makes it seem all too real. I just thank god that I didn't mention to Julian that Om and Nano were considering doing that *Vain* cover. What the heck am I going to do now to convince Coz to get Julian that spread? And who am I going to get to replace Namo at Cannes? "We are so screwed," reverberates over and over in my head.

I'm midcrawl into the fetal position when my cell trills. It's Ivan from IMG Models. At least we still have Nadia. I walk into the back bedroom to take the call.

"What is it, Ivan?" I ask as sweetly as I can muster. "Is there something else Nadia needs?" Kangaroo cutlets? Papaya wrapped in twenty-four-karat gold leaf? First-press extra-virgin heroin poppy seed oil?

"I was actually calling you because Nadia has the chicken pox and isn't going to be able to do the show," Ivan says. No! She *has* to do the show. "She was shooting the new Burberry campaign with Mario Testino and a bunch of toddlers and one of the little nightmares gave her the chicken pox. Can you believe it? I have to clear her schedule for the next two weeks at least. You can't *believe* how much money I'm losing on commission alone."

"I . . . I . . . I," I fumble. Deep breath. Pull it together, Lola. "Ivan, we were really counting on Nadia. Are you sure there's no way she'll be better by then?"

"I just saw her and there's definitely no way. She looks worse than Jessica Simpson before the Proactiv. I'm sorry, darling," he says. *Click.*

I hate my life. What are we supposed to do now? I put my head in my hands. I feel like I'm thinking through cotton wool. But I will not give up here. We're just too close.

And then it comes to me. I walk back into the living room where Julian is still rocking back and forth in front of the TV. "Who was that on the phone?" he asks.

"Ivan," I say. "Bad news. Nadia can't walk your show. Chicken pox. I mean, you've almost got to laugh, right?"

Julian gives a strangled cry. "Oh my god, what else? Lola, what are we going to do? We are so screwed. So screwed."

I walk over to him and grip his shoulders. "Stop it, Julian. We're not screwed. Not yet. I have an idea. What about Aria Fraser?"

"What about her?" asks Julian. "She's retired. Presumably sleeping on those huge piles of cash." Aria was one of the nineties' most visible icons, one of the original supermodels, who out-Linda-ed Linda by proclaiming, "I don't wake up for less than twenty-five thousand dollars a day." Who out-Naomi-ed Naomi with her tantrums, including bashing Grace Coddington's assistant with a crocodile Birkin.

"Didn't she model in your graduation show when you were at Central Saint Martins?" I ask. That was that glorious minute when Julian was being touted as the Next Christian Dior—enough pandemonium to prompt not only Aria, but Naomi, Cindy, Christy, *and* Linda to forsake retirement for a single afternoon flogging his frocks.

"Yes, but you know she hasn't walked since then. And it was a total fluke getting her in the first place."

"Well, then, what could be more perfect than having her model in another Julian Tennant show?" I say.

"Do you know how many requests she gets a day for her to walk? She says no to *everyone*. Giorgio even offered her a hundred fifty grand and she turned him down," Julian says. "She doesn't need the money."

"But you know what she does need? Publicity."

"For what?"

"I read somewhere that Aria wants to launch a line of biodegradable stilettos. We could offer to preview it on your runway. It's a win-win for both of us."

"Biodegradable shoes?" Julian breathes.

I flip open my laptop and tap furiously. "Look. Here are some of her designs. They're actually kind of pretty. She's making them out of cardboard made from sustainably grown softwood pines certified by the Forest Stewardship Council. Here's a quote from her: 'I want to make beautiful shoes so that women don't have to feel guilty about buying next season's shoes now that last season's are biodegradable.'"

"Lola, that's just nutty," Julian says.

"Okay, fine, maybe, but that's what everyone said about Natalie Portman's vegan line and now everyone loves them! And besides, Natalie's people aren't getting back to us and here's a chance to horse trade for something that Aria actually needs."

Julian shakes his head. "I don't know, Lo."

"Here's the kicker: Grace Frost *loves* Aria. They go way back. We get Aria back on the runway and we'll get *Vain*'s attention. We're definitely not going to get there with Coz constantly road-blocking us." I hold out my cell. "So, do I call Ivan or not?"

This time Julian doesn't hesitate. "Give it a shot, Ms. CEO. It's totally nutty, but right now I'll take nutty over nothing."

"Wish me luck," I say. "And keep watching. Maybe they'll get back to Oprah and Cricket before the end."

A half-hour later I emerge triumphant from the bedroom. "I just booked Aria Fraser for the show! How do you like your Ms. CEO now?"

But Julian just sits still, stone faced, in front of the television. He raises a sepulchral finger toward the screen.

"Om and Nano just released the following statement on their Facebook page," Diane Sawyer is saying. " 'To our beloved fans; words cannot express how deeply saddened we are by today's devastating events. Our thoughts and prayers go out to the family and friends of Stephen Smith, who lost his life today. After four years of collaboration, we have decided that the best way to achieve a sustainable world is through our separate paths. While we deeply love and respect each other, we believe that our new creative journeys are best explored as individuals. We want to thank the fans who have enjoyed and supported our music and express the hope that others will move the breatharian movement forward in the absence of our restaurant. Om leaves tomorrow for her six-month deeksha training. Nano will spend the next six months renouncing all earthly possessions with the sadhus in Nepal. We will keep you posted separately with our new ventures. Peace out, Nano and Om.' Of course we'll continue to follow this story as new developments arise. For now we'll take you back to your regularly scheduled programming. This is Diane Sawyer for ABC News."

9

return to cannes-dy land

onjour, Mademoiselle. How may I help you?" the concierge at
the ultra chic Art Deco Hotel Martinez asks from his desk an-
chored within the large marble lobby. Julian and I arrived a couple of
days ago. Of course, we had to stay at the Hotel Martinez on the Boulevard de La Croisette since all the fashion folk stay here, all the better to
bump accidentally into the writers from *Harper's Bazaar, Elle,* Style.com,
etc., who might deign to mention Julian's show in their Twitters or Facebook updates. Or, like Marcy Medina from *WWD,* tell us that she never
received her invitation to the show, which could explain why we have
no RSVPs. Chili mailed out the invitations weeks ago and he's supposed
to be calling everyone to follow up. But since he clearly can't be trusted

to do anything, I've been making more calls than a Tea Party robocaller to try and remedy yet another epic Chili screwup.

I gaze past the concierge and out onto the sparkling Mediterranean. Sure, we're in the South of France, but don't let the idyllic setting fool you into believing that this is a vacation spot for most of us. There's not going to be any lounging on cushioned recliners Med-side with young bronzed French garçons offering up Bellinis and salad Niçoises. Not unless there's a deal memo on the platter. This is the biggest twelve days of the year for international cinema.

If you thought Oscar Week was over the top, in Cannes there are no tops. Not even on the starlets running around outside on the white sand beach in front of the hotel. Think the *Vanity Fair* Oscar party—on a yacht—for twelve straight nights. And unlike the *VF* party, you don't *want* to get there until 2:00 A.M. Every year umpteen thousand agents, managers, studio execs, publicists, producers, directors, and actors (and the hordes of international media who cover them) armed with iPhones, Ray-Bans, Missoni bathing suits, and plenty of attitude descend upon this upscale French Riviera city along with jet-set veterans, fashion icons, music moguls, and lookie-loos. They're all here to discover, sign, screw, or become The Next Brad Pitt. And a three-picture deal would be nice. Of course the *official* reason why everyone's here is for the *films*— whether you're premiering one, promoting one, selling one, buying one, or you're one of the lucky *twenty* flicks that's in the competition, with a shot to win Cannes's most coveted award, the Palme d'Or. Or, like me, staging a full-blown couture show on a yacht—in the middle of the Mediterranean. And hoping to use the worldwide press coverage off the costumes in one of the hottest movies of the festival with the hottest star in the world to launch a wedding dress line for a designer in desperate need of another big break.

I can't believe what I'm about to ask the concierge. I force out the words. "Mademoiselle Fraser is checking in tomorrow, and I just wanted to confirm that you were able to move the bed in her suite so that it's facing east and remove the television and any plants from the bedroom and also have the lavender sheets that her feng shui master Fed Ex'd put onto her bed."

"It's all been taken care of, Mademoiselle. Is there anything else we can do for Mademoiselle Fraser or you?" the concierge asks with a straight face. Then I remember that everyone from Naomi Campbell to Andre Leon Talley has stayed here. God only knows what *they* asked for. I contemplate asking the kind concierge if he can get Grace Frost to actually call me back *before* Julian's show and *before* Stefano and LVMH yank our financing since it seems he can do *anything*. But why should she? I mean, she's Grace Frost. And I'm me. I wouldn't have even dreamed of calling her except that Coz sent me a dozen Big Macs and a note that said, "My deepest condolences for losing Om and Nano and the cover of *Vain*." She left me no choice. I *had* to call Grace myself!

"That's all. Merci beaucoup," I say and then head across the lobby to meet Julian, who's my date for Christopher's big premiere since Lev is still in L.A. Even though the place costs a fortune, the Art Deco furnishing is a little bit shabby when you look closely. I really, really wanted to stay at the Hôtel du Cap (Heaven on the Côte d'Azur) but there was no way we could afford it. Especially not after all that money we lost on Om's gowns. We can barely afford this hotel, but since *le tout* of the fashion world are staying here, it's unquestionably our best bet at drumming up publicity.

I'd longed for a room overlooking the French Riviera—but the concierge informed me unblinkingly that that would be double the rate. And forget the mountain view—same deal. And there will be no swimming at the hotel's pool because of the twenty-five-euros-a-day surcharge. I'm certain that these steep prices have garnered us the shabbiest room of the four hundred available here—the only view we have is of the hotel's loud, thrumming air conditioners, unless you count the Lamborghinis, Maybachs, Mazzeratis, and Aston Martins in the parking lot. And I'm terrified that if Julian's bridal collection doesn't work we may have to swim back to NYC—this is, if we could afford the fifty-euro surcharge from the Hotel Martinez merely to step onto the beach.

Julian Tenant Inc. isn't the only one hemorrhaging money around here. The Oscars are all about picking up fabulous free swag; *nothing* in Cannes is gratis. Certainly not your room at the Riviera's most outrageously expensive hotel, the Hôtel du Cap—which you can only get if you're a Jeffrey Katzenberg, a Kate Winslet, a Jonas Brother, a Gossip Girl, or Oprah. And yes, the hotel has a strict *twelve-night* minimum, nonrefundable, payable up-front—provided that Monsieur Perd, the hotel's uber-manager, deems you *Worthy* of a room. And forget the free limos during Oscar season. At Cannes it'll set you back 125 euro to limo to Dolce & Gabbana's dangerously lavish annual fete. But, really, what's 160 bucks compared to the soiree's budget of one million? You'll get to dance with practically every star alive, watch a hundred-thousand-dollar fireworks display, munch on hors d'œuvres off human platters (naked supermodels "wearing" food), and see Lady Gaga perform in the flesh—hopefully something fresh from the butcher block this time. A diet Coke costs twelve dollars for crying out loud. And a ticket to AmFar's black-tie dinner at Moulin de Mougins will cost you more than six months' rent. Everything in Cannes costs—and some places only take *cash.*

I pass by the L'Amiral Bar off the lobby. It's jam-packed. Keanu Reeves is leaning up against the grand piano as the jazz pianist nimbly races his fingers around the keyboard. I'm so nervous for my brother that I wish I could just grab that Manhattan out of Keanu's hand and down it; L'Amiral's championship bar team serves up some of the best cocktails in Cannes—cocktails I have expressly forbidden Julian to order because we can't afford the thirty euros.

"Darling," Julian yells across the lobby, striding toward me in his tux.

"Hi Julian," I say, kissing him hello.

"Does my hair look okay?" Julian says, patting his slicked-back raven locks. "I'm freaking out without my flatiron."

"Julian, you're lucky you didn't burn down the entire hotel. I don't know what you were thinking trying to splice the wires of your flatiron with the hair dryer in the room."

"The concierge was out of adapters and I was desperate. Does it look okay? I was channeling Christian Bale in *American Psycho*," Julian says.

"It looks great," I say as we walk through the buzzing lobby.

"That dress is what looks great. No offense, Lo, but I wish you were Beyoncé. That dress deserves to be photographed. And it would look so good with her skin tone," Julian says of my cobalt blue, one-shoulder minidress Julian made especially for tonight.

"No offense taken," I say. "I wish I was Beyoncé, too."

"You seem eerily calm. Are you okay?" Julian asks. "Your calmness is making me nervous. It's been three minutes and you haven't said anything about the show or *Vain* or Saffron's movie premiere."

"The next two hours are about my brother. I just want to spend two hours being happy for Christopher and not worrying about anything other than reveling in his moment," I say as the doorman swings open the hotel door and we step out onto La Croisette.

Inside the Palais, I lean back in my plush red velvet seat and clutch Julian's hand. *Please let Christopher get a positive reception. Please.* I'm unbelievably nervous for my brother as his premiere is about to begin.

The theater goes dark and "Forgetting Petunia Holt" appears in simple Courier font against a black screen. "All These Things That I've Done," by The Killers plays over the opening credits. Brandon Flowers's slick, sultry voice croons, "Another head aches, another heart breaks; I'm so much older than I can take." The camera pans across framed photographs of a young man and a woman who seem to be very much in love. There are pictures of them kissing in front of the Grauman's Chinese Theatre, smiling at the top of Runyon Canyon, a black-and-white shot of them laughing at what can only be an inside joke, a solo shot of the woman peeking out from under the bedsheets, and finally a solo shot of the man holding a homemade sign that reads, I LOVE YOU PETUNIA HOLT.

My eyes immediately get moist as I'm reminded of the time Christopher held out that same sign in front of Kate's apartment before they'd moved in together. He'd been planning to take her to the Hollywood Bowl to see Radiohead for their three-month anniversary. Kate had a signing meeting with Zoe Saldana and ended up being two and a half hours later than planned. Christopher stood there with that sign for *three hours.* I take a deep breath and wonder how I'm going to make it through the entire movie and can't help but wish they were still together. I really thought they were going to make it.

I sit forward uneasily in my chair as the music ends and the screen cuts to a close-up of bubbling water and then smoke encompassing the water. The camera pulls back slowly to reveal that the murky smoke and gurgling water are part of a very tall—bong. The actor playing Justin Cooper, a.k.a. my brother, dressed in forest green Adidas sweats, lifts his mouth from the bong and a huge stream of smoke exhales from his lips. He leans back on a pristine white modular sofa and closes his eyes. As the camera holds on his closed eyes, we hear a woman's voice.

"I'm leaving you. Or actually, you're leaving me . . . this is my apartment," says Gigi, the actress playing Petunia Holt. She's stunning and bears an astonishing resemblance to my BFF, except that the legs emerging from her form-fitting structured black skirt suit aren't nearly as lovely as Kate's.

Justin Cooper's eyes widen in shock. "What?" he says, struggling to take in the gravity of what Petunia is saying.

"Look, I'm sorry. We tried, we really did, but I'm just not good at the whole relationship thing," she says. "I already called the movers to help you pack. I'm really sorry."

"You already called the movers?" Justin says, sitting upright. "Please don't do this. I love you." He crumples into a ball, slipping off the white sofa.

I feel angry all over again at Kate for breaking my brother's heart as I watch his character fall to pieces on screen.

"Please don't do this. I love you," Justin repeats, more softly, which only makes me madder at Kate.

I watch the movers onscreen pack up all of Justin's eclectic belongings from around the world—including an African drum, a Moroccan carpet, an Australian didgeridoo—which stick out like a sore thumb against the modern slickness of Petunia's all-neutral apartment. With all of Justin's possessions shoved into a friend's garage, he hops into his beat-up convertible, a chocolate Mercedes he converted to run on grease, and drives to the Mojave Desert to forget Petunia Holt and find himself.

By the end of the first act, when Justin is in a sweat lodge chanting with some shaman, I've somehow forgotten that I'm watching my brother's story or even that Christopher is the director. I've gotten that lost in Justin's poignant, at times wickedly funny and heartfelt journey. By the halfway point, when Justin's Mercedes breaks down and he and the shaman he's now traveling with start hitchhiking, I remember, and take a look around the theater. The packed audience seems just as engrossed as I am. Nobody's checking their watches or tapping on BlackBerries or shifting in their seats. They're all crying and laughing and rooting for Justin right along with me. It feels like one of those instant classics that you want to watch over and over, and that people will be quoting for generations to come. My very own brother could be the next John Hughes or Cameron Crowe or Judd Apatow.

By the end of the movie, as the lights go up, I know that we're safe, that Christopher's not going to be booed out of the theater. But what I don't expect is the entire audience bolting to their feet in a thunderous round of applause. And as I join the room in a standing ovation for my brother, tears of joy are streaming down my face and I'm smiling so wide I can feel my jaw getting sore. I look around the huge theater to take it all in, beaming with pride, and my smile instantly fades when I spot Kate, standing in the back of the theater alone. She must have snuck in when the lights went down. When we lock eyes she's already bolting for the door.

"Oh my god, she came," Julian says, following my eye line.

"I've got to go," I say, scurrying through my row. "Kate," I yell once we're outside. "Kate!" I catch up with her and lay a hand on her shoulder.

"What?" she says, finally turning to face me in the most beautiful black slip dress, her brown hair sweeping her shoulders in soft waves, and her olive skin glowing.

"Am I really that bad, Lola? That ambitious? That heartless?" But before I can reply, she says, "On second thought, don't answer that, I don't want to know." Her face is tight, her smile frozen in place.

Now it's Christopher I'm suddenly mad at as I look at Kate, trying desperately to mask the pain and heartbreak I know she must be feeling. This is one of those moments where words just aren't going to do it. Instead I wrap my arms around my best friend. Part of me expects her to push me away. But she doesn't. She melts into my arms.

"I love you," I whisper in her ear.

"Thank you," she says, not letting go of our embrace. "What if your brother actually *wins* the Palme d'Or? *Everyone* is going to know that movie is about me," Kate says.

"What?! You really think he could win? The Palme d'Or? No way. Really? Kate, *no one* is going to know it's about you."

"Really? How come *People* and ET have already asked me if I know who Petunia Holt really is since they know Christopher and I just broke up?"

"They did?" I say, feeling a pit in my stomach. "What'd you tell them?"

"I told them they'd have to ask Christopher," Kate says. "I still can't believe your brother did this to me. The entire time we were together he wasted his time on commercial shoots, and now that we're broken up his movie is in the fucking dramatic competition at Cannes and ICM is getting to rep him."

"Kate, Christopher made the movie for you originally, remember," I can't help but remind her. "And he's not going to breathe a word to anyone. *No one* is going to know that you're Petunia Holt," I say and hesitate before adding, "Christopher said he called you a bunch of times and you never called him back."

"Because there's nothing to talk about. And I thought I was feeling nauseous before the movie."

It's me who's suddenly violently ill when I spot another of Christopher's movie posters above Kate's head, one I haven't seen before. MY SISTER SAID IT WOULD NEVER LAST, it reads. Kate better not see that poster. How could Christopher approve *that*? My life feels like it's become a bad black comedy. As my cell trills, I see that it's about to get even darker—and less funny.

"I just left Grace Frost's office," Coz says over the phone line. "I simply cannot imagine why you've been calling her. I'm returning the call on her behalf."

I feel my stomach plummet to the floor along with our chances of being in *Vain*.

"I, um, well, I can explain," I stumble and imagine Coz on the other end of the phone basking in this moment from behind her big black sunglasses.

"As much as I'd derive immense pleasure from listening to you grovel for the next few hours, I'm actually really busy so I'm going to cut to the chase," Coz says.

"We're going to give you the cover and a twelve-page layout inside to coincide with the release of *Four Weddings and a Bris* in August."

"You're *what?!*" I ask, flabbergasted. Could it possibly be that Coz is our miracle worker after all? "Is this a joke?"

"Does it sound like I'm joking?" Coz says icily. "Just so we're clear, I'm not doing this for you or Julian," she says, as if she's *ever* done anything for me—or Julian. Except waterboard our careers. "I'm doing it for Chili."

"Chili?" I repeat.

"Grace agreed that it was a complete travesty that Chili's divine wedding gowns ended up on Baz's cutting room floor so she thought it was a wonderful idea to let his gowns see the light of day in *Vain*."

I know that Coz is speaking but I can't compute what's she's actually saying.

"What about Julian?" I'm finally able to get out.

"Saffron and Cricket will do the cover together. Saffron will wear Chili and Cricket can wear Julian," Coz says. "I've already booked Patrick Demarchelier, Gucci Westman, and Orlando Pita and called the Du Cap and arranged to shoot in their gardens. Chili and I are flying out tomorrow. *Jusqu'à demain. Bisous. Bisous,*" she says and then just as abruptly hangs up.

I try and recover from the Coz tsunami that just hit me. So what if Julian has to share the cover of *Vain* with little Chili Lu? At least Julian is going to *be* on the cover of *Vain*. This could catapult Julian into becoming the *next* Vera Wang. He could rule the Hollywood brides. Everything I've killed myself for as CEO of Julian Tennant Inc.

Oh god. Oh no. I still haven't actually *asked Cricket* or Saffron if they'd be willing to pose for the cover of *Vain*. What if they say no?

My head is spinning. I feel faint. I speed-dial Cricket. It goes straight to voice mail. I leave her a very long rambling, bumbling, begging message.

I contemplate hurling myself down the Palais steps, the most prestigious red carpet in the world, but decide against it.

When I finally arrive back at the suite I'm sharing with Julian I flop onto the canary yellow upholstered bed. I'm still reeling from the standing ovation my brother got tonight and Coz's call telling me that Julian and Chili are going to be on the cover of *Vain*.

My eyelids feel like lead weights. I'm practically deep in REM when my laptop trills. It's Lev calling on Skype.

"Hello," I say groggily, turning on the video. I struggle to focus my eyes and sit up. "Oh my god. What happened? Are you okay?" Lev's face and scrubs are covered in blood. He looks like something out of *Saw IX*.

"Oh this," he says, wiping at the mess. "It's fake. I'm on the set."

"Oh," I say, trying not to visibly shudder despite the chills running down my spine. It's just *one* season. As soon as he hears back from Lenox Hill hospital he's going to move to NYC and forget all about *Para-Medic* and this whole acting thing. It's not like I'm marrying Ben Affleck, right? I need to be supportive. *Say something supportive,* I urge myself. "The blood looks so real. You totally freaked me out."

"Sorry, I didn't mean to scare you. The makeup artist went a little wild. It's this crazy scene where what looks to be a tumor I'm removing from a patient's belly turns out to be the spawn of an alien *and* a vampire and it attacks one of the nurses and I have to try and stop the bleeding before the baby turns the nurse into a vampire," Lev says.

"Vampires are the new black," I say. "I mean, who even heard of Stephen Moyer or Robert Pattinson before all this?"

"Who?" Lev asks.

That's my Lev. The only guy in the world who's never heard of *Twilight* or *True Blood* or *The Vampire Diaries*.

"I really miss you," I say. "I can't wait to see you. I'm so happy that you're coming in a couple of days."

"Me too," Lev says. "I wish I could have been there for Christopher's premiere. How'd it go?"

"It was amazing. He got a standing ovation. I'm so happy for him," I say.

"I've been so nervous. I didn't want to call him until I spoke to you but I can't wait to talk to him. That's such great news," Lev says.

"Kate thinks he could win the Palme d'Or."

"Kate was there?" Lev asks.

"Yeah, she snuck in after the lights went down. I still can't believe she came."

"How's she doing?" Lev asks.

"You know Kate," I say. "She's pretending like she's okay but I know she's not. I know she's still in love with my bro—"

"Hey man," a man's voice interrupts our conversation from out of the camera's view. I can just make out the man's hand patting Lev's shoulder. "You were really great earlier. Let me know if you want to come by my trailer and run lines for our next scene." I try and place the man's voice. It sounds so familiar.

"Thanks. I appreciate it. I'd love to," Lev says.

"So what're you up to? Working on the cure for cancer between takes?" the man teases Lev. That voice. How do I know that voice?

"I was actually just Skyping with my fiancée," Lev says.

"Sorry. I didn't mean to interrupt," the man says. "Sorry about that," he says, popping into frame to apologize to me. "Hi, I'm Patrick." Dempsey. Oh my god. Lev is going to run lines with Patrick freaking Dempsey. Mc-Dreamy himself! What's next? An onscreen kiss with Ellen Pompeo? This cannot be happening. This cannot be happening.

"This is Lola," Lev finally says after a few very awkward beats.

"Hi, sorry, I don't usually get starstruck, you just took me by surprise," I say.

"Well, it was nice to meet you, Lola," Patrick says, flashing me one of his famous smiles. He exits the camera's frame.

"Bye, Patrick. It was so nice to meet you!" I yell, feeling like a refugee from *Tiger Beat* with Bieber Fever.

"See you in five in my trailer, Lev," I hear Patrick say.

"Sorry about that," Lev says to me. "Is everything okay? You were kind of weird to Patrick."

"Really?" I say. "I guess I was just so shocked to see him. I didn't realize he was on the show," I say.

"He's doing one episode as a favor to Chandra. His character from *Grey's* comes over to do a special neuro consult on a patient," Lev says. "And it's gonna turn out that the patient has two brains—one human, one alien—and they're gonna ask me to operate with him assisting. But the alien brain is psychic, so the patient knows all about it already and he's gonna try and kill us both by using telekinesis to stick the anesthesia needles in our arms from across the room. But don't tell anyone, 'cause we're all sworn to secrecy, okay?"

"That's just so . . . *great*," I say, forcing a smile and trying to *act as if*

I'm a supportive fiancée and not some loony mess who's spiraling into a massive panic at the thought of her doctor fiancé acting opposite Patrick Dempsey. What if Lev wants Patrick at the wedding? What if he wants him to be a groomsman—or best man!—instead of his own brother! *Jump. Off. The. Crazy. Train!* I order myself.

"Thank you for trying to be supportive, Lola. I really appreciate it—even if you don't really mean it," Lev says.

"What do you mean?" I ask.

"Don't take this the wrong way, but you really are a terrible actress," Lev says.

I feign mock shock. "Well, maybe you can give me some pointers," I tease.

"I still have no idea what I'm doing," Lev says.

"According to Patrick, you were really great."

"I wouldn't say *great*. I think he's just being kind," Lev says. "Look, I'm really sorry, but I've got to run."

"Yeah, yeah, you go, no worries, good luck rehearsing with Patrick," I say.

"Wait, I feel badly, I haven't even asked about you. How's it going there? Is everything okay?" Lev asks.

"It'll be a miracle if Julian and I don't kill each other. He fired the DJ we flew in from Hotel Costes in Paris because he thought his rendition of 'Here Comes the Bride' was too techno, so now I'm trying to get Sam Ronson. I've had to redo the seating chart a dozen times because the French Gwyneth Paltrow has broken up and gotten back together with one of the Monaco royals at least twice over the last week. Orchestrating the seating so that everyone's *happy* is harder than putting together a UN resolution for Iran. We only have one hundred RSVPs—we sent out over two hundred fifty—and the *Next* Giselle *murdered* the finale gown at her fitting yesterday. She decided to *breast-feed* her kid *in* the ivory chiffon hand-beaded goddess gown and got breast milk all over it."

"DOB, huh?" Lev says.

"What?" I ask.

"Dead On Breastfeeding."

"Very funny. This is *serious*," I say.

"You're right. I'm sorry," Lev says. "You're going to find a way to sort everything out. You always do."

"I hope so. That was only the Spark Notes from the last forty-eight hours," I say. "I can't wait for you to get here."

"Me too. I'm sorry again that I couldn't be there tonight. Please give Christopher a hug for me and tell him I'll call him later. And I'll be there for your mother's party."

"You mean Cirque du Santisi," I say. "I don't think I could survive it without you! Anyway, you should go; you don't want to keep Patrick waiting and I need to get changed."

"I'll Skype you later," Lev says. "I love you."

"Love you too," I say, shutting down Skype.

10

hope you're decent in there, Julian," I say, tapping on his bedroom door. "I know you're exhausted, but we need to go over a few things before I head out for the lattes. And I'm going to get you a special treat because you've been working so hard. I tracked down a patisserie that does vegan croissants *and* mille-feuilles."

Silence. The poor dear. He must be completely worn out; I could hear the sewing machine whirring late into the night. I tap again. "Julian? Julian?" I'll just sneak inside and make sure he didn't fall asleep on top of any of the wedding gowns, like he did the night before. I ease the door open.

Julian is standing there in a blindingly bright gold swimsuit, tucking copies of *Voici, Closer,* and *Choc* into a bamboo tote.

"Julian, what are you doing? Why are you wearing a *Speedo*?! You can't go to the beach—we have so much work to do!"

"Honey, it's a Tomas Maier and in case you haven't noticed, we're on the French Riviera. And I'm gay," he says. "Besides, I was up until four undoing all the so-called work Chili did on the gowns back in New York and I need a break. You don't want me to develop carpal tunnel syndrome again, do you? Come on, Princess, we both need a break. Go put on your Missoni bikini and come join me Med-side. We'll order Bellinis and check out the French tabs. Which are sublimely filthy. One of them has a shot of the most gorgeous man having sex with a scorpion. And wait till I show you the topless shots of Kate Moss—goodness, how our little waif has grown!"

"No, Julian," I say. "Did you forget that the Martinez charges fifty euros just to step on the sand? And no Bellinis before eight a.m. Actually, at thirty euros a pop, no Bellinis at all!"

"I'm still trying to digest the *Vain* news," he says. "And a Bellini and Jacques, the très adorable bartender on the beach, are going to help me do that. Princess, you just have no idea how stressed out I am."

"Fine, but only *one*. Aria's plane should be landing in a couple of hours, and I scheduled a fitting with her at noon and I'd very much like it if at least *you* were sober since I'm sure Aria's going to be completely Klonopined out from the flight."

He lets out a vexed sigh. "I still can't believe you convinced me to debut her shoe line on my runway. Why is it that people who merely *wear* fashion suddenly think they can *design* fashion? And remember that dreadful line from what's-her-name, that Hills-billy? And you know I adore Giselle, I really do, but did the world really need her Gazelle jeans? Who has mile-long legs like her, and who pays three hundred fifty dollars for jeans anymore? And god, Dina Lohan's Shoe-hans? *Horrible.* Although next to Aria's shoes, they'll probably look like Choos."

"Julian, no one's going to focus on the shoes; don't worry," I say. "Let me just do a quick food run for us. Then I've got to get back to the room and keep calling everybody. It's the strangest thing. It doesn't even seem as if half these people even *got* our invitation."

"It's that damn Chili," Julian says. "I don't know how I'm going to be able to keep working with him. I thought we were rid of him for good when we left for Cannes."

"In a few days, we will be," I say. "Just keep reminding yourself that your dress is going to be on the cover of *Vain*."

"Only if Cricket and Saffron actually *agree* to the cover," Julian says despairingly. "Any word from Cricket?"

"No. Cricket's phone keeps going straight to voice mail. But they're flying in tonight and I'll handle it then," I say.

"What if they say no?" Julian asks, his voice tinged with panic.

"They won't," I say. "Cricket's the most supportive friend in the world, and she'd do anything for us. And you know she'll convince Saffron."

"But what if she can't convince Saffron? She could totally say no, Lola." Julian's voice is getting an octave higher with every word.

"Stop being so negative. You're totally stressing me out and so is that bathing suit," I say. "I've got to go. And remember: only *one* Bellini," I say, trying to shake off the image of Julian's gold-clad backside.

Five minutes later I'm walking along La Croisette, Cannes's main palm tree-dotted drag. The famous promenade that hugs Cannes's coastline is already crowded with gawkers and tourists who are lining up, presumably hoping for a celebrity sighting, of which there promises to be plenty during the festival. I feel a hand on my arm and turn. A young man eagerly pushes a pamphlet into my hand. "Require financing for my film. Can you help me?" The requisite mimes are imitating the tourists snapping photos and jostling for autographs. Oblivious to it all are the grande dames walking their tiny pooches swathed in tiny Hermès coats, twin noses pointed high at the sky.

Up ahead are bleary-eyed partygoers staggering back to their hotels, stumbling past journos gearing up for the first screenings of the day. And there's Rihanna, a drink in one hand, flipping off a photog with the other and wearing a sheer black dress sans panties. And here I thought the Moonie Noonie was so fifteenminutesago.com.

As I continue walking, I'm bombarded with gigantic movie posters of all the films in competition as well as the ones premiering here. I spot a huge promo banner for my brother's movie ten feet away from one for my father's film. I didn't realize they were remaking *Shampoo* until I see the poster with Taylor Lautner and Emma Stone. And who cast Zac Efron as Ben-Hur?

I spot Miley Cyrus, who's playing a young Meryl Streep in the *Out of Africa* prequel opposite Joe Jonas, being escorted out of the uber-luxe Carlton Hotel by a slew of bodyguards. And is that the real Kate Winslet, or merely her sosie? (Some of the stars or their agents pay for a look-alike to throw the paps off the scent.) It looked like the Carlton beefed up their security ever since Madonna reportedly refused to pay her ninety-thousand-dollar bill because a French TV crew managed to get footage of her suite while she was staying there. I simply had no idea kabbalah water was that expensive, but if that's what it takes to support the Malawi orphans and keep your complexion that dewy, I'm all for it.

I do a double take at a newsstand when I pass it and backtrack. The same photo is plastered across practically every magazine and newspaper on the rack.

I pick up one of the papers to get a closer look. It's a shot of my BAF and Saffron Sykes. They're in a lip lock—an outtake from the very scene I saw them filming in Australia! "Saffron Sykes Est Gai!" screams the headline.

Someone must have leaked a picture from the set or rehearsal or something. I look for a mention of *Four Weddings and a Bris* or that Saffron Sykes is *playing* a gay woman in the film, but don't find any. I wonder if Cricket has any idea that she's international front-page news. I try her cell but it goes straight to voice mail again. So does Kate's Black-Berry. Kate must know though, right? Oh my god, what if she's the one who leaked the photos to create more buzz around the premiere? No, no, no, no, no. She wouldn't do that. Or would she?

I grab a stack of papers and head back to my hotel. It isn't until I'm back in my room that I realize I never even got my morning latte. But these headlines are way more jolting than coffee. I pick up one of the papers and attempt to read the accompanying article. With my rudimentary French I'm only able to decode the following words: vacation, boat, Crete, Cricket, Saffron, Markus, and après filmer. Wait, that can't be right. *After* filming? Are they implying that this photo was taken *after* filming, or is it saying that they took a vacation together after filming, which they did? I'm so confused. I flip open my laptop and decide to search the Web.

"If She Were a Gay Man We'd Say: 'The Queen of the Screen Really Is a Queen'," blares TMZ. "Saffron Sykes Kissed a Girl and Liked It," DListed declares. "WTF?! Saffron Sykes Is Gay?!" XI7 exclaims. "Markus Livingston nowhere in sight. Seems the real love affair is between Saffron Sykes and Cricket Curtis," claims JustJared. "Markus Livingston Is Hollywood's Hottest Beard," Defamer insists.

Is this some kind of nutty marketing campaign for the movie? So what's the deal with Saffron and Markus, not to mention all those other Hollywood hotties she's been with? But wasn't Kevin Spacey on that list? I'm so confused. Cricket would have told me if any of this was true. Wouldn't she?! She's my BAF, for crying out loud. I force myself to keep reading.

"Who Likes Vagina?" Perez Hilton asks. "OMG, you guys! OMG!! Can you believe it? Are you hyperventilating yet?? Saffron Sykes is GAY!!" Perez says. "Perez Hilton has discovered the big plot twist in Saffron Sykes's new movie—and her life. We all thought that Saffron's character was marrying Markus Livingston's character in *Four Weddings,* but sources close to Saffron confirm exclusively to Perez that she's—gasp— marrying her maid of honor, newcomer Cricket Curtis. And Saffron Sykes, who's been linked to everyone from George Clooney to Bradley Cooper to Chace Crawford and we thought was dating Markus in real life is actually playing tonsil hockey with—gasp—Cricket Curtis. Art really is imitating life. The queen of the screen is getting a new crown: Queen of the Va-Jay-Jay!"

I'm frozen in front of the computer screen. Could any of this nonsense actually be good for Cricket? They say any publicity is good publicity. Maybe it'll just get her on a bazillion talk shows to deny the rumor, and they'll play clips from the movie and she'll get even more offers! On the other hand, I have no idea how Saffron or Cricket will take all this attention. What if they're incredibly embarrassed or furious about it? How am I supposed to ask Cricket and Saffron to pose together for the cover of *Vain* now?

There's a knock on the door. I toss the newspapers into a drawer and slam my MacBook shut. When I open the door I'm surprised to see my brother standing in front of me.

"Mom doesn't actually expect us to follow this script, does she?!" Christopher says, barreling through the door and throwing a sheaf of papers down on the couch. "Have you read this shit?"

"I buried my copy in the bottom drawer of that dresser the second I got it," I confess, gesturing toward the 1930s' dresser the plasma TV is resting on. "I was scared it would throw me over the edge."

"Mom's the one who's gone over the edge," Christopher says, sitting down on the couch in a pair of beat-up jeans, a gray T-shirt, a black linen blazer, and his red Converse high-tops. "There's actually a scene in there where Mom has a heart-to-heart with Gigi and," Christopher makes air quotes, "welcomes her into our family."

"What?! Please tell me that you're kidding," I say, instantly thinking of Kate.

"I wish I was. She sent Gigi her own copy of the script," Christopher says. He rests his head in his hands and looks up at me with worry in his eyes. "She's gone too far this time, La-La. What are we going to do?"

"I don't know, Chris, but I'm scared to even ask what she wrote in there for me."

"It seems that Gigi is the sister you never had. You two are very close. Which is surprising, given that I think you met for about fifteen seconds last night," Chris says. What is my mother thinking? Other than about her ratings. "Mom needs to be stopped."

"Yes she does. It's like she wants to be the next Caroline Manzo. Don't worry, we'll find a way to rein her in," I say. Poor Christopher. He looks so distraught. "How *are* things with you and Gigi?" I ask with trepidation.

"Good, I guess," he says. "She's good for me. She . . . supports me."

"Kate supported you. She was your biggest fan." I can't help but interject in my best friend's defense.

"It's different with Gigi. Kate was always pushing me to do more. She thought I was wasting my time on all the commercials."

"No, she thought you were wasting your talent. She thought you were better than all those commercials. Which you are," I say.

"Gigi doesn't push me. She lets me be me and she's not always rushing off to make a million phone calls or scream at her assistant. That's new for me." I can't tell if Christopher's trying to convince me or himself.

"Do you love her?" I ask.

"It's still so new, I don't know," he says. "Have you talked to Kate? Do you think she'll ever forgive me? I've left her a bunch of messages but haven't heard back. Did she hate the movie?"

"Everyone loved the movie, including Kate. Look, Chris, your film is really, *really* good. This is just the beginning for you. I'd hate to see you not able to soak in all of this because of Kate. Because you really deserve it. You've worked hard," I say, stopping myself there. But I could go on. Because it's true. Chris has worked hard. His whole life, not just at work, but at being a good person. And that's why he's not letting all this buzz around his movie affect him. My brother may be exceptionally cool looking on the outside, but he doesn't care about any of it—he knows it's all just a passing show. He's my brother, so I'm biased, but there's a thing or two I know about men since I've been around so many doozies. He's one of the rare ones. So I start making excuses for Kate because I'm holding out hope. "I think Kate's just got a lot going on with Nic Knight and Saffron and Cricket," I say, unable to bring myself to show my brother the story on Perez Hilton. I'm not ready to talk about it out loud yet.

"So what? She's always got a lot going on with work," Chris says.

"Chris, you know Kate; she can't talk about her feelings," I say.

"Stupidly, I guess I thought it was different with me." My brother's voice is tinged with sadness.

"I know she still loves you," I say. And as I look into my brother's eyes I am certain that he's still in love with her.

"Don't start, La-La, please. She ended it with me, remember? Listen, let me know if you talk to her. And read Mom's script but make sure all the windows are closed first. You're gonna want to throw yourself out of one. I've got to run, I'm meeting a reporter from the *International Herald Tribune*."

"Wow. The *Tribune*. I'm so impressed," I say. "You know, I really think you have a chance to win the Palme d'Or, Chris."

"No way," says Christopher. "My money's on Papa, unanimous first-round vote from the judges. I'll see you at his screening tonight, right?"

"Yep. I'll be there," I say, walking my brother to the door.

"Bye, La-La," he says, planting a kiss on my cheek before heading out.

"See you later, Chris."

I close the door behind Christopher and walk back over to my laptop. When I refresh the Perez Hilton homepage a new story pops up. It's a picture of Nic Knight with the caption: "What's that up his nose??"

Perez has drawn his trademark squiggly circle around a damning close-up of Nic's face. I continue reading.

> *"A very happy Nic Knight—with what appears to be white powder in his nostril—stepping off a yacht party in Cannes at 4:00 A.M. Maybe it's just snot? Or perhaps 'frosting from his most recent tart'? When will the pAArty stop? What a waste of his talent!"*

Where the heck was Nic's AA sponsor? Or NA sponsor? Or parole officer? Or Kate? I grab my cell and speed-dial Kate. Not surprisingly, her voice mail picks up. I wouldn't be answering my phone, either, if I were her. Heck, if I were her, I'd be on the first plane out of here.

I continue scrolling down, trying to get back to the story on Saffron and Cricket.

> *"Meet the new McDreamy—McSexy!"* catches my attention.

I feel like I've just been punched in the gut by Chuck Liddell. There's a picture of Patrick Dempsey and—*Lev, my Lev*—together, and Perez has scrawled one of his infamous hearts around Lev's face.

I make myself read the accompanying text.

misunderstanding. We need to get Aria out immediately and make sure that the press doesn't know about it," I say, my mind racing at the potential damning press.

"Let me talk to my boss and see what can be done," he says.

"We have to get her out of jail is what needs to be done," I say. "Please, you have to help me. Your boss will know what to do, right? I mean, she can't be the first celebrity that's stayed at your hotel to be thrown in the slammer, right?"

"We will do everything we can to help you," he says. "I'll call you back as soon as I know anything."

Click.

As the seconds turn to minutes and the minutes turn to *hours,* I've gnawed my fingernails to the nubs and Aria is *still* behind bars despite *everything* I've done to try and get her out. Apparently the passenger she assaulted was a minor who allegedly required a few (seven) stitches on her face. That means there is *nothing,* and I mean *nothing,* that I can do to get her out today. I even tried to bribe the unfriendly police officers with premiere tickets and a private dinner with Saffron Sykes and Nic Knight at La Columbe d'Or, which frankly might have actually worked if we were in L.A.

As we're driving along the windy road back from the precinct in Nice, I can't help but fantasize about asking the driver to plunge his Mercedes straight off the seaside cliff and into the Med. I wonder how you even say that in French? Just as I'm thinking about whether my funeral would get more RSVPs than Julian's show so far, and if my mother would allow her cameras to film my memorial, my cell trills.

"Cricket, finally! How are you?"

"I'm freaking out, Lola," Cricket's whispering. "I'm not prepared for any of this."

"Patrick Dempsey had hearts swooning outside of the U2 concert at th
Rose Bowl in El Lay where he was spotted with Luke Levin, the sexy
new doc on Para-Medic. *Ya, Luke may not have McDreamy's lovely*
locks, but he's a doctor in real life, which makes him even sexier!"

I slam my laptop closed and make a solemn vow never to look a
Perez Hilton ever again.

Compartmentalize, Lola, compartmentalize, I tell myself. Be the CEO of
JT Inc. now, not the daughter of crazy narcissists, friend of beleaguered
starlets, or fiancée of The Next McDreamy. I check the desk clock. Aria
should be here by now. I phone the front desk to see if she's checked in
yet, but she hasn't. I try her cell; there's no answer. I call the car service
I arranged to pick her up at the airport, and the driver tells me that he
hasn't seen her yet. Too early to call Ivan in NYC. I finally decide to call
the concierge and ask him to call the airport to see if Aria's plane landed
on time and to make sure she was on said plane.

It feels like forever before the concierge finally calls me back.

"Mademoiselle Santisi," he says with his très adorable French accent.

"Oui," I say. "Have you located Mademoiselle Fraser yet?"

"I'm afraid she's being taken to prison," he says.

"Prison?" I wail.

"Oui, prison," he says. Even with a French accent there is nothing
pleasant about the word "prison."

"I don't understand, what happened!?"

"I'm not entirely certain, but it seems Mademoiselle Fraser punched
a passenger when they were trying to take a photo of her in the middle
of the flight. They wouldn't tell me anything else," he says.

This officially could be one of the worst days of my life. And it's not
even noon.

"Can you take me to the prison? This has to be some miserable

"Where are you?"

"We just got to the Du Cap," she says quietly. "Can you come over?"

"Yeah, of course. I'm supposed to be at my dad's screening in an hour, but I'll be right there," I say.

"Thanks, Lola," Cricket says. "Oh, and I'm staying under Cameron Streep."

"You have an *alias*?" I say.

"Yes, I have to because the press keeps trying to call my room and someone knocked on my door pretending to be room service and it was a paparazzi. Please hurry, Lo, I need you."

Click.

Minutes later my driver is pulling up to the sprawling, immaculately landscaped palm-shaded grounds of the Hôtel du Cap, the Riviera's most outrageously expensive hotel, hidden away in a twenty-five-acre pine forest on the rocky coast of the Cap d'Antibes. It feels for a moment as if all my woes are lost among the delicious-smelling pines. And then I spot a paparazzo trying to climb through said pine trees. I look around. There's a whole phalanx of them, sneaking among the trees, lurking outside the jewel box of a chateau. Each one of them armed with telephoto lenses thick as Louisville Sluggers. I picture all of them aimed at my Cricket and feel a rush of protectiveness.

I've barely set foot inside the grand, white-and-black, marble-floored, Grecian-columned reception area when a security guard blocks my path.

"I'll need to see a room key, Mademoiselle."

"I'm sorry, I don't have one."

"This way, then, please." He escorts me over to the front desk where another black-suited gentleman greets me.

"I'm here to see Cameron Streep," I tell him, trying to stifle a grimace at the ridiculous alias. But if the clerk shares my sense of the absurdity of the situation, he is far too well trained to show it. "Your ID, Mademoiselle," he says before placing a call to the room. He then waves me in the direction of the ultra exclusive Eden-Roc, an all-suite annex of the hotel nestled in a secluded spot by the water's edge, which is almost like staying on one of the mega-yachts with the three Tom's (Cruise, Ford, and Hanks) on the world's most pricey floating parking lot in front of the hotel.

As I make my way through the cavernous lobby it feels like I could be in a Fitzgerald novel or back visiting Sofia Coppola on the set of *Marie Antoinette*. No sign of a recession here. I just pray that I don't run into my parents, who are also staying here. I'm sure my mother's been in hair and makeup since 10:00 A.M. getting ready for my father's screening tonight. The lobby, with its white marble fireplaces, chandeliers, and canary yellow and robin's egg blue upholstered furniture, is like the living room of some uber-wealthy aristocrat's country estate if Michael Smith had decorated it before rushing more fabric samples for Malia and Sasha's bedrooms and Bo's new doggie bed to the White House.

I pass by Le Bellini bar, with its limestone Corinthian columns and carved crests, and wonder if one of the white-jacketed waiters serving Bellinis by the dozen to everyone from James Cameron to Diane Kruger to Carla Bruni can make me one to go. Hopefully Cricket will have already ordered a giant vat from room service.

I exit the lobby and walk along the palm tree–lined wide, gravel walkway to the Eden Roc. As I go past the pet cemetery that's been here since the 1930s I can't help but think that I wouldn't mind spending the hereafter right here. At one of the clay tennis courts I spot Gavin Rossdale rallying with Roger Federer and wish I could take a seat beside a flawless Gwen Stefani and that darling Mirka to watch.

The scene at the hotel's saltwater, infinity-edge swimming pool built into a rocky cliff over the Med is straight out of a Helmut Newton photo. I feel like the blond Shrek as I scurry past all the half naked supermodels soaking up the last of the day's sun and cheering on Chris Pine as he does a Tarzan-like swing into the Med from a jetty down below.

I finally arrive at Cricket's suite, a contemporary, airy, white-on-white seaside affair that's a stark contrast to the rooms in the main hotel with their stodgy Louis XV and Louis XVI furniture. Cricket's curled up on a cheery floral print armchair, looking the opposite of cheery, practically disappearing inside one of the hotel's plush terry robes. Her porcelain skin is lackluster and her golden locks are in a messy ponytail. I sit down on the edge of the armchair beside her with a million questions swimming around inside my head. I'd be lying if I said that one of them wasn't: "Is there any chance in hell that you and Saffron will agree to pose on the cover of *Vain*?" But right now I need to be Cricket's friend and not the CEO of Julian Tennant Inc.

"How are you doing?" I ask.

"I just didn't expect any of this, Lo," Cricket says.

"Are any of the stories true?" I ask my BAF tentatively.

"Well, um, I wouldn't say that the stories are . . . um . . ." Cricket's fumbling as Kate walks out of the bathroom.

"Hey," I say to Kate. "I've been trying to reach you, too!"

"Are you okay?" Cricket asks Kate, her voice full of concern. "It sounded pretty bad in there."

"I'm fine," Kate says, despite the slightly green hue to her skin. "This is ridiculous. I simply cannot afford to be sick right now. Everything's falling to shit as it is." She reaches into her clutch and pulls out another motion sickness patch to add to the four she's already wearing.

"Are you sure it's okay to put so many of those things on?" I ask.

"These stupid things don't even work," Kate says. "I'm wearing one of every brand the drugstore had."

"That can't be good for you," I say, worried.

"Neither is vomiting on your clients," Kate says. "Or letting them go to a party on a yacht without you, like I let Nic do last night." I debate asking her if she's seen PerezHilton or whether she's aware that it seems Nic's fallen off the wagon—again. But I decide against it. I'm sure she knows. She *must* know. And besides, we're here to focus on Cricket now. "If your father doesn't kill Nic, I just may," Kate continues. "God, I hate boats. And of course the afterparty is on *another* one tonight, but we're not here to discuss my health or my crap life. We're here to figure out how to handle the Saffron and Cricket situation."

I turn to my BAF. "Cricket, you still haven't answered my question. Are any of the stories true?"

"Well, um, I wouldn't say that the stories are . . . um . . ." she starts bumbling again.

"Oh geezus, Cricket, you pulled a Lohan," Kate says. "Just say it already. It's okay. You're not the first actress to have a fling with a costar."

"Whoa, whoa, whoa," I say shaking my head to try and make some sense out of things. "Is Saffron Sykes even gay? Do you think you're gay? What about Markus?"

Cricket looks down at her candy-apple-red toes.

"Saffron Sykes isn't gay and neither is Cricket," Kate says emphatically. "Need I remind you of Yoga Guy, who spent eight months realigning Cricket's chakras? Or that dude from the freecreditreport.com commercial you did? And why would Cricket constantly be hocking me to set her up with all my male clients if she's lesbian? Or drooling all over Viggo from the pool house?"

"Cricket?" I say.

"Look, sexuality is more fluid than that," Cricket announces.

"Oh geezus," Kate sighs and takes a seat as if readying herself for a lecture.

"I feel like I'm back in Human Sexuality class at Scripps," I say.

"Try telling all of those people who can't get married right now that sexuality is fluid. Call it experimentation if anything. Frankly, it's insulting," Kate adds resolutely.

"I'm very aware of that." Cricket finally snaps up from her prone position and begins pacing. "But what I find insulting is that I've finally done some really good work and this is what the world wants to focus on. These freaking tabloids?! It's disgusting and . . . disappointing. I've worked too hard for this to overshadow what I've done here. And that it's hurting Saffron! Look, she isn't like anyone I've ever known before, and when we were filming our scenes together, I just felt something that I've never felt before and—"

"Of course you felt something, Cricket," Kate says briskly. "You are an *actress*. If you didn't *feel* something, you wouldn't be a very good actress. Look, you don't have to convince us that you're not gay."

"I think what Kate's trying to say, Cricket, is that you can be a bit . . . fickle in this area," I say. "You do tend to go from . . . well, it's been man to man in the past."

"I know, I know," Cricket says, placing her hands over her face. "It's just been such a whirlwind that I haven't had time to think about things, I've just gotten so wrapped up. I really care about Saffron and I know she's freaking out about all of the publicity." Cricket looks like she's wearing the weight of the universe on her slender shoulders.

Kate crows with laughter. "Are you kidding? I couldn't have timed it better myself. Do you realize how much buzz there is behind the movie now?" she says.

"It's just that suddenly the whole world is saying that Saffron's gay and I'm gay and Saffron's worried about her career and mine . . . but making this movie and playing a lesbian has really made her think about honoring her true self . . . and Prop 8 . . . and she hates all the lying and so do I . . . but I just wasn't prepared for all of this," Cricket says.

"What are you saying, Cricket?" I ask. "That Saffron Sykes *is* gay?"

"Of course she's not gay," Kate says. "She's my client; don't you think I would know if she was gay?"

"Cricket? Is Saffron Sykes gay?" I ask.

Cricket looks at me and then over to Kate. Me. Kate. Me.

"Yes," Cricket finally says.

"Just because you two rubbed vulvas does not mean that she's gay," Kate says.

"Jesus, Kate, do you have to be so crass?" I say.

"Oh please," Kate says. "I thought Saffron was in love with Markus. Isn't she?"

There's an eerie silence in the room.

"No, she's in love with me," Cricket says.

It's way too much for my brain to comprehend. I feel like I'm trying to put a thousand-piece jigsaw puzzle together without all the pieces. The only piece that's clear is playing like a marquee in flashing bright neon: *There is no way that Saffron and Cricket are going to agree to pose together for the cover of* Vain *now.*

"Just so we're clear, you're telling me that the biggest female movie star in the world—who also happens to be my client—is *gay* and in love with *you*?" Kate says.

"Yes," Cricket says, her voice so soft it's barely audible.

"That's just freaking great," Kate says.

"Oh my god, Cricket," I gasp. "Are you in love with her?"

"I . . . I . . . I don't know," Cricket says.

I look over to Kate. Her steely façade seems to be cracking. I guess this is just too much to digest—even for *Kate*. But just when I think she's full-throttle Humpty Dumpty, she puts herself back together again. I can practically see the wheels inside her head turning.

"We'll do what we always do: deny, deny, deny," Kate says. "Everything will be fine, I promise." Fine for whom exactly, I wonder. Is it really such a big deal that Saffron's gay? Now that I've had a moment to think about it, I'm wondering why Kate's having such a major freak-out. Kate claps her hands together briskly. "Now, I've got to get to Nic's premiere and so do you, Lola. Let's go. Cricket, do *not* pick up the phone. Do *not* answer the door. I will handle everything from my end, okay?"

"Okay," says Cricket, but she's staring off into space.

"I don't feel right about leaving you here," I say to Cricket. "You know we love you no matter what, right?"

"I know," Cricket says. "I'm fine. I'm just . . . I'm fine. Go, you have to go, we can talk more after the movie."

"Are you sure?" I say.

"Yes, go, please," Cricket says. The final glimpse I catch of her as I close the door behind me is of her sinking helplessly into the gigantic chair.

My father is basking in the glory of all the bulbs exploding around him, puffing away on his cigar from the red carpet of the Palais steps, trying to ignore my mother scurrying about with her cameras in tow. She's dressed in a magenta silk chiffon Chanel couture gown that's displaying a little too much cleavage. Just as I try to duck behind the hordes of journalists waiting for a turn with my father, my mother spots me.

"Sweetheart," she calls out in that newly acquired stage voice. "Come, come," she says, waving me over as though she's Dame Judy Dench and the red carpet is the Old Vic on an opening night.

"Not tonight, Mom," I whisper as she tugs me toward her, but not before I wriggle free from her grasp.

"Oh, you're such a poor sport, Lola" she singsongs after me as I make my way over to my father.

"Congratulations, Papa," I say, giving him a quick kiss on the cheek.

"Thanks, Toots," he says, distracted by a sudden shift of attention from him to ten feet up ahead of him.

"Nic! Over here! Nic!" the photogs and journalists shout in a mad frenzy as the star of Papa's movie is lit up by the explosion of flashes going off all around him. Suddenly the scrum around my father evaporates and he's left without a single camera aimed at him. Even my mother's cameras are jockeying for a shot of Nic Knight, hidden from view by the throng shrouding him. "Nic! Over here! Nic!" the crowd continues to yell.

"How nice of him to finally show up," my father says. "Forty-five minutes late. I'm going inside. This is ridiculous."

"Wait, Paulie," one of the photogs says, grabbing my father by the arm. "Can we get a shot of you and Nic together?"

"Fine," my father says as Nic finally breaks free of the frantic swarm and is face-to-face with my father. Papa instantly turns seething red. Nic's in full drag, wearing a floor-length shimmery silver halter dress that looks like molten metal suspended from a thick crystal choker. His eyelids are painted a pale violet pastel, and his lips are in a matte red pout. His dark chocolate Lauren Bacall soft-waved wig is blowing in the slight night breeze. He actually looks—*pretty*. And so is that dress. If it weren't for all the cameras surrounding them, I'm certain my father would knock Nic out.

"That's enough. No more pictures," my father says, breaking away. Moments later my mother steps into his place to pose with Nic, pulling in her ex-flame Mick Jagger for a three-shot. My mother could stand here all night posing for the cameras, but I can't bear to watch her for even one more second. I head inside.

When the lights finally go down forty-five minutes later, my body is in the plush red velvet seat in the Palais but my mind is on Cricket. It isn't that *San Quentin Cartel* isn't brilliant; it's that I just can't stop worrying about whether Cricket is strong enough to withstand the waves of prurient publicity rolling her way. It isn't until somewhere in the middle of the movie when the projector cuts out suddenly and I hear my father yell, "What the fuck is going on?!" that I'm startled back into my body. All the lights in the theater come on, and a thin gentleman in a tux rushes to the front of the theater.

"Mesdames and Messieurs, please forgive this interruption. Our projector just broke but we are trying to get it fixed immediately," he says in a thick French accent. Oh dear. Poor Papa.

"How could this happen during *my* movie?" my father rants.

"I'm sure they'll get it fixed right away, darling." My mother tries to calm my father, placing her hand on his knee. "Are you still rolling?" she whispers to Alex, who's seated on her other side with a tiny video camera tucked in his palm. How on earth did she smuggle Alex's camera *inside* the theater? If she gets thrown in jail for pirating her own husband's movie, I'm not bailing her out. As my father gets increasingly upset, and the crowd becomes more restive with every second that passes without the projector being repaired, I watch as my mother's face fills with a twisted pleasure at the potential ratings windfall this could create.

I pull out my phone to check on Cricket and see the following text message.

JUST LANDED IN CANNES. MEET ME AT NIC'S AFTER-PARTY. ASSUME YOU'VE READ TABS. GRACE REQUIRES IMMEDIATE CONFIRMATION THAT THE SHOOT IS ON. COZ.

||

did you know that Cricket and Saffron are the most Googled people in the world right now?" Kate says over the phone line from her room at the Du Cap. "They have more hits than Nano eating that steak or that baby panda sneezing."

"I'm still not sure if my brain has fully computed the fact that Saffron Sykes is gay and our best friend is her lesbian lover." Even as I say the words, I'm not sure I really believe them.

"That's because Saffron *isn't* gay, and neither is Cricket," says Kate. "I spoke to Saffron. We're just going to put it out there that they lost themselves in the role, full stop. Anyway, Cricket's . . . just confused."

"But what about Saffron? Are you saying she isn't gay or are you saying you're just going to deny it?"

Kate's tone turns instantly steely. "We are talking about the biggest movie star in the world here," she says. "I've got her career to protect. That's my job. If Saffron were gay, do you know what that would do to her box office? She'd be DOA."

"Kate, that's ridiculous. No one cares about that kind of thing anymore. Look at Ellen DeGeneres. Portia de Rossi. Anne Heche. Wanda Sykes. Everybody *loves* them!"

"Lo, please give me the name of a single actress who's had any kind of decent movie career after coming out."

"Jodie Foster!" I announce triumphantly.

"Four words," Kate intones. "Mel Gibson. *The Beaver.* Case closed. Look, Lo, you know me. I don't care who's doing whom, I really don't. But I do care about keeping my clients at the top where they belong. And right now my job is to stop Saffron from sabotaging her career, and I'm going to do whatever I have to to make that happen."

"Kate," I begin, then pause. I'm not quite sure how to say what I want to say.

"What?" Kate demands.

"It's just that . . . I mean . . . maybe this is the right time for this to happen. I mean, I think it's awful—and I know you think it's awful— that directors wouldn't cast a leading lady because she's a lesbian. That's got to change. And isn't Saffron the perfect person to lead the way? The whole world loves her. It just isn't right that she can't be who she is and do what she wants and be accepted for it. Look at Ellen, she's the face of Cover Girl for crying out loud. Why shouldn't Saffron join her in paving the way."

Kate sighs. "Lo, you know I agree with you. And yes, I wish we lived in a less stupid world. I *hate* Don't Ask Don't Tell. I *hate* those assholes who don't let gay people marry. I *hate* that anybody gives a shit whether an actor's gay or straight. But I've talked with Saffron about it all, and she's just not ready to be any kind of poster child for the cause right now. I get where she's coming from. She gets the final say here. You're going to have to trust me on this one."

"Okay, okay, I hear you," I say. "I just feel queasy about the whole thing."

"You're not the only one," Kate says. "That's all I'm feeling at the moment." I hear the sound of furious tapping on computer keys. "Shit. You *have* to log on to usmagazine.com right now," she says. "They dredged up Cricket's prom picture. Did you know that she was the homecoming queen? You should see the crown."

"I've gone cold turkey off online gossip sites after yesterday," I say, staring at my closed laptop on the hotel desk. "Do you see anything on there about Aria? Actually, forget I asked. I don't want to know. Listen, Kate, Coz has already called me like fifty times this morning. I know this is the worst possible time, but have you talked to Saffron about the cover? Cricket said she'd do it, but I really need them together."

"Oh my god," Kate exclaims. "TMZ has an interview with some woman who claims to have kissed Cricket in the third grade and the guy who popped Cricket's cherry. Poor Cricket. This is crazy."

"Where do they find these people?" I say, stunned. "Wait, forget TMZ, are you even listening to me? This is *really* important. Julian and I *need* this cover."

"Gawker just posted that Saffron's high school boyfriend is saying that they never even had sex and Defamer interviewed Saffron's devout Catholic mother, who believes being gay is a sin and lobbied for Prop 8," Kate says.

"What?" I say, taken aback. "That's awful! Do you think she really said that?"

"Defamer isn't exactly *The New York Times,* but who knows? Saffron and her mother haven't spoken ever since she auctioned off Saffron's childhood diaries and her baby clothes on eBay."

"That's disgusting. So not-*WWJD*," I say.

"Well, lucky for Saffron's mommy there isn't anything in the Bible about eBay," Kate says.

"Kate, so about the *Vain* cover—"

"Jesus, where the hell is Adam? I'm getting more calls than the Pentagon. Hang on," Kate says.

I look down at my iPhone resting on the hotel desk, which has also been buzzing off the hook, all thanks to Coz. There's a new flurry of texts.

CALL ME!!

CALL ME!!

CALL ME!!

WHERE THE HELL ARE YOU??

911!!

I'M CALLING GRACE!

I shove my cell into the desk drawer. What's taking Kate so long? My neck is starting to cramp. I switch the hotel phone receiver from my left shoulder to my right.

"That was Anderson Cooper. He's in town and wants an interview," Kate says.

"What'd you say?" I ask.

"I told him when he comes out publicly, he can have an interview," Kate says.

"What'd you *really* say?" I ask.

"*That,*" Kate says. "And then I tried to pitch him a Nic Knight story."

"Did he go for it?" I ask.

"No. No one wants to talk about Nic without talking about his stints in jail, drinking and drugs, and if he'll ever be able to stay sober. I spent hours this morning with his publicist. We're putting out the story that

that white powder in his nose from the yacht party was a new naturopathic cold remedy. Not that I know what the hell it really was; Nic won't take any of my calls. God, I'm going to kill Adam. Where the hell is he? I put him on babysitting duty with Nic and he's *still* not back. This is a disaster," Kate says.

"So . . . um . . . about the *Vain* cover," I try again.

"Look, Lola, I'm sorry but I can't let Saffron pose with Cricket," Kate says. "I just can't."

"What? No! You *have* to. You can't do this to me!" I say in disbelief.

"Do this to *you*? This isn't *about* you, Lola. This is about protecting my biggest client and doing what's best for Saffron."

"Kate, you know how much I've got riding on this cover!"

"*Vain* will understand; they can't possibly expect that Cricket and Saffron would pose together now," Kate says matter-of-factly.

"They're already on the cover of every magazine, what's one more? And we're talking about *Vain,* not *Maxim.* I can tell Coz that she can't broach the gay thing. It will be strictly about the movie," I say. "Please, Kate. I really need this."

"I'm sorry, but this is *business,* Lola," Kate says, no trace of my BFF, speaking solely as Saffron's agent.

"Kate, you said you would make this happen for me," I say.

"That was *before,*" Kate says. "It would be PR suicide for them to pose together now when we're denying that they ever had any involvement."

"But what about the pictures?" I ask.

"What about them? It's called *Method* acting and we're going to say that they were rehearsing for the movie," Kate says.

"But they were taken *after* the movie ended," I point out. "Everyone knows that."

"Markus was on that trip, too; maybe they were reenacting a scene from the movie for fun. Who cares? The point is, we're saying that Saffron is in love with Markus and we're denying the gay thing. And posing with Cricket on the cover of *Vain* doesn't factor into that," Kate says. If she had a gavel I imagine she would bang it.

"I can't lose this cover, Kate. I just can't," I say desperately. "What if Saffron posed alone?" As I say the words I can't help feeling like I'm betraying Cricket. But this isn't going to be her last chance to grace *Vain*, though it may be mine. She'll understand, right?

"I'm just not sure how it helps us right now. It's not like Saffron needs the extra publicity," Kate says.

Think, Lola, think. And then another idea strikes me. "What if she posed with Markus? She's never publicly admitted that they're a couple. We could give *Vain* the exclusive."

"Now you're sounding more like me," Kate says. I don't know whether to be proud or scared. But what I do know is that I've worked too hard to let this cover slip through my fingertips.

"So should I call Coz and pitch her the story?" I ask.

I can practically hear the wheels in Kate's head turning through the phone.

"Yes, tell Coz she can have the exclusive with Markus and Saffron," Kate says finally.

I let out a long sigh and expect to feel more relieved than I actually do. Please let Coz go for it. Please.

"And Markus is on board?" I ask, trying to avert any potential problems.

"Please, Lola, wake up. Sure, Markus was a big action star before this, but now he's *Markron*."

I wince at the mash-up; it's no Brangelina or TomKat. But it's not like Saffkus or Smarffron would have been any better. So: Saffron and Markus on the cover of *Vain*. I know that this is what's best for me and Julian, but I can't help but wonder if this is what's best for everyone else. I push the thought and the sinking feeling in my gut away.

"Great. I'll call Coz now," I say. "Thanks, Kate. And listen, have you talked to Christopher?" I ask, even though I know from my brother that Kate still hasn't returned any of his calls. "I know that he really wants to talk to y—"

"That's my other line again. I've gotta run," she says quickly. And before I can even say good-bye, the dial tone does it for me.

"We're not the *Enquirer*, Lola, we're talking about *Vain*," Coz says after I pitch her the Markron cover. She uncrosses her mile-long translucent legs and peers at me over her trademark black sunglasses. We're sitting on the balcony of her oceanfront suite at the Martinez. The Med sparkles just beyond us, lined with yachts gently swaying on the water. I spot Paul Allen's superyacht, the *Octopus*, a twenty-four-hour-a-day party palace. The sound of the Microsoft mogul jamming with Bono wafts toward us. I look longingly at the bikini-clad women sunning themselves on the upper deck, their only care which cocktail to sip. How I'd love to trade places with one of them. Coz stands up on her chunky woven leather sandal stilettos and repoufs her purple-and-white printed super-short, tiered lampshade skirt. Class is about to be dismissed. "In its hundred-eighteen-year history, *Vain* has only had *three* men on the cover."

"Exactly," I say. "And we both know that Markus has every bit as much heat as Clooney and Gere. You put Beckham on because you wanted controversy, and controversy sells copies. Don't tell me a little controversy with Saffron and Markus won't sell. Besides, you were willing to put Om and Nano on the cover."

"Om and Nano are both style innovators and they're launching their own clothing line. Or at least they were. Who knows what's going to happen to that now. Anyway, it's totally different," Coz says, pacing around the balcony.

"It's not like I'm asking you to put Khloe Kardashian and Lamar Odom on the cover. Saffron is *the* biggest movie star in the world," I say. "Look, Coz, do you want to sell magazines or not? 'Cause I'm pretty certain we both know that a Saffron-Markus cover would sell out."

"What if they break up before the issue comes out?" Coz asks icily.

"They won't," I say emphatically.

"Just like Om and Nano?" Coz says. Thank god she's still wearing those sunglasses; otherwise I'm pretty certain her steely gaze would vaporize me with the flames of ten thousand suns. "Lola, we'd already sent out an announcement to our advertisers about the Om and Nano cover. We based our ad rates on that cover. Do you have any idea what an embarrassment that whole thing was for me and the magazine?" And me.

"I still feel horribly about that, but that was a totally freak thing that was out of all of our control," I say.

"And who's to say that another *freak thing* won't happen? We're talking about *actors,* Lola," Coz says. She's right. Which really pisses me off.

"Saffron and Markus are different," I insist-slash-fib.

"So she's not a lesbian?" Coz asks.

"Of course not," I lie. "She's totally in love with Markus," I lie again.

"I don't buy it," Coz says. Is it because I'm a bad liar or is Coz's intuition that good?

"Coz, they are *not* going to break up. Every magazine wants this story and I'm giving it to *you.* Call all of your editor friends and ask," I say. Last time I bluffed, Coz caught me out. But I think I've got a pretty good poker face and I'm just going to keep bluffing until I win this hand. What other choice do I have?

Coz finally stops pacing and stands directly above my head like the freaking Crypt Keeper, if the Crypt Keeper got his three-thousand-dollar hair extensions at Sally Hershberger.

"I want it in writing that they're not going to break up before the issue is on newsstands," Coz says.

"Fine," I say.

"And I want to shoot a solo of Saffron as an alternative."

"Okay," I agree.

"And Saffron's going to wear Chili on the cover," Coz says. Oh no. Oh no, she's not. She's wearing Julian. Period. Exclamation point.

I stand up to face Coz, who's still a good foot taller. Even when I'm on my tippy toes. Be diplomatic, I urge myself. Do not rip Coz's sunglasses off her face and scratch her eyes out with her Tom Fords. "Coz, the main reason for Saffron to do the cover is to promote *Four Weddings,* and considering that Chili's gowns didn't actually make it into the movie, it really doesn't make any sense as to why she would wear one of Chili's reject wedding gowns on the cover." Coz's nostrils flare. Maybe I shouldn't have used the word "reject."

"*R-e-a-l-l-y?* Is that so?" Coz says. "Well, here's why it makes sense: Because I said so."

"Coz, Saffron won't do the cover at all unless she wears Julian and I'm sure Grace wouldn't want to lose this cover because of Chili." Checkmate, Coz.

There's an eerie silence. The only sound I can hear is my thumping heart. I wonder if Coz can hear it too. *Say something,* I try and will her. *Say anything.* The silence is deafening. I feel like I'm back in an elementary-school staring contest, and damn if I'm going to blink first. I'll let my eyes shrivel up like Courtney Love's after a bender with Shaggy before I blink.

"We'll see about that," is all she says when she finally speaks.

"Oh-kay," I say, confused.

"Now if you'll excuse me, I've got to go check out the venue with Patrick, and you need to go get it for me in writing that Saffron and

Markus are not going to break up before the issue comes out," Coz says. Will ink be acceptable or only blood?

"Okay, so the shoot's still on," I say.

"I think it'd be really beautiful if we had some ostriches running around the lawn for the photos," Coz says.

So the shoot is on. "Great," I say in agreement.

"That's not why I'm telling you," she says flatly.

"Oh-kay," I say, starting to understand just how difficult she is going to make this.

"You need to find them," she states.

"Find ostriches?" I ask in dismay.

"Yes, Lola, find ostriches," she says. "And not just any ostriches. I want Masai ostriches."

"Excuse me, Coz, what makes you think I'm going to be your props master on this?"

"We only have a few days to pull this off. Naturally I have to spend every moment with Patrick. Or did you think I should simply allow Patrick Demarchelier to wander around La Croisette unescorted?" Coz doesn't wait for my reply. "I'll only have a skeleton crew as it is. If you want this to happen, you're going to have to help *make* it happen. Is this clear?"

"I'm on it," I say through gritted teeth. Do Masai ostriches even exist, or did she just make that up?

"Great," she says, though it's clear the subtext is: "I'm going to make your life a living hell and relish every single solitary moment of it." "I'd also like six dozen Bornean orchids," she says with a conniving Cheshire grin.

Yeah, I saw *Adaptation* too and I know those will be impossible to find, but I say, "No problem." Does she want a partridge in a pear tree too? Or maybe the freaking Ring? Or Cher's old lips?

"And the sand on the beaches here is too beige; I want pink sand. It has to coordinate with the ostriches's legs and the orchids or the shoot won't make any sense at all," she says. I'll give her this; she deserves an Oscar for keeping a straight face for that one. I want to hurl her over her balcony. But instead I'm going to focus on the fact that Julian's gown is going to be on the cover of *Vain*. And considering we're only on the second floor, propelling her over the balcony wouldn't harm her nearly enough. With her tarantula legs, Coz could practically touch the ground from here.

"Anything else?" I ask.

"I've really got to run. I'll e-mail you the rest," she says.

"Perfect," I say, with clenched fists. God, I hate this woman. I hate her even more than Bill O'Reilly, Ann Coulter, the inventor of MBT shoes, and the way my ass looks in boyfriend jeans all put together.

After doing a quick check-in with Julian to make sure that all of the fittings with the models are going okay, stopping by the concierge to check on the status of Aria's release—hopefully later this afternoon—and leaving Cricket a very long, rambling apology message, I decide to step outside for some fresh air and another latte. As I walk along La Croisette, it feels like no amount of air is enough to calm the snake I feel writhing in my stomach. I set the intention to start doing yoga again, to start sleeping, and to get off the coffee. I just can't believe that this is my life. How did this happen? I can feel that I'm hanging on by a thread—from a Julian Tennant dandelion yellow chiffon sheath. And it doesn't help that Lev *still* isn't here. I really miss him. When I see Julian's dress on the cover of *Vain,* it will all be worth it. Right?

I decide to set another intention right here, right now: no more private pity parties. As I resolve to stop feeling sorry for myself, I spot Adam, Kate's assistant, on the street.

"Adam, hey, where have you *been*? Kate's freaking out," I say when we come face-to-face.

"I've been up all night with Nic. I still haven't slept," Adam says. He looks like crap. His tux and shirt are completely rumpled and his bowtie is missing. He's wobbling slightly beneath the weight of several huge shopping bags.

"Adam, you were out shopping? You were supposed to be babysitting Nic! Where is he now?"

"Oh these," he says gesturing toward the bags. "These are for Nic. And don't worry, he's back at his hotel, out like a light. Tucked him in myself."

"You went shopping for Nic at Petit Bateau?" I say. What does a forty-something Method actor want with twee French $180 rompers and $80 hoodies?

"Nic's going to adopt a baby," Adam says casually.

"Nic Knight is adopting a *baby*?" I gasp. Who in their right mind would let him do *that*? I wouldn't even trust him to babysit Julian's dog—for five minutes. "Does Kate know about this?"

"Kate doesn't know yet and you can't tell her. Please, Lola, I'm begging you not to tell her. She asked me to handle Nic and that's what I'm doing," he says.

"By letting him adopt a baby?" I say in horror. "What happened on that yacht last night, Adam? Did Nic force you to take acid?"

"I'm not on acid, Lola. I'm totally sober. Nic hooked up with one of the Jolie-Pitt's nannies a few nights ago and it got him thinking. Angelina is practically a saint in the eyes of the world because she's adopted all those kids. No one even mentions that she's a husband stealer who used to wear a vial of Billy Bob's blood," Adam says. "Nic and I realized that if Nic adopted a baby, it would totally change the public's negative perception of him."

"Adam, this is insane. Please tell me that you realize that you sound even crazier than Nic," I say.

"If it worked for Angelina, then why can't it work for Nic?" Adam asks. It's all aboard the crazy train, but he's making it out like it's the most sensible decision in the world, like rotating your tires or doing Master Cleanse for New Year's.

"Because for starters no one is going to give Nic Knight a baby," I say.

"Nic and I are working on that," says Adam. "I'm not at liberty to discuss the details at the moment."

I just stare at him.

"Lola, this is my chance to finally prove myself to Kate," he says.

"Yeah, prove that you're totally crazy," I say.

"Okay, look, I know it may sound a little crazy, but unqualified people become parents every day, I mean look at those kids on *Glee,* and they let Madonna adopt a baby. Actually two. This story is totally going to transform Nic's image. Plus, we totally plan on donating all the money from the sale of the first picture to charity."

"Nic doesn't even have a baby and you're already selling the photos? Are you absolutely sure that Nic didn't slip you something? You can't be serious. Have you lost all of your morals?" I ask.

"Who said I had any to begin with? Morals are overrated. Kate taught me that."

"Adam, you know I have to tell Kate, right? I can't keep this from her."

"You can't do that. Lola, please. I'm begging you. I've already leaked the story to the tabloids, and there's a bidding war for the exclusive story and first pic of Michelle. I've already got *People* magazine up to three *million.*"

"*Michelle?* You don't even have the baby but you've already named it? And did you say *three million?*" I spit out.

"Yes. Nic wanted to name her for the first lady. And all of that money is going to go to charity. Please, Lola, don't tell Kate. She's already got enough to worry about with Saffron and everything else going on. Please," Adam says, practically on his hands and knees.

"I don't know, Adam. She'd kill me if she found out that I knew and didn't tell her. Besides, you and I both know that if the *People* magazine bid is legit, it's going to be up on TMZ in about two nanoseconds, and then *everyone's* going to know. I *have* to tell her," I say. "I'm sorry. If you really want to help Nic and his career, why don't you try keeping him *sober,* because the only way the press is going to stop writing stories about him falling *off* the wagon is if he actually stays *on* the wagon."

"Lola, you have to trust me. I know what I'm doing," Adam pleads.

"Adam, the only thing you should be doing right now is taking those baby clothes back."

"Just don't tell Kate, okay. She'll go ballistic and the doctor said she has to try and keep her blood pressure down or she could risk losing the baby," he says.

"What baby, Adam?" I ask, utterly confused.

"Oops," Adam says.

"What baby?" I repeat again, still confounded.

"I don't know," Adam says flustered. "I thought you knew. I shouldn't have said anything."

"Thought I knew what?" I ask.

"You should talk to Kate," Adam says.

"Adam, *what baby*?" I yell.

"Kate's," he finally spits out.

"*Kate's?!*" I repeat.

"Yes," he says, looking at the floor. "I thought you knew. I shouldn't have said anything. Kate's going to kill me. I—"

I know that Adam is still speaking, but I can't hear a word he's actually saying. This can't be happening. There is no way that this is happening.

"Kate's . . ." I can't even say the word. It doesn't make any sense.

"*Pregnant,*" Adam finally finishes my sentence.

12

"I'm surprised you even found my room," Kate says, opening her hotel room door for me. "I've dreamed of staying at the Du Cap my entire career, and now that I'm finally here they put me in the fucking *annex* next to Matt Damon's personal trainer's assistant."

I didn't even know that the Du Cap had an annex—a.k.a. the Du *Crap*—until I read Brett Ratner's flame of the place in *Variety* after New Line had the temerity to exile him there. This is where you go, bags in hand (no bellhops for The Annexed) after your comeback movie fails to beat *Saw XVIII* at the box office. After you're Exhibit A on www.awful-plasticsurgery.com. After you lose roles to Lindsay Lohan.

"At least the view is nice," I joke as I gaze out of the one small window at a dying shrub. The room is so Jeffrey Katzenberg–minute that you can basically touch all four walls at once from the doll-size bed. Kanye West's *hot tub* is bigger. I sit down next to Kate on the Pepto pink floral bedspread, the only place to sit other than the floor.

"Do you know anyone who has a room here who's leaving early?" Kate asks. "Bryan's assistant told me that CAA has an extra room but then he called me back to tell me that Justin Bieber's mother decided she wanted to stay longer. Think of who you know. I want to pull a Ratner."

During the festival, Hotel Du Caps's rooms are in such high demand that you have to pay, in advance, for all twelve nights—even if you only stay for two. And the hotel can re-rent your old room to someone new who also has to pay, up front, for all twelve nights—even if they're only staying two. But there's a get-out-of-jail-free card for the big cheeses who paid in full. Since practically no one stays for all twelve nights, they can send a letter to the front desk and give their permission for someone else to stay in their room after they check out. After serving purgatory in the Annex, Brett wrangled *four* such letters and sucked up valuable real estate with *four* primo rooms—an artful dodge that caused the hotel to try to ban him for life.

"I'll ask Mom and Papa if they know anyone. But why don't you just stay with Cricket?" I ask.

Kate wrinkles her nose in disdain. "No way. The paparazzi are *insane*. I'd rather stay *here* than have to listen to Cricket talk about her *feelings* and Saffron twenty-four/seven. And now TMZ is saying that her mother's trying to get Joel Osteen to come to Cannes to counsel Saffron."

"Where do they even come up with these stories?" I say.

"That's not even the craziest one," says Kate. "Nikki Finke posted—"

"No more," I cut Kate off. "Please. Real life is crazy enough right now. . . . Speaking of which . . ." I take a deep breath. "Can we please talk about what we're not talking about, which is the only thing worth talking about? When were you going to tell me about the baby?" I ask softly.

Kate exhales as if she's been punched. "I can't believe Adam told you. Damn it! I really *should* fire him, he's completely useless," Kate says, looking down at her buzzing BlackBerry, then gasping in distaste. She starts dialing furiously. I wonder if they make BlackBerries for babies. Adam picks up after one ring.

"Hi Ka—"

"Adam, what are these pics of Nic in a *gown*?!"

"They're—" Adam tries to answer.

"You're supposed to be making sure that Nic wears a *suit* tonight." For yet another party celebrating my father's movie. Diddy, who produced the movie's theme song featuring Ke$ha, is hosting the fete on his yacht.

"I know, but—" Adam attempts to interject.

"The reporter from *The New York Times* is going to be there, and Paulie Santisi will serve both our heads on a silver platter if Nic pulls another stunt like at the premiere and shows up in a dress again."

"Ka—," Adam tries again.

"He *cannot* wear another goddamn dress. This is Cannes, not the freaking *Crying Game*."

"Ka—," Adam stammers.

"Adam, if you do not get Nic to wear the Zegna suit they made especially for him tonight, you're fired! Do you understand me?"

"I'm not wearing a goddamn monkey suit," Nic's voice booms out of Kate's speakerphone in his thick, fake Colombian accent he's still insisting on using until the movie is out in theaters. "And if anyone is getting fired, it's you, Kate, for not supporting my artistic process or my main man, Adam."

"Nic?!" Kate says, the color draining from her face.

"I've been trying to tell you that you've been on speaker," Adam pipes in meekly.

If looks could kill, Adam would be a goner.

"Look, Nic," Kate says, putting on her best kindergarten teacher voice. "I believed in you when no one else did and I've always supported your process, but it's not in your or the film's best interest to show up in drag again. It's important for you to try and separate yourself from your character and let the movie stand on its own."

"The character is a part of me, Kate, and I can't release him until after I'm finished promoting the film," Nic says. Is this guy for real?

"And I want the audience to see your character, too, Nic," says Kate. "But if you keep swanning around in gowns and pissing off Paulie Santisi—the only director who would work with you while you were in rehab—that's all anybody's gonna write about. *Not* your incredible come-back performance. *Not* whether you deserve the Prix d'Interpretation. Just you and Paulie bitch-slapping each other. And then it's back down to the minors you go. And then if you're lucky—*lucky*—it's *Sober House with Doctor Drew* for you."

The silence on the speakerphone is so thick it's almost a physical presence. Then Kate lays down the coup de grace.

"And Nic? Kathryn Bigelow is doing a sequel to *The Hurt Locker,* and there's a great part in the script for you. She's going to be at the party to-night and she's not going to be able to envision you as part of an elite bomb squad if you're dressed as a woman."

There's another long pause.

"Is it for the lead?" Nic asks, taking Kate's bait.

"Of course," Kate says.

"I should have had Jeremy Renner's part. I would have been great in that role," Nic says.

"You could be great in the sequel, but you're not going to get the part if you wear another gown tonight, okay?"

"Okay," Nic finally acquiesces. Man, is Kate good. "But I'm not happy about it. I really love the gown I was going to wear."

"You can wear it another night, just as long as it's not tonight," Kate says. "And drop the accent. I want everyone to see Nic, the actor who can do any role. I don't want you to limit yourself."

"Fine. Adam and I have to go mentally and emotionally prepare for being in men's clothing," Nic says. I wonder what exactly *that* entails.

"I'll pick you up at eight p.m.," Kate says, clicking off her Black-Berry.

"How do you do it?" I ask Kate.

"Despite what a complete and utter prick the guy is, he's just so talented and I actually really believe in him—and all the money I hope to one day make from him. And that was nothing. That was Nic in a *good* mood," Kate says, reaching for a carton of saltines on the bedside table. "Is this nausea ever going to end, because the only thing that seems to help is *bread,* and the last time I ate a carb was 2002." I look down at her stomach. It still looks as flat as ever underneath her gray-and-white abstract floral tank dress. "You know if any of the agents from the other agencies find out that I'm pregnant, they're going to see it as a weakness and start calling all of my clients," she says.

"That's absurd. Who would do that?" I ask, horrified.

"Me. How do you think I signed Kellan Lutz?"

"You're sick, you know that, right?" I say.

"No, I'm just a damn good agent," Kate says.

I take a deep breath. "So . . . have you told Christopher yet?"

Kate pops another saltine into her mouth and ignores my question. Finally she manages, "How did you know?"

"Oh, please. I saw you two sneak into the bathroom the night of my engagement party. I was hoping it meant you were getting back together."

"Well, we're not."

"But you still could," I say. "Especially now that you're pregnant."

"Lola, this isn't some Sandra Bullock romantic comedy where we're going to end up together, okay? We tried and failed. Period," she says.

"Have you told him about the baby yet?" I ask again.

"No. And I don't plan on it."

"Kate, you have to tell him," I say.

"What's the point?" Kate asks. "I'm not keeping it and he's with Gigi now."

"He doesn't love Gigi, he loves *you*," I say.

"Just promise me that you're not going to tell Christopher."

"There is no possible way that I'm not going to tell him if you don't tell him first. You know you can't ask me to choose between you."

"Fine, okay, I'll tell him," she says, although I don't really believe her.

"Listen, Kate, I really can't imagine what you're going through right now, but whatever happens between you and Christopher, I just want you to know that I'm here for you," I say, hugging her. And she actually lets me.

"Thanks, Lo," she says. "Can you believe I'm fucking *pregnant*," she says, and for half of a nanosecond I swear the Great Wall of Kate crumbles. "I . . . I better go. I don't trust Adam or Nic. I'll see you tonight, right?" And just like that the wall is back up.

"Yeah, see you tonight," I say, standing up to leave. "Good luck with Nic."

In the taxi on the way back to my hotel, I can't help but hold out hope that Kate and Christopher's story will have a different ending than the version in my brother's film: Justin Cooper meets a smart, carefree, funny, sexy photographer at the Joshua Tree and Petunia Holt is left with only her clients and a—vibrator. Which is at least better than the version he was thisclose to going with: Justin ends up with the aforementioned photog and on her way to a signing meeting with Jessica Alba, Petunia gets into a near fatal car crash from BlackBerry-ing while driving.

I try and push Kate and my brother out of my mind. With Julian's show just days away and the *Vain* shoot hanging on by a teeny tiny thread, I have to focus on work. I pull out my cell. There's a voice mail from Coz. When she starts talking about wanting to dye the wedding gowns a "pale, pale, pale Tiffany blue" because she's feeling like "there's too much white," I click off my cell. Her list of demands for this shoot so far is even crazier than Lady Gaga's backstage rider. And now she wants Julian to dye the gowns?! They're *wedding* dresses. They have to be *white.* Don't they? That woman is going to give me a heart attack. Thank god that Lev is coming tomorrow so if I do have a heart attack at least he'll be able to resuscitate me. That is, if he can still remember how to actually *be* a doctor as opposed to just playing one on TV. Still, I can't wait for him to get here. No more video chat or Skype. Lev is going to be here in the flesh. My stomach flips at just the thought.

When I walk into my hotel room my stomach flips again. And not in a good way. I expect to find Julian frantically fitting Amazonian stunners for the show and little Chili Lu hunched over his sewing machine while Barbra Streisand's "The Way We Were" bellows out of Julian's iPod. Instead, Julian and Chili are seated in silence in front of Chili's laptop lying open on the brass coffee table in the center of our small living room, and there's not a single gangly model in sight.

"What's going on? And where are all the models?" I ask.

"O-M-F-G, Lola," Chili screeches, practically jumping out of his red vintage Air Jordans. "O-M-F-G!"

"Julian, I need a Chili to English translation please," I say.

"Just watch," Julian says, pointing to the laptop and pressing play on a YouTube video.

Shaky handheld footage of the inside of an airplane cabin fills the screen. The camera pans around what looks like first class, judging by the plush, spacious seats, and lands on a female passenger eating a hot fudge sundae. As the camera zooms in on the woman's face my stomach drops. Even without a stitch of makeup and her signature red boyish crop held back by a gray headband, I recognize that otherworldly Sophia Loren-meets-David Bowie face that's graced every magazine cover in the world and I know what's coming next. I force myself to keep watching as Aria Fraser polishes off her sundae. Suddenly she realizes that's she's being filmed.

"Are you fucking filming me right now?" she says in a high-pitched Valley Girlesque shriek, all six feet of her climbing out of her seat in black leggings and an oversized tee, her empty sundae dish falling to the floor. "Stop fucking filming me!"

"Turn it off, Julian. I can't watch anymore. I know how it ends," I say.

"Keep watching," Julian insists.

"Give me that fucking iPhone," Aria demands.

"I'm sorry, I'm sorry, I'll delete the footage if you want, I'm just such a big fan of yours," a young girl's voice says nervously off camera, which is now filming the floor.

"Give me that phone," Aria persists, the cell still shooting the floor.

"Ms. Fraser, you need to return to your seat," a flight attendant says.

"This little twat has been filming me," Aria hollers.

"Ms. Fraser, please calm down and return to your seat," the flight attendant says, the camera catching a corner of her fried peroxide platinum ponytail. "Plea—"

The footage cuts out and when it starts up again it's a blur of images:

the floor, part of the stewardess's sun-strewn face, the back of someone's head, a section of someone's bright yellow Goyard carry-on, the cabin ceiling.

"Give me that phone," Aria screams, the camera zooming in on her plump lips.

"Ms. Fraser, please calm down," a second, male flight attendant is saying.

"I want that fucking ph—" Aria is yelling when the camera cuts out again. And then the moment I knew was coming happens and it's as though Michael Bay shot it himself. Aria lunges at the young girl and her flailing fist connects with her face.

I stare at the screen in horror. It's even worse than I thought. I look at the video's title: "Aria Fraser Smacks a Girl Down." There are 700,050 views, and the video has only been up for a few hours. I peruse the comments.

HAS-BEEN!

SHE LOOKS LIKE A MESSED-UP DRAG QUEEN!

SHE NEEDS TO BE IN A MENTAL INSTITUTE.

IF SHE'S SUCH A DIVA, WHY DOESN'T SHE HAVE A PRIVATE PLANE?

HMMM . . . GUESS SHE'S A BROKE DIVA.

SHE NEEDS TO RETIRE FOR REAL AND GO AWAY!!

SHE IS GETTING FAT!

SOMEONE NEEDS TO SMACK THAT BITCH!

"O-M-F-G, right?" Chili says, and I suddenly understand his need for abbreviations as there are no words for what I just watched.

"I seriously hate the Internet," I finally spit out, slamming Chili's laptop shut.

"What are we going to do, Lola?" Julian says.

"Where are all the models? Aren't you supposed to be having your final fittings with all of them right now?" I ask.

"They're all probably still out partying, it *is* only noon," Julian says.

"Completely unacceptable. I'm going to call the agency," I say.

"Lola, stop trying to ignore the supermodel in the room. How can we let Aria walk in the show after seeing *that*," Julian says, pointing to the closed laptop, his voice tinged with panic.

"Julian, do you have any idea how much work it's taken on my part to even get Aria out of jail in time for your show? I now know the numbers of the American and French consulates by heart," I say. "She's walking in the show."

"But there's a new Facebook page already: People for the Ethical Treatment of People by Aria Fraser."

"They already have thirty thousand fans," Chili chimes in.

"Seriously?" I ask.

"F.R.," Chili says.

"Huh?" I say.

"For reals," Julian translates.

"That's ridiculous. George from *W* magazine told me they want to put her on the cover in a 'Free Aria' T-shirt, so not everyone is against her," I say. "And that little girl was totally filming her without her consent."

"She punched her in the face," Julian says. "She needed *stitches*."

"I know, I know. It's horrific," I say, trying to erase the grimy footage from my mind. "So she has an anger management problem. So what? Naomi's had one for years, and people toss blood diamonds at her. You can't believe the number of calls I've been getting about wanting to come to the show just to see Aria post prison."

"Really?" Julian asks, perking up.

"F.R.," I say. "Now I'm going to go call the agency. Fingers crossed that none of the other models are in jail."

"What size shoe are you, Mademoiselle?" asks a chiseled French man dressed in head-to-toe white. He looks like he belongs on the cover of *L'Homme Vogue* or a Tom Ford campaign as he holds out his tanned hand to help me climb aboard the steps to Diddy's gargantuan gold-hued yacht. I wonder if the Titanic was *this* big? "Monsieur Diddy requires everyone to wear proper deck shoes."

"These *are* my deck shoes," I say, pointing to my beloved emerald suede strappy sky-high stilettos that I've paired with my Julian Tennant long-sleeved sequin camouflage micro minidress. "Look, I even had rubber soles put on."

"I'm sorry, Mademoiselle, but Monsieur Diddy does not allow anything that has touched the ground to touch the hand-carved Tibetan teak decks. Would you mind wearing a pair of these instead?" he asks, gesturing toward rows upon rows of next season's neon-colored monogrammed Vuitton leather-and-rubber flip-flops. I think I saw those on Sea of Shoes. No wonder Jane said they're impossible to find. Did Diddy buy *every* pair ever made?

I look down at my gorgeous suede numbers and then over to the Louis flip-flops.

"Please take good care of these," I say, handing off my stilettos and slipping into the Vuittons. Ooooh, these feel nice. Would it be weird to ask if I get to keep them?

"I'm not taking my shoes off." I spin around to find Nic Knight on what appears to be the brink of a major tantrum. "Can't you see that my shoes make my entire outfit?" he says, without any trace of his fake Colombian accent, his voice escalating with each word.

"I wouldn't want to part with those either," Julian whispers in my ear, moving in for a closer look at Nic's size fourteen custom-made orange, turquoise, and black tribal-beaded five-inch Manolos.

"Me neither, but at least he's wearing a *suit*," I say of Nic's tailored-to-perfection tan linen suit that will look even better with the Louis flip-flops and not those ridiculous Manolos.

"Do you even know who I am? This party is for *me*! Adam! Kate!" Nic screams.

"Quick, Julian, let's get out of here," I say.

"Heidsieck, Mademoiselle?" a waitress asks once we make our way onto the sacred teak decks and into the party.

"I'm sorry, what?" I ask.

"Heidsieck champagne, Mademoiselle," the waitress says. "Bottled in 1907. Salvaged from a shipwreck off the coast of Finland. They rescued only two hundred bottles." She leans in. "It's two hundred seventy-five thousand dollars a bottle!"

"No, merci," I say.

"Oui, merci," Julian says, plucking a flute from the waitress's tray. "There's Rihanna. Go invite her to the show," Julian says, nudging me with his elbow toward the barefoot Barbadian beauty bedecked in a Balmain nautical sequin number and standing next to our host, resplendent in a spotless white dinner jacket. I watch as she playfully tries on his diamond pinky ring. It's so big Evan Lysacek could skate on it.

"I already did and she can't come. Her publicist told me she just signed a huge contract with Dior so she's totally exclusive to them," I reply.

"What about Anna Paquin?" Julian asks, surveying the sea of guests.

"She's flying out tomorrow morning," I say of the actress lounging on one of the white tufted sofas with a chinchilla throw strewn across it. "She was only in town for two days to promote the *True Blood* movie."

"Did you invite Julianne Moore?" Julian asks of the flawless screen siren in a beaded platinum sheath deep in conversation with my father, who's puffing away on his contraband cigar underneath his straw fedora.

"She's on the jury, and there's a screening during your show."

"Should I just throw myself overboard now?" Julian asks, his shoulders slumped in his seersucker suit. "Is *anyone* coming?"

"So far it's mostly industry folks, but those are the ones we really need," I say. "And the latest winner of *Croatia's Next Top Model* confirmed today, and Rachel Zoe said she was going to try and come. I'm still trying to convince Baz to stay in Cannes a few days longer so that he can attend."

"Is that supposed to make me feel better, because it doesn't," Julian says.

"Look, Julian, you're the one who told me that you don't need gimmicks to promote your line. Well, you don't need celebrities either," I say.

"You're only saying that because we don't have *any*," Julian says. "We should have had the show here. *Everyone* is here. Your mother would have made an amazing publicist."

"I'm doing the best I can, Julian, and I still have calls out to a ton of publicists," I say. "Don't panic. Aria is bringing in a lot of the magazines and photographers, and they're the ones that really matter."

"Is your mother at least confirmed?" Julian asks as we watch Mom maneuvering through the crowd of megawatts like she's freaking MObama in a breathtaking cream Grecian draped-column gown with hand-beaded black lace down the left side. Her WWW cameras are never more than a few inches from her expertly madeup face.

"Her and her cameras will be there," I lie because I don't have the heart to tell Julian the truth. I can't even believe it myself. My own *mother* is considering missing Julian's show because George Clooney is auctioning off a kiss to raise money for Pakistan at the same time as the show. Mom is desperate to be the highest bidder, because she believes kissing Clooney in front of her cameras will be the ultimate *Wristwatch Wives* coup d'état.

My mother sandwiches herself between Madonna and God—and I don't mean her Majesty's erstwhile boy toy Jesus. I mean the great, white, ponytailed, fingerless gloved one himself: Karl Lagerfeld. The ex-Imelda Marcos of fans is a vision in purple.

"Ohmygod," Julian shrieks breathlessly. "I didn't know that Karl was going to be here. Do I look okay? Do you think I should have worn my black linen suit instead?"

"No, I love the seersucker," I say.

"Let's go say hi," Julian says. "Do you think he'll remember us from when we interned for him? What if he doesn't? Maybe your mom can get him to come to the show."

"Whoa, Julian, calm down," I say as we watch Madge, Mom, and Karl playing musical necklaces with Karl's multiple strands of Chanel crucifixes. Too bad Chanel doesn't make Jewish stars. Not that I've seen Mom ever again wear the gold Star of David she claimed to never take off at that crazy staged Shabbat dinner. As I watch my mother puffing out her chest like a show poodle for her cameras I know she's thinking that there's no way any of the other Wristwatch Wives will top this moment. But I can't help but wonder if Madonna is actually going to sign the release form for the show.

I feel a tap on my shoulder. "Lola, hi. I've been looking everywhere for you. I'm so glad I finally found you." A woman in a sculpted nude bustier dress with an electric-lime-green ribbon belt smiles at me.

"Cricket?!" I gasp. "I almost didn't recognize you."

"That's the point," she says, giggling.

"Hey Cricket," Julian says, hugging her. "You look like Uma Thurman in *Pulp Fiction* with that black bobbed wig."

"That's exactly who I was channeling. What do you think?" Cricket asks, shaking her raven wig.

"Stunning," Julian says.

"Very femme fatale," I say. How she really looks: like she's fading away under the pressure of all of this. Like she could use a cheeseburger. And her already pale skin has a hint of purple to it.

"I have a red wig I'm going to try out next," she says.

"That's so Amy Adams of you," I say. "What's with all the disguises?"

"I'm trying to escape the paparazzi," Cricket says. "I had to hide in a laundry cart just to get out of my room. I figured once I made it on board, I'd be home free—and I don't want to miss my very first yacht party!"

"I heard Jennifer Aniston has to be driven out of her house in the trunk of her car," Julian says.

"I've spent my entire life fantasizing about what it would be like to be famous like Jennifer Aniston, but I never imagined it would be like *this*," Cricket says, freeing her signature blond hair from beneath the shackles of that black bob now that she's clear of the photographers' prying lenses.

"It could be a lot worse than *this,* Cricket," Julian jokes, throwing open his arms and gesturing around the party that Diddy told my mother is one of his most lavish fetes ever, even more over-the-top than his annual White Party in East Hampton. The man knows how to throw a party that would make even Colin Cowie weep. We're not just talking vats of caviar, all-you-can-eat lobster, filet mignon, and truffle risotto and champagne that costs more than double my yearly salary. We're talking Diddy-imported Thai masseuses and Chinese reflexologists, since lifting all that champagne to your lips can be so taxing.

"Besides, as soon as another Jonas brother loses his virginity or the next season of *The Jersey Shore,* everyone's going to forget about this whole Saffron scandal anyway," I say.

"Do you think they're going to forget about me too?" Cricket asks, a little wistfully. What must it feel like to get everything you thought you ever wanted and to realize it wasn't remotely what you thought it would be—and that it could vanish in a second?

"Of course not," I say. "Are you excited about the *Four Weddings* premiere tomorrow night?" I ask.

"Kate isn't letting me do any interviews. Only photos," she says.

"Then it's a good thing you have a fabulous gown picked out," Julian says.

"Thanks to you, Julian," she says.

"And Lola," Julian says.

"I can always count on you two to make me feel better," she says, pulling us in for a group hug.

"Who'd you come here with?" I ask.

"Markus. Tom Cruise loaned him one of the masks that he wore in one of the *Mission* movies that he sometimes wears when he wants to go out without being hounded by the paparazzi," Cricket says. "Markus is the nondescript, average Joe-looking guy blending in by the bar."

"That's so creepy," I say, wondering if I've ever been face-to-face with a masked Tom Cruise and not known it. The mask looks so real. "Is Saffron here too?" I ask, looking around the party for a possibly masked Saffron.

"No, she's back at the hotel, but Markus needed a break from it all too. He's been so great. He really understands what I'm going through," Cricket says. "Listen, I'll catch up with you guys later, okay? I'm gonna go remind Markus he can take off that mask now."

"Yeah, good idea. It's a little weird," I say, and give her a quick peck on the cheek before she disappears into the crowd.

I wind my way through the jam-packed party in search of Kate. Suddenly I feel the boat swaying, which is strange considering it's docked. Oh god, is it going to sink?

"Excuse me, sir, do you know why the boat is swaying?" I ask a passing waiter with a tray full of Beluga.

"Monsieur Diddy has chartered the *Christina O* for the after-party, and we're going to meet the yacht in the middle of the Med," he says.

"We are?"

"Don't worry, Mademoiselle, Monsieur Diddy has also arranged speed boats to meet us at the *Christina O* so you can leave whenever you want," the waiter says, somehow sensing my rising sense of dread that I'm going to be stuck on this thing all night long. I wonder if anyone would notice if I slipped into one of the cabins and took a quick nap. I'm sure they're even nicer than my room at the Martinez.

I pop a blini into my mouth and continue looking for Kate.

Ke$ha's and Diddy's "White Powder," the theme song to my father's movie, blares in Surround Sound through the speakers. It's so clear that it feels like Ke$ha is actually here. It isn't until I hear, "Nic, get your ass up here and sing with me and Diddy," that I realize that Ke$ha is in fact on the boat, in the flesh. I swerve through the crowd to get a better view.

It looks like Picasso painted her face there's so much makeup on it. Over half of her face is covered in silver sparkly glitter. As she grips the microphone with her chipped black polished hands I notice the giant pavé diamond-letter rings on every finger, thumbs included, that spell, "White Powdr." She writhes around Diddy in shredded black lace stockings and a sheer white lace bodysuit with a skimpy black lace bra and panties underneath.

"Diddy, thanks, man, for throwing this amazing party," Nic slurs slightly as he jumps up onstage and hugs Diddy. Is Nic loaded? Again? "Ke$ha, you're so f-ing sexy that I want to marry you," he says, grabbing her wavy untamed blond mane and pulling her in for a kiss. Did he just slip her some tongue? Eeeew. I can't tell if Ke$ha is turned on or horrified when she finally breaks free from Nic, who reels back and stumbles.

I hold my breath, hoping he doesn't tumble to the floor. Thankfully he regains his balance. "Paulie, where are you, man?" Nic asks, looking out into the crowd.

"He's right here, Nic darling," my mother shouts. "Alex," she hisses to her cameraman. "Make sure you get this." A spotlight throws her and my father into its blinding glare. She's grinning so widely I'm certain she'll be phoning Dr. Novack for an Aquamid booster shot as soon as she's stateside. My father's lips, on the other hand, are in a grim straight line. He looks pissed off.

"Paulie, I just want to say," Nic says, his Colombian accent back in full effect. "Shit. My agent over there told me to lose the accent so I'm going to try, but this part is so much a part of me that it's really hard," Nic says with a strange half-American, half-Colombian accent. "Paulie, I just want to thank you for taking a chance on me and making such a great fucking movie. I love you, Paulie Santisi," Nic shouts into the microphone. "I'd like to raise my glass to you," Nic says. "Shit, I don't have a drink, can someone get me a glass of something, nonalcoholic of course," Nic says, though it's obvious he's already had a glass—or five—of something he's not supposed to. "I'd like to raise my glass to you, Paulie," Nic says raising the drink someone's just handed him. "To our maestro. Salud," he wails as everyone at the party cheers furiously. Everyone except my father.

"To Paulie," Diddy says, clinking glasses with Nic and trying to usher him off stage. Unsuccessfully.

"You know, Paulie," Nic continues, wriggling out of Diddy's grasp. This is turning into a bad, weird drunken best man wedding speech. "I had this amazing gown that I was going to wear tonight. This frothy gold tulle thing with a spray of orchids made out of feathers. And I was going to sing a mash-up of Johnny Cash's 'San Quentin,' and the Beastie Boys 'Fight for Your Right.' And I wanted these Robert Palmer 'Simply

Irresistible' like chicks to back me up in mini-short versions of orange prison jumpsuits but somehow I let my agent convince me not to go through with it. But you all want to hear it, don't you?" he slurs, waiting for the crowd to respond. "Don't you?"

"Yeah, Nic," someone shouts.

"Go for it, man," someone else shouts as the crowd starts to egg Nic on.

"Nic, let's let Ke$ha finish out her set and then maybe you can sing later," Diddy says, trying again to get Nic off the stage.

"Let's all sing together," Nic says. "Come on, San Quentin, you've cut me and burned me," Nic starts to sing a cappella. "But you got to fight, for your right—"

"To paarty," Ke$ha joins in.

"To paarty," Nic wails, jumping up and down.

My father storms away despite my mother's efforts to stop him.

I spot Kate in the distance practically hanging off the side of the boat.

"Are you okay?" I say, rushing up to her side. She looks chartreuse.

"How did this happen?" she says. "I gave Adam *one goddam job* while I was in the bathroom puking: Do NOT let Nic near the champagne, tequila, or vodka. Looks like he's hit on all three. We'll be lucky if Diddy doesn't make us swim to shore. I don't even know where to start damage control on this one. Jesus, I'm gonna be sick again."

She promptly pukes over the side of the boat.

I grab her hair and rub her back.

"Please tell me that Javier Bardem didn't just see that," she says, sheepishly wiping her mouth.

"I think you're in the clear," I lie because I'm not sure how he could have missed it.

I follow Kate's gaze across the floor where I spot Gigi clinging to

Christopher like a handbag. "Oh no, I can't handle this right now," Kate says. "Do I have vomit on my face?"

"No, you're good," I say. "Are you going to be okay?"

"I'm not sure," she says, her voice on the verge of cracking as she watches my brother and Gigi deep in a lip-lock. I look back at Kate, but it's as though she's left the party. I recognize that leaving-your-body look, although it's not one I've ever seen on my best friend before. My heart sinks. I feel like I may hurl off the side of the boat too.

"Now do you get why I'm not going to tell him, Lo?" she asks. Before I can answer, she pivots away. "I've gotta get out of here," she says, but suddenly my father is blocking her escape route.

"How could you let this happen?" my father yells.

"I'm so sorry, Paulie," Kate says.

"Papa, it's not her fault," I insist. "She got him to wear a suit but you know Nic, he's totally unmanageable."

"Stay out of this, Lola," my father shouts.

"Paulie, I've been looking everywhere for you!" Nic says, charging up to my father. "Did you love it? I *killed* up there, right? I think we should do a *San Quentin Cartel* musical. I've got a lot of ideas I want to discuss with you. What'd you think?"

"A musical?! Are you out of your fucking mind? This isn't *The Sound of Music,* Nic. Francis didn't make a fucking musical of *The Godfather.* You're making a mockery of my film," my father bellows.

"Didn't you hear everyone cheering, Paulie?" Nic says. "They *loved* me." He runs up to the side of the boat and hangs off of the railing, shouting, "I'm the king of the world."

"You're a fucking lunatic," my father shouts.

"Nic, get down," Kate insists. "I'm sorry, Paulie, I'll handle Nic."

"It's clear you're not capable, Kate," my father says. "Anyone could have played that part, Nic. You'd be nothing without me."

"Papa, let's go," I say when I realize that all of the guests are starting to stare. And then I notice something even worse: my mother and her camera crew. Oh god. Oh no.

"Get those fucking cameras out of my face, Blanca," my father shouts, batting away my mother's camera crew with the fury of a scorned Sean Penn.

"Mom! Stop filming," I yell. As I stare into her azure eyes it's like she's forgotten that this is our *life*. All she can see is the potential ratings bonanza. "Mom, stop. Please."

"Paulie Santisi, I hate every inch of you. You've cut me and you've scarred me thru an' thru," Nic starts singing at the top of his lungs.

"Nic, stop!" Kate shouts.

My father doesn't say a word. He lets his fist speak for him. I watch in horror as it connects with Nic's face. As Nic reels back, I jump in front of my father.

"Stop!" I scream, trying to restrain him.

"Let go of me!" my father hollers. "You're finished in Hollywood," he yells at Nic. "Do you hear me? *Finished!* Someone stop this fucking boat! I want to get off right now!" That makes two of us.

And before I know it, suddenly Nic is charging my father and the fact that I'm standing between them doesn't seem to faze Nic. And then everything goes black.

13

"Ow," I mumble as I struggle awake, trying to focus my eyes. It feels like there's a vise grip around my head. I look around the small, white room, trying to get my bearings. This isn't my room at the Martinez. Where am I? As I lift my arm to wipe the sleep from my eyes, I feel a tug. Why is there an IV in my arm? Why am I wearing a hospital gown? What happened to me?

"Hello?" I call out, feeling a *wow* of pain as I try to sit upright. "Hello?" I call out again. "Bonjour?"

I look for a call button on my bed but don't see one. What I do notice are lots of flowers. There must be over a dozen bouquets crammed into my tiny room. Where did they all come from? Are those white carnations?

Uh-oh. This must be serious. Don't they send white flowers when some-one dies? What happened to me?

As I gaze at a tall vase of Casablanca lilies, suddenly Nic Knight charging me like a bull in Pamplona flashes in my mind. It plays on a loop over and over and over. I try and wipe the image away but it won't stop playing. "Hello," I croak. Ow, my head really hurts.

"Bonjour, Mademoiselle," a bony, gray-haired nurse says, coming into my room. She has a kind face.

"Do you speak English?" I ask.

"*Un petit peu*," she says, pinching her index finger and thumb together.

"Why am I here? What happened to me?"

"*Excusez-moi*, Mademoiselle?"

"What happened to me?" I repeat, trying to channel Marion Cotillard's perfect accent.

"Mademoiselle, you have un commotion."

"A what?" That sounds serious. "What's a commotion? I mean, um, uh, *quel est un commotion?*"

"*Comment je dire en English?*" she asks.

"A concussion," Kate says, suddenly appearing from behind the hospital curtain. "I can't believe I fell asleep in that," she says, looking in confusion at the tiny hospital chair that was her makeshift bed for the night. "I've never been so exhausted in my life," she says, one hand unconsciously resting on her belly, hair disheveled and last night's makeup smeared beneath her eyes, a rare sight given Kate's usual airbrushed state. I wonder who looks worse: me or Kate. "Nic Knight gave you a freaking concussion," she says furiously as she plunks herself down on the end of my hospital bed and places a protective hand on my knee.

"No wonder my head hurts so much," I say, trying to sit up. "I don't have time for a concussion. Do you know when I can leave?" I ask the nurse. "I've got to get back to my hotel. I need my laptop. I have so much work to do.

Julian's show is in two days and I have to check on the RSVPs and all the fittings and the seating chart and I still need to get Aria out of jail. I need to leave. Please," I beg. The nurse just blinks at this gush of words.

"You're not going anywhere," Julian says, walking into the hospital room with two foam cups of coffee. He hands one to Kate. I wonder if they can add some to my IV. "Thank god you're awake. We've all been so worried about you, Princess," he says. He sits down on the edge of the bed opposite Kate and grabs my hand.

"Julian, you need to get me out of here," I say. "Kate, please," I plead.

"Lola, you took a really hard blow to your head. You're not going anywhere until the doctors say you can leave," Kate says.

"Julian, Aria's supposed to be getting out of jail today. I have to go and make sure that she actually does, and then you need to have a fitting with her. The show is in *two* days. I need to leave *now*," I say, trying to climb out of bed before another wince of pain assaults me. "Ow, my head."

"Lie back down," Julian instructs, gently pushing me back on the pillow. "The doctor told us that you need to rest. Chili and I already spoke with the concierge and they've talked to the precinct and taken care of all the arrangements. They're going to let us know the second that Aria is back at the hotel. You just rest."

"But—" I protest.

"No buts, Lola," Kate says. "I know how much you want to go to the *Four Weddings* premiere tonight, so we spoke with your doctors. They said *maybe,* but only if you stay here for observation for a few more hours. So please, just rest."

"Chili and I will handle everything today," Julian adds.

"Julian, I don't trust Chili to handle anything. I need to do it myself. I've worked too hard to let things fall apart because of a stupid concussion. Please," I beg.

"No," Julian says.

"At least bring me my laptop," I plead.

"Fine. But you can only have it for an hour and then I'm confiscating it. I know you don't trust Chili and neither do I, but you can trust me and I promise that I will hold down the fort today. Lola, you need to rest," Julian says.

"What happened? Did Nic Knight really—" I try to piece together the surreal, fragmented events of last night.

"Honey, it was like an episode of *The Cannes Shore*. You're lucky that you're alive. You totally saved your father's life, you know," Julian says.

"I did?" I say.

"Nic was totally bombed off his ass," Kate says, shaking her head in frustration. "He and your dad were yelling at each other and then your dad hit Nic in the face with a right hook. I thought he was down for the count, but then he jumped up like freaking Rocky and started coming after your dad."

"That's when you stepped right in front of him and Nic ended up clocking *you* on the head by mistake. You went down like a shot. We all thought you were dead," Julian says.

"Oh my god, is Papa okay?" I ask.

"He's fine, a little scraped up and totally pissed off, but otherwise fine, thanks to you," Kate says. "Your parents have been here all night. Your dad just left because he had to go back to the hotel for an interview that he tried to get out of but couldn't, and we forced your mom to go with him."

"Papa tried to cancel an interview?" I ask in disbelief.

"You totally took the hit for him, Lo," Kate says. "He's been worried sick. We all have," she adds, grabbing my hand and squeezing it.

"Do you want to see the video?" Julian asks.

"Video?" I mutter.

"Yeah, someone caught the whole thing on video and leaked it to TMZ," Julian says.

"Jesus, Julian." Of course there's video. Will anyone ever have another private moment again?

"You have even more views than Aria going Naomi Campbell on that girl on the plane and almost as many as Nano eating a steak," Julian says.

I flop back down in bed. I can't help but wonder if that someone is my mother and her WWW's camera crew. No, she'd never leak that footage—not when she could save it for Sweeps Week.

"So how did I end up here?" I ask.

"It was so scary. Thank goodness Diddy keeps a doctor on his staff. He totally stabilized you until the paramedics got there and transported you here," Julian says.

"And all of this is on TMZ?" I ask.

Julian just nods his head yes. I'm totally humiliated. As Banksy says, "In the future, everyone will be anonymous for fifteen minutes." I can't wait for mine.

"Did you come in the ambulance with me?" I ask.

"They would only let your mother ride with you, so Diddy's driver brought me, your dad, Christopher, Cricket, and Kate here," Julian says.

"Christopher and Cricket were here too?" I ask.

"Yes, but once you were stable, the nurses kicked them out. Technically you're only supposed to have one visitor," Julian says.

"Please tell me that Mom didn't let her cameras film the ambulance ride," I say.

"I'm not sure," Julian says, a trifle uneasily.

Oh god. "What if she filmed it for her show?" I yelp.

"She wouldn't do that, would she?" Julian says.

"Julian we're talking about my *mother*."

"She's furious it's all over the Web," Kate says.

"Yeah, she's probably furious because it didn't break on her show," I say. "What happened to Nic? Are all these flowers from him?" I ask.

"I think he'd send you every flower from the Tuileries if he could," Kate says. "He refused to break character and now look where he is: in the slammer. He should feel right at home there," she adds sarcastically.

"Nic's in *jail*?" I say.

"Yep," Kate says. "Same jail as Aria. Your father tried to go after him after he took you down, but Diddy stopped him and Diddy's bodyguards grabbed Nic. Then your dad called the police. I tried to convince him not to press charges, but he did, and of course TMZ has all the footage of Nic getting carted off to jail."

"My father's right. Nic's a lunatic. I don't know how you represent him, Kate," I say.

"Well, he committed career suicide last night, that's for sure," she says. "He probably sabotaged any chance he had at any acting awards. I'm sure the judges weren't too thrilled when this hit the news this morning."

"Does that mean it'll kill Papa's chances for the Palme d'Or too? He's going to kill Nic. Oh no. He's going to kill you too, Kate! Julian, where's my cell? I need to call my father," I say.

"You need to rest. Seriously, Lola," Julian says.

"Give me my cell!" I say. "Kate, he's going to kill you!"

"Lo, please, don't worry about me right now. I'm fine. We managed here all night together. I'm a big girl. Besides, Nic's safely behind bars. And you need to relax now," Kate says matter-of-factly.

"What about my laptop? You promised I could have it," I say to Julian. "Where's my laptop?"

"I'll call Chili and have him bring it over, but you really need some quiet now. I promise I'll handle everything with Aria today and I already told Chili to start calling about the RSVPs," Julian says.

"I already told you that I don't trust him," I say.

"Enough, Lola. If you don't get cleared by the doctors, no premiere tonight and I really, really need you for the show, so will you *please* just take it easy? I promise you that I will have Chili bring over your laptop and I'll go check with the doctors now about when you can get out of here," Julian says.

"Fine, okay, fine. Thank you, Julian," I say.

"Now please relax," Kate says. "We'll come check on you in a couple of hours."

"Okay, don't forget to have Chili bring my laptop," I say.

"Rest," they say in unison as they walk out of the door.

"Leave me alone, I've got to *resht*!" wails Aria, as she trails an arm languidly from the Doyer hydrotherapy bathtub in the Spa Givenchy. Her face is slathered with some thick gold-white cream. "They treated me like an animal in that jail. I'm filthy . . . and exhausted. I need to *relax*!"

"Please, Aria," I say. "We're two hours late for the fitting!" I wince as the esthetician flips a switch and 180 jets start churning the water furiously around Aria's very, very naked body. Her famously long, olive legs and arms are spilling over the side of the tub and the hair she changes as often as most people change their underwear is now a cropped bleached blond. Maybe one of the other inmates was a hair stylist? Without a speck of makeup on, her pouty lips are a perfect shade of rose and her infamous Bowie eyes—one dark green and one hazel brown—are stunning.

"Mademoiselle," the esthetician says to me sternly, "I am telling you for the last time, you must go! You do not have an appointment here!"

I wish I did. My head is throbbing. There's nothing I'd like more than to be one of the lucky ladies enjoying the Slimming Massage or No Surgetic facials on the *tres* exclusive seventh "Prestige" floor of the Hotel Martinez. I can hear the tinkling of Hawaiian music, muffled behind closed doors, as some lucky starlet avails herself of the Lomi Lomi massage. If I had a spare 160 euros, I'd treat myself to the "Exclusively Givenchy" spa treatment—two hours of utter, hydrating bliss—but after making Aria's bail, I can't even afford a copy of *Le Monde* to find out what the Obamas are up to. Maybe I could just lie down for five minutes on the gleaming cream granite floor glowing softly beneath the oh-so-flattering lights. Just five minutes. I'm so tired. But I've got a job to do. I didn't browbeat those doctors to release me from the hospital only to fail now.

"Aria, we've got to go—this instant!" I tell the supermodel, who simply closes her startlingly mysterious eyes and sinks deeper into the bubbles.

"*C'est imposible.* Mademoiselle cannot leave now," the esthetician tells me. "Now I must remove the gold and calf placenta. It is ze most important part of the treatment."

"The . . . what?" I ask in dismay.

"It'sh the Golden Calf treatment," says Aria. God, is she slurring? Has Aria been drinking? "I absolutely require it if you wan' me to walk your little show. Don' worry, darling, I charged it to your suite."

"H-how much is it?" I ask.

"It is only three hundred euros," says the esthetician. "With gold at a thousand euros an ounce, it is a steal!"

"But we can't af—" I start to say, then stop. Why bother? When will this end? This is the woman who wants the models to wear her hideous vegan shoes on Julian's runway, and she's smearing *calf placenta* on her face? "Aria, enough. I paid your bail. Now I need you at the fitting. Right now!"

"Fine, fine," Aria mutters, rising out of her bubbles like a tipsy Venus on the half-shell. I look away while the esthetician finishes wiping her face clean and wraps her in a plush, pristine, white robe. "I'll do it for Chili. I simply *adore* his designs!"

Is she kidding me! "Aria, you're walking for Julian. *Julian Tennant.* Remember, you did his graduation show? At Central Saint Martins?"

"Yesh, right, right," she says, swishing away this pesky detail with a flick of her slender hand. "I simply *adore* him too."

Ten minutes later I've deposited her on the sofa of our suite and drag Julian into the bedroom. "Julian, I wish I could stay and babysit, but I've got to get to the premiere. I'll be back as soon as I can. Make sure you've got Chili for backup. And don't let Aria out of your sight and do *not* let her order anything else to drink!"

"Darling, we need some champagne—now!" Aria trills from the living room.

Above the faint coos of turtledoves, the gentle whoosh of Kleenex being pulled out of Bottega clutches, and the whir of cameras flashing, is the sound of Sting himself singing "Every Breath You Take." His ivory embroidered tunic seems to glow as he stands flanked by a thousand flickering candles and a twelve-piece orchestra. I tuck a rogue lock of blond hair behind my ear and smooth out the skirt of my little ombré fringe Julian Tennant number. I just can't believe this is really happening. I've waited so long for this moment. And to think I almost missed it.

There's a stirring at the back of the cathedral. The guests in white dinner jackets and designer gowns spin on their white chairs trimmed with alabaster satin bows, craning for a closer look. There are audible gasps as all eyes fall upon Saffron Sykes resplendent in a Julian Tennant antique Valenciennes rose point lace wedding gown. It's even more magnificent than the gorgeous gown Grace Kelly wore on her wedding day. Saffron seems to float up the aisle strewn with white rose petals. She looks out from beneath a tulle veil that's covered with appliquéd lace lovebirds and thousands of seed pearls. Saffron pauses when she reaches the front row of chairs to hand off her bouquet—a simple yet elegant spray of calla lilies and white roses wrapped in antique silk ribbon—to her maid of honor: my BAF, Cricket.

Every woman who's been forced to wear a hideous peach bridesmaid pouf (me at Posh and Becks's wedding, in a rare Vera Wang face plant) is currently salivating at the sight of Cricket, who is rivaling Saffron's radiance in a flowing, blue-gray georgette Julian Tennant gown. Her blond hair is twisted in a chignon and her flawless pale skin is practically luminous. Her eyes glisten with tears as she watches Saffron stride toward Markus Livingston, where he waits for her beneath the chuppah in his own JT creation—a yarmulke appliquéd with lovebirds and ivy.

Saffron lifts her veil and there's another audible gasp. Those startling Aegean blue eyes. A modest blush staining those sky-high cheekbones. Those perfect pillowy lips that even Angelina would kill for. But it's not just that she's breathtaking; it's that mystery behind her eyes, the depth there, the intrigue. Saffron's face tells stories that the world wants to lose itself in.

How I wish that Julian were by my side now like he was supposed to be instead of back at the Martinez with Aria, to see how this internationally beloved superstar bride has made his wedding gown seem even more sensational. Tears well in my eyes despite the fact that I promised myself I wouldn't cry. I feel like such a sap as I dab at my eyes with a tissue, wishing I had worn waterproof mascara.

The sound of clacking beside me breaks me out of my Saffron reverie. I glance over to my left to Kate in a black tuxedo jumpsuit with a plunging neckline, chestnut hair slicked back in a low ponytail, red painted lips pursed, unabashedly *typing* on her BlackBerry. I throw her an "Are you for real?" look, but she doesn't even have the decency to look repentant.

"Are you seriously crying?" Kate whispers, rolling her blue eyes at me.

"It's just . . ." I sniffle. "The gown looks so good."

I sink into my red velvet seat and dab my eyes again as I think back on everything it took to get Saffron into that gown. Then I turn my attention back to the big screen. Markus Livingston's groom lovingly strokes the radiant cheek of Saffron Sykes's bride. Other than totally thrilled to see that our gowns are absolutely spectacular up there in mega-pixel splendor, and that my BAF has finally *become* the next Cameron Diaz instead of parking her Prius, I'm feeling like a complete cliché. How can I watch this movie wedding and *not* picture myself and Lev under that same chuppah?

The sound of a soft snore to my right distracts me from mooning like a twelve-year-old. I peer to my right at a reporter who's fallen fast asleep atop her notebook. This is probably her third or fourth screening of the day, not to mention umpteen press conferences and the requisite dinner party or two, but dead asleep? No, no, no, no. Not during *this* movie. I give the slumbering reporter a not-so-gentle nudge.

Write about the wedding gown, I will her as she struggles awake and poises her pen over her pad. *Check out the workmanship on that bridesmaid's dress! That's Tennant. T-E-N-N-A-N-T.*

The reporter scrawls something on her pad. *Please let it be something about the gowns. Please! Or at the very least how wonderful Cricket is as Saffron's wisecracking sidekick.* I crane my neck to see what she's written. *Pick up script. Dry cleaning. Drinks at Hotel du Cap.* Oh god. Oh no. Screw telepathic communication. "Isn't that gown amazing?" I burble at her. "I heard it's a Julian Tennant. You know, that designer everyone's talking about. Aren't you going to write about the—"

"Shhhh!" Someone behind me cuts off my desperate plea.

What I want to say: "*Please.* You have *no idea* how important this movie is to my career. Could you please just write a little something about the world's most talented but still unknown designer? Please?" Instead I bite my tongue so hard the metallic taste of blood fills my mouth as I murmur an apology. I look around the massive theater at all of the reporters frantically scrawling notes and pray that at least one of them is writing about Julian's divine wedding gown. My attention is snapped back to the screen. "Is there anyone here who has a reason why this marriage should not go forward?" the rabbi asks as he surveys the guests from behind Saffron and Markus. "If so, speak now, or forever hold your peace."

Cricket suddenly steps forward. "I object!"

Markus looks at her, shocked, then smiles slowly, broadly.

The audience starts buzzing frantically at the sudden plot twist. And so does my cell phone. It's a text from Julian: "Disaster. Call immediately!"

What now?! The word "disaster" reverberates over and over and over in my head.

"I've got to go," I whisper to Kate, whose focus is still trained on her BlackBerry. She doesn't even bother to look up as I stumble over approximately ten reporters who give me the hairy eyeball despite the fact that their own BlackBerrys are casting the theater in an eerie Day-Glo white. "Write about the wedding gown. Please write about the wedding gown," I beg each reporter in turn in a final, desperate whisper as I make my way over them. But my words seem to fall on deaf ears and scowling mouths.

I rush up the aisle, throw open the theater lobby doors, and make my way outside and onto the top of the red-carpeted steps of the Palais des Festivals.

Movie posters are splattered everywhere, and so are the yachts as they bob gently on the French Riviera just beyond. I take in a huge gulp of the sultry Mediterranean air and dial Julian's cell.

"Julian, what's happening?" I bark as soon as he picks up. "Is everything okay with Aria?"

"That damn Chili sent the LVMH yacht to the wrong place, and they're not going to hold the slip for us much longer." I can picture Julian raking long fingers with chewed nails through his glossy black hair. "Apparently Paul Allen's superyacht screwed Geffen and Ellison's super-superyacht, and they need to find room for the little baby yacht, because Harvey Weinstein has suddenly decided to have yet another party. Which means we've got a huge show in two days and nowhere to hold it. Not that it matters; no one's coming anyway."

"Yes, they are, Julian, of course they are," I say, in an attempt to talk both Julian and myself off the cliff. That damn Chili. How is it humanly possible for one assistant to screw up as much as he does?

"Julian, everything is going to be fine, I promise." I say it emphatically because I don't really mean it.

"You always say that," Julian mutters.

"And we always are. We're always fine," I say in yet another attempt to convince myself as much as Julian.

I contemplate hurling myself down the Palais steps, but decide against it. The last thing I want is another concussion. Or another video of me all over TMZ.

"Julian," I say, forcing myself not to hyperventilate. "I'll deal with the yacht. Is there anything else? You just made me miss Cricket's big scene where her character gets to profess her love for Saffron's character."

"Anything *else*?" Julian shrieks. "Lola, we might have no venue."

"I think I know who can help us with the yacht. We're going to make this work, don't worry," I say soothingly. "I just had a great idea. I'm going to hang up now—I've got a phone call to make."

"Thanks, Lola," Julian says. "You really *are* amazing."

"Just get back to work and I'll see you soon. Movie's getting out, I gotta go."

I slip my cell back into my purse and hear a commotion behind me as the doors of the theater burst open.

I'm met with a tsunami of indecipherable French phrases and the crème de la crème of Cannes on the Palais steps, all flanked by international reporters with notepads and digital recorders. As I take in the scene I can't help but wonder: Is there anyone even left *in* Hollywood? I turn around and am just about to abandon my last shred of dignity and ask (read beg, plead, bribe) Charlize Theron to come to Julian's show when I'm accosted by two 20′×20′ billboards that are surrounded by the other Cannes movie posters splattered along the Palais steps: FORGET YOU, PETUNIA HOLT and YOU WERE NEVER *THAT* GOOD IN BED, PETUNIA HOLT. I shudder at the sight of them. I'd like to blame it on the ocean air, but it's a spectacular May night on the French Riviera and 70 degrees at 9:00 P.M. It's those damn movie posters of Christopher's that send a chill down my spine. They're *everywhere*.

Cricket, Saffron, and Markus appear at the top of the steps and are swiftly engulfed by reporters and paparazzi.

"Is it true?" one of the reporters begs as the lights of the paps' cameras blare on Saffron's face. Cricket is blinking rapidly next to her in the sudden glare.

"Saffron Sykes, are you really *gay*?" a reporter asks.

"Are you in love with your costar Cricket Curtis?" another reporter demands. "Is your relationship with Markus just a beard? Have all of your relationships with men been a cover? What about Clooney? Was that a front? Is Clooney gay? Have you been lying to your fans? How long have you known you're gay?"

The questions are rapid-fire. I'm surprised not to see gun wounds. Or blood. The only explosion is the blinding lights and my friend caught in the middle of it all.

"Cricket, can we get a shot of you kissing Saffron?" another reporter wants to know as Cricket stands there frozen in front of the blinding glare.

"Cricket, over here!"

"No, over here!"

"Cricket!"

"Cricket!"

"Cricket!"

Jesus. You'd think she was Angelina Jolie. This is nuts.

I attempt to make my way through the throng surrounding Cricket, Saffron, and Markus, but it's no use. I get an elbow to the ribs for my trouble from the mosh pit of yelling reporters and paparazzi I'm now stuck in. These people are piranhas. I've got to get out of here. Someone's going to get hurt. And I don't want it to be me. I've already had one concussion on this trip.

As I struggle to break free, the reporters and paparazzi continue to swarm my BAF.

"Cricket, are you gay?"

"Are you a lesbian?"

"Are you in love with Saffron?"

"Cricket, over here!"

"Cricket!"

"Cricket!"

"Cricket!"

My BAF just stands there like a deer in headlights. Someone needs to save her before she gets run over. How can anyone live like this? She's not ready for it.

Meanwhile Saffron and Markus, who are used to the paparazzi's glare, seem to thrive in its blinding light. It's like they have on magic shields that prevent the reporters' invasive and inappropriate questions from penetrating their souls. The reporters keep the barrage of questions coming as Markus and Saffron stand there smiling for the photogs, arms wrapped around each other, acting every bit the golden couple they're pretending to be. But when I look closely, really look, I can see beneath that smile plastered on Saffron's face that she's looking like the wax replica of herself in the Museum on Hollywood Boulevard.

"Markus, over here!"

"Saffron, over here!"

"Markus, what did you think of watching your girlfriend kiss Cricket Curtis?"

"Saffron, what was it like kissing a girl?"

"Saffron, are you gay? Have you ever been with Ellen DeGeneres? Have you spoken to Ellen?"

"Saffron, over here!"

"Saffron, can we get a shot of you kissing Markus?"

"Saffron, Cricket, Markus, how about a shot all together?"

I finally tear myself free as Cricket, Markus, and Saffron are whisked away by bodyguards to an awaiting limo. And just like that, it seems they've made their escape. For now. But I can't help wonder if Cricket's life will ever be the same again. Will my BAF ever be able to go the grocery store again without being hounded by the paps? Is this really what she wants?

Kate materializes from amid the scrum and threads her arm through mine. "Let's go. You can ride with me," she says.

"Sorry, I can't. I have to go back to the hotel and try and clean up our latest disasters," I tell her.

"You have to come. Cricket really needs our support. Did you hear what those asshole reporters were yelling at her? She needs us," Kate says.

"I'm sorry, I really can't. I've got to work. Will you give Cricket my love and explain why I couldn't be there?"

"Fine." Kate jerks a thumb toward the *Petunia Holt* billboards. "Those posters are every fifteen fucking feet. I still can't believe Christopher did that to me. I can't believe you let your *own brother* do that to me!"

"Oh, Kate, I'm so sorry. You *have* to believe me. I just didn't know. He didn't do it to hurt you. He still loves you. Have you told him about the baby yet?"

"Lola, when are you going to realize that he's with Gigi and he loves *her*?" Kate snaps. "I've got to go. The whole thing makes me sick to my stomach. I need to puke before I get on yet another boat. See you later."

I'm about to resume Mission Charlize when I get a text from Saffron: LOLA, HELP! IT'S ALL A BIG LIE. I'M SORRY I CAN'T GO THROUGH WITH THE *VAIN* SHOOT.

No. No. No no no no no no. I cannot lose this.

I'm about to tap out a reply when a hand clasps my shoulder and spins me around. It's Papa, in a volcanic fury.

"Where's Kate?" he hisses, his voice quaking.

"You just missed her," I say. "She just left."

"I heard she posted bail for that fucker. How could she do that? How could she do that to *us*? I'm gonna—Blanca, dammit, turn those goddam things off!"

I don't know what's worse, my father yelling or my mother by his side with her camera crew. It's like a hall of mirrors—the camera crew shooting me, shooting my father, shooting us. Are we in Cannes or Versailles?

Suddenly the paps, drawn like moths to the bank of lights behind Mom's crew, come streaming toward us. They've lost their big celeb quarry, but sniff blood in the water with Papa's screaming fit.

"Mom, please, turn those things off! Can't you see what's happening?"

But she's too busy adjusting her tissue-fine silvery pink lamé couture Chanel and fluffing her blond hair to pay attention.

"Mom, stop!" I shout.

"Oh, Lola, what's the big deal?" she says.

And that's when I realize my mother's officially become Madonna. It's like Warren Beatty said in *Truth or Dare*: "She doesn't want to live off-camera." Is it any coincidence that Warren dated Mom *and* the Material Girl?

As the paps descend, my phone buzzes yet again. Oh thank god, it's a text from Lev. His plane must have just landed in nearby Nice. In just a few hours he'll be in my hotel room. I close my eyes and picture putting all the cares of Cannes—Julian's show, the *Vain* shoot, Nic Knight and my concussion, Saffron's meltdown, Papa's tantrum—on hold while I dissolve in his arms. Lev. I want Lev. Lev will make it all better. I'm practically on the verge of tears as I open the text.

STUCK IN L.A. DISASTER IN ER. HOPE TO FLY OUT SOON. SO SORRY. LOVE YOU LOTS. LEV.

Breathe. Breathe. Do. Not. Cry. I bet DVF and Donna Karan don't collapse at the sight of a few glitches. I can handle this. I am the CEO of Julian Tennant Inc., and I'm not here for romance anyway. I'm here to make my company work, dammit! *Focus, Lola, focus!*

My phone buzzes again. Dammit! It's all I can do to force myself to look at the screen: Julian *again*. Turning my back on the boil of paps engulfing Mom and Papa, I press the phone to my ear. "What is it now, Julian?"

Julian's voice is so high and pinched I'm amazed that it hasn't summoned every poodle within a ten-mile radius. "Why is Coz on the phone telling me that they're pulling the *Vain* cover? Why? *Why?* Lola, *you've got to fix this!*"

I rush inside the lobby of the Martinez and beeline for the elevator when something stops me dead in my tracks: Nic Knight standing on top of one of the marble and wrought-iron coffee tables. The image of him charging toward me like a bull in Pamplona immediately flashes in my mind. I push the image away and try to steady myself on my stilettos.

"Take it off!" a raucous, drunk man shouts at Nic. He's one in a small crowd that's gathered around Nic.

"Come on!" a young blond Victoria's Secret model type in a barely there hot-pink slinky number squeals, springing up and down on her five-inch strappy sandals.

"Show us what you've got!" someone else hollers.

"For fuck's sake, take it off already," a woman screams. I know that voice. I crane my neck and stand on my tippy toes but it's no use, I can't see her face. There are too many people blocking my view. "Come on!" That voice. I know that voice. Oh my god, it's Aria!

The small crowd cheers wildly as Nic slowly strips off his light blue shirt, taunting them button by button. At least he's wearing men's clothing, I can't help but think. Once his sweat-drenched shirt is off, he swings it around and around in the air like he's at freaking Chippendale's and then flings it into the air, where it lands on Blake Lively.

Gross. Nic's so caught up gyrating his pelvic bone in front of his hooting friends that he hasn't bothered to see where his shirt landed or even notice me at all. He seems so blitzed I'm not sure he's aware of anything at all.

"Your turn, baby," Nic says, pulling Aria, barely clad in a super-short lace ruffled skirt and little camisole, up onto the coffee table with him. Oh god. Oh no.

"To freedom," Aria bellows, holding up a magnum of champagne. Where did she get that? And how did she get out of our suite?

"To freedom!" Nic echoes as Aria takes a long swig from the bottle and then opens up Nic's mouth and pours some bubbly down his throat. Doesn't she know he's supposed to be *sober*? What the hell is going on? I have to do something.

I shove my way through to them.

"I'm sorry to break up this little get-out-of-jail party, but what the hell is going on?" I ask once I'm standing in front of them.

"Lola, holy shit, are you okay? I'm really sorry about last night," Nic blubbers. "But I can't believe your dad had me thrown in fucking jail. That was totally uncool."

I look at him standing up there on that coffee table in the middle of the Martinez in the middle of the night, a sweaty, drunken mess. I want to feel sorry for him, he looks so pathetic, but then I remember last night and the hell he's put Kate and my father through despite everything they've done to help him. And you know what? He doesn't deserve their help anymore. Or my pity. For the first time in forever, I actually agree with my father. I feel my cheeks flush.

"What's uncool, Nic, is your behavior. What the hell are you doing? Last night should have been a wake-up call. I spent the night in the *hospital* because of you. I have a *concussion*. You need help. You need to go back to rehab—or jail," I say.

"No way, man, I've got it all under control," Nic says.

"Shtop being such a party pooper, Lola," Aria says. "Here, have a shwig," she says, shoving the magnum in my face. "To freedom!"

"No thanks—and it seems like you've had enough already," I say, trying to take the bottle from her.

"Give that back," Aria says, grabbing the bottle from my hands and taking a hefty swig.

"Aria, Julian's show is in two days and you just got out of jail. Don't you think you should be resting and keeping a low profile? The last thing you need is another incident," I say. I wonder how many cell phone photos have already been snapped tonight.

"Lola, I've been locked up like a caged animal, I need to spread my wings and fly. We're just having a little harmless fun!" Aria says. "Woohoo," she wails, taking another swig. "To freedom," she squeals, taking off her top—and bottom—to reveal the teeniest tiniest pink lace bra and matching thong. This cannot be happening. This is a nightmare.

"Okay, that's enough," I say, forcibly prying the bottle from her grasp. I pour out the remaining champagne on the marble floor.

She jumps down off the coffee table and onto the floor where she proceeds to lie down and roll in the puddle, pausing to lap some up with her tongue. I try and pick her up, but she's so slippery that she manages to kick me away.

"Champagne Slip-n-Slide!" Nic screams in approval. He grabs another bottle of champagne out of someone's hand and pours it all over the floor next to Aria. What the hell is he doing? What? No, no, no, no, no, no. What have I done?

Nic stands behind Aria and gives her a hearty push. I watch in abject horror as Aria shimmies across the lobby in a pool of champagne in her bra and panties.

"Ahh!!" Aria's scream is piercing as she nose-dives straight into a marble wall.

The room starts spinning and I try to steady myself. Do not pass out. Do not pass out, I urge myself as a pool of blood starts to puddle around Aria.

When Aria finally lifts her head, it's immediately clear from the gush of blood and her already purpling eyes that our star model has just broken her nose.

14

my ringing cell phone startles me awake, and for a suspended moment I've forgotten everything: that Lev's not here,
that Aria's nose is broken—it's a miracle that no footage has appeared yet
on YouTube—that we have no venue for the show, that Saffron has called
off the *Vain* shoot, and that I'm probably going to lose my job.

"Hello," I say, jolted back into my bleak reality as I sit up in bed.

"Have you ever seen a *Vain* cover with no one on it?" demands a
frosty female voice I don't recognize.

"Huh?" I say, confused.

"Have you ever seen a *Vain* cover with no one on it?" The British accent has taken on an even more arctic tinge. I'm surprised my ear doesn't
have instantaneous frostbite.

"Um, uh, no," I mutter.

"Neither have I and I don't plan on it," the voice pronounces. And then it hits me. Oh god. Oh no. It's Grace Frost *herself*. Holy editor-in-chief.

"Ms. Frost," I choke out, "I—"

"What's going on with the Saffron Sykes and Markus Livingston cover? Are they in or are they out?"

My voice catches in my throat. Fear courses through my veins.

"Hello?" Grace Frost says in a tone so cutting that I'm not certain I'll ever be able to hear the word again without shuddering. "You do understand that we have a contract, correct? And the advertisers took ad space based on Saffron Sykes and Markus Livingston being on the cover. And what this will mean to Julian Tennant Inc., and most especially your career if Saffron Sykes and Markus Livingston aren't on the cover as planned."

"I understand."

"Do you?" she asks as though I'm mentally handicapped.

Cricket's old mantra to me, *Act As If,* surges through my mind. *Act As If* everything is fine. *Act As If* I will figure out a way to get Saffron and Markus back on that cover. *Act As If* I'm not utterly and completely screwed.

"I don't know what Coz said to you, but everything is fine, and we realize what a tremendous honor it is to be on the cover of *Vain* and how valuable it is to our company. I apologize that you even had to make this call," I say, hoping that I can somehow will it to be true.

"Good. Marc Jacobs is holding on the other line, I have to go," she says, and the line goes dead just as the cell is about to slip through my hands from the slick of flop sweat.

I stare at my cell in my glistening palm. The career that I've worked so hard for, the career that I so dearly love, is hanging in the balance, and I don't know how to save it. But I'm going to try. I've got to figure out a way to convince Saffron that she has to do the *Vain* cover, but first I have to find a new venue for our show tomorrow. I furiously start dialing.

"I think we land it here," Sergei Crimini says to the pilot as he points down to the flight deck of the aircraft carrier he's converted into a floating mansion for the duration of Cannes. From the caramel calfskin seats of Crimini's custom McDonnell Douglas helicopter high above the Mediterranean, his vessel looks like a whale among the guppies floating at the old port next to the Palais des Festivals. It makes David Geffen's mega yacht look like a dinghy.

"Sergei, I can't thank you enough for this," I tell the Russian financier. "First you bailed out Chris's movie, and now you've just saved our show. If anything, Julian's show is going to make even more of a splash on your ship than on the LVMH yacht! What would we have done without you?" I've already made all of the arrangements to have everything moved here. Chili's calling everyone to tell them about the new venue now.

"It is my pleasure, Lola," says Sergei. "After all, it is thanks to you that I am now a Hollywood producer. And thanks to your brother that my daughter is going to be a big movie star."

"Well, I know that Chris was absolutely thrilled to cast her." Who wouldn't be? Alexandra Crimini, age fourteen, is already six feet tall and stunning. Chris would have been happy to give her that small but pivotal role in *Forgetting Petunia Holt* even if her father *hadn't* shelled out several million dollars to underwrite the movie. "And of course, Julian was more than happy to make Alexandra a special gown for the premiere, weren't you, Julian?"

"Oh, absolutely," pants Julian, "I hope she was pleased with it!" Julian releases his death grip around my thigh only long enough to swipe the sweat dripping down the side of his face. "Just tell me when we land," he whispers, sinking into his seat and clenching his eyes closed.

Moments later, the helicopter alights gracefully on Crimini's flight deck. Julian stumbles out, his tan Gucci cigarette pants shaking vigorously. He grabs my arm to steady himself. "Don't make me get back on that thing ever again," Julian hisses. "I'd rather swim back to the hotel."

I pinch his hand to shut him up and throw him a warning glare. "Behave!" I hiss back.

"Welcome to my home away from home," Sergei says. "Of course my personal chef will take care of all the food and drinks."

"Mr. Crimini, again, I don't know how to thank you enough," Julian says. That's more like it.

"Of course, it is nothing," Crimini says. "Lola tells me that you're a huge fan of Hermès. I modeled the boat after the Hermès store in Tokyo. She is called *Magic Lantern* after Renzo Piano's design. She glows—like a floating lighthouse. See," he says, gesturing toward the undulating walls of glass that are catching the light off the ocean. "The walls of hand-blown cubes of glass are inspired by a Japanese lantern. The reflection of the blue of the ocean mixed with the interior colors creates an aura of light."

"It's like an impeccably designed piece of jewelry," I say in awe.

"May I give you a tour?" Crimini asks.

The doors in front of us seem to magically slide open, as if on cue.

"This is the great room," Crimini says.

"I'd say," Julian says breathlessly at the expansive room before us that's probably twice the size of Julian's loft in New York.

"When do I move in?" I say, sliding a hand along the wood wall. Its dark grain is so intricate it looks like an abstract painting "Is this . . . ?"

"Cashmere," Julian finishes my sentence in awe as we both kneel and caress the flawless, creamy floor.

"My god, no red wine in here," I say, our feet sinking into the plush cashmere carpeting as we make our way through the room. I have to resist the urge to curl up in one of the orange cashmere blankets strewn on the soft, navy couches lining the walls.

"Champagne? Pellegrino?" A deck hand appears with a tray of drinks.

"Thank you," Julian says taking a glass of champagne as I grab a Pellegrino in a wine glass.

"Please, follow me," Crimini says, guiding us toward a staircase.

"I'm pretty sure that's not a poster," Julian whispers to me as we pass a Rothko painting.

"Oh my god," I say, clutching the beige, woven banister as we make our way down the steps, "it's gorgeous, it's like a Bottega handbag."

"These are the guest rooms," Crimini says, gesturing down the long hallway of wood doors. "All of the wood used on the boat is from old wine vats from our winery in Tuscany. That's how we get the deep, rich, red tones in the wood. All of that gorgeous color comes from soaking in wine over years."

"I've always wanted to float in a glass of cabernet," Julian says, whispering, "de-lish!" as he runs a hand along the wall.

"Each of the guest quarters is designed after a jewel. This is the sapphire room," Crimini says, pushing open the gorgeous cherry-colored wood door to reveal a blue jewel of a room, with a sumptuous bed made up in Frette linens, a giant flat-screen television, and a marble bathroom beyond. The pieces of Italian blown glass on the desk facing out to the Mediterranean are all a sapphire blue, and even the collection of books lining the bookshelf have all been chosen for their blue book jackets. Clearly the only thing of Crimini's affected by the recession is his lighting.

"This is the most outrageous spot for our show, Lola," Julian says, grabbing my arm and pulling me toward him. "If we can pull it off, this is going to be gorgeous. Our guests will be blown away."

"And this is my daughter," Crimini says as he guides us into the emerald room. Sitting on the bed is Alexandra, her endless legs stretched out beneath a computer, sun-kissed hair down her back looking like she's just stepped off the beach. That we're in the emerald room isn't lost on me as I look into those green, almond-shaped eyes as startling as the Mediterranean peeking through the window behind her.

"Hi Alex," I say, reaching out my hand to her, to which she stretches long, graceful fingers in my direction. "You're really good in my brother's movie." It was a small part but she made an impression. And even more stunning in person, I think to myself.

"Oh, I was so happy to get the part. It was fun," she says shyly.

"Julian? What are you doing?" I whisper, waving him in from the doorway where he's cowering like a five-year-old on the first day of kindergarten.

"Oh, I'm sorry," he recovers, reaching a hand out to introduce himself. Now I've seen Julian in many incarnations, but blushing? This is a first. "I have to say, you just took my breath away. I'm not sure I've ever met anyone so beautiful." Which is saying a lot, given that Julian has spent most of his adult life surrounded by models, Turlington, Moss, Crawford, Evangelista among them. I look to Julian and if I know my BGF at all, we're both thinking the same thing: This girl is going to be *huge*. And we're going to be the ones to introduce her to the world.

"Alex, I'd like you to meet Julian Tennant," I say.

"Oh, Mr. Tennant," Alex breathes, "thank you so much for the incredibly gorgeous dress you made me. I felt like a model wearing it!" Julian made Alex the most romantic, flouncy chiffon dress with itsy bitsy strawberries embroidered all over it. Style.com called it "magical" and *WWD* said it looked like Alex walked straight out of a fairy tale. Of course, no one other than Crimini could afford that dress right now. The embroidery alone was over a thousand dollars.

"That's wonderful," I tell her. "Because we have a great favor to ask you. Would you consider modeling in Julian's show?"

"Modeling? Me? In a real show?" Alex blinks in shock and looks at her father.

"That's exactly what we mean. Do you know Aria Fraser?" Julian asks her.

"Of course," she and her father answer in unison.

"Well, she's had an . . . unfortunate accident"—if you can call getting completely blotto and skinny dipping in the most visible lobby in Cannes and smashing up the world's most perfect Roman nose an "accident"—"and Julian and I think you'd be an absolutely smashing"— that word again—"replacement for her. That is, if you're ready," I say, looking her square in the eye. And she doesn't have to say anything for me to know it. Those piercing green eyes say it all.

Julian doesn't even threaten to swim back from Crimini's boat, he's so excited about our new venue and our new model. In fact, not only does he get onto the helicopter without a fight—or a Xanax—but he giddily whips out his sketchbook the moment we take off and starts sketching the new touches he's planning on making to the dresses for Alex. "Now I know what having a muse feels like," he says without looking up from his Moleskine notebook.

"Oh my gosh, Julian, it's already seven o'clock," I say, looking at my watch. "Once we get back to the hotel, we have to get ready and go. I told my mom I wouldn't be late for her party."

"I'm sorry, Princess, but I'm not going. I'm way too inspired. I have to get these dresses done for Alex," Julian says.

I wish I could argue with him that he has to come with me, but he's right. I only wish I could do the same.

"You're right Julian, get your work done. We don't have a lot of time to get ready for the show. Chili's around so he can help you with whatever you need—and will you please make sure that he triple-checks that all the arrangements have been made for the change of venue?"

But Julian's too deep in his sketches to even answer me.

"We Are Family," by Sister Sledge is blaring through the windows of the massive chateau my mother rented for "Fête-ing Santisi." Old home movies of me, Christopher, Mom, and Papa are playing on giant screens throughout the massive gardens, as well as specially cut-together trailers for *San Quentin Cartel* and *Forgetting Petunia Holt.*

As I make my way through the candlelit courtyard hemmed by hundred-year-old towering limes trees and fairy-tale turrets, I hear a loud whooshing sound coming from above my head. I turn to find flame-throwers on eight-foot-tall stilts bounding toward me. I don't know who's more likely to topple over: me in my six-inch Louboutin stilettos, or the men now circling us in this surreal circus. It seems my mother took me literally when I suggested that the party should be called "Cirque du Santisi" instead of "Fête-ing Santisi." She clearly didn't get the joke. Judging by the number of contortionists, fire-eaters, clowns, and trapeze artists, I'm wondering if she actually got Cirque du Soleil to come to Cannes. My mother is obviously trying to outdo the annual Chopard party, the D&G bash, the AmFar Gala—and every other lavish soiree in Cannes—with this party. And of course she's called in extra camera crews to capture it all for her show. I think I even spot a camera in the hands of one of the clowns.

I make a quick beeline for the mosaic marble entryway of the chateau, quickly pinning up my hair as I go. This rat's nest is a fire hazard. I didn't have the time to wash it, let alone do anything with it. And I'm feeling pretty dismal as I pass by Gwyneth, looking perfection as usual in a shimmering silver micro-minidress, with those sculpted legs that go on for days. I overhear her telling Kylie Minogue about Tracy Anderson's new baby food cleanse. Baby food? Really? I'm sure I'll read about it on GOOP next week.

There's no baby food on the buffet, thankfully. On long, ornate tables there are tray upon tray of iced oysters, lobsters, and crab legs interspersed between flickering candelabras that are casting a glow on the honey-colored, thirteenth-century stone walls and exposed timber beams. The chateau's heavy, wooded windows offer views of the Mediterranean beyond, the smell of lavender and rosemary float up from the immense garden stretching out to the sea, and the cobblestone floors are dotted with more stars than there are in the sky.

I pass by Al Pacino, Jack Nicholson, and Mick Jagger huddled in conversation on one of the sumptuous crimson velvet couches. I wonder what it would have been like if one of them had been my father—my mother dated them all at one time or another. On another sofa Russell Brand and Salman Rushdie are seated beside one another. Only my mother could bring those two together. What could they possibly be talking about? Across the room is another odd coupling: Woody Allen and Kid Rock.

I spot my father and Christopher posing for photographs against an ornamental wall hanging by the fireplace. My father looks as angry as the wild boar goring the deer in the tapestry; he's clearly miffed that he's being forced to share his moment and the spotlight with Christopher, who looks no more pleased than the deer breathing its last. Gigi, on the other hand, seems to love the spotlight. I must say she's looking ravishing in a long, slinky, white silk column dress with a daring slit up to her hip, canting her legs this way and that, wrapping and rewrapping her willowy arms around Christopher's waist. I overhear one of the photogs saying, "Can someone get this girl out of the two-shot please?" Mom's *Wristwatch Wives* camera crew, with Alex at its helm, pivots around the herd of lensmen. Cameras taking pictures of cameras. When will the snake stop biting its own tail?

I feel awfully alone at what's supposed to be at least in part a quote-unquote "Santisi family celebration." I look at my BlackBerry. Lev texted me two hours ago that his plane had landed in Nice. He should be here anytime.

"Sweetheart," my mother calls out with outstretched arms as she makes her way across the party looking like a blond Cleopatra by way of Karl Lagerfeld. She seems to float across the antique Persian carpets in her swooping ivory chiffon gown with intricate Egyptian-style gold embroidery across the bodice. Thank god she's not being trailed by her crew. "What's the matter?" she says, hugging me. "You look so sad. Where's Lev?"

"He's on his way, but I'll be surprised if he even makes it."

"Oh sweetie, I'm so sorry," my mother says, continuing to hold me, and I don't want her to let go. "Darling, is there something else the matter?"

"Can I talk to you off camera?" I ask.

"Of course, darling, just as long as you promise me that you'll also talk to me on camera as well. Did you bring the script I sent you? I had cue cards made up in case you didn't have time to memorize your lines," she says.

"Mom, I really need for you to be my mother for one second and not a Wristwatch Wife, okay?"

"Of course, darling," she says.

"I'm really scared that I'm not going to be able to save JT Inc. this time. I finally found a new venue for the show, but with the RSVPs so dismal I'm not sure it even matters. And I don't know how on earth I'm going to convince Saffron to pose on the cover of *Vain*. She was on board with doing the cover with Markus, and then all the tabloid nonsense started and she backed out. Kate says that she's tired of lying to the world and pretending that she's straight." All of it comes gushing out of me like a BP oil spill. And at the word "straight" I suddenly notice a very strange glint in my mother's eye and wonder why she seems to be inching closer and closer to me, practically stabbing me with the giant white tulle Chanel camellia pin on her left shoulder. "Mom?!"

"So Saffron Sykes is really a lesbian," she says.

"Mom, why do you keep shoving that flower in my face?" I say. And then I get it. "Oh my god, Mom, no, no, no, no, no . . . Mom is there a—" I can't even get the words out. I'm scared if I say it aloud it will make it all too real. That I just confirmed on camera that Saffron is gay. "Mom, is there a hidden camera in your camellia?"

"Oh, Lola, sweetheart, come on," she whispers.

"Mom, you *cannot* use that footage! You have to promise me! You told me you weren't filming."

"Darling, it's all going to come out anyway, why shouldn't it come out on my show? Can you imagine the ratings? This is just what I need now!" she crows. "Christine's been lording her footage of her dermatologist's biopsy over me. She's been telling everyone it was cancer, and it was just a measly basal cell—"

"Are you freaking kidding me right now, Mom? This is not happening!" I can feel hot tears burning at the corners of my eyes.

And as though it's been timed, Lev walks into the room. Finally. Lev is here. The man who is going to take me away from all of this. The man who is going to save me from Hollyweird. The man who is going to be my husband. My new family. I want to run to him and fling my arms around him. But something's different, something's not right. No, not right at all. I barely recognize him in his ultra slim-fit black linen suit. I mean, it's a gorgeous suit. And he looks gorgeous. But it's the kind of suit I'd expect to see on Brad Pitt, not my Lev. My Lev who wears jeans and T-shirts and thinks Hanes is a designer brand.

"Lev darling!" my mother calls out.

And that's when a bribe comes to me. I put a restraining hand on her arm. "Mother, if you even *think* you're coming to our wedding, you will make a solemn vow this very second that you will *not* use any of that footage."

"You would really do that?" my mother asks in shock.

"The same way you would use that footage. Yes, you better believe it."

There is the very briefest of stare-downs. "Oh, *fine,* Lola," she says, shrugging her slender shoulders in surrender. But I know better.

"I want you to promise on your life."

"Stop being so dramatic," Mom says. "I said I wouldn't use it but I really don't see what the big deal is."

"Promise me," I demand. "This very minute."

Mom rolls her eyes. "Fine, yes, I promise. But you've got to let me—"

I turn to my fiancé, but he's already been enveloped in a swarm of photogs snapping away. And I feel a jolt to my system, because he looks awfully comfortable there in front of those cameras. It's not until I get closer that I realize that it's not just the flashes that make his complexion look odd. He has a Mystic Tan.

"Yeah, thanks, man, I just flew in on Dempsey's G4," I hear him telling one of the photographers.

This is when the room starts spinning.

Fortunately, Lev picks that moment to cross the room and wrap me in his arms. "Hi honey," he says, kissing me. Okay, now *that* feels like home, I think to myself with relief when I'm folded into him. That's my Lev. But then when I pull back to look at his face, something's not right.

"Lev, what's with the Mystic Tan? And what happened to your eyebrows?" I ask in shock.

"Oh I forgot about that! Yeah, the makeup artist did that," he says, rubbing his fingers along his newly waxed brows.

"Makeup artist?"

"Yeah, for the show."

"Oh," I say, trying to get used to his new brows. "Did I hear you say something about Dempsey's G4?"

"Oh yeah, I ended up getting a ride on Dempsey's plane, because shooting ran over and I missed my other flight," he says before I can fully digest that Lev is calling Patrick Dempsey "Dempsey."

"Oh, that's so great," I force myself to say. "Is that a new suit?"

"Yeah, it's a gift from Dempsey," he says.

"That's quite a gift," I say. "Should I be jealous? Is there a bromance brewing?"

"No, no, Hugo Boss sent him a bunch of suits and he didn't want them all so he gave this one to me. Did you know they're, like, a thousand bucks? I could never afford one of these." He brushes the lapel admiringly.

"Oh," I say and as I look into his green eyes it hits me how much I've missed him. Even though he's standing right in front of me the feeling of missing him hasn't gone away. It's like a gaping hole that I could just crawl into and get buried in.

"And guess what?" Lev says. "I have the most amazing news!"

"What?" I say.

"The Coen brothers were on the flight here with us, and I guess they've been trying to cast this role of a doctor in their next movie. They seemed to be interested in me. It's a small part, but I think it could be fun," he says with a big smile. I didn't think he even knew who the Coen brothers were. "It's about a Jewish Orthodox gynecologist who has a midlife crisis after falling in love with his nurse. He decides to leave his wife and family and converts to Catholicism because that's the only way his shiksa nurse will be with him. I'd be playing the brother he shares a practice with who tries to talk some sense into him."

"A gynecologist in a Coen brothers movie?" I ask in shock, shaking my head in disbelief. With as much calm as I can muster, I ask, "What about Lenox Hill Hospital? Have you heard back from them yet?"

"Not yet," he says as Kate comes up to us.

"Hey, guys," she says, giving me a quick peck on the cheek. She glows in a simple white dress that traces the outline of her perfect body. "Lola, you'll be happy to know that Nic Knight is on a plane to Clean and Sober Detox in California. I'm making Adam fly him there. I told Nic the only way I was going to bail his sorry ass out of jail was if he agreed to go. Thanks again for not telling your father or calling the cops on him last night for violating his parole."

"No problem," I say. "I'm just glad he's getting some help."

"He needed it. He was actually hallucinating. He kept telling me about his new baby! He even said he'd bought actual clothes for it, can you imagine? I almost feel sorry for Adam having to drag him all the way to detox, but I told him that was his penance for blabbing everything to you. I'm just so relieved he's gone. I don't have to worry about him crashing the party tonight and pulling some stunt." Kate looks around the room appreciatively. "Your mom's in rare form, Lo. I almost got impaled by one of her sword swallowers coming in. And I don't think your dad's so happy about those Lipizzaner stallions crapping in the courtyard. Amanda Seyfried just stepped in a big pile of—"

"Kate—" I blurt. "Lev was on the plane with the Coen brothers. They want him to audition for a part in their next film."

"Oh yeah, that's a great part," Kate says, turning to Lev. "You're going to need a good agent. Why don't you call my office so we can get you set up with the paperwork?"

I don't give Lev a chance to respond. "Sweetheart, would you mind getting me a glass of champagne," I say to him. Once he's out of sight, I turn to my best friend. "Are you fucking kidding me right now, Kate?" I say. "I already told you you had my blessing to agent him. I just asked you to leave me out of it. Do you really have to throw this in my face tonight of all nights?"

"Why are you being so touchy about this? Wouldn't you rather he be with me than someone else? I'll get him the best deal."

"You're my best friend!" I say between teeth clenched so hard my jaw is aching. "Don't you understand what's happening?! I'm losing him— to Hollywood. He's a *doctor,* not an actor."

"Are you sure about that?" Kate asks.

Everything seems to come to a screeching halt, as if the pause button on life has been pushed: the fire outside being thrown up in the air by the flamethrowers, my mother with her cameras holding court with Demi and Ashton, my father puffing away on a cigar while holed up in a corner with Julian Schnabel, my brother, giving an interview as Gigi drapes a long arm over his knee. As the voices and music drone in the back of my head, I realize we're all just putting on the show and hoping the pieces fall together. The room sways back into focus and so do I.

"Kate, look, what's it going to take to get Saffron on the cover of *Vain* in Julian Tennant? Just get me in a room with her. I'm drowning here and I have to do something or this ship is going to sink."

"Lo, I wish I could help you. I really do. But with everything that's happening, Saffron just doesn't want to do it. I'm sorry. It's a no," Kate says simply.

But I know I can't take no for an answer. "Kate, no, wait! You can't just say . . . I mean, if you want to represent Lev . . . I mean . . ." I trail off miserably. When did Fête-ing Santisi become Extortion Night?

All of a sudden Kate looks worse than I feel. "Kate, you okay?" I ask. Her face has turned pale, and I wonder if she might vomit again right here in the middle of this party. "I'm sorry, I didn't mean to . . . I mean, I understand your position completely. It's just that—" I trace her eye line to land on my brother and Gigi, still stapled to Chris's side. Kate's dark eyes are like lasers trained on my brother.

"So we hear there's a bidding war going here at the festival for your movie," the reporter says to Christopher. "Where do you think it will land?"

"I can't speculate at the moment," he answers, then adds, "but stay tuned. I'm anxiously awaiting the outcome myself."

"Are you two an item?" another reporter asks. Christopher demurs, but Gigi bats her eyes like a lovesick doe and coos, "I'm crazy about this guy."

"I can't listen to another second of this," Kate says, pulling her Black-Berry out of her clutch.

"Kate, would you just go talk to him, for crying out loud?" I beg. But she just continues to ignore me, pounding so furiously on her Black-Berry I think her thumbs may go into a spasm. I'm going to have to take matters into my own hands. I make a beeline for Gigi.

"Gigi," I say with a big fake smile as I unwrap her arm from my brother. She has a surprisingly strong grip, like Jill Zarin at a J Mendel sample sale. "Can I steal you?" I ask. "Come, come, Patrick has been try-ing to find you to get a photo," I say, pulling her toward a *Vanity Fair* photographer and urgently mouthing to Chris as I do, "Kate wants to talk to you."

Just as soon as I deposit Gigi right where she wants to be, in front of the camera, I run into Lev, who hands me my flute of champagne and pulls me toward a private corner beneath a very large, dark painting of a rather stern-looking woman who I have the creepy impression is staring at me

"I have a confession," he says. "It wasn't my work at the hospital that made me late for Cannes yesterday. It was *Para-Medic*."

"Why didn't you simply tell me that?"

"I'm not even sure myself," he says, looking down at his shoes, a pair of John Lobbs whose uppers are so shiny I can practically see the chandeliers reflected in them. Another gift from Dempsey? "I think I knew that it would upset you and that you have so much work to do here. I didn't want it to distract you from your job. I'm so sorry about everything that's going on. The *Para-Medic* thing has been a total fluke," he says, taking my hand and then dropping it. He starts pacing back and forth in that damn Hugo Boss suit.

"I wish you could take that thing off," I say, waving in the general direction of his ensemble. "You just don't look like you."

"That'll probably have to wait until we get back to the hotel," he jokes, but I'm not feeling very amused at the moment. "You really don't like it?" he asks, moving toward an antique gold mirror hanging on the wall and smoothing back his hair before he turns back toward me. Lev is checking himself out in the mirror. I don't think I've ever in the entirety of our relationship seen him do that. "I know, this trip is about you and your work," he says, coming over to me and resting his hand on my back. "Don't freak out about this Coen brothers movie. It's not like they've even offered me the part, although it would be so cool if they did," he says. "I mean, *No Country for Old Men* was incredible."

"I thought you never went to the movies before you met me," I say.

"Oh no, I saw it last week with Dempsey. He's giving me a little lesson in Hollywood 101," Lev says, taking a sip from the tumbler in his hand.

"Well, has he given you a lesson in what it's like to shoot a movie?" I say, wishing we were anywhere but here at this damn party having this conversation. "Twelve-hour shoot days—in Vancouver—or Albania—or Timbuktu. Who's going to do your surgeries then?"

"I know, I know, you're right, it's totally unrealistic. I'm a doctor first. Forget it. Let's talk about this when you've gotten through with this week. This week is about you," he says for the second time in this discussion. And for the second time I can't help but feel that that isn't close to being true. "I love you and everything's going to be just fine. Let's get back to the hotel and get a good night's rest. You've got a big couple of days ahead of you."

And as he pulls me into him, I try to feel like everything's going to be fine. Only three more days and we'll be back on the plane and this week will be over. And I'll figure out how to get the *Vain* cover shoot back on track, even if I have to bend over as far backwards as those gymnasts doing a tableau vivant near Mom's oyster buffet. And as the din of the party fades away, my old mantra repeats itself in my ear, *Act As If, Act As If, Act As If* . . .

But when I reluctantly release myself from Lev's arms, I find that he suddenly doesn't have eyes for me anymore. Once again, his gaze is fixed on the mirror as he studies his own reflection. He seems to really, really like what he sees there.

15

"Julian, everyone's in their seats, are you ready?" I ask anxiously over my headset from the end of the long runway where I'm stationed next to Sam Ronson, out of everyone's view. I've inspected the models, double-checked their outfits and accessories, directed the makeup artists for final touch-ups, made sure Chili seated and greeted the guests and doled out the programs, and run the sound checks with Lex and the rest of the tech crew. I feel like Kelly Cutrone, except I'm not in head-to-toe black. I'm wearing a gorgeous floaty silk yellow, purple, and fuchsia color-block dress that Julian made especially for me. As I look out at all of the guests and the phalanx of photographers crowding the runway, I know that I've done everything in my power to make this show even better than any couture show in Paris. So what if Aria's not walking in it—or Nano—or Saffron? So what if there were a million more celebrities at my mother's party last night than here right now? I'd like to see even John Galliano top this venue. Or Vera Wang try and top Julian's divine gowns.

"We're ready," Julian says with a shaky voice. "Father in Heaven, thank you for this runway show. Bless the hands that prepared it and please let it be a huge success. Amen."

"Amen," I echo, although I'm a bit puzzled. The only gods I've ever seen Julian worship are Robert Pattinson and Tom Ford. *And please, please, please let me keep my job,* I think. "John, we're good to go," I say into my headset, cueing Crimini's pilot.

"Copy that," John says.

It feels like there's an army of butterflies in my stomach as Crimini's G-550 swoops through the air like an eagle and touches down on the tarmac just beyond the catwalk. There are audible gasps over the plane's engines as Crimini's plane taxis along the tarmac until it reaches the runway on the flight deck of the aircraft carrier. I nod at Sam Ronson, who fires up a techno, trance mix of "Here Comes the Bride" as the door to the plane opens and Alexandra Crimini steps out like an ethereal angel in dreamy white satin that's been whipped into a masterful ball gown dusted with crystal. It makes Princess Diana's wedding dress look like something off the clearance rack at Loehmann's.

Everyone in the audience rises to their feet and cheers wildly as Alexandra seems to float down the runway that is actually a people mover. I'm certain no one has ever seen an entrance like this before. I look over to Stefano from LVMH, who's grinning ear-to-ear as he stands there applauding voraciously next to Charlotte Casiraghi, Princess Caroline's daughter, standing on her Roger Viviers in the front row. I kept the models' entrance a secret from everyone, including Stefano, which wasn't that hard considering I only just thought of it yesterday. I can't believe we actually pulled it off. Alexandra poses as expertly as Giselle at the end of the runway, looking absolutely magnificent and as if Julian hadn't given her walking lessons late into the night.

One by one the models step off of the plane and glide down the runway, each wedding confection more beautiful than the next. The catwalk is an orgy of hundreds of yards of beaded and swagged white lace, organza, tulle, silk, and duchess satin. My breath catches in my throat at the sheer beauty. Say "Yes to That Dress," Vera Wang. And Monique Lhuillier. And Pnina Tornai. Every bride from this day forward is going to want to wear Julian Tennant.

Finally the moment arrives that has my heart pounding against my chest. "Hit it, Lex," I say into my headset. "Here Comes the Bride" slowly fades out as U2's "Beautiful Day" begins to play. An enormous screen is erected in front of the plane at the beginning of the catwalk. Scenes of Cricket in *Four Weddings and a Bris* play behind her as Cricket herself steps out on the runway in the finale gown, a long-sleeved, backless Chantilly lace number embroidered with scads of pearls that bustle in the back. It's the very gown she's wearing in the scene playing up there on the giant screen, with Saffron beside her, who looks absolutely resplendent up there in her Julian Tennant bridal gown. If we couldn't have Saffron here in person walking in the show, at least we can project her larger-than-life image for everyone to see how smashing she looks in her JT creation. The sight of Cricket in that dress makes my heart pitter-patter. She looks even more magnificent than at her final fitting. As she strides down the catwalk she's doused in a meteor shower of flashes.

Suddenly the footage from *Four Weddings* cuts out. Damn it! "Lex, what's going on?" I bark into my headset.

Then just as suddenly grainy footage of Cricket kissing Markus Livingston fills the screen. What's going on? Terror washes over me. I don't remember that scene from the movie. But I do remember that unforgettable yacht in the background. Why is she kissing Markus? And on Diddy's boat, out in public?

"Lex, turn it off! Turn it off!" I shout through my headset, feeling the blood rush to my face.

"We're trying," Lex barks back at me.

"What's going on?" Julian shrieks from inside the plane.

Cricket continues to swan down the runway, oblivious to the footage behind her and the weird stares and whispers of everyone in the audience. The photographers' flashes are blinding, and it looks like everyone is getting their own footage on their cell phones. I'm sure everyone from Harvey Levin to the AP will have them in seconds. This is a disaster.

"What's taking so long? Cut the film," I scream into my headset.

"Jesus, I'm trying! What the—"

"What's happening?" Julian squawks over his headset.

What *is* happening? Where on earth did this footage come from? Oh god. Oh no. Please don't let it be my mother's cameras. Please. But why would she play the footage here and not on her show, for the ratings? She's not even here; she's too busy bidding for a kiss from Clooney. It can't be her, it just can't. Besides, there's no way Mom would want to sabotage Cricket's career; she loves Cricket as much as I do.

But . . . what if this isn't about Cricket? What if Cricket isn't the target? What if someone's trying to sabotage Julian? Or me? Who would do that?

It can only be two people: little Chili Lu and Coz. But how did they get the footage?

I scan the first row until I find Coz's seat. I can't help but notice that she looks *exactly* like the devil in her body-hugging, lipstick-red cotton suit, red platform pumps, and matching stupid smirk on her red painted lips.

"Lex, get somebody to pull down the screen," I shout. "Hurry! Please!"

Cricket reaches the end of the runway, poses for the photogs, and then spins around. I can't see her face as she turns, but I'm certain it's ashen as she sees the footage and stiffens in midstride. I half expect her to crumple to the ground but she continues walking with her head held high.

"Got it," Lex wails into my ear as the footage of Markus and Cricket is stopped and scenes from the movie start to play again.

"Julian, get ready, that's your cue. Show's over. You have to go out and take your bow," I say.

"No way, not after that," he says, his voice full of panic.

"Julian, get out there," I insist.

"No, they're going to boo me!" Julian shrills.

"No they're not, just get out there," I say. "Don't make me have someone push you out."

"Fine, fine," Julian says and seconds later he's on the runway hand in hand with Alexandra Crimini. They're met with modest applause amid a low murmur as everyone seems too busy gossiping about Cricket and Markus to give Julian the recognition he really deserves. The applause he would have gotten if someone—Cozili—hadn't leaked that footage. I wonder if Stefano is going to fire me right here in front of everyone. I have to go talk to him and try and explain. But first I have to find Cricket and Julian.

As I maneuver through the dispersing crowd, trying to make my way to one of Crimini's vast drawing rooms that we're using as the backstage area, it's clear that the guests have only one thing on their minds.

"Is that chick gay or not?"

"So what's the deal with Saffron and Markus?"

"I'm confused. So the fashion show's just a big publicity stunt for *Four Weddings and a Bris*?"

"I heard Saffron was supposed to be in the show. Guess she chickened out."

I don't know whom I feel worse for: me and Julian or Cricket. Julian killed himself over those gowns, and no one's saying a word about them. Cricket didn't even really want to walk in the show today, but she did it for us.

When I finally find Cricket in the hallway behind the makeshift stage, she looks like a teeny tiny bird that's broken its wings.

"Lo, I'm so sorry. I ruined everything. I didn't mean for any of this to happen. What have I done? I'm so sorry," she says, falling into my arms amid a puddle of lace. I hold her in my arms as she cries. As the crying turns to sobbing, I continue holding her.

"Cricket Curtis, was this whole relationship with Saffron a sham?" a journalist shouts, trying to shove a mic in Cricket's face as a photog starts snapping photos of her. How did they get in here? Suddenly there's a swarm of journalists surrounding us and they're all yelling at Cricket.

"Are you straight or are you gay?"

"Was this just a publicity stunt?"

"Are you in love with Markus?"

"Does Saffron know about this?"

"You need to leave, Cricket has no comment," I shout, shrouding Cricket protectively in my arms. "Security!"

Where the hell are all of Crimini's security people? I feel Cricket shaking in my arms and continue to try and protect her from the piranhas that are still yelling questions at her. I've got to get her out of here.

"Cricket, we have to make a run for it. Don't let go of my hand," I whisper into her ear and then we both start running. The journalists and photogs try and follow us, but thankfully Crimini's hulking security team shows up and blocks their path. I pull Cricket into one of the bedrooms.

"Are you with Markus?" I ask when we're finally alone.

Cricket can't even meet my eyes. "I don't know. I'm just so confused. I wasn't prepared for any of this and Markus, he really understands what I'm going through, and well, one thing led to another . . . I can't believe someone was filming us the whole time. I'm just so freaked out."

"Why didn't you tell me?" I ask, feeling a little bit betrayed. Cricket tells me everything. At least she used to.

"I'm so sorry, Lo. I haven't told anyone. Markus didn't want it to become public given his deal with Saffron," she says.

"Deal? What deal? Wait . . . so, I'm the public now?"

"Of course you're not. I didn't mean it like that. It's just that Saffron and Markus swore me to secrecy. She's so afraid that her being gay is going to kill her career, and Markus just really loves her and wants to protect her. The three of us were hanging out all the time, and then Markus and I started talking a lot, and then everything just kind of happened." Cricket shoots me a pleading look. "But I didn't mean for *any* of this to happen. You have to know that, right?" she says, but suddenly I'm not so sure anymore. Cricket's turning into someone I don't recognize. "Lola, I'm so sorry for all of this. I'm scared I've totally lost myself. I never meant to hurt anyone—most especially not you and Julian. Are you guys going to be okay?"

"I don't know," I say. I'm not at all sure. "I better go find Julian. Are you going to be okay here by yourself for a little bit?"

"Yes, go. Tell him I'm so sorry," she says.

"I'm sorry too," I say. "For all of this."

It takes me forever to find Julian on a boat this big but when I finally do he's hanging off the railings in a quiet corner.

"We're ruined. It's over," Julian says. "I feel like jumping overboard. No one is even talking about the gowns. All anyone wants to talk about is Saffron and Markus."

"It's not as bad as you think," I say. "I know it seems that way right now, but I'll find a way to spin this. Kate's always telling me that any press is good press. It's going to be okay. We've overcome worse than this before."

"It's not going to be okay. Not this time," Julian says, his voice so somber, so serious. How can he be so sure? "I can't believe anyone would do this to us."

"Not anyone. Chili and Coz," I say.

"Are you sure it's them?" Julian asks.

"Who else would do this?" I ask. "Coz has wanted to sabotage us ever since her little Chili's stock started falling. Have you seen Stefano? I need to find him and try and explain."

"He already left," Julian says. "Coz got to him before I did and told him that the *Vain* cover is off since Saffron and Markus don't seem to be a couple. Stefano said he'll see what the buyers say, but he wants me to fire you, Lola."

"Oh," is all I'm able to get out. They want me fired. LVMH wants me fired.

"I told them they'd have to fire me too if they were going to fire you. But LVMH owns my name, Lola. If I walk away, I'm walking away from my name."

"There's no way you're quitting," I tell him. "Your work today is genius, Julian, and when people stop yapping about Cricket and Markus, they're going to recognize that and reward it. There's no sense in us both losing our jobs over this."

"I'm so sorry," he says, wrapping me in his arms. And I'm thankful he's got me. Because I'm about to fall on the floor from the oppressive weight of all of it. No tears come, even though I want to cry. It's as though my body knows not to let me fall apart because that would be too much to take on top of everything else. So instead the shock kicks in. Pure shock. With our Oscar success from last year, I thought we were going to make it, but that red carpet just got ripped right out from under me. When I finally break free of Julian's embrace, the pain in his eyes is too much for me to bear.

"Julian, I just . . . I need a minute alone, do you mind?"

"Of course not. Come find me when you're ready," he says and walks away, blowing me a silent kiss.

I slide down the side of the boat and onto the deck. Even if it's just for a minute I need something solid beneath me. I can't believe that LVMH really wants me fired. I mean, I don't really blame them, but I can't believe it's actually happening. I'm about to lose everything that I've worked so hard for.

I don't know how long I've been sitting on the deck when I feel a steadying hand on my shoulder.

"I've been looking everywhere for you. Julian told me everything. I'm so sorry about all of this," Lev says, sitting down on the deck next to me.

"I can't believe I'm about to lose everything," I say, my head spinning.

"You still have me," Lev says, kissing me and as I look into his green eyes—right below the alarmingly groomed brows I still can't get over—I want desperately to believe him. I want it more than anything I've ever wanted. I want the doctor I fell in love with in the emergency room at Cedars and not the one on TV. Do I still have *him*? I want to ask Lev. But as I look into my fiancé's eyes, really look, I feel like he's right in front of me. So what if his eyebrows are waxed? He's still my Lev, my love.

"I love you, Doctor Luke Levin," I say.

"I love you too," Lev says, kissing me again. "I know that you'll figure out a way to save your job. You'll think of something."

"I wish I had as much faith in myself as you have in me," I say.

"Hey Lev, are you ready, we really need to get going." I look up to see a man with salt-and-pepper hair and a tan Varvatos suit standing over us.

"Lola, this is Buzz," Lev says, standing up.

I struggle to my feet. "I know who this is," I say, reaching my hand out to Buzz Keating. And I don't need Lev to tell me what he's about to say, because I already know it in my bones.

"Buzz represents the Coen brothers. He was on the plane with us and he wants me to meet with them right now. Do you mind, we'll only be an hour," he says with trepidation.

"Right now?" I ask. Is this a joke? Lev wants to go and meet the Coen brothers right now? Could a worse time even exist? *I* need him now. *Me,* his fiancée. Not the Coen brothers.

"It was really hard to arrange the meeting at all. The Coen brothers have a very tight schedule, so I'm afraid it has to be right now," Buzz says, sounding genuinely apologetic, which only makes it sting more. "This is an enormous opportunity for Lev's career."

"Which career would that be?" I ask. My suddenly screechy voice sounds foreign in my ears. I try to gulp the words back but they keep coming.

"Lola, please don't do this right now," Lev says. "Buzz, I'm so sorry. Is there any other time we could meet them?"

"I'm afraid not," Buzz says.

Lev looks at me and I can see in his eyes how badly he wants to go to this meeting. How is it that everything's going so horribly wrong? What's happening to Lev? He's about to lose himself to Hollywood and I don't know how to get him back. The existential crisis I'm having seems to be flooding my body, lifting me above the boat, above the Mediterranean, it seems to be lifting me into the sky, though I know I'm right here standing in front of Lev and Buzz.

When it comes to me, it's as if my body comes back down to the ground too with a strangely inaudible crash. I've got it. I know how to save my job. I know how to save our company. I have to get to Saffron. I have to talk to her. Lev will have to save himself.

"Lev, you go. Go meet the Coen brothers. I've got to see someone right away," I say.

"Are you sure?" he asks.

"Yes, I'm sure," I say. "Buzz, it was nice to meet you," I say, shaking his hand. "I'll see you back at the room," I say, kissing Lev good-bye.

He's not ten feet away when I dial Kate. It goes straight to voice mail.

"Call me as soon as you get this," I say. "You've got to get me a meeting with Saffron. I'll explain why when we talk."

Once I'm back in my room at the Martinez I turn on the bathwater. I'm desperate to rinse off as much of this day as I can. My cell trills as a new text appears.

WHAT I'D LIKE TO KNOW LOLA IS WHAT DO YOU PLAN TO DO WITH
ALL OF THOSE OSTRICHES?
—COZ

I hit DELETE. I see my laptop open on the desk. It's sheer masochism, I know, but I have to find out what people are saying about the show. When the darkened computer screen comes to life, I find myself gasping for air. It's Perez Hilton, and there's a photo of Lev with one of Perez's hearts scrawled around his image. I'm not sure what's more disturbing: the fact that Lev is on Perez Hilton again or that he was *looking* at Perez Hilton. He didn't even know who *Paris* Hilton was before we met. I recognize the photo. It's a shot from my mother's party last night. A photograph that I've been removed from—airbrushed out as though I don't even exist in the life of Doctor Luke Levin. The man I'm marrying. The love of my life. All of a sudden I feel so small, and so dispensable. I feel like I could just vanish and no one would care. Not LVMH. Not Lev. No one.

I opt to skip the bath and go straight to bed. Where are my pajamas?

I can't find them anywhere. I decide to grab a T-shirt from Lev's suitcase. When I see the Lenox Hill emblem at the top of the piece of paper peeking out from a stack of Lev's clothes, my heart starts beating as though I've just finished running a marathon, which in a way I have. As I pull the stationery out from the pile of clothes, the words start to blur together on the page:

> *Dear Dr. Levin,*
> *We at Lenox Hill Hospital are very pleased to offer you the*
> *position of Resident in Emergency Medicine. . . .*

I can barely think above the blood pounding in my ears. I scan the date on the letter. Lev has known about the offer from Lenox Hill for more than a week and has been lying to me about it. Just as I'm spinning out into how he could possibly have done this, I hear the key in the door.

"Hey hon," he says. "The Coen brothers are going to screen test me when we're back in L.A. Isn't that so coo—" He stops as he sees me holding the letter in my shaking hands.

"How could you do this?" I ask, then melt down onto the lounge chair that is luckily right next to me. My legs just can't hold me up anymore.

"Were you going through my things?" he asks, shocked.

"That's kind of beside the point, isn't it? But no, if it makes you feel any better, I was looking for my pajamas and instead I found *this*." I shake the letter in his face.

"We need to talk," Lev says as he collapses onto the edge of the bed. And for the first time I realize that he's been carrying around the weight of this as well. "I keep waiting for it to be the right time and now I've learned the hard way that there's never a right time. I just know how much pressure you've been under and I haven't wanted to add to it. And now I've caused you pain because you think I've been lying to you. Really, I've just wanted to protect you from what I know won't make you happy. But Lola, I'm not sure I want to be a doctor anymore. I want to pursue this acting thing. All my life it was just *expected* of me that I was going to become a doctor. Both my parents are surgeons. Their parents are surgeons. I feel like I never really had a choice. My first word was 'scalpel,' for god's sake. I can always go back to being a doctor, but I'm really happy when I'm acting. I've never felt this kind of happy before . . . except with you."

"But what does this mean?" I beg and feel pathetic as I'm doing it.

"I'm going to resign from Cedar's."

I feel the walls to the world I've created coming down in a giant heap, the castle crumbling in around me, the moat that I thought protected our world invaded, and the sword of the invader going right through my heart.

"I didn't sign up for this," I say, my head drowning, my hands the only thing keeping it afloat. "I can't do this," I say through tears that are coming out in gasps, in a fight for the oxygen that seems to have left my body.

"Why can't you support me and love me for who I am?"

"Because this isn't who you are," I say. And then the red-faced monster suffocating in my chest lets out a scream. "You're not an actor!"

"But maybe I am!" Lev yells back. And this is when I realize, as I look out the window beyond the pool, beyond Diddy's and Paul Allen's yachts, beyond this week, beyond Cannes, out to the horizon where the sun is just about to set, that this isn't about who Lev is. This is about who I am and what I'm willing to give up, what I'm willing to risk to stay true to myself. Even if I'm not entirely sure who I am, in my guts I know what I want and I'm going to have to love myself enough to risk it all.

"I'm sorry, Lev," I say, turning around, "I'm sorry, but I just can't do it. It's not right for me, for my life, for the life that I want, that I've wanted for us. I love you," I say, smoothing my hand gently across his forehead. "You should have your dreams. You should fulfill every last one of them and I shouldn't keep you from them." And as I slip the beautiful princess-cut diamond ring from my finger, I give it a kiss as I look into his eyes. Then I hand it back to him and give Luke Levin a final kiss good-bye.

16

I can't believe you found a Ferris wheel here," I say to Kate, who's seated beside me, our little passenger cart swaying gently to and fro as we look out at the Med sparkling way down below.

"I know how much you love them. Remember our first one?" she asks.

"Of course I do. In Texas, when you were PA-ing on Papa's movie."

"God, remember how much I hated you then?"

"Well, you *were* an uptight asshole," I remind her. We had the kind of catfights you can only have when you're sixteen and ambitious, but it was Kate who'd picked me up off the ground after a big fight with Actor Boyfriend No. 1—the very first time I'd succumbed to Actorholism.

We'd cemented our friendship atop the Ferris wheel nearby, and ever since it's been our post-breakup ritual. We must have racked up a million Frequent Flyer miles on the wheel in Santa Monica.

"Thank you for bringing me here," I say, my spirits lifted already.

"That's what best friends are for, right?" Kate says and despite everything that's gone on between us, I know that she means it.

"From up here everything looks so small and insignificant. Somehow losing Lev and probably my job doesn't sting as much," I say.

"Lo, I'm so sorry that I ever tried to sign Lev. I realize now how selfish that was, and that there are some things that are actually more important than work," Kate says.

"Thanks, Kate. And don't think it's gone unnoticed that you haven't checked your BlackBerry even once," I say.

"It's not easy, but I'm trying."

"Thanks," I say. "How could I be so wrong about Lev?"

"Hollywood is seductive; it can suck even the best people in," Kate says.

"I just never thought it would happen to *him*. But if that's what he really wants, I don't want to keep him from it. I just can't be a part of it," I say. And as we spin around and I look down at all the festival-goers who are just tiny specks from way up here, I feel myself getting even clearer. "I don't want a life in Hollywood. I know that now. I'm really happy in New York. Where I'm free of my family's shadow. I finally feel like I've found myself. And I don't want to lose me again."

"I hate that I'm losing you to New York, but I really envy you for figuring out what you want and staying true to yourself," Kate says. "You're going to be okay, Lola."

"Yeah, I'm going to be okay," I say, surprised to find that I actually believe it. "But what the hell am I going to do in New York if LVMH fires me?"

"They're not going to fire you," Kate says.

"Have you seen the papers today? *No one* is talking about Julian's divine wedding dresses. All anyone is writing and blogging about is Cricket and Markus and Saffron. It's a disaster. It's all over. I even saw it on the BBC and CNN. I feel like I've let everyone down. Julian won't get out of the fetal position, and Stefano won't even return my calls or e-mails. And without the *Vain* shoot, what am I supposed to tell Stefano? I would fire me too," I say. "I just hope they don't want to pull Julian's financial backing. I want to kill Chili and Coz. I don't have any proof yet, but I know it's them. I just know it."

"That's why you have to convince Saffron that she still needs to do the *Vain* cover," Kate says.

"What do you mean? You told me she said there's absolutely no way she'll do it," I say.

"And you told me that you could change her mind, so I convinced her to at least hear you out. She's expecting you at her place this afternoon," Kate says.

"What?! Oh my god, Kate," I squeal. "That's amazing! I can't thank you enough."

"Don't thank me until she's on the cover," Kate says.

"It doesn't matter what she says, thank you for getting me the meeting and sticking your neck so far out for me," I say in awe of my best friend.

"It's the least I could do after everything that's happened," Kate says.

"Thank you," I say. "Have you talked to Cricket? Do you think she's going to be okay?"

"Yeah, she's going to be okay. She just needs to lay low for a while, but she's going to be fine," Kate says.

"Do you think this thing between her and Markus is real?"

"I have no idea. You know Cricket; the girl loves being in love. I think she just got totally overwhelmed by everything, and Markus was there to sweep in and save the day."

"Who would have ever dreamed that our little Cricket would be headline news?" I say.

"I know," Kate says.

We continue to spin around and around in silence.

"What am I going to do without you in New York?" I ask.

"It's going to be hard," Kate says so softly I can barely make out the words.

"You know, maybe it will be good for us. We *are* oddly codependent," I joke—kind of. "I mean, you're not my mother; I can't depend on you for everything."

"No, I'm not your mother, Lo. And yes, you can always depend on me for every last thing. Because I'm not your mother," she says, looking me deeply in the eyes, then looking out at the water. "I'm going to miss you," Kate says.

"I'm going to miss you too," I say. I look into her eyes. "Are you crying?" I ask in shock. I mean, I haven't seen Kate cry since she got that B-minus in Physics at Harvard her freshman year.

"It's these damn hormones. I'm a pathetic pregnancy cliché straight out of *Knocked Up.*"

I grab Kate's hand, we look at each other, our eyes pooling with tears, and then out into the distance—it has nothing to do with pregnancy hormones—we both cry, long and hard. We spin around for a few minutes like that, long enough for me to summon the courage to ask what's been weighing on my mind since Kate first told me she was pregnant. "Have you reconsidered keeping the baby?"

"No."

"Don't you think Christopher should have some say in that?"

"What for? Isn't it the woman's right to choose?"

272 | *Amanda Goldberg and Ruthanna Khalighi Hopper*

"Kat—"

"Look Lo, I don't do babies. When my sister forced me to play Barbies with her when we were growing up I was always Ken. I never understood why they made a Dream House but not a Dream Office."

"You know, Kate, you can have the dream house *and* the dream office."

"But not the dream man because he's found another dream girl. No one gets to have it all."

"That's not true," I say, unsure whether I'm trying to convince Kate or myself.

Then Kate pulls an envelope out of her bucket bag. "Christopher gave me this last night," she says. "I think I'm ready to open it. Will you do it?" She passes me the envelope.

"Kate, Christopher gave this to you. You should really be the one to open it," I say.

"Please, Lola, just open it."

"Okay," I say, tearing open the envelope. There's a DVD inside along with a note.

> *I shot two endings to my movie, and this is the one I prefer.*
> *—Christopher*

"Kate, we have to go watch this immediately."

A half hour later, Kate and I are huddled together over her laptop on her tiny bed in the annex of the Du Cap. She gingerly puts the DVD in and presses PLAY.

The camera pans through a grove of bougainvillea and lands on the two actors in *Forgetting Petunia Holt* exchanging vows in a simple wedding ceremony. It's the most romantic thing I've ever seen. I can't believe my brother never told me about this. Tears well in my eyes and as I steal a glance at Kate, I see them pooling in hers too. It's as though I'm watching Kate and my brother up there. Kate and Christopher belong together. They just do.

Of course, I really believed that Lev and I belonged together too. That was supposed to be *us* up there. An unbelievable ache washes over my entire body. I push the pain away and turn to Kate, who's sitting as straight as a rod.

"Kate," I say tentatively. But she doesn't move. "Kate," I say again. She's looking out as if to an imagined horizon, her hands turned up on her lap and tears pouring out of her eyes like a busted open pipe.

"It's like quicksand," she says softly, "a thick, heavy blanket over me. I can't move. I can't breathe." Then she looks at me finally. "That's how much I miss him, Lola. I'm good, I'm really good at my job, but relationships, I don't know how to do relationships."

"Oh, Kate. No one does," I say. "Everyone is just trying to figure it out as they go. Stop shutting Christopher out. He loves you. You guys belong together."

"How can you be so sure?"

"Kate, I've known since we were sixteen," I say.

Kate starts crying again. "Geezus, what's the matter with me? I don't think I've ever cried this much in my life." She says it just as I'm thinking it. I've never seen Kate like this. "Fucking hormones. Fucking baby." She looks down at her stomach and takes her hand and rubs it across her belly. I put my hand on top of hers and let it linger there for a few moments. Before I can say anything, she says,

"I'm scared, Lo."

"It's okay to be scared, Kate. Love is scary but it's also the greatest thing on the planet. And Christopher loves you. He really loves you," I say.

"I love him too," Kate says.

"Then *tell* him."

Winding my way in a taxi toward Juan des Pain from the Du Cap, I don't need to practice what I want to say because I feel it in my bones.

When I finally find Saffron's rented cottage tucked away into the olive trees like a small bird's nest, I'm surprised by its humbleness. But I also understand it. No one would expect to find the biggest female movie star in the world hiding away here. The only tiny tipoff is the large bodyguards standing at the small front gate.

"Hi, I'm Lola Santisi," I say to the one standing closest to the gate.

"May I see some identification please," he says somberly. I show him my passport.

"Go ahead." He waves me in.

And as I make my way down the small path and open the front door of what seems like a hobbit hole, I understand completely why this is where Saffron wants to be. It's a tiny gem of a place. The light cascading through the windows is throwing beams off the crystal candlesticks that are lit throughout the place on antique tables. The air is subtly perfumed with the wildflowers and roses scattered in vases throughout. All around are soft couches to be curled into.

This is where I find Saffron with a cashmere throw wrapped around her, lost in a profusion of pillows on an oversized white couch. My first instinct is to turn away; she seems so fragile. I also think she could be sleeping. But then she surprises me by readjusting herself on the couch. It seems like the weight of sitting up is too much for her, and this is when I go to her and wrap her in my arms.

I take in the scent of her unwashed hair wafting toward me in all of its humanness, the semicircles of her unpolished fingernails, the purple veins peeking through the soft skin of her forearms. Once her shaking sobs subside, she pulls her head up from the crook of my arm, her usually porcelain skin blotchy from crying. And I realize that despite how loved she is by the world, she is utterly alone.

"Lola, I feel like such a fraud." She finally gets the words out, her voice hoarse and cracking as she does. "I pretend to be someone else for a living, but I'm tired of doing it in my real life," she says, seeming to sink even farther into that couch. "It wasn't fair to Markus, it wasn't fair to Cricket. And it wasn't fair to me. I've been scared. I've been a coward. I forgot who I was."

"Saffron," I say gently, not letting go of her hands. "We all get lost in our different ways. All of us," I say, thinking about myself, Saffron, Cricket, Kate, my mother, Lev, Nic, all of us. "We all get caught up in searching for what's out there and lose what's in here," I say, touching my hand over my heart. "It's hard and it hurts like crazy, but we have to find a way back to ourselves," I say, looking into her magnificent blue eyes. I want to save the *Vain* cover and my job more than anything I've ever wanted, but sitting here across from Saffron, staring into those eyes, I want to try and help her save herself most of all. "I think you should still do the *Vain* cover, but without Markus. On your own."

"What?" she says, bewildered.

"Marriage is about a commitment to your partner. You vow to love, cherish, and honor your partner till death do you part, right?"

"Yeah," she says tentatively.

"But how can you vow to do all of those things with another person before you do them to yourself? We all need to vow to love, honor, and cherish *ourselves* first. So I think you should do the *Vain* cover in the gorgeous gown that Julian made for you, but instead of a wedding story it should be about you committing to yourself," I say squarely. "We're all programmed to believe that another person can save us or complete us, but the truth is, it's an inside job," I tell her. "You have this amazing opportunity to send a message to the world. We don't have to act *as if* anymore. It's time to *be*." I lift my head. I repeat the words softly but strongly, "A commitment ceremony to *yourself*." This time both of our eyes are filled with tears and it's my turn to sob in Saffron's arms.

When I finally lift my head up, "Okay," is all that she says.

"Okay," I repeat. "Okay."

Back at the Martinez, I feel eerily calm as I dial the number.

"Grace Frost's office," her assistant picks up.

"Yes, hi, it's Lola Santisi."

"I'm sorry, she's not available," she says coldly and without hesitation.

"Look," I say. "Tell her that it's really important. Tell her that she'll want to hear what I have to say. My job, my life, everything is on the line. Please."

After a long pause, the assistant finally says, "Give me a minute." Which turns into more like fifteen.

"Yes." Grace Frost's voice could cut through butter.

"I need to talk to you about the Saffron Sykes cover," I say.

"I don't have time for this. You should be dealing with Coz."

"Actually, I don't deal with Coz anymore. In fact, I'm pretty sure that you aren't going to want to be dealing with Coz anymore either," I say, "but right now I want to talk about Saffron."

"I'm listening," she says matter-of-factly.

"Well, it starts with Saffron. But really it's about all of us," I say, and I'm surprised by the strength of my own voice as I go on to pitch my lifeline. When I'm done, all she says is, "I like it."

"Good. I'll set everything up. And about Coz? I'm also going to be sending you some footage that I think you'll be very interested in."

"I'll expect the cover try in two days. No longer." And the line goes dead.

"I'm so sorry I'm late," I say to my mother as I sit down beside her in the Palais for the closing ceremony of the festival and the announcement of the Palme d'Or winner.

"I'm the one who's sorry, Lola. I feel terrible for what happened at Julian's show. I should have been there," she says.

"It's okay, Mom," I say. "What was it like kissing George Clooney?"

"Some Russian woman outbid me. Can you believe it?" she says. "It's probably my karmic retribution for missing Julian's show—and for so much other stuff," she adds softly, shaking her head remorsefully, then placing her hand on my face before reaching in her clutch for her lipstick.

"You're forgiven," I say. "You're the one that proved that Chili was able to hack into the server and steal that footage."

"Yes, darling. That Chili really is a technical whiz. I still don't understand how he did it, but we really have Alex to thank for figuring it out. Julian got Chili on the phone, and he said that Coz made him do it. I think we should press charges."

"I never liked that little shit," my father leans over my mother to whisper to me. "I knew he was trouble."

"I thought you loved him. Isn't that why you used his designs in your movie instead of Julian's?" I ask.

"I used Julian's gown for the prison break scene," he says, looking straight ahead.

"You did?" And then I remember that the film cut out during the screening of Papa's movie. I never actually saw the prison break scene. So Papa chose Julian after all. He chose *me*. "Thanks, Papa," I whisper, tugging on his arm. "Thanks for pulling through."

He gives me a sheepish smile, reaches across my mother's lap, and kisses me on the forehead.

"I still think we should press charges," my mother says.

"Mom, Chili's *sixteen* years old and all he is, is Coz's puppet. For whatever reason all Coz wants is to see me and Julian fail. Succeeding is going to be the best revenge of all," I say. Not that a teensy bit of karmic retribution won't be lovely too.

"Is there anything I can do to help?" Mom asks.

"Actually, there is," I say. "Do you know if you can get Doctor Singh here by tomorrow?"

"I'll certainly try," she says.

"Thanks," I say. And as I look at my mother, I realize that something's missing.

"Where's Alex and your camera crew?" I ask.

"I told them not to come," she says, which surprises me. "Tonight is about your brother and father, not my show," she says.

A tuxedo-clad Sean Penn takes the stage, a small envelope in his hands.

I clasp my hand in my mother's. "Good luck, Papa," I whisper.

"It is my great honor to announce the winner of this year's Palme d'Or," he says, ripping open the envelope. I look past Papa and Mom and scan down the aisle for Christopher, who's a few seats away. I catch his eye and give him a nervous grin. I'm pleased to see that he's somehow surgically removed Gigi from his side and that it's Kate instead who's seated beside him. I can't help but smile. And I suddenly realize it doesn't matter if Christopher wins the Palme d'Or or not because he's gotten what he wants most of all: Kate.

Sean Penn pumps his fist. "And the winner is . . . Christopher Santisi for *Forgetting Petunia Holt!*"

Oh my god! He won! He actually won! My brother just won the

freaking Palme d'Or! Christopher bounds down the aisle and runs toward the stage. And my father is the first person to jump to his feet to give Chris a standing ovation. And not only is he standing, but he's actually crying. And suddenly, so am I. Yes, because I'm proud of Christopher, but also for all of us, because I'm proud of all of us. My brother, my father, my mother, Kate, and me. All of us.

17

the sun behind Saffron reveals itself as if on cue, backlighting her so that she appears to be surrounded by an aura of soft golden light. Her Julian Tennant gown is magnificent, wafting in ivory billows in the gentle breeze off the French Riviera as she stands at the top of a secluded bluff. I fluff the skirt of her frothy bias-cut chiffon gown with a ruffle-edged, plunging V-back, not as the CEO of Julian Tennant Inc. but as Saffron's woman of honor at her commitment ceremony to herself.

There are no trumpeter swans or ostriches or Arabian stallions or imported pink sand from the Sahara Desert. And most important of all, there is no Coz or Chili. There is a simple white linen chuppah decorated with white camellias and a few scattered white rose petals on the floor. I cancelled Patrick Demarchelier's lavish lighting package, and he doesn't have any assistants with him as he discreetly snaps photos of Saffron.

Saffron hugs me before she takes her place in front of Dr. Singh, my mother's crazy mystic healer-slash-spiritual guide-slash Best Guru Forever (BGF), whose real name is Bernie Freedman from Brooklyn. My mother got him to fly in from L.A. this morning. Dressed in his white kutras and turban, he rings a Tibetan peace bell to commence the ceremony.

"Saffron, before we begin, I'd like you to take a moment to turn around and look out at the people who came here today with deep love in their hearts to support you," Dr. Singh says as Saffron spins around to gaze out at me, Julian, Kate, Christopher, my mother, my father, Cricket, and Markus.

Saffron's eyes fill with tears as she looks at all of us. In some ways her ceremony is for all of us, not just her. We're all, each one of us, finding our way back to ourselves. I smile to myself as I realize that somehow, some way we've all survived this insane trip at Cannes. Saffron mouths a quiet "thank you" to us and then turns back around to face Dr. Singh.

"Do you, Saffron Sykes, vow to love, honor, cherish, and be true to yourself, in sickness and in health, in all of the ups and downs of life, through all of your successes and failures and in all of life's impermanence?"

"I do," and as she says it, I make a vow to myself as well. *Lev,* I tell myself, *Don't think about Lev.* I miss him so much it's like a thunderbolt through my heart. But it's not just that I lost Lev; I was losing myself as well. And as I stand here next to Saffron, I vow to never lose myself again.

"Saffron, in the Jewish tradition the groom breaks a glass at the end of the ceremony as a symbol of the fragility of life," Dr. Singh says, placing a glass wrapped in cloth at Saffron's ivory satin Louboutins. "In a gesture of appreciation for each fleeting moment and in recognition of the imper-manence of all things, please, Saffron, go ahead," Dr. Singh says.

Saffron stamps on the glass with all of her might, looking up to the clear blue sky with her eyes squeezed shut as she does. As we hear the crunch of the glass breaking, we all yell "Mazel tov!" and start cheering, all the while Patrick capturing every moment with his camera.

I spin around and look over to my brother, Kate, Julian, my parents, and Cricket and I'm suddenly flooded with gratitude for all these people that help hold me together just like that cloth wrapped over the glass that's holding all those broken shards in one spot.

Dr. Singh rings his peace bell to close the ceremony, and as the ring-ing reverberates over and over and over, it feels as though peace among us has finally been restored.

"Thank you for helping me find the courage to do this," Saffron says, hugging me.

"No, thank you for doing this, not just for yourself but for all of the women out there who don't have the courage that you do," I say. "Maybe now they will."

"I really hope so," she says.

"That was a beautiful ceremony," Cricket says, coming up to us.

"I had nothing to do with it," Saffron says. "It was all your friend, Lola."

"There's no better friend," Cricket says with a smile.

"Thanks, Cricket," I say and I can't help but notice she looks more like herself than she has in a very long time. "I'm going to go get us some champagne. I feel a toast is in order."

As I make my way over to the champagne, I suddenly see Kate drop-ping down to her knees beside Christopher. Oh god. Oh no. I hope she's okay. I rush to her side and as soon as I do I can't believe what I'm wit-nessing.

"Christopher," Kate says, with a tear rolling down her cheek, gazing up at him with her deep, dark eyes. Everyone's gathered around them as she clasps Christopher's hands in hers. "I love you, Christopher Santisi." Christopher tries to pull Kate up off the floor, but when she won't budge, he joins her on the ground. It's as though they have no concept that we're all standing here watching them.

"Chris, I've been so stupid and so scared, but I've missed you so much. I even miss your stupid messes. I have this perfectly designed house without any life in it, and you're the life that's missing," she says, cupping Christopher's face. "I guess what I'm trying to say is, will you marry me, Christopher Santisi? I want us to be a family. You and our baby."

"Yes, of course, yes," Christopher says kissing Kate.

"Baby?" my mother yelps.

"Yes," Christopher says, as he and Kate stand up, wrapped in each other's arms. "Mom, Papa, Kate, and I are having a baby. You're going to be grandparents."

"Oh my god, Paulie, we're going to be grandparents," my mother says, pulling in Kate and Christopher for a hug. "Do you think we can film the delivery for my show?"

"NO!" Kate and Christopher shout in unison.

"I was only kidding," my mother says, and I decide to take her word for it. I steal Kate away from Christopher and wrap her in a hug.

"I'm really happy you decided to keep the baby."

"I'm terrified that I'm going screw this kid up but I finally realized that I'm more afraid of letting all this pass me by. You were right, I guess sometimes you do get to have it all."

"You're going to be a great mother," I say.

"And you're going to be a great aunt."

Suddenly Cricket's arms are wrapped around us both and the three of us hug tight.

"I'm really proud of you both," she whispers. "The way you've taken a stand for yourselves. Thank you for being such good friends. And for showing me the way back to myself." Kate and I both look at Cricket expectantly from our huddle. "It's time for me to take a break from this whole falling in love thing. I'm not confused anymore. I know what I want. And that's to focus on my craft. I'm an actress. Period. And I've got a shot at a career now. My love life's going on the back burner," Cricket looks over to Markus as she says this. "Even if he is awfully cute," she teases. "Time to focus!"

"I've got just the agent for you to do that," Kate jokes.

"We need to celebrate," I dash over to the champagne and pass out glasses to everyone. Then first raise them to the girls.

"To us," I say to my best friends before turning out to the room, "To Kate and Christopher," I say, raising my flute.

"To Kate and Christopher," everyone echoes as we clink glasses.

"There's no forgetting you, Kate Woods," my brother says, beelining toward her and wrapping her in a kiss.

"I'd like to propose a toast to Lola," Julian says. "Thank you for always finding a way to make everything okay and saving me and our company over and over again."

"Thank you, Julian," I say with watery eyes.

"Thank you, Lola!" says Saffron, raising her flute to me.

"To all of us," I say. "And honoring yourself."

Several months and many downward dogs later, my arms are full with grocery bags from Gourmet Garage as I make my way up Bleecker Street. I contemplate stopping at Magnolia Bakery for some banana cream pudding for Julian and me, but keep walking when the long line decides for me. As I make a right up Perry Street to my little brownstone rental, I think of how nice it is to get to *invite* Julian over rather than work and live under the same roof with him.

As I unlock my apartment door and step into the small foyer, my last box unpacked, a huge smile washes across my face as I think about how much I love it here. I pull a bunch of peonies from one of my bags and fill two vases with water, one for the small kitchen table beneath a small window where I like to read in the mornings—there are nothing but small windows in this small apartment—and one for the coffee table in the living room. I throw on my sweats and my slippers. No more playing dress-up for Julian. For one fleeting moment, I imagine the feel of my feet sliding into those comfy Crocs, then shake the thought away. A moment later I'm buzzing Julian up.

"Hey sweetie," Julian kisses me on my forehead as he steps through the threshold with a beautiful orchid plant.

"Thanks. This is gorgeous, Julian," I say, taking the orchid from him and heading into the kitchen.

"The place is looking great," he says, throwing himself onto my couch.

"Here's some bubbly for you," I say, resurfacing from the kitchen with a bottle of Dom and two glasses.

"Turn it on already," Julian says as he takes the bottle from my hands and uncorks it. "I can't wait one more minute."

"Okay, here we go," I say pressing play on the TiVo. "It started five minutes ago." It's been all I can do not to watch Oprah's latest primetime special until Julian arrived.

"Today's guest has caused quite a stir," Oprah bellows from the screen. "Since we last saw her, she's not only come out, but she's been at the forefront of the hottest new trend sweeping the nation: solo commitment ceremonies." Oprah pauses and looks around at her guests. "Y'all know how I feel about marriage," she says out of the side of her mouth.

"So you can guess how I feel about the commitment ceremony to your-self. I'm all about it. In fact, don't be surprised if I get on the bandwagon and have a big old bash myself. But first, here today to talk all about it is . . . *Saffron Sykes*!" Oprah howls as shots of Saffron in Julian's gorgeous gown on the cover of *Vain* beam onto the walls of the stage.

"Oh my gosh," Julian says as we both move closer to the screen to get a better look at Saffron's breezy Julian Tennant persimmon-hued dress that shows off her long, golden legs as she strides across the stage. "She looks fantastic!"

"So, Saffron," Oprah says placing her hand on Saffron's knee once they take their seats. "How are you?"

"Never been better," Saffron says.

"So tell us how this commitment ceremony frenzy you've embarked upon all began," Oprah asks.

"Actually, Oprah, the truth is that I can't take credit for the commit-ment ceremony craze. I'm just kind of, well—you could call me the spokesperson," Saffron says humbly. "Lola Santisi, the mastermind behind my favorite designer, Julian Tennant, is truly its creator. If we're lucky, a bit of light shows up in our darkest hour to guide the way. And for me, that was Lola."

"Isn't that always true," Oprah interjects. "If we're paying attention when we're in that dark night, there's usually an angel standing in the wings," she says, turning to the audience for emphasis.

"If angels stand on five-inch Louboutins," Julian says. "With a fabu-lous little JT number, of course." He wraps his arm around my shoulders and pulls me toward him.

My eyes fill up with tears. I can't believe that this is really happening. To get this kind of acknowledgment? From Oprah? In prime time?

We turn our attention back to the screen.

"Saffron, during the Cannes Film Festival and the aftermath of *Four*

Weddings where you play a gay character, there was a lot of speculation about your sexuality and you stayed quiet. Until this latest issue of *Vain*. Which, by the way, has been *Vain*'s best-selling issue of all time. So, Saffron, why come out now, in *Vain*?" Oprah asks.

"Because what the commitment ceremony taught me, what Lola taught me, and Oprah, you're known for preaching about living one's truth, is that it was time for me to honor my truth."

"The truth will set you free," Oprah says, grabbing Saffron's hand in hers in a gesture of support. "Although I hear you're not exactly free these days. A little birdy told me you just got twenty million for your next role."

"That's right, Oprah. I absolutely cannot *wait* to work with Christopher Santisi. My big fear was that no one would want to hire me if they found out I was gay. I guess I didn't give people enough credit."

"And what was all that fuss about you and Cricket Curtis?" Oprah says. "Give me that dish, girlfriend."

"I look at Cricket and I see myself ten years ago. I'm telling you, Oprah, that girl is going to be a superstar. I knew it the minute I saw her. It's going to hit the papers tomorrow, but I don't think she'd mind my telling your viewers that she's going to be starring alongside Julia Roberts in the sequel, *Eat More, Pray Harder, and Love Hotter*."

"I'd buy a ticket to that!" Oprah grins. "Now Saffron, I believe you have a surprise for everyone in our studio."

"I'm so excited," Saffron says. "I'm getting to pull an Oprah. I'm sending each of you audience members home with a gift certificate for a custom-made Julian Tennant commitment gown! It doesn't matter if you're gay or straight, single or married, everyone should commit to honoring themselves and have a fabulous Julian Tennant gown to wear while they do it!"

The audience erupts into a frenzy of cheering. Julian and I look at each other in shock. My head is spinning as I try and tabulate how many people are in that audience and what this could mean for our company. Not to mention all of the people watching the show. This is mammoth. This is monumental. I feel like the particles in the room just shifted—along with our lives—forever.

I look over to Julian expecting: a gasp, a scream, a yelp, a hug, a dance? Instead what I get is an eerie stillness from my BGF like I've never seen before, and a solitary tear spilling down his cheek.

Finally Julian breaks the silence. "Lola," he says, turning off the television and turning to face me. "Thank you. I feel like I should have a commitment ceremony for you. For your commitment to us," he says.

"Thanks, Julian." What more is there to say? Actually, there *is* one more thing: "Cheers to that, cheers to me." I laugh but at the same time, really, in the depths of my bones, I *really* mean it. Cheers to me. I don't need a Julian Tennant gown or a party to have *this* commitment ceremony. Right here. Right now. Cheers to *me*.

"You know what makes this moment even more perfect?" Julian asks with an evil grin.

"What?"

"Knowing that Bitchitor Coz is watching *Oprah* far, far from the kingdom of Condé Nast."

"Two can play at *Cut-Throat Couture*," I say. "I would have given a lot to see Grace Frost's face when she watched the footage Coz and Chili hacked for your show. If you ask me, Coz got off easy and Grace knows it. We really could have sued. But getting Coz canned—"

"—from *Vain and* her reality show!" Julian crows.

"*And* making *Vain* pay for all those ostriches!" I say. "That's good enough for me."

"And now Chili's out of her clutches," Julian says. "He was annoying as all hell and I wanted to throttle him half the time, but I have to admit, the kid's got talent. It really wasn't his fault. Coz was a master manipulator. She's the one who convinced him to trash all those invitations."

"Chili Lu is going to be just fine," I reassure him. "Stefano told me that LVMH is hiring him to design a whole line of virtual clothing for preens."

"What are preens?"

"Pre-teens. They're the hot new demographic. He's doing a line called 'Out of the X-Box.' Watch for him on a *Guitar Hero* nearest you."

"*Guitar Hero*? Out of the X-Box?" Julian groans, slumps back on the couch, and covers his eyes dramatically. "I'm too young to feel this old."

"And guess who's gracing the next cover of *Vain*? Our very own Alexandra Crimini," I announce. "Grace Frost called me herself to thank me for discovering the *Next* Kate Moss."

The phone trills. "Hello?" I can't hide the grin spreading across my face. "It's Stefano," I mouth to Julian as I cover the receiver. "He wants to congratulate me on Oprah!"

"I'll see you tomorrow, then," Julian whispers, pushing himself up off the couch. "I think we're in for an interesting day." He blows me a kiss, then closes the door behind him.

"Wait, your scarf!" I hiss, but he's already gone.

Curling into the couch, I pour myself the last bit of bubbly as Stefano murmurs sweet nothings about orders and grosses in my ear.

Who would have ever thought that a commitment ceremony dress would be this millennium's little black dress? I've barely hung up with Stefano and tipped the last of the Dom in my flute when my phone rings again.

"Hey, Lo," Kate says. "What'd you think about Oprah? How fucking amazing is that?"

"I know!" I say. "I can't believe Saffron did that for us."

"Don't worry. She can afford it. After all, I'm the one who got her twenty against twenty on her next film," Kate says.

"And I hope you got the director a nice piece of the action," I say. "I hear he's going to be a dad soon." My other line beeps. "Kate, I've got to run. That's Mom on the other line and I'd better get it."

"Okay, call me when you can so we can talk about your maid of honor duties," Kate says. "Did I just say that?"

"I'm pretty sure you did, Soon-to-be-Santisi," I say before clicking over.

"Hi darling," my mother says. "I just saw Oprah and I'm so so proud of you!"

"Thanks, Mom!"

"I always knew my Lola was going to make it big. And I've got some big news of my own. The ratings for *Wristwatch Wives* are enormous. It's a huge hit!"

"Congratulations," I say, not quite knowing whether I mean it.

"But that's not my news," my mother says and then pauses. "I've decided to go behind the camera."

"You've what?! Have you told Dad?" Just what the Santisi family needs: three directors in the family!

"That's right, darling. I'm going to be directing my own documentary about fame. It's all about stars and the paparazzi and I'm calling it *Camera Carnivores*."

Okay, that's actually not a terrible idea. "Mom, I have to admit, that's your sweet spot. Just promise me that you'll leave the family out of it, okay?" The downstairs buzzer rings and I quickly buzz Julian up to retrieve his scarf. "Have you told Papa yet?"

"No, darling, but he'll be thrilled for me, I know it," Mom says.

I hear a knock on the door. "Mom, I gotta go. Julian's at the door. Bye now."

"Bye, darling," she says and clicks off as I swing my front door open. I freeze in my tracks.

"Lola," he says softly, standing there like he's been waiting for a million years.

"Lev," I say in shock. "How did you get here?"

"I drove," he says.

"You drove all the way from L.A.?" I ask, dumbfounded.

"Yes," he says. "Lola, it's been killing me. I miss you. I miss us. You were right. I'm a doctor, not an actor. I drove here in a U-Haul. All of my belongings are in that van, but there's no place to put them because there's no home without you," he says. "I don't know what happened to me. I'm so sorry. I got caught up in the illusion but I don't want to lose my shot at something real because of it."

I peer at him closely. He looks—well, he looks . . . real. No Mystic Tan, no eyebrow wax, no gel in his hair. Just Lev. The guy I fell in love with. The guy I think I'm still in love with.

"I turned down the Coen Brothers gig. I've taken the job at Lenox Hill Hospital," he says. "And I hope you'll take me back. I hope you'll give me one more chance because what you and I have is real."

"So. . . . No more acting?" I ask. "No more playing a doctor, just being a doctor?"

"No more acting," he says, dropping onto one knee, "Lola Santisi, will you be my wife?" he asks, pulling out the engagement ring and trying to slip it back on my finger. But I stop him and pull him back up to his feet.

"Lev, I don't need you to save me anymore," I say, holding both of his hands in mine.

"Lo," he says, looking me squarely in the eyes, "you never did." And my life rushes by like a slideshow and I realize that he's right. And I realize that the last images I want in my life, I want to be full of pictures with him. That I get to choose how this story ends. And I want it to end with us. But I don't need a diamond to prove our commitment to each other.

"I don't need a wedding," I say, handing him back the ring. "Thank you for finding me."

"Thank you for helping me find my way back to myself," he whispers in my ear as I throw my arms around his neck and then pull away so that I can look into those green eyes that look like the closest thing to home I'll ever know. There's one thing in life that I've learned isn't an illusion: it's love. So I say to my Lev, "Now let's go play doctor."

acknowledgments

---

deepest gratitude to: Steve and Ella, for every beautiful day together, you are my heart; Daria, Khosrow, and Jahan, for all you've taught me, for your patience and unconditional support; Amy, Angela, Chelsea, Emily, Liz, Marin, for being my sisters; Jane, DeBorah, and Mary, for your generosity; Amanda, for persevering, for the "growing up" together, for showing up in the rough times, and for becoming family through these years; and my father, Dennis, and my grandfather Larry, two challenging warriors whose creative lives moved us all.

Heartfelt thank you to: Philip, for our love through it all; Wendy and Leonard, for your incomparable love, support, and wisdom; Richard, John, Magdalena, and Belen, for always being there; Toni and David, for teaching me to find the humor in life; my friends, for being like a second family; and Ruthanna, for forever altering the course of my life and believing in us.

Thank you to Deborah Schneider, Jennifer Weis, and everyone at St. Martin's Press for championing us, and to Betsy Rapoport for guiding us with her brilliance, and to Glenda Bailey for being our fairy godmother.